She was soaking wet, fr weight jacket and…her wedding dress. It was dirty and ripped at the bottom. Her hair covered her face like a veil, her hands were clenched together, and her shoulders slouched. Swallowing, he reached out and swept the hair out of her face.

Slowly, she raised her head. When their gazes met, he was hit with an overwhelming urge to hold her, which wasn't really new. It just wasn't normal. But he'd do anything in that moment to make it better. Her bottom lip trembled and he inched closer to her. When she let out a whimper, he pulled her to him in a tight hug.

As she cried into his chest, he whispered that she'd be okay, that he'd protect her, that he'd help her. But the more he assured her, the louder she cried. His chest tightened as he rubbed her back. His thoughts were spinning. What the hell had happened to her?

HER KIND
OF MAN

ALSO BY ELLE WRIGHT

The Forbidden Man

His All Night

HER KIND
OF MAN

An Edge of Scandal Novel

ELLE WRIGHT

FOREVER
NEW YORK BOSTON

Copyright © 2016 by Elle Wright
Excerpt from *The Forbidden Man* copyright © 2015 by Elle Wright
Excerpt from *His All Night* copyright © 2015 by Elle Wright

Forever
Hachette Book Group
1290 Avenue of the Americas
New York, NY 10104

HachetteBookGroup.com

Printed in the United States of America

First Edition: April 2016
10 9 8 7 6 5 4 3 2

OPM

Forever is an imprint of Grand Central Publishing.
The Forever name and logo are trademarks of Hachette Book Group, Inc.

The Hachette Speakers Bureau provides a wide range of authors for speaking events. To find out more, go to www.hachettespeakersbureau.com or call (866) 376-6591.

The publisher is not responsible for websites (or their content) that are not owned by the publisher.

To my mother, Regina. I'm so thankful you encouraged me to feed my imagination through reading and writing. It is because of you, and everything you've instilled in me, that I do this. I created Sharon Parker (Allina's mother) with you in mind. You were the best mother I could have: beautiful, intelligent, funny, and real. You protected me, nourished me, and loved me unconditionally. Love you eternally. You are missed.

ACKNOWLEDGMENTS

The journey to "The End" for *Her Kind of Man* was one filled with winding roads, rough terrain, and inclement weather. It was definitely a challenge. In the midst of it, as with every journey, I found clarity. I was able to see the beautiful scenery, have lots of laughs, and sit with good company. I'm so thankful for this experience. And I appreciate the love and support I've received while on Allina's and Kent's adventure.

First and foremost, all thanks and praise to God. It is because of His Grace and Mercy that this is possible.

To my husband, Jason, you are my *one*. I love you more than I could ever fully express. Thank you for having my back.

To my children, Asante, Kaia, and Masai; I hope you all know how much I love you. You're smart, driven, beautiful, and mine. Thanks for inspiring me daily.

To my father and my brother, thank you for your unwavering support. No questions asked. I can't imagine my life without you.

To my Nanay and Tatay, I love you both very much. Thank you for accepting me in your life all those years ago and loving me like your own.

To my sister LaDonna, thank you for being you. And thanks for loving me for me. I appreciate you and love you BIG!

To my sister Kim, thanks for listening to and loving me. Your unwavering support means the world to me. I can't thank you enough for always being #TeamElle. Love you.

To my brother Joe, thank you for never putting an "in-law" at the end of my title. You are my true brother. When I created Kent, I'd always think, "What would Joe do?" LOL, I love you, and I'm so proud to be your sister.

I would be remiss if I didn't thank a few special people. These people let me vent, helped me focus, and cheered me on the whole way. To my writerly boo, Christine Hughes, you rock! I'm glad that we're still on this journey together. Thank you, Sheree, for being my insight. You are a godsend. Another special thanks to Crystal for being on my team. You have been a true friend to me and I'm so thankful to have you in my life. To my sis, Sheryl Lister, God knew what he was doing when we hooked up on Facebook. It has been a pleasure getting to know you. I'm blessed to call you my friend. To Tanishia Pearson-Jones, thanks friend. Who knew, at forty-one years old, I'd make new friends. I sure didn't. But I feel so blessed to count you as one of them. To Keshia, who knew you were right around the corner from me for all these years? I'm so glad that we connected. I also want to thank Danielle, Kimberley, and Shannon for being there for me in everything. I'm so happy I wrote a book you wanted to read.

To all of my friends and family, I can't name you all. Really. There are so many wonderful people in my life, people who've encouraged me, sat with me, cried with me, laughed with me...love you all.

To my agent, Sara Camilli, thank you for your calming presence. I definitely had some moments with this book.

To my editor, Megha Parekh, at Grand Central Publishing, thank you for pushing me always. I've learned so much from you. Thanks for supporting me the way you have. I also want to give a shout-out to the Forever Romance team. I've truly enjoyed this experience.

I also want to thank King Brooks from Black Page Turners, Sharon Blount from BRAB (Building Relationships Around Books), LaShaunda Hoffman (SORMAG), Orsayor Simmons (Book Referees), Tiffany Tyler (Reading in Black and White), Delaney Diamond (RNIC), Wayne Jordan (RIC), Radiah Hubert (Urban Book Reviews), and the EyeCU Reading and Social Network for supporting me. I truly appreciate you all. Also, thank you to Black Stone Bookstore.

Thank you, Beverly Jenkins, for everything. You have no idea how much you continue to inspire me. You've been so welcoming and supportive, I can't thank you enough. Thanks to all the many author friends who have been such a support to me; authors who have supported me, given good advice, written a blurb; you've all inspired me to keep going. I'm forever grateful.

Last but not least, I want to thank all my readers. It makes me feel good to know that you love my characters the way I do. I hope you keep reading.

I hope you enjoy the wild ride that is *Her Kind of Man*! It is definitely an experience.

Thank you!

Love,
Elle

HER KIND
OF MAN

CHAPTER ONE

$\mathcal{J}$'m leaving," Allina Parker announced, standing up.

Allina had spent the day with her friend Kent. Dinner and a movie. It had been hours since they'd returned to his place. They'd chatted about nothing in particular, but it was good. Easy. She'd missed hanging out with him. Things had been strained between them since she'd moved away months earlier. But now...now they seemed to be back to normal. It wouldn't last, though.

Kent looked up from his phone and smiled. "Okay. I'll see you tomorrow?"

"No, I'm leaving town," Allina explained. "I've decided to go back to Ohio. Isaac and I are going to be married as soon as possible,"

Allina's gaze dropped to a piece of lint on the plush taupe carpet. Gripping the bottom of her sweater, she steeled herself for his response.

Kent didn't care for Isaac. That much was obvious. In fact, her friend had made it known on numerous occasions, announced it every single time he got the chance, no matter who was around, oftentimes without regard for her feelings. She expected a similar reaction to this news. But they needed to talk about it; she couldn't leave without telling him.

Seconds passed with no response. Allina finally met Kent's pensive gaze. His dark eyes traveled over her face. It was no different from any other time he'd looked at her like that. It felt like a tender caress, the way his gaze seemed to take every part of her in and hold her. Her stomach tightened and she couldn't help but wonder if that feeling would ever go away. Lord knows, she wanted it to. She'd spent the better part of her adult years loving Kent, only to have him reject her time and time again. Unrequited love was not the life she'd envisioned for herself. She had no choice but to move on.

"Say something," she croaked.

"Why?" he asked.

Allina wondered if it was a trick question, if Kent was playing some sort of game with her. Only he didn't play those types of games.

"You know we're engaged, Kent." That had been another day, another argument. It felt like a lifetime ago. "I believe this is the best decision for me. He loves me and wants to spend his life with me," she answered, holding her chin up high.

"Do you love him?" Kent asked.

Allina's mouth fell open. She hadn't expected him to ask her that. Even so, it was a valid question—something she would have asked her friend in the same situation.

"Yes," she said simply.

It wasn't a lie. Once she'd decided that waiting on Kent was a lost cause, she met Isaac. The future minister had courted her like her father told her a man should—with candlelit dinners, walks in the park, trips to the theater... Isaac Hunter was exactly what she'd prayed for in a husband—kind, intelligent, caring, handsome. He was a man of God, the one who'd been groomed to take over the church his father pastored. One thing she was sure of was Isaac's love for her. He told her every day how much she meant to him.

Kent arched a brow. It was a trademark, yet something only she seemed to notice. It made her pulse race. His smooth, dark skin seemed to glow in the dim light of the room. "How could you?" He inched closer to her and she slowly backed away. The faint waft of his cologne surrounded her. "You don't even know him. How can you love someone you don't know?"

"I do," she insisted.

"Right." The sarcasm in his voice was unmistakable.

He reached down and grabbed her left hand, surveying the ring that she had pulled out of her purse only that morning. Allina couldn't deny the warmth that spread over her like a wildfire in a dry forest as his fingers brushed over hers and twisted the ring around.

Unable to concentrate with him standing so close to her, she gently took her hand from his. "I don't understand why you're being so rude about it. I know sarcasm when I hear it."

He took a deep breath. "You're making a huge mistake."

"Tell me why," she pressed. Time and again Kent had told her she was making a mistake with Isaac, but he never elaborated, never gave her a reason. Allina didn't know what she expected from Kent in that moment. Did she want him to beg her not to marry Isaac? Would she marry Isaac if he told her not to?

Kent took a step back and ran a hand over his bald head. "He's not for you."

Frowning, Allina stepped toward him. "Why do you keep doing this to me?" she asked. "Every single time, you give me some half answer. But you never tell me why."

He shrugged. "For starters, I know you. I know how much you want the dream—the wedding, the kids."

Allina folded her arms across her chest. What he said was the truth. Becoming a wife and mother had been her dream since she'd watched *Cinderella* as a child. Even though her life seemed bleak at times, she still wanted the fairy tale.

"Why shouldn't I?" she asked, throwing her arms in the air. "Why is it so wrong to want a family of my own? I found someone who adores me, who treats me well—"

He grunted.

She blinked and a lone tear fell down her cheek. "Stop," she hissed. "You don't know him."

"I know you're struggling with this," he argued. "You've been here for months."

"My friends needed me." Allina had arrived after Christmas for her best friend Sydney's baby shower and ended up staying through the birth and afterward to help out.

"Allina, it's April," he pointed out. "If this guy is the one for you, why are you still here?"

Allina swallowed.

"No need to answer. I already know. There is something about him, about marrying him, that is wrong. And you know it."

"Don't tell me what I know," she grumbled. "Isaac is good to me."

Kent frowned. "How? If he treats you so well, why are you broke? Hm?"

She didn't have an answer for that. Not one that she could tell him. It would make his case even stronger. Isaac had offered to foot the bill for her trip to Michigan, but Allina had turned him down.

"You don't know him," she whispered.

"I don't need to know him," he said, unfazed by her weak response. "When is the wedding?"

Originally, they'd decided to wait until next year to marry, but the church had voted to install Isaac as an associate pastor. He'd told her that being married before he was promoted would be best. Agreeing to marry so quickly would put her own career ambitions on hold. After all, she'd still been struggling to find gainful employment since her abrupt move. But it was a sacrifice she was willing to make. Kent wouldn't understand, so she wasn't going to mention it to him.

Allina dug her fingernails into her palms. "In a few weeks. There's a convocation at the beginning of the month, and he wants the ceremony to take place before that. My mother is planning everything."

"Why are you doing this again?"

Allina couldn't tell him that she'd given up on him ever loving her, even though she suspected he already knew. There was only one reason she wouldn't marry Isaac, one person who could really stop her. If he told her not to marry Isaac, to stay with him, she would. It always had been Kent—in her heart, in her thoughts. She knew she'd never love anyone the way she'd loved him.

Sucking in a deep breath, she approached Kent tentatively. "Tell me why I shouldn't," she pleaded. "I'm asking you, please."

* * *

The room descended into silence. Kent surveyed Allina, standing before him begging for an answer. Her big, normally expressive eyes asked him for a reason. He wasn't sure he could give her the one that would satisfy her, though.

All he knew was that marrying the preacher man, Isaac, would be the worst thing she could ever do.

Since the minister had bulldozed his way into her life, he'd influenced Allina to change everything about herself—everything that made her the unique, ambitious, self-sufficient person he knew. The woman in front of him was not the woman who'd moved to Ohio less than a year ago. She was a shell of herself, and Kent could only assume the minister was to blame.

Kent had never met Isaac, had only seen a profile picture on Facebook. But he didn't like him, and he certainly didn't care for the hold he had on Allina. And he'd let her know that every chance he got.

How could she love someone she didn't know? More importantly, *how could she marry someone she wasn't in love with?*

Because Allina couldn't love the minister. She loved *him*. Kent had known it for years. But he wouldn't say that to her. He'd made a decision a long time ago to keep things strictly platonic. The friend she was to him, the confidante she'd always been, wasn't something he wanted to risk for a relationship that might or might not work. The last time he'd taken one of his *friends* to bed, the resulting drama had almost destroyed him after his childhood friend tried to kill herself right in front of him.

Raking his eyes over her thin frame, over her hair styled in a way he knew she hated, he shook his head. "Allina, you can't tell me that you're so in love with this man that you would leave your entire life behind—your career, your friends—to become the dutiful wife. You're so busy trying to turn yourself into the perfect preacher's wife that you can't see that he's systematically and deliberately turning you into a different woman altogether. Pretty soon, you'll be wearing church hats and directing the church youth choir."

Her beautiful, light brown eyes widened, and she took an uneven step back. He'd hurt her. "Okay," she murmured. "That's it?"

"What? Do you need another reason?" he blared, unable to help himself. Sometimes the truth hurt; better now than later—after she was married to the jerk. "He's controlling you right now, demanding that you come home and marry him before the damn convocation. And you can't tell me you don't feel that this is wrong on so many levels. Look at you: you're wasting away. You've lost so much weight. You barely eat. What the hell is wrong with you?" he roared. "You're a goddamn fool if you marry him."

She blanched; a shaky hand covered her mouth.

"I'm sorry." He cringed at the dejected look on her face, not that he regretted *what* he'd said. It was the shitty delivery that had taken it to another level. Scrubbing a hand over his face, he apologized again. "I didn't mean to yell. I'm just trying to help you. You're my friend, one of the best people I know."

"Friend," she mumbled with a snicker. "I'm done with this conversation, Kent. I'm going to marry Isaac. You don't know him like I do. He loves me, I love him."

"That's bullshit," Kent grumbled.

"Stop, Kent!" she shouted, slicing her small hand through the air. "It's almost like you don't think I'm worthy to be loved or something. You've been against him from the beginning. And you've never even met him."

Her words pricked his heart. Allina thought he didn't think she was worthy of love. That couldn't be further from the truth. "Why would you say that?" he asked incredulously. "Of course I think you deserve love. But I don't need to meet him to know that he isn't the right man for you. I only have to look at how you act."

"How do I act?" she asked, fire in her eyes.

"Not like a woman in love." He pointed at her ring. "This is the first time I've seen you wear that thing since you came here—over three months ago."

She opened her mouth, but nothing came out.

"You don't even talk about him," he added. "It's like he's a ghost."

"Why can't you just support me the same way I've always supported you? If I'm your friend, why can't you accept my choice?"

Her emphasis on the word "friend" wasn't lost on him. Peering up at the ceiling, he muttered, "I can't."

"So you're telling me you won't come to my wedding?" Her voice quaked as she sniffled. "You're so angry with my decision, you won't even be there?"

When he met her gaze again, he noted the tears standing in her eyes. But he couldn't stop himself. "I won't watch you marry him."

CHAPTER TWO

3 Weeks Later

Do you love him?"

The large door slammed behind Allina as she entered Christian Dreams Church, startling her. The simple question had haunted her the entire way to the church. This was her wedding day. It should be the happiest day of her life. But melancholy had set in the night before, and stuck with her throughout breakfast, her hair appointment, and the slow drive to the sprawling church.

The weather wasn't cooperating either. It had rained for three days in Cleveland, Ohio. The temperature had fallen to record lows. Her friends couldn't come, and her dress wasn't as perfect as she'd wanted, but she was getting married to the man of her dreams. *Right?*

Frozen in place, she flashed back to the conversation she'd had with Kent before she left Michigan. The answer should have been obvious. *Right?* She'd uprooted her life for her fiancé, turned down a business opportunity to move back to Ohio and marry him.

But that conversation—*well, argument*—with the man that she'd once thought she'd love until the end of time had etched itself into her mind. Kent had challenged her to look at her motives, and to really think about taking the big step of marriage with a man she'd met only months before. She had to admit Kent was on to something. As wonderful as Isaac was, as perfect as he presented himself, there was a nagging feeling that something was off with him. But nobody was perfect. *Right?* In the end she'd decided that Isaac was the man for her, and she would become Mrs. Hunter before the day was out.

One of the church mothers stopped in front of her. "Are you okay?" the elderly woman asked, a concerned look on her face.

Allina swallowed and nodded quickly. "I'm good, thanks, Mother Bell."

The older woman patted her arm gently and tucked a roll of tulle under her arms. "Great," she said in a caring tone. "Do you need help with your things?" Mother Bell eyed Allina's dress bag and the small suitcase that sat next to her.

Shaking her head, Allina told her no. "Have you seen my mother?"

The woman craned her head around and turned back to her. "I saw her earlier," she explained, "but she disappeared. I can go find her for you and send her into the changing room, if you'd like?"

Allina thanked the woman and watched as she hurried into the ceremony space. There was a flurry of activity around her as people scrambled to prepare for the ceremony. Shaking off her umbrella, Allina started toward the hallway leading to the changing room. "Bride's nerves" was what her mother had called it a few hours ago when she'd called to make sure she was on schedule. It was normal to feel this way.

She turned toward the foyer again. Since the wedding was

kind of last minute, her mother hadn't had much time to prepare. But Sharon Parker had worked a miracle and managed to transform the church into an elegant yet whimsical space. There was an art to planning and Sharon had it down pat. It didn't matter if she had two years or two hours. Anything she put her name on would be lovely and evoke emotion. It had been that way since she was a child.

Allina would have preferred an outdoor wedding, though. There was something about the natural beauty of a garden that appealed to her—the sound of the wind, the feel of the sun on her skin. The sanctuary wasn't a bed of grass with beautiful wildflowers, but it was a close second. Looking around at the mint green and coral decorations with shades of peach accents, she felt a calm wash over her, a peace. What did the venue matter? The wedding was only a day; she and Isaac would have the rest of their lives together.

As she approached the large Sunday School classroom that would become her changing room, she heard voices coming from the church secretary's office—a woman...and Isaac. The boom of his voice sounded like an echo and she stopped in her tracks. In all the time she'd known Isaac, she'd never heard him yell at anyone. He was mild mannered and rarely lost his temper. Curiosity got the best of her and she glanced behind her before she tiptoed toward the room.

"You need to leave this alone," she heard Isaac say. The harsh edge of his voice stopped her mid-step. It was a threat. He wasn't yelling anymore. His voice was calm, a whisper; but the intent was clear.

"You don't know him."

Kent's words flooded back into her thoughts. She hadn't given him the satisfaction when he'd accused her of marrying Isaac for the wrong reasons, telling her that she couldn't love someone she didn't know. But listening to the quiet yet menacing tone of the man on the other side of the door—*her* man—she thought maybe Kent was dead on in his assessment.

There had to be an explanation. *Church business? Maybe a bill collector?* Determined to find out, she set her dress bag on top of her suitcase and raised her hand to knock on the door.

"I'll never leave it alone," the mysterious woman snapped. "You don't deserve to live, let alone inherit this great church. You destroyed lives, and you won't get away with it. You're an evil man. I've kept quiet long enough."

A heavy feeling settled in her stomach and she let go of the doorknob as if it were a hot coal. *Evil man?* Surely the woman didn't know Isaac. This was a man who was respected in the community by men, women, and children. He volunteered at the hospital's pediatric wing three days a week, had pioneered the church food drive and clothes exchange to help out the homeless. How could this woman call him evil?

Leaning her nose against the door, she waited for Isaac to respond, hoped he would say something that would alleviate the dread that had crept in. This wasn't the first time she'd felt this way, either. There was *something* that felt off with him.

Allina had noticed subtle changes once she'd accepted his proposal. Isaac had started to become possessive, controlling. He didn't want her to go anywhere, hang out with anyone but him. She'd exerted her independence by spending a couple of months in Michigan with her friends. Her best friend, Sydney, had just had a baby and she'd used that event as an opportunity to get some time away, think about if this was what she really wanted. In the end, she'd decided that there was more right than wrong with their relationship.

And things between them had seemed fine since she'd returned home.

"How much?" she heard him say.

A slight shiver crept up her spine.

"I don't want your money," the woman said. "Your father tried to pay me off, and I can't be bought."

The sound of glass breaking startled Allina and she stumbled away from the door. The door swung open and the woman rushed out. Allina scrambled backward, pressing herself against the wall. *Oh God.* As the woman stomped to the front of the church, Allina exhaled. She tried to get a good look at her, but the young woman was sporting huge shades. Odd, since the sun hadn't shined in days. Frowning, Allina noted her thin frame, light skin, and long weave. The woman didn't seem familiar, but she had to know who she was and how she knew Isaac. The urge to catch up to her shot through her and she started after her.

"Excuse me?" Allina called as she rushed forward. "Wait."

Allina caught up with the woman and grabbed hold of her arm. The woman turned to look at her. "What?" the woman spat, crossing her arms in front of herself.

"I'm sorry," Allina said, trying to get a good look at the woman's face. Unfortunately, the thin woman seemed to purposefully avoid a direct gaze. "I'm Isaac Hunter's fiancée, and I—"

The woman froze, lowered her head, and gripped the belt of her huge purse. "I know who you are."

"Okay." Swallowing, Allina thought about how to proceed. "You were just talking...I overheard you in the room talking to Isaac."

"Wow," the woman said, lifting her head up finally, but turning away just as quickly. Allina was able to see her face long enough to note the streaks of mascara running down her cheeks, signaling the woman had been crying. But what stood out to Allina was the angry, red scratch peeking out from under her shades. "This is just great. Get out of my way."

"Wait," Allina blurted out. "I just want to talk to you, ask you some questions. Who are you?"

"I have to go." The woman pushed past her. Allina, not wanting to cause a scene, backed away. Just as the woman reached the door, before she pulled it open, she sighed. "Don't do it," she warned, without turning around. "If you know what's best for you, get far away from that man. He's not who he seems. And neither is his family."

Allina let out a haggard breath she hadn't realized she was holding. "But—"

Her words were cut off by the slam of the door. Allina quickly tugged it open, but the woman had already jumped into her car. The woman sped off, her tires screeching as she rounded the corner.

Running a shaky hand through her hair, Allina went to search for her mother. She needed to talk to her, tell her what had happened. Sharon Parker would know what to do.

Something was definitely not right. She opened the door to the sanctuary. A handful of workers were decorating pews and setting up floral arrangements on pillars. But her mother wasn't there. Maybe she'd left the church?

Patting her pockets for her cell phone, she realized she'd left everything in the hallway. She raced to get her stuff. Her purse, suitcase, and dress were right where she'd left them. She picked up her small clutch and pulled out her phone.

"Allina?"

She gasped and the phone slipped from her sweaty palms and crashed to the floor. When she picked it up she noted the cracked screen. *Shoot.*

Slow, hesitant footsteps neared her and she fought back the surprising urge to flee. She'd never had a reason to be scared of Isaac before, despite his controlling ways. He'd never shown her anything other than kindness. He had his faults, but he'd never been cruel. But she couldn't deny that overhearing that conversation earlier had changed her perception of him. He'd threatened that woman and offered to pay her off. That alone was enough to make Allina question everything she thought she knew about him

Then there was the warning from the mystery woman before she'd bolted out of the church. Too much to sweep under the rug.

The feel of his breath on her neck made her hair rise. He touched her shoulders and she held her breath. "What's going on?" he asked, his voice low.

Her heart pounded in her chest. "Nothing," she croaked. "I dropped my phone." She made a show of rubbing the face of her phone and tapping the screen.

"We can get you a new phone," he offered in the same loving and concerned tone he'd used with her so many times before. It was hard to reconcile that with what she'd heard from him earlier.

Unable to turn around and face him yet, she shrugged. "I know. I just...I'm not due for an upgrade and I..." Allina struggled to finish her sentence, to say something. No luck.

"Are you okay?" His voice seemed far away, but she heard everything else, from the clang of a hammer to the sound of furniture being moved.

Allina's first thought was to pretend she hadn't heard anything, which would give her time to talk to her mother and maybe her father.

On second thought...

"Who was that woman?" she asked finally.

He turned her around to face him. He looked normal enough. His short hair was freshly cut. He smelled like Isaac. Gucci Guilty, his signature cologne. But the man in front of her wasn't the man that she'd gotten to know. This man was a stranger.

"Shouldn't you be getting dressed, sweetie?" He grazed a hand down her cheek. Instead of the warmth that normally accompanied a touch from Isaac, she felt a chill. "We don't want to be late for the ceremony. I can't wait to make you my bride."

Frowning, she asked, "Are you going to answer my question?"

He paused as if he was thinking it over. Finally, he said, "No. It doesn't matter. She's nobody."

The man in front of her lied to her face without even a hint of remorse in his brown eyes. Assessing him, she thought about what the other woman had told her...that scratch. *Did he do that to her?* Allina didn't have to see the woman's face to know. It was in her mannerisms, her movements, and her voice. Mystery woman had tried to play it off, but her fear had been unmistakable.

Hugging herself, she moved back to put some space between them.

But he only stepped forward, crowding her, hovering over her. Allina was a tall woman, but he had a couple inches on her.

How can you love someone you don't know?

Allina had thought she had all the answers. She had a plan—marriage, family, happiness. Now, she wasn't sure if she knew anything. There was a reason that woman was scared of Isaac. And Allina needed answers.

Here goes. "That woman...I heard her." Her thoughts scrambled as she tried to decide whether she should come right out with it and tell him that she'd not only heard their exchange in the classroom, but she'd talked to the lady. But the blank stare on Isaac's face, the dangerous air that swirled around him, prevented her from revealing everything she knew. Who was this man in front of her?

"You offered to pay her off," Allina accused, finally finding her voice. "Then you lied to me and told me it was nothing. How can I trust you if you can so easily lie to me?"

"What exactly did you hear?"

"What happened between you two?" Allina pressed. "Who is she?"

"Can we talk about this later?" Isaac grumbled through clenched teeth. "Shouldn't you be getting dressed?"

"Just answer the question, Isaac," she demanded. "What is going on?"

"It doesn't matter," he told her again, in a stern tone. "It's church business. Nothing to concern yourself with. Let it go."

"It matters to me," Allina hissed. "That woman said she couldn't be bought. And I'm not going to—"

Marry you died on her lips when his fingers dug into her cheeks. He pulled her to him, his eyes boring into hers.

"Allina," he whispered.

She gasped as he squeezed tighter. To anyone who should happen to pass by it would probably look like they were sneaking some time in with each other before the ceremony. But Allina was terrified. The tight grip he had on her jaw and the glare in his eyes took her back to another time in her life, to a similar threat from someone who was supposed to love her. A few minutes earlier, she'd bargained with herself that Isaac would never hurt her and now she was sure he would. Pushing against him, she ground out, "Let me go."

"Allina?" The sound of her name on his lips had once made her feel treasured, but now she felt trapped. Tears welled up in her eyes. "I'll never let you go. You *are* going to marry me."

"I won't," she cried softly, whimpering when she felt the sting of his fingernails against her skin. Her response sounded hollow to her own ear. Allina squeezed her eyes shut and tried to shove him away. She had to get away from him. She needed to call her father.

"You don't want to play with me. I know too many people. I'll ruin you and your father's precious reputation with one phone call."

He leaned closer. "I can make your life ten times worse than you think it is now. And I *will* hurt you if you leave me. If you even think about not going through with this wedding, you're dead." With his mouth against her ear, he whispered, "Don't cry. Go put on that wedding dress. And make sure you smile wide for the camera."

"Minister Hunter," a voice called from behind them. Allina recognized Mother Bell's kind voice immediately.

Allina opened her mouth to scream, but Isaac's other hand dug into the muscle of her arm. His height and broad shoulders, along with the hold he had on her, prevented her from seeing past him to meet the woman's gaze. Not that anything she said to the woman would be received well. The truth was everyone in the church thought Isaac and his family walked on water. No one would believe her if she told them what had happened.

"Yes," he replied without looking at the woman.

"Your father is looking for you," the older woman said. "And don't you know that seeing the bride before the wedding is bad luck?"

Isaac laughed then, a terse chuckle. "I know. We just can't seem to help ourselves. I can't wait to make Allina my bride."

The older woman giggled. "We're all so excited."

"Can you do me a favor?" Isaac asked, glancing at the woman over his shoulder and flashing her a devious smile. "Do you mind taking my love's suitcase and dress to her changing room?"

"Sure thing," the lady chirped.

"Leave her purse," he added.

The woman shouted "Okay" and rolled the luggage away from them. Allina bit down on her lip and tried to push Isaac away again.

Then he let her go, and she fumbled backward. Leaning against the opposite wall, she rubbed her face where his hands had been and frantically looked down the hall for help. She heard voices toward the front of the church, but the hallway was empty; the woman had disappeared.

His threat was more of a promise. She believed every word of it. She eyed Isaac as he picked up her purse and pulled her cash out.

"If you say anything about what you heard," he continued, "you won't like what I do." He snatched her phone out of her hand and tucked it into his pocket. Without another word, he pushed her empty clutch into her arms and walked away.

CHAPTER THREE

*S*afely in her changing room, Allina sagged against the door and ran a shaky hand over her hair. She rushed to the mirror, leaned in, and ran a finger over her jawline where Isaac had grabbed her. No marks yet.

She scanned the empty room. Spotting the phone on a small table, she hurried to it. Before she could dial her mother, Mother Bell walked in after a short knock. Right behind her was another, younger woman.

The younger woman waved. "Hi."

"Baby," the older woman said. "This is Toya. She's going to help you get dressed. I didn't see your mother. One of the other ladies said she had to run to the flower shop. So I figured we'd help you get dressed."

The women went to work, the younger one opening a small makeup bag and plugging up a curling iron while the older woman unzipped the garment bag holding the gown.

Allina walked over to the dress hanging on the closet door, ran a hand over the soft material. She'd designed it herself for another bride, one who'd changed her mind about getting married. With the short notice, she hadn't had time to make the wedding dress she wanted, so she'd gone with something she already had. The dress was a beautiful A-line, but it wasn't her. She'd always envisioned wearing a ball gown.

Designing wedding dresses was Allina's passion. She'd done so happily for the last several years. She'd had dreams of opening up her own bridal shop. She'd even had the opportunity to take over the one she'd worked in for years when the owner retired. But she'd left it all behind to follow Isaac, to give love a chance. *Now look at me.*

"All right, now," Mother Bell said. "Let's get you into this beautiful dress."

Sighing, Allina took the dress off the hanger. Her hands shook as she dressed. Could she go through with this? The warning in his tone, the hard glimmer in his eyes, told her he would *hurt* her and her parents. She warred with her thoughts. *How can I be so sure he won't hurt them anyway?*

Once she was dressed, the smiling women nudged her toward the full-length mirror on the bathroom door. Allina studied her reflection. She'd straightened her natural curls for the occasion and put a simple, decorative clip at the base of her scalp. The women had suggested a light foundation and blush, but Allina had decided against it. Makeup wasn't her thing.

"There you are," her mother said, entering the room.

Allina's gaze snapped over to the doorway. She let out a sigh of relief at the sight of her mother fiddling with a handmade bouquet as she made her way to the far corner of the room. When Sharon looked up, she gasped. "Oh my goodness. You're beautiful."

Sharon's chin trembled and she gave Allina a wobbly smile. "I hate that I missed helping you get dressed." She waved the bouquet in her hand. "It took longer than I thought at the florist."

Allina rushed over to her and hugged her, holding on to her as if her life depended on it.

She closed her eyes as her mother's arms wrapped around her. The smell of her mother's signature cologne comforted her as it always did. Sharon told the two women to give them a moment and Allina heard the sound of the door closing.

Can I tell her what happened? But Sharon Parker was a worrywart, and she knew her mother would be crushed. Isaac had told her that he'd hurt her, but he'd also threatened her parents. If anything happened to them because of her—

"Allina? Babe, are you okay?" her mother asked, leaning back to meet Allina's gaze, concern in her eyes. "I tried to call your cell phone. Sydney called, too. She's been trying to reach you. Is your phone dead or something?"

She smiled sadly at her mother. "Mom, I…"

Her mother caressed her face, brushing her thumb over her cheek. "I remember when you were a little girl, and you would dance around the house with my white towel on your head. You told me it was your veil. Now I have the honor of watching you realize that dream. I always knew you'd make a lovely bride."

Stepping back, her mother dabbed her eyes with a piece of tissue and fiddled with the bouquet she'd brought in with her. Sharon Parker was beautiful from head to toe. Her long gray dress flattered her small frame and loose tendrils of her light brown hair framed her face. Sharon used to joke that Allina was her "mini-me," and as she grew older, Allina had to agree. They had the same fair skin and light brown eyes. Both were thin, but Sharon was petite while Allina was pretty tall at five-foot-nine. And both had heads full of thick brown hair.

They'd been through so much together and shared a special bond. Allina remembered her mother showing her how, after her sixth birthday, to sew a button on a blouse. Growing up, her mother had always told her she'd do anything for her—and she had. The woman had risked her own freedom to save Allina. Watching her mom, standing before her with a straight pin in her mouth and a determined look in her eyes as she wrapped gray ribbon around the stem of the bouquet, Allina choked back a sob. Calling off the wedding would devastate her mother. Ever since Isaac had asked her father's permission for Allina's hand in marriage, Sharon had been giddy with excitement and the prospect of grandchildren.

The situation was a mess. Sure, it was her wedding, but whatever she did would affect her parents. If she called off the wedding, her parents would be smack dab in the middle of the scandal. What if Isaac was serious? What if he made good on his threats? The thought of running, getting the heck out of there without looking back, appealed to her. But she couldn't put her parents through that. They'd be worried sick about her if they came to get her for the wedding and she was gone.

Her mother's hands stroked her back slowly. "Oh, baby. You're still nervous?"

Nodding, Allina stepped away, averting her gaze. "Yes. Mom, what if I can't do this?"

"Why wouldn't you be able to do this? Isaac is a good man. The members here love him. Everyone was willing to pitch in on decorations, food. The church is excited about this wedding."

Yep. Everyone was excited about the wedding—except her. Looking at her mother standing before her, pride in her eyes, Allina knew she couldn't tell her right then. She had to come up with a plan of action first. Eyeing the clock on the wall, she knew she had to make a move fast.

Her mother reached out and wiped Allina's eyes, gave her

a loving smile. "You're going to be fine; you'll see. When you see Isaac standing at the end of the aisle waiting for you, everything will become clear and you'll race toward him."

Allina wanted to throw up. The thought of seeing Isaac made her sick. "Mom, I—"

"You've overcome so much. I know that you thought you would never find love. But you have, and you deserve to be happy."

Allina thought about her mother's words. As much as she'd wanted the dream, there was a part of her that feared it would never happen. She'd spent years alone until she'd fallen for Kent. Then she'd spent years hoping he'd actually *see* her.

Briefly, she considered calling Kent. After the argument they'd had, she doubted he'd want to talk to her. He had refused to come to her wedding.

"Mom," she said, her voice hoarse. "Do you think I could have a minute? I really need to get my nerves under control."

"Sure," her mother said. Sharon took a slight step back and tilted her head, peering into Allina's eyes. "Are you sure you're okay?"

Allina nodded, just a little too fast. "Yes," she lied. "I'm fine."

Her mother bit her thumbnail and stared at her for a few seconds. Allina wasn't sure how much longer she could look at her mother and not tell her everything that had happened. But Allina wasn't ready yet.

"Okay," Sharon said finally. "Just call me if you need me."

A few minutes later, a knock on the door drew her from her thoughts. She walked to the door and opened it. Her father stood on the other side in his gray tuxedo, his salt-and-pepper hair slicked back, a smile on his face. He ducked as he walked through the door, pulling her into a

warm embrace. She took in his smell and immediately felt
at ease. Old Spice. Judge Owen Parker, or simply Judge,
had always made her feel safe. He was tall and slender, but
strong.

"You look beautiful, baby," he said, tears welling up in
his eyes. "I'm so proud of you."

Allina couldn't help but tear up. The love that shone in
her father's eyes comforted her. She knew what she had
to do.

"Daddy, I love you."

His eyes lit up. "I love you, too."

Allina took a deep breath. "There's something I have to
tell you."

Judge frowned. "Baby, is everything okay?"

"I don't know if I can do this."

Allina told her father about the scene in the hallway,
everything from the overheard conversation to the mystery
woman's warning to the not-so-veiled threats Isaac had leveled against them. By the time she finished, Judge was staring at her, his mouth a straight line.

"Daddy, say something."

Her father sighed, long and low. "I've spent my life trying
to protect you from the things that would hurt you. I haven't
always succeeded. We know this. But you don't have to
marry Isaac, or do anything else that would make you uncomfortable. Please don't feel like you have to do anything
to protect me or your mother."

"But he said he could ruin our lives. What if he knows—"

"He doesn't." Her father's voice left no room for argument. "I think he's just desperate because he doesn't want to
lose you. So he's making baseless threats, hoping to intimidate you into staying with him. That's what a coward does,
baby. Plain and simple."

"I don't...I can't do this. I can't marry him."

Judge stood up and pulled an envelope out of the inside pocket of his tuxedo. He handed it to her. "Take this."

Allina met her father's gaze. "What is this?"

"Open it."

With her eyes still on her father, she opened the envelope and pulled out the card. Dropping her gaze, she ran her thumb over the beautiful design on the front. Her father always picked out the best cards. The heartfelt words reminded her of the love and bond they'd always have; the unwavering support they'd provided throughout her life. When she opened the card, she gasped at the check sitting inside.

"Don't say anything," he said as if he'd read her mind.

Allina was as stubborn as the man standing before her. She'd never asked her parents for any help, even after she moved back to Ohio and struggled to find work. So seeing a check of this amount immediately made her want to give it back to her father.

"Read the rest," Judge ordered.

Under the check, in her father's impeccable handwriting, were the words *Remember to always keep a stash.*

It was the same thing he'd often told her growing up. He'd taught her to "pay herself first," to save money and keep it hidden from everyone else, including any future husband. And she'd followed his instructions to the letter, until she'd recently had to dip into that stash to support herself.

"Thank you, Daddy," she breathed as her tears fell down her face. "I don't know how to handle this. Should I just call off the wedding?"

"I'll support you in any decision you make."

Allina thought about that for a minute. Calling off the wedding, telling everyone who had donated time and energy to making her day beautiful, made her want to throw up. They wouldn't understand. This was Isaac's church, Isaac's family. As much as she hated leaving her parents to deal with the fallout, it was the only way. She'd just disappear for a while, give Isaac time to calm down and save face.

She blinked and looked at her father. "I have to go."

Her father took his handkerchief and brushed it over her cheeks. "Take this," he said, wrapping her hand around the soft cloth. "And this." He pulled out a few hundred-dollar bills and placed them in her other hand. "Now, I'm going to step outside and give you a minute. You take that money and do what you have to do. Just call me in a few hours, let me know where you are."

Allina nodded.

"Hurry." He placed a tender kiss on her forehead.

"What about Mom?" she asked, imagining the disappointed look on her mother's face. She wished she could at least lay eyes on her again, give her a parting embrace.

"Don't worry about your mother. She'll be all right."

"And Isaac?"

"You let me handle him," he grumbled before he pulled her into a tight hug. "I'll do a little investigation of my own. I love you."

She swallowed past a lump in her throat as she watched him disappear around the corner. Picking up her purse, she stuffed the money in there. Opening the inner pocket of the clutch, she said a silent prayer of thanks that Isaac hadn't thought to take her driver's license or her debit card earlier.

Taking a deep breath, she walked to the door and down the hall. But instead of heading toward the foyer, she turned and rushed down the back hallway, through the cafeteria, to the side exit. Her heart raced as she neared the door.

She glanced back to make sure no one saw her. Pushing the door open, she stepped outside and took off to the limo. She pulled the door open and slid inside.

The driver turned, his eyes widening when he saw her. "Ma'am?" he asked with a questioning look.

"Just drive, please," she ordered, clutching her purse against her chest when he sped off. Allina needed to go where she felt safest, to the one person who would protect her from the fallout.

* * *

Kent Smith gripped the tumbler in his hand and gulped down the contents. Closing his eyes, he relished the burn of the liquid. It was his second drink of the day—and it was only eleven thirty in the morning. He'd tried to go to work, but he couldn't concentrate so he'd ended up at the Ice Box. The bar wouldn't open for a few hours, so he had the place to himself. *Perks of being one of the bosses.*

In less than an hour, Allina would be married to the preacher man. And he was sick about it. He'd told his friend of many years that getting married to that man would be the biggest mistake of her life. The argument they'd had a few weeks earlier seemed to have had lasting effects, and he couldn't stop thinking about it. He'd been so furious that he'd told her he wouldn't be there. He wouldn't see one of his best friends walk down the aisle.

Even now, he didn't regret telling her how he felt because she *was* throwing her life away for a man she'd known only for months. Not even a year. She'd already given up her dream of opening a bridal shop, going into business with a friend. For what? The chance to have a church wedding and some dream life with a white picket fence and a gang of

kids? That was noble and all, but walking away from everything she'd worked hard for was stupid.

Okay, maybe I was a little harsh.

He couldn't get the look in her eyes out of his head,
how disappointed she'd been when he'd basically called
her stupid. He was desperate. In a way he hadn't been in
years…or ever. He was a jerk, plain and simple. But she'd
known that all along. At least that's what he'd told himself
after she left and went back to Ohio.

"Starting early, huh?"

Kent clenched his jaw. "Well, the last time I checked, my
father was dead."

"Ouch," Morgan said, walking over to the bar where Kent
was seated.

Kent watched his brother pull a clean glass from behind
the bar and sit down on the barstool beside his.

"I figured you'd be here," Morgan said, as if Kent hadn't
just basically told him to fuck off. "And you'd better be glad
I'm feeling too sorry for you to respond to that comment."

Kent snickered. He probably *shouldn't* have brought their
father into it. It had been years since his death. The family
hadn't been the same since then, but they'd had each other.
Which made it better.

He glanced at his brother out of the corner of his eye.
When Morgan's biological parents had been arrested, Kent
had convinced his mother and father to take Morgan and
Morgan's brother Caden in, and he'd never regretted it. Doing so only proved that biology didn't matter. Kent didn't
have siblings, but when he'd met Morgan that day on the
playground all those years ago, he'd realized what it was like
to have a true brother.

"Syd's been calling her," Morgan said. "She's a little
concerned because she hasn't heard anything. I take it

Allina is the reason you're working on a fifth of cognac before noon?"

Kent swallowed. "I guess I was hoping she wouldn't go
through with it."

His brother shrugged. "Well, she has to live her life,
Kent. If the minister makes her happy, why shouldn't she
go for it?"

"That's just it. She's not happy. She hasn't been for a
while."

"Look, Allina is an adult, capable of making her own decisions. As her friend, you should be there for her even if she
falls flat on her face."

"I guess," Kent mumbled. Needing a change of subject,
he asked, "How's my ladybug doing anyway?" Kent was an
uncle. Who knew one tiny baby would be able to wrap him
around her finger before she could even utter a word?

"Fever went down and she's not crying so much. We're
exhausted. But that goes with the territory."

Little Brynn had an ear infection. Morgan and his future
sister-in-law Sydney were beside themselves trying to nav-
igate parenthood. And both had been terrified when Brynn
got sick because they didn't know what was going on. Kent
was with them when they rushed the baby to the emergency
room, Syd in tears and Morgan trying to comfort her while
maintaining his own composure.

"I'm glad she's better." His mind wandered back to Allina. "So Syd hasn't talked to her?"

Morgan shook his head. "Nope. She talked to her mother,
but not Allina. Cali hasn't talked to her either."

In hindsight, Kent thought he should have put his own
feelings aside to support his friend. After all, it must have
been hard to find out none of her friends could attend the
wedding. Syd had planned to go, but the baby's sickness

prevented her from going. Cali was on the other side of the state supporting Jared, who had a court date to finalize custody of his daughter. *I mean, who gets married on a Friday afternoon anyway?*

"Why wouldn't you just tell her how you feel about her?" Morgan asked.

As for his feelings, who knew what they were. The only thing he ever knew for sure was she was too good, too nice, and too important in his life to fuck up their friendship. But he feared he'd done just that.

Grumbling, Kent said, "I told her how I felt about her marrying him. She didn't want to hear what I had to say." He knew what his brother was insinuating, but Kent refused to respond to it.

He glanced at Morgan out of the sides of his eyes again. His formerly cynical, commitment-phobic brother had seemingly been recruited to the Kent-needs-a-woman Club, headed by Sydney and Cali. Being in a relationship with Syd had turned Morgan soft. Instead of shooting pool and drinking cognac, he was playing Scrabble with Syd by candlelight and drinking Pinot Grigio. It wasn't his fault, though. Kent knew all too well what the love of a woman would make a man do. He'd been there, done that. And it was all good—until it wasn't.

Morgan sighed and finally poured a healthy shot of cognac into his empty glass. "That's not what I meant, but whatever. Why don't *you* call her?"

Before Kent could respond, the buzz of Morgan's cell sounded.

"Syd?" Morgan answered. "Is everything okay?"

Kent listened as his brother asked about Brynn and exchanged conversation about medicine, milk, and diapers. Then Morgan got quiet. If Kent hadn't been paying attention, he would have missed the quick glance his brother shot his way. A few tense minutes later, Morgan hung up.

Kent had an uneasy feeling in his gut. "What's wrong?" he asked.

"It's Allina…"

He sat up straight, his stomach rolled. "What happened? Is she okay?" Only he knew the answer before he even asked. She wasn't okay, or Morgan wouldn't be beating around the bush.

"She didn't get married," Morgan said, his voice low.

Kent let out a sigh of relief. But then…he looked at his brother, who still had a solemn look on his face. Confused, he frowned. "Wait, why didn't she get married? And where is she?"

"They don't know. Apparently, her mother called Syd to see if she'd heard from her," Morgan explained.

"She's missing?"

"Not exactly. Allina…"

Kent clenched the edge of the bar. "What? Just say it, Roc." They'd called Morgan Roc since grade school.

"Her father knew she wasn't going to go through with it, told her to call him in a few hours, but her mother panicked when they hadn't heard from her and assumed she'd show up here. So they're just wondering where she is right now."

Kent stood up, tipping the bar stool over. "What do you mean, they don't know where she is?"

Morgan shook his head. "No one has heard from her since she left."

Anything could have happened to Allina. And he wasn't there, because he was being a prick. He'd let his anger keep him from supporting his friend. If he'd been in Cleveland, at least she would have had him to turn to. But he'd been too stubborn to be there. "Something must have happened.

Does *he* know anything? Why did she decide not to marry him?"

"According to Syd, her mother didn't say. She just told Syd she was sure Allina would show up here and to call her when she heard from her. But that's it."

Where the hell is she? Glancing around the bar, Kent thought about everything he'd heard. His first thought was to drive down to Cleveland and look for her. This wasn't like her. She was dedicated and loyal and determined. She wouldn't leave unless something had happened. And that led Kent to think that *something* was the groom himself.

"I have to go," he said, grabbing his briefcase.

"Where are you going?" Morgan asked, a frown on his face. "What are you going to do? We don't know anything."

"I have to find her. Obviously, she's in trouble. He did something to make her run." It was as simple as that in his mind. He had to find her.

CHAPTER FOUR

*K*ent was going crazy. It had been a few hours since he'd found out that Allina had run away from the church. He'd been tempted to drive to Ohio, but Sydney had convinced him to stay close in case Allina returned to Michigan. Running a hand over his bald head, he sighed. The rain had been falling for hours, beating against the roof and the gutters. The storm was the first severe one of the season. He dialed Syd again, asked her if she'd heard from Allina. Of course, she hadn't. It hadn't been that long since his last call.

The doorbell rang. He rushed to the front door and swung it open. Allina stood before him in the doorway, her head down, clutching her purse against her chest. Closing his eyes, he slumped forward in relief.

"Allina?" He tilted her head to get a good look at her face.

Letting his gaze wander over her, he took in the lightweight jacket she wore and the ... wedding dress. It was dirty and ripped at the bottom. She was soaking wet, from head to toe. Her hair covered her face like a veil, her hands were clenched together, and her shoulders were slouched. Swallowing, he reached out and swept the hair out of her face.

"Allina," he called to her softly. "Are you okay?"

Slowly, she raised her head. When their gazes met, he was hit with an overwhelming urge to hold her, which wasn't really new. It just wasn't normal. But he'd do anything in that moment to make it better. Her bottom lip trembled and he inched closer to her. When she let out a whimper, he pulled her to him in a tight hug.

As she cried into his chest, he whispered that she'd be okay, that he'd protect her, that he'd help her. But the more he assured her, the louder she cried. His chest tightened as he rubbed her back. His thoughts were spinning. What the hell happened? He had so many questions, but *God, please let her stop crying.* It was pure torture. And he'd had the nerve to think Morgan was soft. He hated to see anybody he loved cry. But Allina...she wasn't an overly emotional person. In all the years he'd known her, he'd only seen her cry a handful of times. That last time had been here, the last time he'd seen her. An ache settled in his throat as she sobbed.

When the tears finally tapered off, he glanced out the door and noticed the cab still sitting in the driveway. Reluctantly, he tapped her arm lightly. She pulled back and her big, glassy orbs stared back at him. He swept his thumbs under her eyes.

"Let me go take care of the fare, okay?"

She nodded, setting her purse on a small table by the door.

"I'll be right back," he said gently.

He pulled his wallet out of his pocket and ran out to the cab. After he paid the driver, he returned to the house and kicked the door closed behind him. Wrapping an arm around her, he led her into the living area.

She tugged off her small jacket, giving him a complete view of the form-fitting silk dress. Without a word, she dropped down on the couch. He sat down next to her, their knees touching. "It's going to be okay," he murmured, rubbing her arms. "I'll take care of you."

Peering up at him, a pained expression in her eyes, she let out a slow breath. "I didn't get married. I ran. I didn't even think to change clothes. I just had to get out of there. I bought a train ticket, and then I fell at the station. My dress is ruined," she cried. "Everything is ruined. I'm ruined."

He grabbed a box of Kleenex off the coffee table. "You're not ruined. Stop saying that. Can you tell me what happened?"

"I don't have anything with me, obviously," she continued. He could tell she was trying to pull herself together. She cupped a hand over her mouth and let out a muffled sob. "My phone broke. I dropped it, and then Isaac took it."

He'd replace her phone in the morning, but he had to know... "Did he... hurt you?" he asked. Kent steeled himself for her answer. *If he hurt her, I'll hurt him.*

Allina closed her eyes and hugged herself. Shaking her head, she said, "Not really, not physically." Her hands gripped her elbows.

Her tears continued to fall unchecked. He grabbed a few tissues and wiped her eyes, then her cheeks. "What did he do?" he asked.

"I'll tell you. I promise. But do you mind if I take a shower, get out of this dress? I can't stand being in it another minute."

Sighing, he nodded. "Whatever you need." It wasn't a surprise that she'd changed the subject without answering his question. Allina did things on her own time, in her own way. And he'd wait. He always did.

He stood up and headed to his bedroom. He fumbled around in his drawer for a dark T-shirt and some basketball shorts. Allina was thin, so anything he had would likely fall off of her, but he figured something with a drawstring would help. When he turned toward the door, he stopped in his tracks. She was standing there watching him.

His gaze flitted around, from his closet to his chest to his...bed. As long as they'd been friends, he'd never brought her into his bedroom. Most of their interactions were in the living room or the kitchen. Glancing at her quickly, before focusing his attention on anything else, he searched for the right words.

Finally he told her, "I'll go and get you a towel. And..." He cleared his throat. "You can use my bathroom."

After he got her set up with towels, lotion, and an extra toothbrush, he left her. In the kitchen, he started a pot of tea and turned on the fireplace to take the chill out of the room. It was colder than normal in southeast Michigan. Instead of the mild temperatures usually associated with early May, the temperature had dropped with the rain.

Kent couldn't get the look in her eyes out of his head. She didn't just look hurt; she looked devastated, humiliated. She'd avoided eye contact and seemed to crumble into herself. He hated it. And he hated *that asshole* for making her feel that way. Picking up his phone, he was tempted to call Syd to let her know that Allina was there, but something told him to hold off. He couldn't explain it, but he felt he needed to talk to her first before he told anyone else where she was.

Hearing that the preacher man hadn't hurt her physically made him feel better on some level. But that only lasted a minute. Physical wounds healed faster than emotional ones. Whatever he did could have lasting effects on Allina. It wasn't like she hadn't had plenty of pain already in her life. Some things she'd shared with him. Others, he knew he'd never know. It was okay, though. That's why their relationship was the way it was. They accepted each other, not only for the things they said, but for the things they didn't say.

He glanced at his phone when it vibrated. Jared, or Red, was calling. His friend was on the west side of the state, preparing for a court appearance. A few short months earlier, he'd been reunited with his young daughter Corrine. Tomorrow, he'd get permanent custody of her since the girl's mother was set to serve a twenty-year prison sentence. Cali had accompanied him for support. Kent knew their friends were worried and Red was likely calling for an update.

The crew had all gone to college together at the University of Michigan. They were one intertwined group with countless connections. His brother, Morgan, played high school basketball with Red. Red was Sydney's twin brother. Sydney had introduced them to Cali and Allina because they were roommates their first year of college. As the years went by, no matter what career or romantic route each of them took, the bonds of friendship between them remained strong. They'd seen each other through the best and the worst times of their lives. That was important to him.

The loud, shrill whistle of the tea kettle pierced the air, and he turned the gas off and poured hot water into a mug. He dropped the tea bag into the cup, and squirted honey and lemon in it. Figuring she was hungry, he grabbed a roll of crackers from the pantry and cut a few pieces of cheese—her favorite snack.

As he padded back into the living room, he heard the sound of his bedroom door closing. He set the plate on a table and sat down. Rubbing his palms against his pants, he waited. She appeared in front of him, wearing his oversized T-shirt and black shorts. Her natural curls were pulled back into a loose braid. Allina was usually pale, but in the dim light of the room, she looked almost translucent.

He motioned for her to take a seat. "Here," he said. "I

made you some tea." He wrapped a throw around her shoulders.

Taking a sip, she closed her eyes and moaned softly. Allina was the only person he knew who loved herbal tea. Tea was something she treated herself to often, since she didn't drink alcohol.

"This is good." She took a few more sips, and then relaxed into the couch. "Thank you."

He took a deep breath. "Are you ready to talk? You know you can tell me anything."

"I know." With a heavy sigh, she nodded. "You were right," she whispered, a lone tear falling down her cheek.

He closed his eyes, unable to take seeing her cry again. "Lina, what did he do?" he asked again.

She swallowed visibly. "I was so wrong about him. He's not the man I thought he was. I knew I couldn't marry him." She tucked a leg under her. "I can't believe I thought he would make me happy."

The thought of her being *happy* with Isaac—after Kent had told her it was a mistake—still stung. He'd said some hurtful things to her in an attempt to make her see reason. They hadn't even known each other for a full year when the man proposed. There was no way she knew Isaac well enough to marry him. It hadn't been Kent's most shining moment; he'd acted like a jealous boyfriend instead of a supportive friend.

Morgan had told him he was a jealous ass, and Red had ordered him to admit his feelings for Allina, but it wasn't that simple. Allina was his friend. Above all else, he wanted her to be happy. And he'd had a lingering feeling that Isaac wasn't what he seemed. Kent read people. That was what he did best. He could spot a fake a mile away, and he made it known that the pastor-to-be was not the saint he pretended to be.

"I heard him," Allina continued, staring at him, but not

really looking at him. "He was talking to a woman. They were arguing."

She explained to Kent the conversation Isaac had had with the mystery woman, the subject of money and the threats. While she told the story, rage began to build inside of him. His ears pounded when she told him that Isaac wouldn't explain to her *why* the woman wanted money. He clenched his fists when he heard about the threat to make her life hell and destroy her father's reputation.

"Then he grabbed me," she mumbled.

Kent bolted to his feet, unable to sit still any longer. His heart seemed to be beating out of his chest. "He what?" he asked, careful to keep his voice even, controlled. "You said he didn't hurt you."

Dropping her gaze, she said, "He grabbed my chin and told me to get dressed and smile for the cameras."

Fuck that. Kent wanted to hurt Isaac, in front of the entire congregation. He paced the floor like a caged animal. Violence never solved anything. That much was true. But, damn it, it would make him feel better.

"Kent?" her soft voice pulled him from his desire for vengeance.

He glanced at her, his gaze softening when he met hers. "Yes," he grumbled.

"I'm okay."

"No, you're not," he said incredulously. "You're here. Crying. On what should have been the happiest day of your life. You're not okay."

"I *am* okay. Or I will be. God will—"

"Allina, I know that you trust the Lord and everything, but this is a big deal."

One of the things he loved about Allina was her faith in God. She was steadfast with it and a devoted Christian. But she wasn't one of those churchgoers who bombarded people with her views.

She dabbed her eyes with a piece of tissue. "You're right. It's a big deal. But I'm not there anymore. I left."

"I'm glad you did," he said, finally sitting next to her again. He squeezed her hand. "Your mom called Syd, looking for you. Syd, Cali…everybody is worried about you."

She froze, then gripped his sleeve. "Oh God. I forgot to call my dad. I told him I'd call when I was settled. He's probably worried sick," she said, panic in her voice. "I need to check on them, see if they're good."

"Calm down, okay? You can use my phone to call your parents."

"Thanks," she said. "Oh, Kent? Can you please not tell anyone else I'm here?"

Frowning, he asked, "Why?"

Shaking her head quickly, she said, "Because. My plan is to lay low, give it some time. I know Isaac will contact Syd or Cali. It's better if they don't know I'm here. That way they don't have to lie." She blinked rapidly. "Promise me," she begged.

Honestly, he'd do anything for her at that point—even lie to everyone. Especially if it would stop her from crying and looking so damn terrified. Before he realized it, he nodded his agreement. "I won't tell anyone right now. But you have to tell me something…"

Wanting to hide out for a few days was understandable. Allina was downright scared, though. Something wasn't right. "From what you've told me, he's a dirty bastard," he continued. "You know I won't let anything happen to you. That's why you came here, right?" He gazed into her damp eyes. "But is there something else you're not telling me? Does Isaac have something over you and your family?"

CHAPTER FIVE

Can I just...let me call my parents first and then we'll talk?" Allina asked.

"Of course." Without a word, he got up and left the room. Moments later, he returned with his cell phone. He placed the phone in her outstretched hand and headed toward the door.

"Wait," she called, stopping him in his tracks. He turned slowly. "Will you stay with me while I make the call?"

Kent nodded. "Okay."

He took a seat next to her on the couch as she dialed her father's cell.

"Hello?"

Tears filled her eyes at the sound of her mother's voice. "Mom?"

A soft gasp echoed in her ear. "Allina?" she cried. "Thank God! I've been so worried about you. Where are you?"

Allina let her head fall against the back of the couch before she answered. "I'm okay. I'm sorry. I meant to call you right away."

"Babe, where are you?" Sharon asked again. "Your father said he gave you money and told you to call. I called Sydney and she said she didn't know where you were, I was so…" Sharon paused before she continued. Allina could picture her mother holding her palm to her chest, like she'd done so many times before when she was relieved. "I thought something happened to you. Don't ever scare me like that again. I don't think I could take it."

"I'm in Michigan, Mom. But I'm not with Syd. I'm over at Kent's house." Allina rocked back and forth in her seat. "I just wanted to let you know that I'm safe. Where's Dad?"

Sharon screamed her father's name. "He's coming, sweetie. Do you need anything?"

"You've done enough for me. Thank you so much for the card and the gift. I love you so much. But I need to make some decisions—for me."

"That Isaac…" her mother grumbled. "Your father told me what happened. I'm so sorry, baby. Your father has been inundated with calls all day from that family. Right now, Isaac is playing the distraught, inconsolable groom. Hold on, here's your father."

"Allina?" Her father's baritone voice soothed her nerves. "Are you okay?"

"I'm fine, Daddy. I'm safe. What happened once Isaac realized I was gone?"

"He barked a bunch of orders, demanded we tell him where you were. But your mother put on a great performance. Acted like she was just as surprised as he was when you disappeared without so much as a 'Good-bye, asshole.'"

Allina gasped. "Daddy?"

"What?" he said innocently. "Anyway, I put an end to your mother's charade when Isaac showed up here a little while ago begging us to report you missing. I told him to go to hell."

It wasn't funny, but Allina couldn't help but snicker.

Judge Parker had a potty mouth. It was the one thing that drove her mother crazy.

"I've been checking into some things, trying to find the mystery woman," Judge continued. "But I haven't come up with anything and no one at the church is really talking."

"Mom told me you've been getting calls from his family?"

"Yeah, yeah. I just got off the phone with the bishop. He told me to contact them as soon as I heard from you. Are you staying with Syd?"

Allina peered up at Kent. He had been sitting quietly next to her, offering silent strength. "No. I'm at Kent's house."

There was a short pause before her father said, "Good. Tell Kent to keep his eyes and ears open. I'm not sure how Isaac is going to play this right now. I've had someone tailing him since he left the church. Hopefully he'll just let it go, but if he doesn't... well, I'm glad you're protected."

"Thank you. I'll call you when I get a new cell phone. Tell Mom I love her and we'll talk soon."

Allina hung up. It was torture putting them through this. She prayed her father was right and Isaac was just issuing idle threats to keep her in line. At least now her parents knew she was safe and not lying dead in the Cuyahoga River.

She brushed her palms together. "That was hard," she told Kent.

"I bet," he agreed, holding her hand between his. "But it's done. Now you can concentrate on you."

I'll never let you go.

Allina shuddered as Isaac's promise replayed in her head. She pulled away from Kent to put some distance between them.

I will hurt you.

After a few moments of silence, Kent stroked his low-cut beard. "Allina, I need you to be honest with me. You don't want me to tell Syd or anyone else that you're here, okay. I get it. But something isn't adding up. The only thing that makes sense is if Isaac really has something that can hurt you and your parents."

Allina tucked a lock of hair behind her ear. "It's not like that." She tugged at her earlobe. She understood why Kent was concerned. There was so much she hadn't told him about her past. "I just need some time, a day or two to sort myself out. That's all."

She just wanted to relax, knowing that she was in good hands. That's why she'd ended up on his doorstep. Sydney was her best friend, her sister, but Isaac would call her first. Then he would call Cali. He wouldn't know to call Kent, though.

Early on in her relationship with Isaac, she'd made the decision to not share how much Kent meant to her. It would only cause a problem, she'd thought at the time. Yes, Isaac knew that Kent existed, but she'd downplayed their friendship, made it seem like they just hung out together because of Syd and Cali. It was a blatant lie that she'd regretted from the moment she'd told it. Not only because she wasn't a liar, but because Kent was so much more than a casual acquaintance.

He was everything.

It was the reason their argument had stuck with her, why she'd been so stressed in the days leading up to the wedding. His opinion mattered to her. It always did.

Staring down at her toes, she wished she could go back and do everything over. She felt guilty, like she'd betrayed her friendship with Kent by not acknowledging him. Especially when he'd always made sure every woman he dated knew about her and how important their friendship was to him. He'd once told her that any woman who wanted to be with him would know that Allina was part of the package.

"Okay," Kent said, his voice low. "You've had a rough day, and I can understand if you want to relax. But I want to help you. I wish you'd let me."

You're dead.

Allina squeezed her eyes shut. She wasn't one to let down her guard easily. When she met Syd her freshman year in college, they'd started a tentative friendship because they were roommates. It wasn't until Sydney was brutally attacked one night that Allina and Syd had bonded. And it wasn't because Allina had felt sorry for her. Unfortunately, Allina felt Syd's pain because she'd felt it herself. Only her attacker hadn't been a teaching assistant with control issues; hers had been her aunt. Aunt Laura, her father's younger sister, had molested Allina from the age of ten until her fourteenth birthday.

It had started one night while her parents were gone at a community event. Allina's father was well-respected in their hometown of Akron, Ohio. He was a philanthropist, a person who gave back to those less fortunate. Because of that, her parents were always going to balls, fund-raisers, and other elite events in the city. Her aunt had always been charged with babysitting Allina.

The first touch, the first incident, had been a simple inappropriate touch. Things escalated as time went on, and on her thirteenth birthday, Aunt Laura raped her. Allina didn't tell because her aunt had promised her that her parents would be ruined if she did. Allina believed it. After all, her parents were so high profile that a scandal would surely devastate their reputations. So she'd kept quiet.

Each time, each night, her aunt took a piece of Allina with her when she left, and soon Allina was finding other ways to cope. She started sneaking into her parents' liquor cabinet, drinking herself numb just to get through the evenings. She retreated to her room, rarely coming out. Her school work suffered and she lost so much weight her mother dragged her to countless doctor appointments.

Isaac knew about that part of her past. Aside from Syd, he was the only one who did. After he'd proposed, she'd opened up to him about it. He'd assured her that her secrets were safe with him, that she could trust him. An uneasy feeling settled in her stomach. Unfortunately, Isaac's threat had brought up so many more memories, put her right back in that room with her aunt. That same fear and desperation she'd felt all those years ago had taken her over from the moment he'd grabbed her in that hallway.

She pressed a hand to her throat, warred with herself over telling Kent some things or everything. As much as she trusted Kent, she didn't know if she could open herself up like that to him yet. At the same time, she knew he would keep her confidence.

"The woman in the church? She was scared," Allina admitted. "She called him evil. At first I didn't understand why, but now I do. I believed him when he said he would hurt me. He said he'd kill me. His words...they took me back to a time in my life I'd rather forget, when I..." Allina wanted to tell him, knew she'd feel better if she could just say the words. But she couldn't bring herself to do it.

He rolled his shoulders. "Lina, you don't have to worry about him hurting you. If he even tries to get to you, I'll fuck him up."

She snickered. There was no doubt in her mind Kent could take Isaac in a fight. Even though Kent hadn't played football in years, he was still built like an active player. He

ran every morning and trained in the gym at least three times
a week.

"I know," she told Kent. "I just…it got to me. Now I
can't stop thinking about how I almost…Why didn't I see
it?" Allina had been careful all her life. She didn't date
just anybody, didn't open her house to her friends or intro-
duce her parents to random men. Rubbing her hands on her
thighs, she choked back a sob. "I feel like an idiot."

"You thought you were in love," he said simply. She
didn't miss the way he rolled his eyes.

Their gazes met, held for a second, before she dropped
her head. "I wanted to be."

Kent patted her on her knee. "We all do to some extent.
Shit, both of your friends found love, we're getting older…"
While he talked, she couldn't take her eyes off his hand on
her knee, mesmerized by the contrast of his dark skin against
her pale, light skin. "Don't beat yourself up for putting your
faith in the wrong man."

Peering up at him, she nodded. "He said he'd never let me
go. I'd be a fool to think that he'll give up because I left him
at the altar."

He studied her. "Is there something else you want to tell
me?" he asked.

Her heart raced and her lips parted. "What?"

"I mean, you're here with me." He tilted his head and
paused. "You know he won't come here looking for you.
But you're guarded, like you're on the verge of saying something, but then you stop yourself. You don't have to be
scared. If he comes here, I have something for him."

Unable to look him in the eyes, she admitted, "I *am*
scared. But it's not because he has something over me or
my parents." She swallowed hard, fiddled with the edge of
the blanket. "I never told you this, but when I was a kid…I

was molested by a family member. My aunt Laura," she croaked.

His eyes were on her. She could feel them even though she wasn't looking directly at him

"She did it for years, threatened me every day to keep it a secret," she continued. "Told me she'd hurt me and destroy my father; the same thing Isaac said. I told him about it because I thought it was the right thing to do. He was supposed to be my husband. Then, he used the same tactics on me today; used what I'd told him in confidence to intimidate me. It was like he didn't even care."

"Allina?" Kent wiped her eyes with a tissue.

She hadn't realized she was crying. "I'm sorry," she breathed. "Lost myself in my thoughts."

"You're good," he assured her, sadness clouding his features. "I'm sorry that happened to you. I can't even imagine carrying something like that. Why didn't you ever tell me? I mean, we've talked about some serious things. I'm not saying you had to, but . . ."

Allina watched as he looked away for a second. Telling him about her past was something she'd wanted to do from the moment he'd opened up to her about his all those years ago. In fact, she'd tried on many occasions. But the shame she'd always felt every time she thought about it kept her from saying anything. She was damaged goods, unstable and full of baggage—the one thing he'd told her he wanted to avoid at all costs.

"I just didn't know how to tell you," she answered. "Syd was the only person I told, until Isaac."

Allina recalled sharing this part of the story with Syd years ago. The difference in her friend's reaction was in stark contrast to Kent's. Not that she'd expected him to gasp and tear up like Syd did. One good thing about Kent was his ability to remain calm. She'd only ever seen him lose his cool in a few situations. In this instance, she was glad that he was who he was. Otherwise, she would crumble.

Kent took her hand and brushed his thumb across her knuckles. "I'm sure it helped to talk about it."

Nodding, she leaned in closer to him, needing the comfort and warmth he provided. "It did."

"Allina, none of this is your fault. It's nothing to be ashamed of. What your aunt did to you doesn't make you a bad person."

"But I did things…" She nibbled on her bottom lip. "It was pretty bad. Remember when I told you I used to drink, but I stopped?"

"Yes," he said.

"I almost killed myself." Her lips trembled as she remembered the disappointment in her parents' eyes. She'd taken a fifth of vodka straight and ended up in the hospital with alcohol poisoning. "I ran into a neighbor's garage, caused thousands of dollars of damage. My father used his position as a judge to sweep it right under the rug." It hadn't been the first or last time her father would have to cover up a crime for their family.

He glanced away from her, shifted in his seat. "Do you think Isaac'll use this information to threaten your father's career?"

"God, no," she replied, waving a hand of dismissal. "I never told him about that. But he doesn't need proof of wrongdoing to manipulate me. He knew exactly what to use to make me cower in fear. His last name is enough to get him whatever he wants in that town. His father is the governor's spiritual advisor." Kent's phone blared from the other side of the room. When he made no move to pick it up, she asked, "Aren't you going to get that?"

"No," he answered. "They can wait. I'm concerned about you right now."

"It's fine. It's probably Syd. You should call her back." She scooted to the edge of the couch, but turned back to him before she got up. "I'm sorry I never told you. It wasn't because I didn't trust you, I—"

"What?" he said with a frown. "Don't apologize to me for not telling me your business. That's not how we do. You mentioned that you'd only told Syd before you told Isaac. Did your parents never find out?"

"Eventually. My mother actually walked in and caught her."

"I'm sure they were devastated."

"They were. Especially my father." Her dad had practically raised his sister after their parents died. He'd given her everything in life, from a college education to her first car. When he found out what she'd done, he was heartbroken.

"He probably wanted to kill her."

A chill ran up Allina's spine and she rubbed the back of her neck. "By the time he found out, she was already dead," she said, her voice flat.

He frowned and she knew what was coming next. "So your aunt died in jail?"

"No," she said. "You understand why I'm scared, right?"

He pulled her into his side. She relaxed into him, took in his smell. Kent always smelled like a fresh shower, no matter what he'd done for the day. It amazed her how comforting that smell was.

Rubbing her shoulder, he said, "I do. As much as I hate it, I get it. He sounds like the type who doesn't take no for an answer." He brushed his lips against her forehead and she let out a heavy sigh of relief. "But I'll take care of him," he added, a hard edge to his voice.

She lifted herself up and peered into Kent's eyes. "What do you mean?" She shook her head rapidly. "I don't want you to do anything that will get you in trouble."

"No worries," he said, giving her a quick smile. "I know what I'm doing."

"But, Kent, he—"

"Is a punk?" he interrupted. "I can't stand men who bully women. Sometimes all it takes is a man to get that through to a punk. So..." Kent rubbed her back. "Don't worry about it. I'm going to handle it. Tomorrow, we'll deal with the preacher man. Right now, you rest. You can stay here as long as you need to."

The room descended into silence and Allina tried to relax. Isaac was still in Ohio and Aunt Laura was long gone. There was no reason to ever speak about her again. Allina prayed that Isaac was just issuing idle threats. After all, he couldn't know what had happened all those years ago, the circumstances surrounding her aunt's death—or the fact that her mother had killed her.

CHAPTER SIX

Kent held Allina in his arms for what seemed like hours. It was a first for them—him holding her, being so close to her. Aside from a hug here or there, he'd purposefully kept her at arms-length physically. It was why, through their entire friendship, he'd never allowed Allina to just chill with him at his house. Not after eleven o'clock.

Because there *was* something there, an underlying feeling that scared the shit out of him. He'd been around enough women to recognize when someone wanted him, and he knew how Allina felt about him. But knowing that only strengthened his resolve to *not* acknowledge it or even let on that he could even possibly reciprocate her feelings.

In the process, he'd probably hurt her feelings numerous times and ultimately pushed her straight to the fucking pastor in the first place. But he had his own baggage, his own past to deal with. His reasons for not risking his place in Allina's life—as her friend—were valid, considering his history with women. Maybe it was the example his parents had set? Or the talk that he'd had with his father about the love of a good woman making the toughest man stronger? But he wasn't afraid of, or closed off from, relationships. He just wasn't good at them. Inevitably, he always disappointed the women he became involved with, spent too much time working to pay attention to them, forgot a stupid anniversary... or just got tired of them invading his space. He was impatient, didn't have time to play silly, bullshit games, or coddle anyone's feelings. Not good relationship material.

Women came easy to him, though, and he'd had his share. And he'd had enough ass thrown at him from chicks who wanted his money. Kent wasn't rich, but he lived comfortably. Allina would say he had multiple streams of income because he had a day job, owned a business, and had invested part of his inheritance very well.

Finding a woman who was on his level, someone who could talk to him about anything from the stock market to conspiracy theories to the NFL playoffs, appealed to him. Even though she fit the bill, that person couldn't be Allina. They'd been friends too long to ruin it over a failed romance. And she was too important to him, too good, to take a chance on something so uncertain. Despite the long-lasting enduring love his parents shared, he'd seen the dark side of love as well.

His mother had once told him it was the Smith charm that made otherwise sane, independent women lose their minds. She would know. She loved his father with everything in her, and he loved her desperately. When he died a few years earlier, Kent didn't think she would make it. Apparently Mama was right about him, though. Watching your girlfriend throw herself off a building because you'd hurt her feelings was awful. The guilt alone had eaten him up.

Allina had been there for him after that. Prior to that, they'd been cool with each other, only bonded through their common relationship with Syd and the rest of the crew. As they'd spent more time together, their friendship deepened, and it became more about their connection to each other than the people who connected them.

Then it was...more. Still, there was no reason good enough to change what made them Kent and Allina—acceptance and a comfortable, genuine friendship. Complicating it with love and expectations would undoubtedly disrupt the ease they had with one another.

But now she was sleeping in his arms, in his shirt and his shorts—after midnight.

Tracing the outline of her cheek, he took in the soft lines of her face, the flush in her skin. She had come to him, shared her deepest secret with him, after everything. He couldn't deny that made him feel good, to know she trusted him. He didn't like that she'd been hurt in the process, but he was glad that she hadn't ended up Mrs. Isaac Hunter.

Yet, he couldn't shake the feeling that she was holding back. He wouldn't push her to tell him. Obviously, she had her reasons for keeping whatever it was under wraps. It wasn't as if that would change anything. No matter what she told him, he would always be there for her. That was a given.

His attention drifted back to her, the rise and fall of her chest as she slept. She'd been through more in her life than most people. Her childhood wasn't church all day on Sundays, Wednesday night Bible study or choir rehearsals like she would have him believe. It was dark, twisted, perverted.

If her aunt were still living, he was sure he'd confront her. The woman had taken Allina's innocence and terrorized her for years. Thinking back, he realized her experience affected everything she'd done up until that point. The way she seemed to close herself off to new people, how she always seemed on guard, and even how committed she was to God.

Kent understood why Allina acted the way she did. She'd had enough heartbreak to last a lifetime. Now she had to deal with Isaac. One day soon, Kent would meet the minister face-to-face. The man had threatened to kill her. The thought of anything happening to her chilled him to the bone. Because a life without her was not something he was prepared to live.

Sighing, he finally stood, lifting her into his arms. She nuzzled her face into his neck and his skin tingled. The soft scent of his soap on her skin was driving him crazy. Carrying her through the house, he wondered if he'd have the self-control to just deposit her in the guest room and leave her. Already, he was tempted to watch her sleep, stay with her through the night, and fight every demon or nightmare she had.

After he entered the second bedroom, he paused. Shaking his head, he snickered at the argument he'd had with his mother about even buying a two-bedroom condo. He'd told her time and time again that he was comfortable with one bedroom. Hell, he'd actually wanted a loft. What the hell did he need extra space for? His brothers, if they needed to, could crash on the couch. Any woman he deemed important enough to bring home would share his king-sized bed. But Mama was more pragmatic. She'd insisted to the point where he agreed just to shut her up. Shifting Allina in his arms, he realized two bedrooms had been a good idea. He'd never admit it to his mother though.

Scanning the room, he took in the neutral colors. He'd given Mama free rein to decorate the space. The queen-sized bed sat in the middle of the room with pillows and a comforter that looked like something right out of a magazine. A dresser lined the wall next to the door, a chest sat in the corner, and a flat-screen television was mounted to the wall across from the bed. It looked like a hotel room. There was nothing of him in there, and he could count on one hand the number of times he'd actually stepped foot in it. The cleaning service he'd hired took care of it every week so he knew it wasn't dusty. That's all that mattered to him.

Kent stepped over to the bed and gently set Allina on the mattress. He tossed a pillow on the floor and pulled back the heavy comforter. There was a small alarm clock, a box of Kleenex, and a lamp.

Once again, he let his gaze wander over Allina's still body. A desire to climb into the bed and wrap his arms around her washed over him and he shook it off. *What the hell?* Had he missed her so much that he was reduced to ogling her sleeping form?

"Kent?" Her raspy voice jarred him from his thoughts.

"Yes?" He focused on her closed eyes, then her plump lips.

"Thank you for everything," she murmured. "You're always there for me. I should have listened to you."

Allina's eyes opened and a few tears escaped the corners and drizzled down her face onto her pillow. He brushed a thumb under one glistening orb. "You know I'll do anything for you," he grumbled, his voice hoarse.

"You could have turned me away, especially after my last visit here."

Leaning down, he placed a tender kiss against her cheek. He clenched his hands together, resisting the urge to touch her or worse—kiss that mouth of hers. *Get it together, Kent.* Shaking his head, he willed himself to stop thinking about her lips against his. Finally he stood to his full height and pulled the covers over her.

"I'm tired." She let out a slow, shaky breath. He knew she wasn't just talking sleepy tired.

"I know." He rubbed the top of her hair, traced the wrinkle in her forehead with his thumb. "Get some sleep. We'll figure this out in the morning."

Before he could walk away, she grabbed his arm. "Will you promise me something?" she asked.

Without looking at her, he asked, "What is it?"

"No matter what, you won't ever stop being my friend."

Frowning, he met her concerned gaze. "Why would you ask me that?" There it was again, that feeling deep in the pit of his stomach that there was something else going on.

"You hate drama. I brought it to your doorstep." Her eyes welled with fresh tears. "And it's not..."

Dropping to his knees, he took her hands in his. "Listen to me. Nothing will make me turn my back on you. Besides, this isn't what I would consider drama." He smiled slightly. "Drama is when your brother sleeps with your other brother's ex-fiancée."

She giggled. "Ouch."

He grinned broadly, happy that he was still able to make her smile. Yes, the joke was at the expense of Morgan and Syd, but it was worth it to see the glow of real laughter in her eyes. Last year, around this same time, his family had almost been torn apart because Morgan and Syd wanted to be together. Syd had been engaged to his other brother, Caden. Den, as they called him, had broken her heart mere months before their wedding and she'd turned to Morgan for comfort. Unfortunately for Kent, he'd been caught in the middle between them. It was a sticky situation, especially since he actually didn't believe Syd and Morgan were that wrong. In fact, he'd even encouraged both of them to follow their hearts and secretly rooted for them to make it work.

"Allina, stop worrying about that. You're my girl; you know that."

"I know. And you're my boy. I just can't say thank you enough. Thanks for letting me stay here."

"Stop thanking me. You can stay as long as you need to. You trust me, right?"

She nodded. "Yes. I trust you," she assured him, closing her eyes and snuggling against the pillow.

"Okay then. We're going to get through this." He paused, taking in the long lashes against her cheeks. "We'll talk more in the morning. Get some sleep."

"Not yet," she said, opening her eyes. "Can I just say something?"

He nodded.

Seconds later, she said, "You know me. Better than most. Over the last few months, I wasn't sure our friendship would survive. The last time we spoke, it was...awful."

Another reminder that he was an ass. Turning away, he replayed that conversation in his mind yet again.

"You told me I was a fool," she said, biting down on her lip.

He wasn't someone who lost his temper a lot, but that night, he'd surprised himself.

"I was so angry," she continued, tracing the stitches on the comforter. "At the time, I embraced it. Because that was the only way I could really walk away from you." His eyes flashed to hers, surprised at her soft admission. "I told myself that what you said didn't matter. But at the end of the day, it mattered. You matter."

"You matter to me, too." Of course she did. More than she could ever know.

"And you were right," she whispered, her voice thick. "Maybe if I'd just listened..." She hunched her shoulders. "Never mind. No sense in bringing up the past."

"It's a good thing you didn't marry him. Maybe now you can start over, pick up the pieces and focus on what you want. That's always been a problem for you."

Allina was a gifted seamstress, and her dream was to design gowns. He wished she hadn't been so willing to abandon that dream for Isaac, but the good news was she could still make it a reality. He was pretty sure Cali was still interested in going into business with Allina like they had planned before she'd started dating that clown.

Reaching out, she grazed his chin with her fingertips, and he almost forgot to breathe. Closing his eyes, he willed that *more* between them away. *She's better off.*

Standing up, he squeezed her hand. He needed to put some space between them. He eyed the door. "I have some work to do," he lied. "Rest now."

"Good night, Kent."

"Night."

CHAPTER SEVEN

*A*llina woke up with a start, practically tumbling out of the bed, arms swinging like she was fighting. She didn't even realize she was screaming until Kent charged into the bedroom. It was the second time since Kent had left her that she'd drifted off to sleep and had a nightmare.

She glanced at the clock on the nightstand, grateful that it was finally morning, albeit early morning. It had been a horrible night.

Kent approached the bed tentatively. "Allina, it's going to be okay. It was just a bad dream." He sat down on the bed next to her, his presence immediately putting her at ease.

"It was so real," she whimpered, clutching the thin sheet to her chest. "I thought he was going to…" *Kill me*. She didn't even want to say the words out loud. It was ridiculous. *Wasn't it?* It made more sense for him to just let her go. Would he?

Kent pulled her into his arms. "I won't let him hurt you," he promised. He'd told her that countless times, but he couldn't be there every minute of every day. Allina didn't doubt that Kent would do everything he could to protect her. She knew he would, but she had to start making wise decisions herself. Staying away would work for only so long.

It just wasn't realistic since her parents were in Ohio. She wouldn't allow herself to let her guard down anymore.

Lying back on the bed, she stared at the ceiling. "I need to get myself together." Even though her words were directed toward him, she was talking more to herself.

"Allina, it hasn't even been twenty-four hours since you left. There's a lot that has to happen. It's going to take time."

Aunt Laura had disrupted her sleep for years. It had taken years for her to work through everything that had happened then. It was hard, but she'd done it.

But now, it seemed Aunt Laura was back, taking up residence in her dreams. Except this time, she was with Isaac. He was chasing her, and Aunt Laura was helping him. Laura had promised to destroy her if she told anyone. Isaac had basically done the same thing. Two people who were supposed to love her had threatened to kill her. It was no wonder she was terrified. For a long time, she'd thought her life was ruined.

"I just don't have it in me to go through this again," she said, her voice cracking. "What did I do wrong? Why did God let this happen to me?" Allina had done what she was told—went to college, worked hard, and didn't turn her back on God, even though there were times when she thought she'd buckle from the pressure. "I've always tried to do the right thing—no cheating or stealing—and I thought Isaac was the man that God sent for me. And even with him, there were things I didn't do. I waited..." She was unable to finish her sentence and reveal that she'd avoided random relationships with men, never even went to second base. "It feels like God is punishing me for something."

A flicker of something passed through Kent's eyes before he lowered his gaze. "I don't know what to say to that, except you know that's not true," he murmured. "You're stronger than you give yourself credit for."

"You don't understand. It has been years since I've felt this . . . fear in the pit of my stomach. I don't know if it's because of Isaac himself or the fact that his words mirrored things that my aunt told me. Now I keep thinking about my past, that night."

It was true. Allina had been transported back in time ten years ago. She remembered it like it was yesterday, because the events of that day had changed her life. Her parents had gone to a charity event. As usual, her aunt had come to sit with her. Allina had been old enough by then to stay home by herself, but her parents had unknowingly encouraged Allina and Laura to stay close.

It had started out like every other night. Allina would lock herself in her bedroom, like it mattered. And her aunt would unlock the door and come in. This particular time, Laura had brought a camera, told Allina that she wanted to take pictures. Allina had decided enough was enough and fought back. She told her aunt that she would tell her mother. Then, Laura told her that if she did, her father's career would be over and her mother would be dead. It was the first time she'd threatened violence against Allina's mother. All this had surprised Allina because her father had always taken care of Laura. She gave in to protect them, but things went horribly wrong when her mother entered the room.

Things escalated quickly when her mother jumped on her aunt. They fought and Allina scrambled to call her father. Everything had happened so fast. One minute, Aunt Laura was punching her mother, and the next her mother was standing over Laura's lifeless body. Allina still remembered how bright the blood had been, flowing from her aunt's head.

When her father arrived he screamed. It was a piercing, loud wail. She'd never heard her father even raise his voice, because he was so mild mannered and even-keeled. Allina had been rooted to her spot, glancing back and forth between her dead aunt and her mother. Mom was holding a bloody baseball bat, chest heaving, tears streaming down her face. There were no last minute apologies, no struggling to survive; her aunt was just gone. Died instantly.

Her father made a decision in that moment that would put all of them at risk. Instead of calling the police right then, he took the bat from her mother's hand and disappeared. A few minutes later, he came back. The bat was gone. He ushered them out of the room and told them to get in the shower. Once they were done, he collected their clothes, gave them money, and told them to leave and not come back for a few days. They did exactly what he said.

A few days later, they returned home to yellow police tape, news trucks and detectives swarming the house. Her aunt's death was labeled a random act of violence by an intruder. The reporters speculated that it could have been a criminal that her father had punished exacting revenge. Soon, with no leads, the case was closed. It was over. Her father, the judge, had covered up a murder. They never spoke of it, or her aunt, again. Every trace of her, every picture, was removed. It was as if her father had never even had a sister. It was that act, that sacrifice, that had propelled her to give her life to God. She didn't want her parents' sacrifice to be in vain. She owed it to her parents to excel, to never do anything that would disappoint them.

"What do you want to do?" Kent's voice pulled her out of that memory.

She shrugged. "What can I do? Before yesterday, Isaac had never done anything to make me feel so afraid of him. Yes, he was controlling at times, but never abusive. I keep thinking about that woman in the church, flashing to the look in his eyes when he threatened me."

"Maybe we can hire a private investigator," he suggested. "Just to keep an eye on him, make sure he stays where he is. Who knows? It might help turn up something on that woman."

We? He kept saying the word, and Allina couldn't help but feel comforted by it. She wasn't alone; that much was clear. It made her heart swell.

Lying down on the bed, she stared up at the ceiling. Maybe Isaac would just lick his wounds and move on. But deep down, Allina knew better. "I know this is going to sound strange, but I have this feeling that he's never going to give me up." She met his gaze. "He's going to come back for me. And that puts you and everybody else I love in jeopardy."

His jaw tightened. "He can try something, but I promise you this... if he brings his ass here, I'll send him to the hospital. I'm not playing. Don't worry about Syd and Cali. I'm pretty sure Morgan and Red will feel the same way. We're not going to let anything happen to you."

Allina turned away, stared out the window.

"I understand," Kent said softly. "Something of this nature has brought up a lot of feelings and memories of your past. And it's because you're afraid in a way that you haven't been in a while."

Kent rubbed her knee and a familiar feeling settled into her stomach. With everything going on, she hadn't had time to really think about how she still felt about him. Sitting there in front of him, staring into his dark eyes, she wondered if her canceled wedding would change anything for them.

Shaking her head as if to clear her mind, she asked, "Do you think I can use your computer? I want to e-mail my boss and let her know that I won't be coming back." It was a spurof–the-moment decision to quit her job, but she knew she'd never go back to the chain bridal store she'd been working at for the last few months as an alterations associate.

"Sure." He stood up, glancing at his watch. "Use the one in the office. I'm going to run out to the store to get a few things. Will you be okay here?"

"I'll be fine. Go ahead."

He nodded and shot her a quick glance before he left her alone.

She stared at the door for a few minutes after he closed it. They'd never been this close, physically. He'd never really invited her to his place much. The majority of the time they'd spent together was at her place or in a public setting. There was a stark difference between how he treated her as opposed to Syd, and even Cali. She used to wonder why, but figured it was because Syd was with his brother and Cali was... well, Cali. And her friend had been firmly and obviously fooling around with Red for most of their adult lives.

She scooted out of the bed and headed down the hall toward the office. Pushing the door open, she stepped inside. Kent was very clean, almost to the point of being obsessive. She knew he hired a service to come in, but he hated dust because of his severe allergies and spent a lot of time cleaning. He hated clutter, so he didn't have a lot of extra stuff lying around. The office was neat, with a drafting table, a large desk, two chairs, and a small cabinet that likely held his files. In the far corner of the room there was an easel with a covered painting on top. Two big monitors sat on the desk.

Kent was a techie, a computer engineer at his day job. But he was also an artist. He loved being in front of a canvas or on his computer designing graphics. She'd tried to convince him to go into business for himself, but he'd balked at it. Which was a shame because he lit up when he was working on his passion. They had that in common, spending evenings curled up with a pad and a pencil, drawing sketches—sometimes together.

She sat down at the desk and powered on the computer. Drumming her fingers against the desk, she waited for the system to come up. After a few seconds, she was able to log in to her e-mail.

The plan was to e-mail her boss, let her know that she would not be coming back after her planned two-week vacation, and apologize for any inconvenience she may have caused. But when she saw the e-mails from Isaac, she felt sick to her stomach.

She clicked on the first one. *Where are you? You better call me as soon as possible or else.*

There were dozens, mostly one liners, ranging from *I can't believe you actually think you're going to get away from me* to *I told you I'd ruin your life. Don't make me.* With each message, the tone grew more menacing, threatening. The one surefire way to hurt her would be to hurt her family. The big skeleton in their family closet involved murder and impeding a murder investigation. If he had somehow found out about her aunt's death it would change everything. She'd do anything to protect her parents.

She moved the messages to a separate folder as she read, but the last and most recent e-mail gave her pause. The hairs on her arms and neck stood up as a shiver ran up her spine. He'd stepped up the intimidation with another one-line e-mail. His intent was clear and she had to do something. She read the e-mail one last time. The sound of her heartbeat thrashed in her ears as each word came into focus. *Don't worry, maybe your friend Sydney will tell me where you are.*

CHAPTER EIGHT

*K*ent had spent the majority of the night pacing the hall outside of his second bedroom door. He'd tried to go into his own room. Really. But the first bloodcurdling scream from the room where Allina slept woke him up, and he couldn't relax after that.

When he'd barged into the room to check on her, she'd held on to him like he was her savior. It took almost an hour to calm her down, but he'd done it with low whispers and soft caresses. Eventually, she'd drifted back to sleep, but he was left with that uneasy feeling.

Once he realized that getting a good night's rest wasn't in the cards for him, he'd tried to work on a project he was painting for the bar. When he couldn't concentrate on that, he'd busied himself cleaning and rearranging his refrigerator. That's when he first realized he didn't have much food. He'd given her the last of the cheese and he was pretty sure she wouldn't want crackers for breakfast. So he'd pulled on a pair of sweatpants, intending to jump in his car and sneak off to the twenty-four-hour Super Walmart when he heard the next scream. This one was louder than the last.

Throughout his lifetime, the urge to beat someone up had come and gone. Sometimes he'd end up fighting, other times he didn't. But there was only one other time when he'd known if he saw the person, he'd do him serious bodily harm. And Isaac was up there with the predator who'd raped Syd years ago on campus.

He wanted to hurt him, envisioned pummeling him until he couldn't stand, let alone walk. Who the hell did Isaac think he was anyway? The fact that Allina was scared and anticipating the day that fool would come back to get her made his blood boil.

Now, Kent was racing back to his condo. He knew he was going to get a ticket. Then he was going to have to explain to the officer why he was doing fifty-five on a twenty-five-miles-per-hour street. He'd taken too long. A simple trip to the store to get yogurt, berries, and granola for his terrified friend had turned into a full shopping trip. Allina had called his cell and told him to get home as soon as possible. He had to get back to her.

Once he made it home, he rushed in, dropping the grocery bags on the floor by the door. "Allina!" He paused to listen for her. When she didn't answer, he started down the hallway leading to the spare bedroom. "Allina," he called again.

"In here," she shouted.

"Hey?" he asked, stepping into his office. Her eyes appeared damp, but bright. "What's wrong? Are you okay? Did something happen?"

"I-I got a…" she stuttered. She swallowed visibly, then sighed. "Isaac e-mailed me."

His hands tightened into fists. "And? What did he say?"

She gestured to one of his computer monitors. Giving her a quick glance, he leaned in and read the e-mail. It was clearly a threat, one that made him want to find that motherfucker and… Sighing, he dropped his head. She didn't need his rage; she needed his comfort.

He extended a hand to her and pulled her up and into his arms. They stood like that for a while, swaying back and forth. When she started to pull away, he let her.

She wiped her eyes and pressed her hands to her cheeks. "We have to call Syd. I told you—"

Kent squeezed her arms. "Look at me," he told her softly. "Don't worry about Syd. She's fine. I talked to Morgan not even an hour ago and he was home with them. Okay?"

"But we have to warn—"

"Allina? We will. Your father has someone on him. He would know if Isaac was here. He would've called you, right?"

She nodded rapidly. "Yes."

"It's just an idle threat, something he's using to manipulate you. It's okay."

She slumped forward, resting her head on his chest. "You're right. I just... I panicked when I saw the e-mail. I'd never forgive myself if something happened to Syd because of me."

"First of all, it wouldn't be *because* of you. So don't put that on yourself." He ran a hand down her back. "And Isaac doesn't want to die. Morgan would kill his ass."

He realized his little attempt at humor hadn't worked when Allina peered at him quizzically. "Oh God."

"I'm just joking," he assured her. "Nobody's going to die."

Allina seemed to suck up all her emotion. She tugged at the T-shirt she had on and scratched her forehead. "I'm sorry. Did you get what you needed at the store?"

Grateful for the change of subject, he replied, "I did, and I got you a few things too."

He grabbed her hand and led her through the house to the kitchen. Once she'd settled into a chair, he went to grab the bags he'd left by the door.

"I figured you would want to change clothes."

He unloaded the groceries and a few necessities that he'd picked up for her. Shopping for a woman wasn't his forte, but he'd managed to grab a pair of yoga pants, a few T-shirts, and some sneakers. He'd passed the bra and panty aisle three or four times, going back and forth with whether he should try to get her something. Finally, he'd just grabbed a pack of Fruit of the Looms and a sports bra and tossed them into his cart.

She eyed the stuff laid out on the table and picked up the pack of underwear. She shot him a quick glance before focusing her attention on the boy shorts.

"I hope I got the right sizes," he said, smiling at the blush that worked its way up her neck.

Allina explained that he'd done pretty good on the yoga pants and shoes. According to her, the panties were a little big and the bra was a little small, though. But they would work.

"Thank you," she whispered. "I appreciate everything you've done." Allina rubbed a hand over her bare leg. "Maybe I should get dressed."

"Good idea," he agreed. "I'll fix you something to eat."

She slid off the high bar stool, giving him an unabashed view of her upper thigh. He turned his head quickly and focused on the clock on the stove. It was still early enough to go for a run. Although he hated to leave her, he needed to let off some of the tension that had set in. Maybe she would go with him?

He knew it was a long shot. Allina did not run. She likened running to walking a plank. As thin as she was, she hated to exercise. And she didn't do it often.

He let out a strained breath when she walked out of the kitchen. Between Isaac, her aunt, and his hormones, it was going to be a long day.

As he waited for her, his phone dinged and he glanced at

it. Syd. His future sister-in-law had texted him an outright threat of bodily harm if he didn't call her back. He sighed. Grumbling a curse, he turned his phone off and tossed it on a table.

Allina came out fully dressed and he smiled at her. There was something about a woman in yoga pants. The ones he'd purchased fit her like a tight glove, showing off all of her curves. "How about we go for walk? Clear our heads a little?" he suggested, food forgotten.

Smiling, she asked, "What about breakfast?"

He shrugged. "We can eat when we get back."

She wrung her hands together and swept a hand across her forehead. "Okay. That sounds good. A walk," she added, pointedly. "Not a run."

He barked out a laugh. "Maybe a little one," he joked.

She shoved him. "You know how much I hate it."

"Okay, okay." He held his hands up in surrender. "No running. Besides, I don't even have on my running gear."

About an hour later, they re-entered his condo. He headed to the kitchen to get two bottles of water. He tossed one at her when he walked back into the living room.

She dropped down on the couch. "Oh my God, you're so wrong for that," she said, taking off her shoes. " 'I don't even have on my running gear,' " she mocked with a scowl on her face. "I knew you were going to do that. These shoes you bought me were not made for running."

He chuckled. "I'm sorry. I couldn't resist. It was just a little sprint." He took a long gulp of his water, then joined her on the sofa. "We have to get you to the store so we can buy you another pair of gym shoes and more clothes."

"Or I can just go with my first inclination and not go on another *walk* with you—ever." She giggled and he smiled in response.

"Lina, stop fronting. You know working out does wonders for your mood. I bet you feel better, don't you?"

She shrugged. "I'll give you that. It was definitely good to get out of the house. I'm so happy the rain stopped. I almost panicked when I thought it was going to start up again."

"I run in rain, sleet, and snow," he said.

"Whatever," she said, untwisting the cap to her bottle and taking a sip. "I don't do inclement weather."

They settled into a comfortable silence as they both finished their water. His stomach growled and he glanced at her.

"Hungry?" she asked, arching a brow.

"I guess so," he said. He started to stand up, but her hand on his wrist stopped him.

"Let me make you breakfast."

Frowning, he shook his head. "Allina, you don't have to cook for me."

"I want to." She scooted closer to him, her eyes on him. She was radiant, glowing. They'd taken the scenic route. He figured getting her to focus on something other than her circumstances made her feel better. On their way back to the house, he took off on her, forcing her into a little race. The walk seemed to have done wonders for her, though. She seemed relaxed, smiling from ear to ear. Her face was flushed and her hair was piled on top of her head in a messy bun. "I want to do something for you."

I can think of a few things. Clearing his throat, he stood up, gently pulling his arm from her grasp. "There's no need." He walked to the thermostat to check the temperature, to make sure it wasn't just him that felt hot. It was.

She walked over to him. "I'm cooking for you. Case closed." Then she hugged him. Tight.

For a moment, he forgot about everything else. All that

mattered was her in his arms, the electricity in the air, and the peace he felt that she was with him. When they finally pulled apart, he stared at her, sucked in a deep breath. A *thank you for offering to cook, I want some bacon* would have been appropriate—if he wasn't tongue-tied like an immature school boy.

She patted him on the shoulder. "I hope you have bacon." She winked at him, as if she'd been reading his mind. "Let me get a shower, then I'll get started."

After she disappeared down the hall, he rolled his eyes, muttered a long curse, and peered up at the ceiling. Since when did he get all giddy about a hug from his friend? Not only was he amazed by her strength, he was drawn to her now even more than he was last night. There was something about her spirit that he couldn't get enough of.

For the first time, he wondered if he'd actually be able to keep his distance and maintain the "strictly friends" status quo.

A soft knock on the front door jarred him from his thoughts. *Who the hell is that?* He glanced at his watch. It was early as hell. He stomped to the door, intent on cussing someone out, releasing some of his pent-up tension. He yanked the door open and whatever curse word he'd been ready to use died on his tongue. Syd was standing there, arms crossed and a deep furrow on her brow.

Sydney Williams had been in his life for many years. They had their own relationship, outside of hers with his brother, based on mutual respect and unwavering support. When he introduced her to people, he didn't feel the need to quantify her as his future sister-in-law. She was his sister in every sense of the word.

The fallout from her "affair" with Morgan had affected the family dynamic, but he was glad his relationship with

Morgan and Syd remained as strong as it ever was. Unfortunately, he couldn't say the same for Den. His other brother had pretty much distanced himself from everyone, except Mama. Kent had reached out to him many times, but Den had refused to talk to him. It saddened him, but he hoped Den would come around eventually.

"Where the hell have you been?" she hissed, stepping past him into the house.

He glanced down the hall quickly, then back at Syd. "What? What are you talk—?"

Syd smacked him on the shoulder. "I've been calling you all night!" she shouted. "All night."

His sister looked like she had been through the ringer. Her dark curls were wet and wild, and she had on a pair of blue jeans, a huge sweatshirt, and a pair of flip-flops. Her cheeks were flushed and her hazel eyes wide.

"I mean, why haven't you answered any of my calls? I've been worried sick. I couldn't sleep." She paced the floor, murmuring curses under her breath. "My friend is missing and you're choosing this time to screen your calls. I can't believe you. Like this is not an emergency," she babbled on. "I just want to punch you."

Her fist against his shoulder startled him. "Ouch," he grunted, rubbing it. "I'm sorry, Syd."

"Sorry?" she asked, throwing her hands in the air. "I don't want your apology. We're supposed to be working together here. We need to find Allina." She huffed as she paced the floor in front of the door.

"Allina is—"

"Anything could have happened to her." She whirled around to face him. "You know, I've been thinking about this all night. She could be lying in a ditch somewhere. And you just decided to ignore my calls and texts."

He glanced back down the hall, hoping Allina would pick that moment to walk out because Syd was not going to shut up long enough for him to get a word in. Not when she was riled up like this.

"Kent?" Syd shouted, snapping him out of his thoughts. "You didn't even hear me."

Nope, I didn't. "Syd, I told you I was sorry. My phone was turned off," he lied. "But—"

"What were you doing?" she demanded. "Why would you turn your phone off knowing Allina skipped out on her wedding and we don't know where she is? I tried to call her parents again, and it keeps going to voicemail."

He rubbed the back of his neck and darted a quick glance down the hall again. "Syd, you need to calm down. Where is Brynn? Does Roc know you're here?"

"They're asleep, okay," She folded her arms across her chest. "I snuck out of the house."

"Did you at least leave a note?" he asked flatly.

"I don't care." She raised her chin. "Morgan doesn't run me. And stop changing the subject," she ordered, pointing her index finger at him. "Who's here?"

"W-what?" he stuttered, scratching his forehead. "What are you talking about?"

"You keep looking over there," she said, gesturing toward the hallway. Narrowing her eyes, she tilted her head. "Please don't tell me you have a woman here, Kent. Because if you do, I'm going to blow a gasket."

He grabbed her shoulders. "Stop," he said, squeezing them gently. "Why would I have some random woman here?"

"You know?" Syd said. "This is probably all your fault."

"Me?" He pointed at himself. "What did I do?"

"Yes, you! If you would have just told her how you really felt in the—"

"Syd, shut up," he ordered, placing a hand over her mouth, glancing down the hall. *Damn it*. And just like that, Syd had innocently revealed something he'd never shared with anyone but her. When it came to Allina, it wasn't his brother or Red that he'd confided in. It was Syd. His sister, and friend, the person he went to the first time he'd ever felt attracted to Allina. She was also the one who'd sat with him, drinking shots, after Allina left Michigan to get married. It was then that he'd revealed his feelings were *more* than a simple friendship.

His sister pushed him away. "Why did you tell me to shut up? Kent, I'm scared for her." Syd sighed.

Syd's chin quivered. *Oh God. More tears*. Until he'd seen Allina crying the night before, Syd had held the record for making him feel helpless when she cried. Last year, she'd spent a ton of time crying after her breakup with Den and developing relationship with Morgan.

Back then, all the drama had taken its toll on her. She'd been a wreck, crying at the slightest thing. Even when she and Morgan said "Fuck it, let's be together," she'd sealed it with a tear—or a river of tears.

"I'm such a bad friend. I should have been there. What if he did something to her? I knew she had doubts. Hell, I had doubts. And you know why?" Syd asked, panic rising in her voice. "We don't know shit about him. He could be a freakin' serial killer masquerading as a pastor. For all we know, Allina could be one in a long line of victims. What if his church is not a real church after all, but a cult? That happens all the time. Women get lured into relationships with psychopaths."

Syd had the frustrating habit of going off on a tangent. And she had the uncanny ability to get him off track. One minute they could be talking about the Food Network and

the next she was talking about...political scandals and conspiracy theories. She was too damn dramatic for her own
good.

Frowning, he quipped, "Syd? Sis, you need to lay off the
Investigative Discovery Channel."

"This is not a joking matter," she said through clenched
teeth.

"If you would stop talking and listen to me," he said, "I
could tell you that Allina is fine, and—"

"You don't know that!" Syd shoved her hair back away
from her face.

He exhaled. "I do. Can you just shut the hell up and let
me finish? Allina is here."

"Here? As in here in your house?"

"Yes!"

"Why the hell didn't you tell me that?" she yelled. "You
just let me go off with conspiracy theories when you could
have said something the minute I walked in here. Or better
yet, you could have picked up your goddamn phone and told
me that."

"Because I told him not to tell you I was here," Allina
said, walking into the living room.

"Allina!" his sister screeched.

The two friends hugged each other.

"You're okay." Syd cried as they swayed back and forth.

"I'm so sorry," Allina told his sister.

Kent slumped forward, sighing in relief. He was happy
the secret was out. Despite Allina's initial wishes, Kent
knew he wouldn't have been able to keep her presence from
Syd for long. It would have been the one time he'd ever
broken someone's confidence. Good thing, he didn't have
to. Allina needed her friends and the support they could
provide.

CHAPTER NINE

Standing there, hugging the friend she knew would always be there for her no matter what life put in their paths, Allina felt centered, supported. After they pulled apart they both wiped their eyes.

"Allina, I was worried sick about you," Syd said.

"Can we sit?" Allina said, motioning toward the couch. "Kent bought me the wrong shoes and my feet hurt."

Syd glared at Kent, who shrugged. "What?" he asked.

"You are such a jerk," Syd said, pointing a finger at Kent. "I can't believe you didn't tell me."

Kent opened his mouth to speak but Allina rushed on. "It's my fault. I should have let you know where I was right away, but I was scared."

Syd blinked, her hand flying to her chest. "Why? What happened?"

It would have been easy to tell Syd that she'd run out on Isaac because she didn't love him like a bride should love her groom. But Syd deserved to hear the truth. Allina began her story, starting with the scene at the church and ending with her showing up on Kent's doorstep. By the time she was finished, Syd was gaping at her, mouth wide open.

"Oh my God," her friend said. "I'm so sorry you had to go

through this. But I'd be lying if I said I was sorry you didn't marry Isaac." Syd gave her a half-shrug. "I should have done more, said more. I guess I felt like it wasn't my place to tell you not to do it, especially when you seemed to be happy for the most part. Who was I to tell you not to get married?"

Allina wasn't shocked. Syd and Cali had voiced concerns from the beginning. She leaned forward, resting her chin on her palm. "You did warn me in your way. I just didn't listen. I thought I was doing the right thing by marrying Isaac," Allina said, glancing at Kent again. "Thought I had something to prove."

"What could you possibly have to prove?" Syd asked.

"That I could be happy. That I could find someone who loved me, someone who wanted to be with me." Allina rolled her eyes, fighting back the tears that threatened to fall. "I couldn't turn back after I'd left everything behind to be with him."

Allina watched as Syd and Kent exchanged glances.

"Syd, I need to tell you something. This morning, I received a few e-mails from Isaac," she explained. "Well, more than a few. Most were threatening, but there was one in particular that…" She swallowed past a lump in her throat. Allina glanced at Kent, but he wasn't looking at her. When she turned to Syd, her friend was watching her intently, waiting on her to speak. "Isaac didn't say it outright, but he threatened you, Syd."

Syd frowned. "What do you mean, he threatened me? What did he say?"

"It wasn't an obvious threat." Allina let out a harsh breath and told Syd what the e-mail said. "It still has me worried."

Kent pounded his fist against the end table next to his chair, startling her. He jumped to his feet. "This is bullshit. I'm going to beat the crap out of that piece of shit."

Allina peered up at Kent, who was walking the floor, grumbling curses as he paced back and forth. She knew that he'd been holding back earlier when she'd shown him the e-mails. She guessed he couldn't hold his anger in anymore. To see him so angry, so willing to fight for her, made her limbs tingle and her heart race. She realized it was a mixture of gratitude, admiration, amazement, and…hope. Her life wasn't as ruined as she'd initially thought, and neither was she. Maybe she would make it through this stronger than ever?

"Kent, please. Stop."

"She's right, Kent," Syd agreed. "Calm down. The last thing we need is you going to jail."

"What the hell do you expect me to do?" Kent shouted. "That asshole threatened to kill her in his church. And now he's insinuating that he might come after you to get to her. I'm tired of him. Period. I'm going to take care of this." He grabbed his phone.

"Wait," Syd said, rising from her seat. "What are you doing, Kent?"

"Calling Morgan and Red. Allina, I'm going to have you stay with Syd because I'm going to Cleveland today."

Allina bolted out of her seat, but Syd got there first, snatching the phone away from him.

"Don't," Syd ordered. "I think we should talk about this before we make any drastic moves."

"Kent, you can't go down there," Allina pleaded. "You said it yourself earlier; we're not in immediate danger. He doesn't know where I am. He won't get to Syd or Cali. And my father will take care of my mother. Those are the people I care about. If something changes, we'll know about it." She ran a hand over his arm. The words left her mouth so fast she didn't have time to think about them. And she meant what she said. Watching Kent lose it had put everything into perspective for her.

Her father would do anything in his power to protect her and her mother, like he'd always done. She was in good hands with Kent. Isaac might be a manipulative jerk, but she had to believe he wasn't a dumb one.

Kent's brows drew together. His gaze darted back and forth between her and Syd. Finally he said, "For now. I'll hold on, for now. But if he contacts you again, he's going to deal with me sooner rather than later. That's a promise."

Without another word, he stomped off, muttering a string of curses. A beat later, she heard his bedroom door slam.

Glancing at Syd, Allina plopped down on the couch. "This is a nightmare."

Syd sat across from her on the coffee table, placing a hand on Allina's knee. "It's going to be okay. Kent is just angry right now. He's not used to feeling helpless."

"I know. I just hate that this is happening at all." She gazed at her friend. "I told Kent about my aunt," she admitted softly.

Syd nodded. "How was that?"

Allina scrunched her nose, bobbed her head from one side to the other. "It was hard, opening up to him. But he was very understanding, gentle."

"How did you think he would be?"

Shrugging, Allina said, "I don't know."

"Sweetie, is there something else going on?" Syd asked.

"I just feel embarrassed, that's all."

"About what? You have nothing to feel embarrassed about, Lina. You can't help what happened to you."

"No, not about that. I just feel like a fool. Here I was thinking Isaac was the man I'd prayed for, that he was somebody that I could spend the rest of my life with. There were signs, but I was so focused on moving on, letting go of my feelings for Kent. I handled everything wrong, even running away."

"I understand why you did. A little distance and a lot of time always helps. Right now, Isaac is upset and lashing out. But I have a question for you. Why not call the police, file a restraining order against him? Red could help with that."

Sydney's twin brother Red was an attorney. He had connections in the Sheriff's Department and other police departments in the area. He even golfed with a few of the county judges on occasion. Allina knew he'd help if she asked him. They were like brother and sister. He was just as annoying to her as he was to Syd. But she could count on him.

"Honestly, I didn't really think about calling the police. I'm just going to trust that my dad will take care of it. For all we know, Isaac will go hide in a corner somewhere and never come out. Besides, he'll know what state I'm in if I file a restraining order."

"Okay," Syd said.

"I hate that he pulled you into this with that e-mail."

"Trust me, I'm not scared."

Allina assessed her friend. With a past full of hurt like Syd had experienced, Allina would expect her to be frightened at the veiled threat. Sitting before her, Syd was calm and strong. Nothing about her seemed afraid. It probably had a lot to do with her relationship with Morgan.

"You've changed so much," Allina said. "Being a mother and future wife definitely agrees with you. You seem…content." When she'd first laid eyes on Syd earlier, her friend had looked stressed, but now that she was relaxed, a visible glow radiated from her.

"I am," Syd admitted. A smile spread across her face, in her eyes. "Girl, let me tell you, I hadn't realized how stifled

I've felt my whole life. It was like I was suffocating in my own circumstances. When I fell in love with Morgan, it felt like someone opened a window and let a soft breeze into my heart. And when Brynn came, my life zoomed into focus even more." Tears stood in Syd's eyes, but Allina knew they didn't reflect sadness. They were tears of joy, and she couldn't be happier for her friend. "Now, I know my purpose. Everything I've gone through, every tear shed, every bit of pain, brought me to this point. Now, I can be there for her the way I wished my mother was for me. Now, I can be with a man who pushes me to be the best Sydney I can be. It's a wonderful, free feeling. I want that for you."

Allina didn't know if that was in the cards for her. After what had happened, she thought it might be easier to be alone. But she wanted it. She wanted to feel that free feeling that Syd described.

Syd cupped one of Allina's hands between her own. "I know it seems far off to you right now. But trouble doesn't last always. You know why I believe that?"

"Why?" Allina asked, her voice thick.

"Because you told me that," Syd admitted. "It was you who told me that when I was at my lowest point. It was the truth then, and it's true now."

Allina cried then. Sydney pulled her into her arms, rubbing her back gently. She'd questioned God on the train ride back to Michigan. She'd wondered what she'd done to deserve so much heartbreak in her life. But hearing Syd's encouraging words made her realize that her faith was justified. And fear was not an option for her anymore.

"It's going to be okay, sweetie," Syd murmured. "We'll make sure of it."

There was that word "we" again. It felt good to hear it. Allina wrapped her arms around her friend. They sat there for a moment before Allina pulled away, dashing tears from her cheeks.

She smiled at Syd. "Thank you, Syd. You have no idea how much you mean to me."

"I definitely do, because you mean the same to me. I just need you to be okay. And you will be. I'm glad you came here. Kent will take care of you, and you know I'm going to be right by your side as well—through any- and everything. I won't bail on you."

"Thank you." Allina tugged at her earlobe. "Can I ask you a question?"

"Shoot," Syd said, pulling a few pieces of Kleenex from a box on the table. She handed Allina one.

"I heard your conversation with Kent earlier, or at least part of it." She studied Syd while she spoke. "You said that it was his fault that I was getting married."

Syd leaned back, stretched her legs out in front of her. "I didn't mean that," she murmured. She balled up the tissue in her fist. "I was angry. I had been up all night worried, and I had to take it out on someone."

"But you sounded so serious."

Syd shrugged, pulled at her collar. "It was nothing," she said, giving a dismissive wave of her hand. Clearing her throat, she stood up. "I better get going before Morgan shows up."

Allina had known Syd long enough to realize she was holding back.

"But I will say this," Syd said. "Kent cares about you. He was so upset after your big fight. More at himself than at you, because he wanted to support you. At the same time, he knew it wasn't right."

"I know that now."

"I know how you feel about him," Syd whispered. "I've

always told you to be honest with him. That was for a reason."

"Syd, I can't." Just the thought of telling Kent how she felt made her feel nauseous. She flattened a hand on her stomach. "Aside from the obvious, I was supposed to be married yesterday. What would I look like, saying anything about feelings that really should have faded by now?"

"Allina, trust me. You should tell him how you feel. You know I wouldn't tell you to show your ass if I believed it would turn out to be a bad move. But I can agree that now is probably not the best time, considering the current situation with Isaac."

Allina thought about Syd's words. Had she basically just admitted that Kent had feelings for her? "Are you saying—?"

"I'm saying, take this time to heal yourself. Let Kent be there for you the way you need—and he wants to be. Let things settle down, and then consider being open with him. I don't think you'll regret it either way."

Syd grinned. "Come on, give me a hug." Allina stood up, walked over to her friend, and embraced her. "I love you."

"I love you, too," Allina said.

Syd grabbed her keys. "Tell Kent to calm down and make you some breakfast. I'll call you later. Maybe I'll bring Brynn over to see you."

"Is she feeling better?" Allina said, following Syd to the door. "I miss her."

Allina had been there during the dramatic birth months earlier. Syd's water broke in the middle of her baby shower, after Morgan proposed to her in front of all the guests. The chaotic scene that ensued was one for the record books, but everyone was ecstatic to see Syd become a mother, especially since doctors had told her she'd never have the opportunity.

"She's doing well. I can't believe she's mine. I have lots of pictures."

"I can't wait to see them. I'm so ready to move on from this."

"And you will. Bye, girlfriend. Call me if you need me. Cali and Red made it back late last night. She'll want to see you too."

Allina nodded. "Okay. Talk to you soon."

They hugged again before Syd breezed out of the house. Allina slumped against the door. Even though her initial plan had been to keep her presence a secret for a bit, she was glad at the turn of events. She needed her friends. She thought about what Syd had told her about Kent. It was good advice, and she planned to take it. Soon.

CHAPTER TEN

The smell of bacon wafted to Kent's nose. "I'll call you back, Roc," he said, ending the call. He'd spent the last twenty minutes talking to Morgan on the phone. His brother agreed with the girls that he should wait before charging down to Cleveland. At the same time, Morgan said he was down for whatever Kent needed.

Even though it wasn't what he wanted, he'd decided to give it a few days at least. It had been less than twenty-four hours since Allina had left Isaac. The situation might blow over after a few days, once Isaac realized Allina wasn't coming back to him. Then they could put this behind them once and for all. But if the minister decided to step up his threats, nobody would be able to stop Kent from getting to Isaac.

He walked toward the kitchen, taking in the smell. It had been a while since someone had cooked in his house, as he preferred to order in or mooch off his family. While he could prepare a few easy dishes, he didn't enjoy cooking by any means. But he loved to eat, and Allina could throw down in the kitchen.

As he rounded the corner, he caught a glimpse of Allina bobbing her head and flipping the thick-cut bacon he'd purchased at the store earlier.

"Smells good," he said.

She let out a yelp of surprise, whirling around, fork in hand. "You scared me. I guess my mind was on the task at hand."

He peeked into the pot of buttery grits. "You're going all out."

"I made you coffee, too."

Damn, she's good. Kent wasn't used to this. Having a woman in his home, cooking in his kitchen—something about it felt right. "How did you know I needed some?"

She grinned at him and he felt the corners of his mouth turn up into a smile. *God, she's beautiful.* From her toes, painted with a soft pink polish, to those damn yoga pants. Even that plain white T-shirt looked amazing on her. What he especially loved was her hair, wild and free.

"I figured caffeine was in order. You left so fast earlier." She leaned against the countertop. "I know you're upset and you have every right to be. You're a fixer. You like to *handle* things."

They both stood there for a moment. The silence between them made the crackling sound of the pork frying seem to echo in the room. She'd called him a fixer, like he was a male Olivia Pope. Really he just wanted her to be okay. His desire was to handle things for her, chase her fears away.

"You were right. I'll wait. It doesn't make any sense to go down there and confront him right now. The only thing that will do is tip him off to your location, and we don't want to do that."

"More importantly, I don't want to have to worry about you," Allina added, before she turned around and transferred the crispy bacon from the pan to a plate on the counter. "Breakfast is ready."

A few minutes later, they were seated across from each

other at his small table. The silence from earlier had returned and neither of them spoke as they ate their food. The only sound in the room was the clink of silverware against their plates. Throughout the years he'd known Allina, silence was rarely uncomfortable for them. They'd spent hours doing nothing together, just enjoying each other's presence. No words had to be spoken. Now the lack of conversation did nothing but amplify his thoughts—about the situation, but mostly about her.

Finally, unable to take it anymore, he said, "I thought maybe we could go to the store and pick you up a few more things later. I have to work at the Ice Box tonight, and if you're up to it, I'd like you to come with me."

The thought of leaving Allina alone when she was so vulnerable made his stomach clench with tension. He'd feel better if she was with him, where he could keep an eye on her.

After they'd opened their bar, the group had decided to make sure at least one of the owners was present during the weekend. They had competent management on staff, but Syd had suggested it would benefit them in the long run if they remained hands-on. It was his turn.

"I'd like that," she said. "I don't want to stay here by myself."

He instantly relaxed. "Good. Do you have a specific store you want to go to?"

She placed a hand on top of his. "Kent, you don't have to keep buying me things. I have money. My father gave me a check."

"I don't mind. The bank won't open until Monday morning." He flipped his hand over and squeezed hers. "Besides, what are you going to do for clothes? The bank may put a hold on the check, preventing you from accessing the funds for a while. You can't walk around in the same outfit every day. I have the money, so why not let me do that for you?"

It was refreshing to do for someone who didn't expect it. Most of the women he met were focused on what he was going to do for them, all the while glossing over what they could offer him. In his opinion, the worst type of woman was one who thought that because she looked good, he owed her the world. Looks faded fast and so did his attention.

She dropped her gaze. "I appreciate it, I really do. Thank you again. I'll pay you back as soon as possible."

"Okay, but there's no rush. I'm not going anywhere."

Allina got up and carried her dishes over to the sink. She turned on the faucet and filled up the basin with water. "I'm going to clean up and get ready to go to the store."

He finished up his plate and joined her at the sink. Not thinking, he dropped his mug into the dishwater, splashing the soapy water on Allina. She screeched and stumbled back. He reached for her, sensing she was getting ready to fall. Instead of preventing her fall, she ended up pulling him with her and they both landed on the floor, her on her back and him on his side.

"Ouch," she groaned from her where she lay on the tile. "That hurt." She wiped her face and pushed her hair back, leaving a few suds on her face.

He chuckled. "That was...clumsy."

She laughed then. "It was crazy. How did I fall? There was no water on the floor." She pointed at him. "It was your fault."

He grabbed her finger. "It was not my fault you can't stay on your feet."

She flicked some remaining soap on him. It was a running

joke with their crew. Syd was dramatic, Cali had no filter, and Allina was clumsy as hell. It didn't matter where they were or what they were doing, Allina always seemed to get hurt.

Before he knew it, they were both laughing in earnest. She turned to him. "I needed this."

He tucked a piece of hair behind her ear. "Glad I could help. I've never met anyone who is more accident-prone than you."

She grinned, her eyes gleaming. "Hey. Don't say that."

He stood up and held out a hand to her. When she placed her tiny palm in his, he pulled her to her feet.

Brushing off her clothes, she murmured, "My body is already sore from that run. Now my back is throbbing."

"Maybe you should go lie down for a little bit before we go to the store," he suggested. "I have a heating pad somewhere if you need it."

She waved him off. "I'm good." Peering up at him, she smiled again. A wide grin. "I need to keep moving."

Kent observed her. Her cheeks were flushed and her eyes dancing and he found himself inching closer to her. A piece of her hair was stuck to her forehead and he pushed it to the back.

"I must look crazy," she said, smoothing a hand over her hair.

One of the things Kent found so attractive about Allina was her sultry, deep voice. She talked like she was singing a lullaby. It was low, even, and sexy as hell. And what made it even better was she had no idea it could have an effect on a man.

As if he had no power or control to stop himself, he leaned closer. She peered up at him and froze. Instead of retreating, she stayed where she was, her eyes on his. The air changed in that instant. He brushed her cheek with his thumb and she gasped. Their noses were almost touching. He knew he should step back, walk away, but he couldn't. His body had a mind of its own.

His nose bumped into hers. Her breath still smelled like the honey from her tea. It was warm against his skin. He wanted to kiss her, more in that moment than ever before. Then her lips brushed against his. It wasn't a full-on kiss, but enough to make him want more. He framed her face with his hands and kissed the corner of her mouth, enjoying her sharp intake of breath. She squeezed his biceps, her nails digging into the sensitive skin.

"Kent," she whispered. "Are you sure you want to do this?"

"Do you want me to?" he asked, unable to keep his eyes off her mouth. It was amazing how one simple touch had opened up the box that labeled them "very close friends." He imagined how it would feel to really taste her, to feel her tongue against his, to touch her the way he wanted.

But then where would that leave them? Confused and awkward around each other? Allina wasn't just any woman. He couldn't do her first and ask the hard questions later, because she deserved better than that. They had never really talked about sex with each other before, but knowing her the way he did, he figured she was careful about who and what she did. Being with her, or even kissing her, was a game changer. *But, damn-it, I want to*.

Sighing, he stepped back. He scratched his head. "I'm sorry. This isn't right. We better get going."

Then he left her standing there in the kitchen.

* * *

The car ride was silent and Allina was getting antsy. It had been hours since they'd almost kissed in the kitchen. Things hadn't been the same since. He still took her to the store and bought her more than enough clothing, as well as other things she needed. But their ease with each other had been disrupted and replaced with stolen glances and forced space between them. The conversation consisted of trivial, surface talk—about weird people in the mall, the basketball game that he wanted to watch, and food.

"Do you mind if we go straight to the Ice Box?" he asked softly. "I want to be there before happy hour."

She gripped the sides of her legs. "I don't mind. I can chill out in a booth and sketch while you're working." Among the things he'd purchased was a sketch pad. She rarely went anywhere without one. Over the years, she'd filled many and kept them safely locked away in a chest at her parent's house. She'd used them to design gowns, but they also served as a journal. In her haste to get out of Cleveland, she'd left her current one behind in the suitcase at the church.

It was the little things that Kent did, things that she hadn't even thought of, that made him so irresistible. Just the fact that he'd thought to replace her sketch pad and even get her a purse big enough to hold it made her love him even more.

"Sounds like a plan."

What possessed me to try to kiss him? Even now, she couldn't believe she'd made the first move. *I broke us.* Covering her face, she wondered if Syd was home. Maybe he could drop her off over there. At least then she wouldn't have to be in the same room, watching him flirt shamelessly with the female patrons or smile at the petite waitresses.

Admittedly, Allina didn't have much experience with men, but it felt like Kent wanted her. The way he looked at her, touched her, made her dizzy. *And brazen, apparently.* But look where that had ended—with her standing alone in the kitchen. The fact that he'd walked out and left her standing there still stung.

"Allina?" he said, his voice low. "I think we should talk about what happened earlier."

Did she want to hear that it was a mistake? A lapse in judgment on his part? It would crush her and she'd been through enough. She couldn't take any more rejection from him.

"No, we shouldn't," she blurted out.

He frowned and shot her a quick glance. "I think that—"

"Kent," she said. "It's fine. No big deal." *Yeah, right.* She rolled her eyes. "Besides, nothing happened. Let's just forget it."

Only she couldn't forget it. Just that little interaction was ingrained in her memory. It was tangible, not a simple dream or fantasy. She'd actually felt his breath against her skin, his hands caressing her. Since he'd walked away from her, she hoped her attempt at blowing it off would keep him from saying anything else about it.

She shifted so that he couldn't see her face. She stared outside, tried to focus on the cars and the buildings.

"Lina," he said after a few moments. "I realize that things are awkward. That's the last thing I want."

"You made it that way," she murmured.

"What?"

"Well, you did stop talking to me, and you left me standing there looking like a fool."

"To who? There was nobody there."

She felt the car slow, then stop at a light. "It doesn't matter. You almost kissed me and . . . you walked away. I guess I shouldn't be surprised."

"What the hell is that supposed to mean?" They pulled into the parking lot at the bar, and he stopped the car. "Can you please turn around and look at me?"

She held her chin up high. "I don't need to. You've made it perfectly clear, more than once, that there can never be anything more between us than what is. My bad for assuming things might have changed."

"Wait a minute. Wasn't it *you* who was on her way down the aisle yesterday?"

Ouch. "You don't have to keep bringing that up," she hissed. "I'm very aware of my predicament, thank you very much."

He exhaled. "I'm sorry. I didn't mean to say it like that." She opened her mouth, but he held a hand up. "But you're on the rebound from a serious relationship—no matter how it ended."

As much as she hated to admit it, he had a point. If she hadn't walked into the church when she had, she would already be married and on her honeymoon. In her defense, though, what she felt for Kent had never changed. She just thought it was a lost cause. Obviously, she was right. She'd practically put a sign on her face that said "kiss me" and he didn't bite.

Maybe she'd misunderstood Syd? She picked at her fingernails. "Okay," she grumbled. "Like I said, let's just forget it. I feel like an idiot."

His fingertips grazed her neck and she leaned into his hand as he caressed her cheek. "You're not an idiot. I wanted to kiss you."

She let out a shaky breath. "You did?"

He shrugged. "How could I not?"

"Because you never have before," she answered.

"There are reasons for that." He scrubbed his face with

his hands. She missed his touch immediately, the way his fingers felt against her skin. "But it's not because I don't find you attractive." He smiled at her. "That's so far from the truth, it's not even funny."

"Then why?"

He shook his head. "It's not right. We're better as friends. That's important to me. I can't lose that."

His words weren't malicious, but they felt like a smack in the face. She swallowed past a lump that had formed in her throat. Suddenly, it felt like she couldn't breathe. She opened the car door. "I have to…go to the bathroom," she said before she jumped out of the car, grabbed her purse, and ran into the building.

CHAPTER ELEVEN

I'll be happy when this day from hell is over. Well, the whole week had pretty much sucked. Actually, the past year had been one of the worst she'd ever had. And that was saying a lot, considering her past.

Allina huddled in a booth on the far side of the bar, her sketch pad open and a glass of water in front of her. She nibbled on her pencil and gazed at the design in front of her. She'd fill in details later, but it was shaping up fine. And she had the perfect bride in mind.

When she'd slid into the booth earlier, she'd wanted to just hang her head and cry until she couldn't cry anymore. He'd rejected her. Again. Not in a mean, just-not-attracted-to-you way, either. That would have been much easier to take. Instead, he'd been very sweet and completely sincere—which made it worse because she wanted him even more because of it.

"You look like you need some of this, girlfriend."

Allina's head snapped up. "Cali!" She grinned at her friend, who set two shot glasses down on the table and waved a bottle of tequila in the air. Allina stood up and embraced her. "I didn't know you were going to be here tonight."

"We just got back to town. I heard you were here with Kent so I figured I'd come and keep you company." When Allina sat back down, Cali slid in across from her and set the fifth of liquor down on the table. "I called Syd and she said she's on her way. What are you working on?"

Glancing down at the fit and flare gown she'd been sketching, she held it up. "I figured I'd start with Syd's dress."

Cali picked up the pad. "It's gorgeous. Syd will love it."

Allina was in her element. Growing up, the only time she'd felt normal, free, was when she was sitting at the small sewing machine her mother had bought her one Christmas, creating her own designs. She still remembered how the fabric of the first shirt she'd ever made felt beneath her fingers, the soothing sound of the needle punching through the material; the pride she felt when her mother had tried it on and it fit.

She could never really leave her love of designing behind, even if she tried. Her major had been Business but she'd taken classes in textiles and kept up her skills by working for a local seamstress. If she hadn't moved back to Ohio to be with Isaac, she'd have had her own shop by now. So many regrets, so many wrong decisions. She had always been taught her gifts would make room for her. The maxim was biblical and she'd never really thought about what it meant. Maybe it was simple? Maybe she could start over and finally realize her dream?

"I have to warn you," Cali said, smiling at the dress. "I talked to her about the wedding and she bit my head off. I don't think she's feeling the planning right now. They haven't even set the date yet."

Allina closed the large book. "Don't tell her I'm working on it, then. I'll just surprise her with it when you give me the go ahead. I'm so glad to see you." She reached across the table and squeezed Cali's hand. "How are you?"

A few months earlier, Cali had lost her uncle. Allina had been there when her friend discovered his lifeless body. It wasn't something she'd ever forget. The man had raised Cali since she was a young child. Uncle Cal had been the only father Cali had ever known.

"I'm good," Cali answered, pouring a healthy shot into a small glass that she'd brought with her. "It's been hard, but Red and Corrine make everything better."

Allina smiled. "I'm happy you and Red finally got it right."

Cali and Red had fooled around for years as *friends with benefits* before they'd actually made it official. Cali was headstrong and said whatever was on her mind, hurt feelings be damned. It was about time Red had called her bluff.

Her friend's mouth curved into a smile. "He's all right," she quipped with a chuckle.

Allina knew Cali was all in with Red. "I would say he's more than all right if you're smiling the way you are."

"Well, if you told me a year ago that I would actually be in a committed relationship with Red, practically living with him and his daughter, I would have fallen out of a chair laughing." Her whole face lit up. "But I can't imagine my life any other way. Corrine...she's a doll. My doll. And Red now has permanent custody of her."

It made Allina feel good to hear the news. Red had recently found his daughter after the child's mother had run off with her. He'd searched for months for her, but it wasn't until Corrine's mother was arrested that he was able to locate them.

Allina rested her chin on her hand and listened as Cali told her about the court date and how it felt to basically be a mother figure to a child when she'd never wanted kids. Allina's eyes glazed over, suddenly overcome with emotion. She had no idea where it even came from.

"Girlfriend?" Cali said, with a concerned look in her eyes. "Are you okay?"

Allina waved off her friend, and discreetly wiped a tear from her face. "I'm fine. Just emotional, I guess. My turn, huh?" They'd each spent months crying due to life events. She felt like a faucet, as much crying as she'd done.

"Aw, I'm sorry, hun." Cali gulped down her shot and filled up her glass again. Then she filled up the second glass and slid it toward Allina.

"No, Cali, I—"

"Wait," Cali said, holding up her hand. "You've spent years doing the right thing. I understand why. But Allina, you went all runaway bride yesterday. You deserve a good shot of tequila."

Allina giggled at her friend's sense of humor. Cali was the feisty one, always ready for a fight. But no one would know it by looking at her. With her short frame, brown skin, and big expressive eyes, she looked innocent. Only she was anything but and would cut anybody down without batting her eyelashes.

Allina twisted her lips as she considered taking the shot. It would be the first time she'd had a drink since she was a teenager trying to cope with her life. Hell, she'd probably fall out. The sound of hearty laughter drew her attention to the bar. Kent was smiling, his dimples on full display. He was standing next to Red.

"You brought that guy with you?" Allina asked, gesturing with her thumb toward the bar.

Cali turned around. "Yeah, you know he wasn't letting me come without him," she admitted, a wistful look on her face. She shifted her attention back to Allina. "Plus, he wanted to see you too. He'll be over in a minute, with his loud ass."

Allina laughed. "He is loud. I heard him over everything in this place."

She stared at Kent—the easy and confident way he moved, the gleam in his eyes. Just thinking about him seemed to flood her with warmth. His gaze met hers across the room, and she glanced away. Her cheeks burned and she skimmed her fingertips along her jawline.

"Allina?" Cali called to her.

She snapped out of her thoughts and looked at her friend, who was eyeing her with a knowing look. "Yes."

"What's going on with you?"

Clearing her throat, she shifted in her seat. Cali would notice right away that something was up. She was like that; could see right through a facade. Allina usually admired that quality in her friend, except when it was directed at her. "Nothing. Well, the obvious, of course. Like you said earlier, I'm a runaway bride and all."

"Yes, but there's more, I can tell."

Allina tapped the still full shot glass. "Remember that conversation we had when you told me that I didn't look happy to be marrying someone I claimed to love?"

Cali nodded. "I do. Is that what happened? You realized you couldn't go through with it because he didn't make you happy?"

"Actually I didn't go through with it because he threatened me." Cali's expression hardened, but Allina rushed on. "But I thought a lot about what you said."

"Wait a minute," Cali said, her brows snapping together. "What do you mean he threatened you?"

"Syd didn't tell you?"

Cali shrugged. "Not that, but we haven't really had a chance to talk."

"He doesn't know where I am. And I don't plan on telling him anytime soon. But if he should try to contact you, act like you have no idea where I am."

"Got it," Cali said, shaking her head. "I can't believe this."

"Last night, I was terrified. I'm a little better today. Earlier I got an e-mail from him implying he would try to get to me through Syd."

Cali narrowed her eyes. "He must have a death wish," she grunted.

"Right," Allina agreed. "Kent wanted to go down there and kick his butt. But we convinced him to stay put."

"Well, I'm sure Kent is filling Red in on the details." Cali placed a hand on top of Allina's. "Aw, sweetie. You know I'm here for you, whatever you need. How are you feeling?"

"Honestly, I'm glad I didn't marry him. Which leads me to what I was going to tell you. I don't think I was in love with *him* as much as I was in love with the *idea* of him."

Cali leaned forward. "What made you come to that conclusion?"

"Kent," Allina said simply. "Because one night with him and all those feelings just bubbled to the surface. We've never been together for such a long time at once. He held me, listened to me, took me shopping...he was awesome." She lowered her voice, "We almost kissed today."

Cali's mouth fell open. "Oh my God. Really?"

"Really, what?" Syd said, approaching the table and sliding in next to Allina.

Allina smiled at her best friend. "Hi, Syd."

"Hey," Syd said, picking up the shot glass and taking it to the head. She slammed it down on the table. "Really, what?"

she asked again, her gaze darting back and forth between Cali and Allina.

"Allina kissed Kent today," Cali announced, a slow grin spreading on her face.

"What?" Syd said, staring at Allina, eyes wide.

Allina covered her face with her hands as a blush worked its way up her neck. "It wasn't a kiss, Cali. I said we *almost* kissed," Allina murmured.

"My bad," Cali said. "What exactly is an almost-kiss anyway?"

Syd laughed and smacked Cali's hand lightly. "Stop."

Hunching her shoulders, Cali yelped. "What? You're wondering the same thing, right?"

"No," Syd said. "Unlike you, I've had many almost-kiss moments in my life."

Cali twisted her lip. "With who? You were with Den for umpteen years. And you and Morgan skipped the almost and got right down to it, Ms. I-made-a-mistake."

Allina giggled. When Syd glared at her, she covered her mouth.

"I'm ignoring you, Cali," Syd said, holding a hand up in Cali's face while she refocused her attention on Allina. "So, what did you mean when you said you almost kissed him? Were you leaning really close to him, so close that you could feel his breath on your skin? Or did your lips actually touch his?"

Allina dropped her head on the table. "Both," she grumbled.

"Fuck yeah. We have some action over here," Cali said, smacking the table.

"Oh my God," Syd squealed. "I told you. I knew it."

Allina glanced up, pushing her hair out of her face. "Don't go too far. We didn't actually kiss."

"Why?" Syd asked.

Allina's feet shuffled under the table. "He stopped it, said he couldn't do it."

Their smiles faded and Syd's face paled. Without another word, Cali filled up the shot glass and slid it toward Allina.

"See, you do need this," Cali exclaimed.

Allina glanced at Syd, who had a pained expression on her face. Then she looked at the full glass on the table. Picking it up, she finally took the shot.

The tequila burned going down her throat, and she shuddered. "That's awful." She scowled. "I don't know how you drink that mess."

Syd poured herself another shot and took it. "This is my last one. I have to be 'mommy' when I leave here."

"Good thing my doll is school-aged," Cali said before she gulped a shot down.

"That really sucks, Allina," Syd mumbled. "Kent needs a smack to the head."

"No," Cali grumbled. "He needs his ass beat, that's what. How could he turn down my girl like that? I need to talk to him."

"Please don't," Allina murmured. "It's okay. He did tell me he wanted to kiss me."

"So why the hell didn't he pucker up and lay one on you? Lord knows you need it," Cali said.

Allina gasped, her hand flying to her chest. "Really, Cali?"

Cali shrugged. "What? I've always said you needed a little something something. And Kent is definitely the guy to give it to you. Look at him," she said, pointing over at the bar. "He's fine as hell. But don't tell Red I said that," she added under her breath.

"He is very nice looking," Syd agreed.

They all turned to watch the three men standing there, each of them attractive in their own right. Morgan and Red were tall and slender. Kent was not as tall, but he was built like a building; and he stood out from the others, in Allina's opinion. Syd used to call them the dimple crew because they all had them. They each had their own personal, fly style. In college, they'd been pretty popular with the ladies.

Cali tipped the bottle in Allina's direction. "Another one?"

Allina lifted her empty shot glass up. "Why not? I can drink away my troubles for the night. Maybe I'll get a good night's sleep out of it."

CHAPTER TWELVE

Kent watched Allina as she chatted with Syd and Cali. He'd hurt her feelings and he hated himself for it. He couldn't even bring himself to run after her when she jumped out of the car earlier. When he finally entered the bar, she was already sitting in a booth, her head down, scribbling something in her sketch pad.

He scanned the crowd. The Ice Box was busy and he couldn't help but feel proud that he was one of the owners. Opening a bar wasn't his dream, but Syd's. She had talked about it since they were in college. When the previous owner of their hangout, the Mic Mac, retired, he offered to sell them the building. It had taken months to get it up and running, but it had been worth it.

Spending time there was the highlight of his week. It broke up the monotony of his day job. Being a computer engineer was what he thought he wanted, and it came easy to him. His father had told him to make sure he worked in a field that would pay, and that's exactly what he'd done. It was high stress and he hated it, but he made a good living.

Over the past hour, Allina had consciously avoided eye contact with him, but he couldn't keep his eyes off her. He never let his gaze linger long, but every few minutes, he'd glance over at her. Kent had just finished unloading on Red and Morgan about the little scene in his kitchen and the later conversation in his car, but it was a complete waste of time to talk to them because they didn't really say anything. Not that he needed advice. He was a man, after all. He should be able to handle himself.

Red clapped him on his back. "I think it's high time we plan a vacation. You look like you need it."

He rolled his eyes. "Whatever, man. I'm good."

"You're good and stressed."

Morgan laughed. "He's right, bruh. You just made a margarita with water," he said, pointing at the glass in front of Kent.

Kent dropped his head to look at the drink he was making. He muttered a curse. "That's why I don't bartend. I drink liquor straight, no chaser. None of this mix shit."

"Nobody told you to volunteer while Peter went on break," Red said. "That's what we have employees for. What the hell is wrong with you?"

"Nothing," Kent said. "I'm just..."

"Distracted?" Red suggested.

"I'd say frustrated," Morgan replied.

Red leaned back in the chair. "Or just plain stupid."

"Maybe it would have been a good idea to just follow through and kiss her. That way you wouldn't have to wonder." Morgan tapped his beer bottle on the counter. "Because you're acting like a punk."

"Shut up," Kent grumbled. "I told you why I didn't kiss her."

All valid reasons, Kent thought. The biggest and main reason was because of their friendship. Next on the long list he'd made—and he hated to even think about it—Allina *was* going to marry Isaac. Sure, he knew how she felt about him, but she must have felt something for Isaac to say yes to his marriage proposal. What if she'd kissed him because she needed to hold on to something constant? Where would that leave him? Hurt, if he decided to invest and things didn't work out. And that brought him right back around to the first reason—she was one of the most important people in his life, one of his closest friends. He was sorry, but not sorry.

Shrugging, Morgan took a swig of his beer. "Yeah, but it didn't make any goddamn sense."

It was just like his brother to be right. Like him, Morgan wasn't someone who beat around the bush. He was honest to the point of not even caring about hurt feelings. And Red was worse than Morgan was, so Kent wasn't sure what he expected. That's why his brother and Red had been friends since they played basketball together in high school.

"You were in the moment," Morgan continued. "Standing that close to her. She made the first move and you—"

"Fell on his sword," Red interrupted, snickering.

"Asshole," Kent mumbled. But his brother and his friend hadn't said anything that was untrue. He *was* officially a punk. "What the hell was I supposed to do? It's not like she wasn't someone's fiancée yesterday. She *is* on the rebound. I can't take advantage of her like that. She's probably just feeling attached to me because I'm there for her. "

"Man, that's a grown-ass woman," Red said, swatting the air. "You're acting like she woke up this morning and decided she wanted you. Allina has been nursing that crush for years. You know that shit."

Morgan finished his beer. "Okay, I'll give you the rebound thing because she was about to get married, but Red is right, too," he said. "Yeah, the timing is crazy, considering she was about to marry that sociopath minister, but it's not like her feelings for you came out of the blue. I'm pretty sure the reason she agreed to marry Isaac anyway was because she gave up, got tired of wanting to be with someone who seemingly doesn't feel the same way she does. It didn't work out, and she came to you because she trusts you. She needs you. And maybe that kind of stirred up something in her that she's wanted all along."

That made sense to Kent. Allina probably didn't come to him with plans to take *their* relationship further.

"Either way, this whole saving-the-friendship thing you got going on is a cop-out," Morgan added. "I understand it, but it's stupid. I mean, I just had a baby with my friend, my brother's ex. If any relationship is doomed to fail, mine is."

"True," Red agreed with a nod of his head. "Look at me and Cali. I feel like our relationship is better *because* we were friends first."

"At the end of the day," Morgan said, "I can't imagine what my life would be like if I hadn't tried to make it work with Syd. At least I know how it feels to be with her, to love her, to have Brynn. If it doesn't work out, I know that I put forth the effort. You can't even say that, because you're so damn rigid. You don't want to do anything that will take you out of the box you put yourself in. It's the same thing with your job. You could be doing so much more, designing all kinds of shit. But you're content to...punch a clock."

As much as Kent hated to admit it, what it boiled down to was that he was a scared motherfucker. His relationships never lasted for one reason or another. He'd yet to maintain any semblance of a friendship with any of his exes. Taking a chance on Allina was appealing, but if he hurt her...He could barely stand to see Allina get a splinter, let alone cry because of something he'd done to her.

Allina was different, too. She didn't fall for just anything or anyone. What made her want him? She was a good girl, almost too good.

"Look at them," Red pointed at the girls. "You've driven

sweet, churchy Allina to the bottle. She's over there drinking tequila. Pretty soon she's going to start cursing and shit."

"Shut the fuck up, man," Kent said. The thought hadn't escaped him, though. He wasn't a churchgoer, hadn't been since his mother had forced him to go to Sunday School as a child. He would corrupt her, no doubt. Yes, he believed in God, but he didn't belong to a church. Allina went to church faithfully, every single Sunday. It was just too much pressure. He considered himself a good guy, but he was a heathen compared to her.

Crossing his arms, he observed Allina. He'd noticed her take a shot earlier. Red was joking, but he was essentially telling the truth. She jumped right in with the Patrón and he'd never even seen her drink a glass of wine at dinner. All because of him, probably. And *that damn Cali*.

"Why don't you go get your woman?" Kent told Red. "She's the one who took the tequila over there. Blame her."

"Hey, it's not Cali's fault that Allina actually drank it," Red argued. "It's not the first time she's offered her a drink. Allina never took one—until now."

Kent rubbed his head. "I'm going to need both of you to go get your women, and take their asses home. Let me deal with Allina."

Tossing a towel on the counter, he stalked over to the table. As he approached them, he heard the giggles and wondered what they were talking about. But once he got to the table, the laughter died and he was faced with two sets of glares.

Syd folded her arms across her chest. "Is there a problem?" she snapped.

"What the hell do you want?" Cali hissed.

"Why are you drinking?" Kent asked Allina, ignoring the two bad influences. "You're actually sitting there knocking back shots with them? You don't even drink."

Allina burped and covered her mouth. "I drink tonight."

Mean mugs forgotten, the women burst into a fit of giggles. Kent grumbled and snatched the bottle of Patrón. "You're all done."

Morgan and Red approached the table. Cali scooted over and Red slid in next to her. Morgan stood next to Syd.

Allina looked up at Morgan. "You're tall," she said, her eyes wide. "I forgot you were so handsome."

Kent gave Morgan a side eye when his brother winked at Allina. "He's not that tall," he retorted with a bitter snort. So what; Morgan had four inches on him in height. *I can still kick his ass if I want to.*

"Someone's jealous," Syd grumbled. When Kent scowled at her, she turned her head quickly.

Red leaned back against Cali. "I never thought I'd see the day when Allina was drunk."

"It's Kent's fault." Cali wrapped her arms around Red's shoulders and kissed him on the cheek.

The more they talked, the more irritated Kent became. He could take a joke, had even been the joker on more than one occasion. But this wasn't funny. *That's because I'm guilty.* The idea that he could be the reason Allina decided to say fuck it and get her drink on didn't sit right with him.

He eyed her, sitting in the booth. She was leaning with her head against the wall and her eyes halfway closed. "Allina," he called. "What are you doing? You're drunk. This isn't you."

"How would you know?" Allina said. "You think you know me. I'm sick of you." She pounded her hand against the table. "All of you! You put me in this box, you cate…cat…catheglorize me as this good girl." She clumsily held up air quotes. "That's not who I am. It's who *you* want me to be."

"Right!" Cali shouted. "You tell him, girlfriend."

"You're no better," Allina said, pointing at Cali. "You're a brass bitch."

Syd giggled when Cali's mouth fell open. It wasn't often Cali was rendered speechless. So not only had he driven Allina to Patrón, he'd driven her to cuss.

"And you, Syd-nee?" Allina was on a roll. Sydney placed a hand over her mouth to hide her grin. "Dramatic, much? You're such a drama queen."

"Hey," Syd said with a frown.

"And Red?"

"Don't bring me into this shit," Red said, an amused smile on his face.

"You're a jerk."

Red laughed loudly. "Thank you."

"No!" Allina shook her hands in the air. "The point is, who cares. I love your bitchy ways, Cali. And what would I do without the drama, Syd? Red? You're still a jerk. But I love you all anyway, flaws and all. Why can't you all love me the same way? Stop putting baby in a corner!" Her head fell forward to the table.

Allina grumbled under her breath—something about boxes, expectations, and being "set free to be me." It was time to go. He needed to get his...friend home to sleep off that Patrón. He rolled his eyes hard at Cali, who shrugged.

Morgan must have sensed his mood because he motioned to Syd to get up. "Let's get back home," his brother said. "I have some work to do."

Once Syd rose out of her seat, Kent leaned in close to Allina, nudged her with his hand. "You have to get up."

Allina smacked his hand away. "Move."

"Come, on," he said, pushing her hair out of her face. "Let me take you back to my place."

She peered up him with hooded eyes. "Don't tell me what to do," she slurred.

"You're drunk, baby."

She pushed at him again. "Go away. I'm talking to my friends."

"If they were really your friends, they wouldn't have let you in that bottle of tequila," he said, glaring at Cali and Syd.

"Hey, I'm her friend," Syd said with a pout.

"I'm her friend, too!" Cali shouted. Red covered her mouth with his hand.

"Damn, you're loud, babe," Red grumbled. He stood up and helped Cali to her feet. "It's time for us to go."

Kent shook his head. There was no way he'd be able to get Allina home without touching her. And he was trying to avoid that kind of contact with her. He needed her to at least walk to the car. If he had to carry her out of here, she'd be mortified in the morning. Muttering a curse, he slid his hands around her and pulled her toward him.

"You have to walk to the car, Allina," he grunted, pulling her to her feet. She swayed a little and he gripped her hips to keep her steady. "Let's go."

"Wait!" she shouted. "I'm not done with you. You didn't kiss me."

He pinched her lips together, glancing around the bar to make sure no one was paying them any attention. Morgan and Red had done a pretty good job of blocking the booth from the other patrons, but that wouldn't last long because he had to pass everyone on his way out.

"Uh oh," Syd said.

"I made a move and you re-rebirthed, re-buffed me," Allina slurred.

Kent hung his head. *How did I get myself into this?* "I told you why I did it."

"You suck." She almost fell back into the booth, but he grabbed her shirt and pulled her to him. Her body crashed against his. *Shit.*

He held a breath as she traced her fingers down his cheek. "Allina," he managed to say. "I'm sorry."

She held a finger against his mouth. "Shut up," she snapped. "Why can't you see what's right in front of you, how I feel about you?"

Then she kissed him, slowly and tenderly. For a minute—a bite-sized minute—he let her. Closing his eyes, he went with it and captured her bottom lip in his. Her lips were as soft as he'd imagined and the tequila on her breath was intoxicating. And it wasn't enough. He wanted to explore her mouth further, but he wouldn't. Call him crazy, but he preferred this moment be shared in the privacy of his home with a sober Allina. Not standing in the bar, surrounded by people. He gripped her shoulder and pushed her back gently.

She grinned at him, her eyes still closed. "Finally," she breathed, before sagging against him.

Clearing his throat, he allowed himself to look at the people surrounding him. His family. The word "friends" didn't do them justice. Judging by the way they all stood around, eyes wide and mouths hanging open, the turn of events had surprised them as well.

"Holy shit," Cali whispered.

"I know, right?" Syd said.

"Um," Kent croaked, adjusting Allina in his arms. She hadn't passed out, but he didn't believe she could hold herself up at that point. "That was ... different. Roc, will you help me get her to the car?"

Nodding, his brother picked up one of Allina's arms and wrapped it around his neck. "Syd, go to the car."

The walk was rough, as Allina kept stopping and making

little comments about wind, cake, and banana fo-fana. If this had been Syd, and Morgan the one dragging her to the car, he would have been rolling on the floor with laughter. But it wasn't. This was his life.

When they finally got her buckled in, Allina gasped. "My phone!" She patted her chest and her legs where her pockets were.

"You don't have a phone," he reminded her.

"Oh," she said simply. She closed her eyes, relaxing into the seat.

Kent turned around and told Morgan, "I'll get with you tomorrow." The rest of the crew was standing off to the side, Cali and Syd with guilty looks on their faces. "Later, y'all."

A little while later, Kent cursed Cali and Syd to hell and back as he stumbled through his front door—with an inebriated Allina in his arms. He'd tried to walk her into the house, but getting her to actually stand up without falling over was impossible. In the end, he'd hoisted her in his arms and carried her.

That wasn't the problem, though. It was her warm, soft skin. Her shirt was a twisted mess and his palms were resting on her bare skin. When he thought about adjusting her in his arms, he realized that the only place his hand could go was her ass. That wasn't going to work.

When he kicked the door closed, her head fell back. Her hooded eyes were open, watching him. The desire in them was unmistakable. Her cheeks were red and her lips parted. Thoughts of kissing her flashed through his mind—the feel of her mouth against his, the smell of Patrón on her breath. In an instant, everything else seemed to fade away.

"It's you," she whispered, tracing the outline of his lips with her finger.

Muttering a curse, he said, "Yes. It's me."

"Hi," she breathed.

His gaze flickered from her eyes to her mouth. "Hi."

She finally closed her eyes and he let out a long, tortured sigh before he made it through the house to her room. He stepped in and deposited her on the bed. But before he could back away from her, she wrapped her arms around his neck and pulled him down on top of her.

Shit. As if being pressed against her so intimately wasn't enough, her fingers crept down his back and over his ass, scorching his skin as they traveled. It was too late; his body had already responded to her touch, to their closeness. Exhaling, he pushed himself up on his arms and peered down at her.

Her thumbs grazed under his eyes and over his forehead. "You're beautiful," she mumbled.

Mesmerized by her mouth, he groaned. *Okay, maybe just one more kiss?* Shaking his mind free from the vivid memories of her lips against his, he slowly backed away. He wouldn't kiss her again—not yet; not when she more than likely wouldn't remember it in the morning. He gripped her wrists and pinned her hands to the bed so he could slide off her. When he was finally back on his feet, he let her go and tried to pull the covers over her. Unfortunately she wrestled with him, pushing the comforter away every time he pulled it over her. Finally she gave up, letting him win their little match.

He gave her one last glance before he went to the door.

"Kent?" she said.

Without turning, he answered. "Yes?"

"I wish you knew how much I need you, how much I love you."

Closing his eyes, he slowly turned to her. But she was already snoring lightly. He let out a ragged breath and walked out.

CHAPTER THIRTEEN

Allina's eyes opened and she sat upright, clutching the thin sheet to her body. She glanced around the room. *Kent's house.* She massaged her temples and groaned in pain. Her head was on fire, throbbing as if she'd spent a whole night banging it against a wall.

Her mind raced to remember what had happened the night before. She'd been at the Ice Box drinking with Cali and Syd. She'd said some things... *Oh God.* She remembered calling someone a bitch. Vaguely, she recalled bumping into Kent and... kissing him? Groaning, she mentally kicked herself. *Way to make a fool of yourself, Allina.*

Liquor was definitely not her thing. She made a mental note to never let Cali talk her into taking a shot again.

She wondered what Kent was doing, if he was even there, just before she heard a soft knock on the door. Kent poked his head in. "You're up," he said, entering the room.

"Yeah," she grumbled. "My head hurts."

She squinted, tried to focus on the label of the bottle in his hand. Tequila? Shaking her head, she pointed at the pint of liquor. "What's that for?"

"It's the quickest way to get rid of a hangover. I figured

you'd wake up with one. Take a shot; your headache will go away."

Which was worse? Throwing up because the smell was making her sick to her stomach? Or taking the shot and getting rid of the massive headache? She took the shot and fell back against the mattress, closing her eyes.

"I'm so embarrassed," she admitted. "I can't even imagine how I look right now. And how I acted at the bar... I... there is really no good reason."

She steeled herself for his response, uncertain she could take another rejection from him. Only he didn't say anything. *Did I screw everything up with my behavior?* Kissing him in front of all of his friends, while he was working, was awful. She'd never been so brazen before. *What if he'd hated it and that's why he isn't saying anything?* Suddenly she felt small.

She lowered her gaze, scraped a nail over a loose thread on the sheet. "The kiss... at the bar..." Her apology died on her lips because she actually wasn't very sorry. The details of last night were hazy but she did recall how his lips had felt against hers and how he smelled——like spices, chocolate, and mint. "Can you just... say something?"

He peered at her then and sat down beside her. "I need us to have a serious conversation about what's going on between us," he said, his voice husky.

She bit her lip. "Okay," she muttered, grateful that the tequila was working and her headache was fading.

Talking about what was happening between them wasn't a conversation she was prepared to have in the haze of the night before, but she would roll with it.

"I know how you feel about me," he admitted. "I've always known."

Allina's stomach dropped; her face and neck felt hot.

Mortified, she resisted the urge to jump out of the bed and lock herself in the bathroom. She knew she wasn't good at hiding her emotions, but she hadn't expected him to actually call her on it.

She sank down into the mattress. "I...well..." *Forget it.*

"But I'm not sure you realize how I feel about you," he mumbled, averting his gaze.

Did he say "feel," as in present tense, current feelings? Just like that the dread in her gut was replaced with flutters.

"I think it's very real," he continued. "I want to explore it, but I'm just concerned the timing isn't right."

Her shoulders dropped. She slowly shook her head. "I don't understand."

"I think we need time to make sure that it's what we both want. Allina, you were going to marry Isaac. I just want you to be sure this"—he motioned between them—"is what you really want. Because despite how we may feel for each other, sometimes it's not enough to make anything more happen."

"How do you feel about me?" she asked hesitantly.

"I think it's pretty clear I care about you. I'd literally do anything for you, and I'm not afraid to admit it. I think you're beautiful, inside and out. I can see myself getting lost in you. And I just want to be sure it's right."

Lips parted, her heart racing, she exhaled slowly. "I can't...did you just say you think I'm beautiful?"

This was better than she could ever have hoped for. In all her wildest dreams she'd never expected him to be so honest, so open, about how he felt. Although Kent wasn't the first man to tell her she was beautiful, it felt like he was.

"You always were. So beautiful. But it's not just that. You've been there for me every time I've needed you, with no hesitation."

"You've done the same for me," she said.

"And that kiss…" He let out a harsh breath. "I can't stop thinking about it. We definitely have chemistry, something pulling us toward each other. It was there before, but it's undeniable now. I was up most of the night trying to figure out a plan. But even the best laid plans don't work. I won't try to force it. If this is going to happen, I need it to happen after you've had a few days to process everything that's still going on with Isaac."

She twisted her lip. "I guess you have a point. And I'm—" His fingertips against her palm rendered her speechless. She lost her train of thought when he lifted her hand and placed a tender kiss to it.

"We're friends," he muttered against her skin. "Good friends. It shouldn't stop us, but it should make us more cautious of the decision we make. I don't want to lose you."

"So what do you propose?" she asked.

"This is going to sound really crazy after everything I just said, but I'm thinking we should just forget about this conversation for a few days. Concentrate on getting you set up here. First and foremost, I want to get you a phone. While I want to believe that Isaac will just let this go, I want to be cautious. I don't want to take anything away from your father, but I'd like to find out more about Isaac myself. There is too much going on for us to start something."

"Okay," she said, surprising herself. He'd given it a lot of thought, apparently. How could she argue with his logic? "But we *are* going to revisit this again?"

"Definitely," he promised. "I think it's pretty impossible to *not* have another discussion very soon. You are staying here."

"Okay," she repeated. "That sounds fair."

He stood up and she immediately missed his warmth. "I

have a meeting at the bar in an hour that I have to prepare for." Leaning down, he brushed his lips against her forehead and hugged her. "I'll put you on some tea, okay?"

When she opened her mouth to thank him, he planted a kiss on her lips before pulling away. They shared one last look before he walked out of the room.

* * *

Kent mentally shook himself. He'd just told Allina that he essentially wanted to take it slow, that there was something going on between them that he wanted to explore. Then he'd kissed her? *What is up with that?*

He wanted to blame it on his lack of sleep, but there was no sense in denying the truth any longer. The reason he said one thing and then turned around and done the complete opposite was because he couldn't *not* do it. Allina showing up at his door, needing him, trusting him, had changed him. It had opened up possibilities that he'd tried hard to ignore. Then she'd opened the door when she brushed her lips against his and kissed him for all the world to see.

But it wasn't even just that. Her voice and the way she looked up and said "finally" were tattooed on his brain. Truth be told, he felt the same way. Waiting for a few days was his failsafe, a way to make sure they tested the waters before they stepped in. Because he wanted to step in, possess her; make her feel everything she'd dreamed of as a young girl, replace every doubt and fear with love and acceptance. And he would. Slowly. There was too much at stake.

He heard a knock on the door and rushed out to the front of the house. The jingle of keys let him know that whoever it was had a key, which meant it was either Morgan or—

"Mama," he said when his mother pushed the door open. "What—"

"Hi, son," Mama said, walking in with a couple of grocery bags. "Here, take these."

Patricia Smith, affectionately known as Mama, was just as busy at sixty-one as she'd been at thirty. She'd had Kent late in life, but she certainly hadn't allowed that to stop her from being an active part of his life growing up.

She was always on the go and she looked damn good. Today was no exception. She wore her workout gear, a lightweight jogging outfit. Her hair was pulled up into a tight ponytail. Recently, she'd decided to forgo the dye and embrace her salt-and-pepper hair color.

Grabbing the bags, he gave his mother a kiss on the cheek. "I wasn't expecting you," he said. "You didn't have to bring me food."

"I figured it was the only way I could see you," she said with a wink. He motioned her in the direction of the kitchen with his head and she followed him. "You haven't even called your poor mother in days. I had to see if you were still alive over here. Besides, it's Sunday. I was thinking we could have dinner at your house today."

He snickered at her attempt to make him feel guilty. It was the same conversation every time she stopped by. "Mom, I just talked to you Friday morning." Unloading the bags, he continued, "You really shouldn't have bought all this stuff. We can't have dinner here tonight."

"Son, you know I've been trying to start up our Sunday dinners again, now that Morgan is back in Michigan, settled."

Sunday gatherings had been a tradition in his family for as long as he could remember. Mama would cook an awesome dinner and they'd all sit down to eat, sharing the good and bad news of the week. It had continued on a regular basis until that whole debacle with Syd, Morgan, and Den. Morgan had been offered a promotion at his architectural firm and he'd taken it, but he and Syd had needed to relocate to Baltimore for a period of time. After Brynn was born they'd moved back permanently, which made his mother very happy. She loved being a grandmother.

Mama didn't say so, but she'd been devastated when the family seemingly fell apart. After his father died, she'd devoted her time and energy to taking care of Kent and his brothers. Even though Morgan and Den weren't her biological children, she loved them as if she'd given birth to them. And she'd grown to love Syd just the same. It hurt her that things weren't the same between them.

"I hate this," she said. "I want my family to come out of this. Have you talked to your brother?"

"Morgan?" he asked.

"Den."

"No," he said, bending his neck forward. There was a heaviness that kind of passed over him when he thought about the fact that he hadn't really spoken to Caden in over a year. They'd seen each other, but there were barely any words spoken.

"I've been trying to reach him. Normally he'll answer for me, but he hasn't. I hope he's okay."

He looked at his mother, noticed the worry lines in her forehead. He would tell her anything to keep her mind off his brother's whereabouts. Talking about Den would only make it worse for her. "Mama, it's not that I don't want to have dinner with you and my family. I have a lot to do. I have a project due at work that I need to work on and…" Hesitating, he wondered if he should tell his mother about Allina. "I have a meeting at the bar in a few. It's not a good day for me."

Frowning, Mama went to the refrigerator, opened it, and pulled out a bottle of water. "I feel like if we don't start it up, we never will."

"That's not true, Mama. I promise I'll do it here next week."

She nodded sadly. "Okay. I'll leave the food. How are you?" she asked, leaning against a cabinet. "You look tired."

"Thanks," he said. "I'm fine. There's a lot going on, but it will be okay."

"Is it work?"

Shaking his head, he said, "Not really. Work is work."

"Well, what is it?"

Before he could answer her, Allina shuffled into the kitchen, clad in one of his white T-shirts. "Kent, I was wondering if... oh my God." Allina tugged at the shirt, trying to pull it down.

Mama's mouth fell open. She glanced at Allina, then at him, then back at Allina. "W-what? Allina? What are you doing here?" Mama stammered.

A pretty blush had started working its way up Allina's neck. "Mama, I was just getting ready to tell you that Allina is staying here," he said.

Allina shoved her hair back off her face with one hand and held on to the shirt with her other hand. "Hi, Mama," she said. "I'm so sorry. I didn't know you were here."

"Baby, aren't you supposed to be married and on your honeymoon?" Mama asked.

"It's a long story, Mama," Kent replied. "I want to tell you about it. Just not now. I have a meeting to get to."

He hated to rush his mother out. But he had to get to his meeting and he wouldn't leave her there with Allina.

Mama cupped her elbow with one hand. Tapping her lips with the other, she asked, "Is everything okay, Allina?"

Allina nodded. "I'm okay."

"Yes, she's fine," he confirmed. "Let me walk you out, Mama. I'll call you later, Allina."

Grabbing his mother's hand, he led her out of the kitchen.

"I'm confused," Mama said as they walked to her car. "So, she's not getting married?"

"No," he said. "The man she was going to marry is dangerous. And she came here to get away from him."

"He didn't hurt her, did he?" Mama asked, concern in her eyes.

"Not physically. But he did do some crazy shit."

Mama smacked him on his arm. "Watch your mouth."

"Ouch. Okay, Ma." He rubbed his shoulder. "I'm sorry."

She waved him off. "It's okay. So, how long has she been here?"

He opened her car door and waited until she was seated before he closed it. "Since Friday."

"Wow. I hope she's able to pick up the pieces quickly and get back to her life. It's a shame."

"She's better off," he said.

"Are you?"

Leaning against the hood of the car, he peered down at his mother. "What do you mean by that?"

"That's close quarters, son. Spending nights with someone can change things."

Deciding to tell her the truth, he said, "It already has, Mama."

His mother jerked her head back, her eyes widening. "Oh my. That fast, huh?"

"Not as fast as you think," he murmured. "Nothing's happened between us, really. Before you got here, we had a little talk about where we see our relationship going."

Mama nodded slowly. "I can't say I'm not concerned,

Kent. I want you to be careful. Breaking an engagement doesn't necessarily break off feelings."

"I know, Ma. That's why we haven't really made any decisions yet."

"Okay. You're a grown man and you can make your own decisions. I like Allina. But I want you to be careful."

"I will." He gave her a peck on her cheek. "And I'll call you about dinner next week."

"Love you, son."

"I love you, too."

Allina was in the office at his computer when he got back in the house. She was sitting, staring at the monitor, a hand over her mouth.

"Oh my God," she gasped.

He walked over to her. "What's going on?" Peering at the screen, he read the headline. "Twenty-eight-year-old Woman Missing. Family suspects foul play," he read aloud. "Do you know her?" he asked.

"That's her," she whispered.

Frowning, he glanced at the picture of the missing lady. "Who?"

"The woman from the church," she said.

"I thought you said you didn't get a good look at her face," he said, leaning in, skimming the article. The woman had last been seen Friday, driving a tan Toyota Corolla, license plate HJU 5744.

"That's her car. When she sped away from the church, I saw her car and caught a glimpse of her plate. Oh my God," Allina breathed before glancing back at him. "He did something to her. She's gone."

CHAPTER FOURTEEN

By one o'clock the following afternoon, Allina still hadn't heard from her father. She'd left him a brief message explaining that Karen Little, the missing woman she'd read about online, was the same woman she'd encountered at the church. She knew her father didn't have court on Mondays, so he should have called her back by now.

Allina dialed her father again. When his voicemail picked up, she left another message: "Daddy, call me as soon as possible. I need to talk to you."

Slamming the phone down, she punched her mother's number in. *Straight to voicemail.*

Kent had made a quick run to the office to grab some work. He'd decided to work from home so he could be close. He'd been gone for only forty-five minutes, but it felt like hours had passed. He'd asked her to ride with him but she'd told him she was fine.

Yesterday had been rough, though. Allina was spooked by the article. According to the Cleveland PD, Karen had last been seen on Friday afternoon around three o'clock. She'd been scheduled to work the afternoon to midnight shift at the hospital but failed to show up. Her abandoned car had been found on Saturday morning.

Allina had been checking for updates on the story every ten minutes or so, praying they found Karen safe and sound. Because if they didn't...

Allina couldn't shake the feeling that Isaac had done something to Karen Little. Kent had dismissed the idea, telling her that he highly doubted Isaac would do something so drastic. She'd agreed with him last night, but now... *now I'm not so sure*. Obviously, the woman had something on Isaac. Maybe she'd threatened him again with exposing whatever it was. And he took care of her.

Groaning, she rolled her eyes. She was starting to sound like Syd, the ID channel junkie. Chances are, she was making too much out of the missing woman. This wasn't a Lifetime movie. But she still wanted to hear from her dad.

Allina was walking out of Kent's office toward the kitchen when Kent's cell phone, which he'd left for her, rang. She recognized her father's number on the screen and picked up.

"Daddy?"

"Allina?" The static on the line made it difficult to hear him. His voice was breaking up.

"Daddy, I can't hear you," she called.

"Hold on." A moment later, he asked, "Are you there?"

"I'm here. Where have you been?" she asked. "Did you get my message?"

"I did. I've been doing a little digging. Isaac has been looking for you around town. Yesterday he went to your job."

Allina closed her eyes, let out a slow breath. She was grateful now that she'd only told her boss that she wouldn't be returning to work. Something had told her to keep it simple. She hadn't even asked for her last paycheck. "I think we should call the police."

"Already done," he said. "I called my friend Tom and told him what you said about the missing woman. They're already on the way to question Isaac."

Thank goodness. "So your guy is still tailing him?"

"Yes. I told you not to worry. I've got this under control."

Her father was her hero. She knew there was nothing he wouldn't do for her. "Thanks, Daddy."

"My guy is still on him," he added. "Nothing seems out of the ordinary. Other than his trip to the bridal store, he's only left his house to go to the church. Nothing more. Like I said, he will probably let it go."

"You're probably right," she conceded. "Where's Mom? I tried to call her, too."

"She's at home," he replied. "Her phone is probably dead. If you need to talk to her, call the landline."

"I'll wait until later. Kent is taking me to get a cell phone today or tomorrow. I'll call with the new number once everything is up and running." Kent used a Google+ number and had told Allina to give it to her parents. He'd told her once he got her a phone, he'd help her set up an account for herself. She agreed it was best to use an untraceable number for now.

"Good thinking. I love you, baby. I'll be in touch."

One more good-bye and two more *I love you*s later, Allina disconnected the call.

* * *

There. Looks good.

Allina pulled two nine-inch cake pans from the oven and fanned them with her mitt. The smell of strawberries and vanilla filled the kitchen. After she'd spoken with her father, she'd called Kent and told him to take his time. She felt a measure of peace knowing the police were investigating Isaac now.

With Kent gone most of the afternoon, she didn't have anything to do, so she'd decided to bake a cake and cook dinner for him. To thank him. After their conversation, they'd turned a corner. Or so she thought. Now she was second guessing herself. Considering everything she'd been through, the earlier conversation with Kent felt almost too good to be true. Was she on the verge of having the man she'd wanted for years? Would it work out between them?

Then there was the lingering issue of her canceled nuptials. Part of her was concerned about starting something new with Kent. Yet she'd waited so long, spent many nights imagining a kiss like the one he'd given her, and she found herself wanting to forget about everything else and focus on him.

He'd shocked her kissing her the way he had, especially after he insisted they take some time. It hadn't been one of those passion-filled kisses that she'd watched on television. But it was sincere, sweet. Everything she'd dreamed of.

She'd only ever heard people talk about butterflies in the stomach, shivers of pleasure described in romance novels, and tingling nerve endings. But to actually feel that for herself—with one kiss?

Closing her eyes, she let her mind travel back to that instant. She was like a giddy teenager, and she wanted more. For the first time in her life, she actually wanted to forget about everything holding her back and move forward. Even though she'd just left a relationship, she wasn't willing to deny herself this chance with Kent.

She heard the beep of the alarm system signal that the front door was open. Biting the inside of her cheek, she wondered if she should greet him or let him come to her. Setting her spatula down, she decided to go to him first.

Walking out of the kitchen, she paused when she saw him standing at the doorway, looking at his work phone. Lowering his brows, he tapped at his screen. Figuring she'd give him a minute, she stood there.

Once he fastened his phone in the holster on his waist, she stepped forward and asked, "Is everything okay?"

He glanced up at her and smiled. "Hey. Smells good in here. Did you bake my favorite?"

Something is definitely wrong. He was smiling, acting like he was fine, but his eyes gave him away. There was a shadow there that hadn't been there earlier. "Just pulled it out of the oven," she replied.

He sniffed, then closed his eyes. Groaning, he said, "Fried chicken, too? What's the occasion?"

"I figured I should at least do something since you've been so good to me." She inched closer to him.

"Yum." He pulled his laptop out of his bag, walked over to the couch, and set it down. She heard his phone buzz again. Sighing, he glanced at it and rolled his eyes. Instead of putting it back on his belt, though, he set it on an end table.

Looking up at her, he asked, "Have you heard anything else from your dad?"

She shook her head. "No." Wrinkling her brow, she asked, "Are you okay? It's just…" She wrung her hands together. "You look like something is on your mind."

The smile on his face wavered, and he sat down on a chair. He ran a hand over his head and leaned forward, resting his elbows on his knees. She took a seat opposite him on the coffee table, folding her hands in her lap.

"Mama is worried about Den," he grumbled. "She just texted me to ask me if I could try to find him. He hasn't been answering her calls and she's worried."

Allina tugged at her earlobe. Den wasn't exactly her favorite person. He'd treated Syd horribly during their relationship, proposed to her after he'd cheated on her to keep her with him. But he was Kent's brother. She cared because *he* did. "Do you think he's in trouble?" she asked.

Den was bipolar. He'd often go through periods when he wouldn't take his medication, which caused a lot of trouble. She'd been around on more than one occasion when Kent and Morgan had had to look for him. And Syd had convinced herself to forgive Den time and time again for the things he'd done to her because of his illness.

Hunching his shoulders, he shook his head. "I don't know. It's not like we've talked much. I've seen him a few times at Mama's house, but other than that, I have no idea what's going on in his life. He could be fine, just keeping his distance."

Knowing what she did about Den, she agreed with Kent. He was kind of an attention whore. He'd always make these awful scenes in order to get everyone to drop what they were doing to come to his aid. Syd used to complain about it often. "I'm sorry," she said. "When you did see him, did he look like he was having an episode?"

He stared off behind her, like he was trying to recall the last time he'd seen his brother. Which in itself was sad to Allina. The brothers had always made it a point to know what was going on in one another's lives. She knew it was important to Kent to spend time with his brothers. Each year on their birthdays, they would go out to breakfast and play basketball. Although Kent was closer to Morgan, she knew he loved Den and wanted him to be happy.

"He looked fine. We actually had a laugh when Mama let out a slew of curse words after she dropped one of her plates on the floor." He clasped his hands together. "That was the first time I had seen him in months. After the first of the year, I thought he might be coming around. Mama said he was coming by every Sunday, calling her regularly. But she told me things changed after Brynn was born."

He bowed his head. They sat there for a few minutes. She chewed on her thumbnail, thinking about what Kent had just revealed. It made a lot of sense that Den's demeanor had changed once Brynn arrived, since Den had been with Syd for so long. He was probably hurt that he wasn't the one to give her a baby, that Morgan and Syd and Brynn were a happy family.

"I'll go with you if you want to go look for him," she offered finally.

He looked at her then, his eyes softening. "No, that's not necessary. I have a lot of work to do. Den..." He sucked in a haggard breath. "He's probably okay, hiding like he's been prone to do in the past." He gave her a half-smile.

Nodding, she said, "Well, let me know if you change your mind. I want to be there for you, just like you're always there for me."

"Please stop saying that," he said. "You've been there for me many times, too. We depend on each other. That's why we're friends. So you don't have to keep thanking me."

"Fine," she said, rolling her eyes. "I won't say it anymore. I'll just fatten you up with my cakes."

He laughed then. "Allina, if you knew what 'cake' meant on the street, you wouldn't have said that."

Blinking rapidly, she asked, "What does it mean?" Her mind raced, searching for possible definitions. Syd and Cali used to make fun of her all the time for getting her slang wrong or mixed up. Or she'd say things that were seemingly innocent only to have them tell her she'd basically said something naughty.

He smirked. "I'll tell you but you're going to be embarrassed."

"Just say it," she told him, smacking his knee playfully.

Clearing his throat, he chuckled. "When someone says 'nice cakes,' it means the woman has a nice ass—shapely, large."

Her mouth fell open and she covered her face with her hands. "Oh my God. I had no idea. Yikes."

"You're funny. It's okay. It also means money," he added. "Either way, what you said is a good thing."

Eyes wide, she laughed. "Stop. I'm going to go finish dinner."

She stood up and he grabbed her wrist. Looking back at him, then at his hand on her, she asked, "What?"

"I missed you," he admitted softly. "While you were gone," he added in a low voice.

Her heartbeat quickened. "I missed you, too."

"Seriously, you make me laugh. I don't think you realize how funny you really are."

That was a first. "I don't think anyone ever told me I was funny." She placed her hand on top of his and squeezed. "But I'm glad I could return the favor."

The fact that Kent made her laugh was one of the reasons she'd been drawn to him. It was his way. Everybody loved his sense of humor, the way he could lighten up the room with his smile and his wit. It made her feel good that he thought she was funny.

"The offer still stands," she said. "If you need me to go with you, or even if you want to talk about Den or anything, just let me know."

"I will." He stood up, peered down at her. "I'm going to go take a shower and get to work. I need to finish this project."

He squeezed her shoulder, picked up his briefcase, and headed toward his bedroom. Sighing, she strolled back into the kitchen.

Syd had once told her that she always held back when it came to business and matters of the heart. She guessed it was true to an extent, except with Kent. Being with Isaac, letting him in, had been a big step for her. Isaac was her first boyfriend, the first *man* she'd ever kissed. In an attempt to cope with what her aunt was doing to her, she'd kissed a few boys in high school, but after Aunt Laura died, she'd backed away from boys altogether. She didn't even go to her prom, instead choosing to go to a church function.

She'd always be grateful for Syd being in her life, because Syd brought so many different characters with her. Having guy friends was something she could never have imagined until Red barged into their dorm room freshman year with Morgan. She and Red were both business majors in undergrad, so they shared a lot of classes. They were able to forge a friendship because they were study partners. He was respectful and protective. As nice looking as he was, other girls assumed she had a crush on him, but he was like a brother to her. And Morgan was elusive, closed off—except with Syd, even then. He preferred to keep his business private, but he was fun to be around. Then there was Kent.

Allina didn't click with Kent right away. He'd been a jock, and played college football for most of his time there. Whenever she saw him, he usually had some groupie with him. But he was the nicest—and finest—player on the team. Eventually, they'd formed a tentative friendship and it grew from there.

When Kent got with Kerri, Allina remembered everyone joking that he'd finally been tamed by a woman. Kerri was a medical resident, and at least five years older than Kent.

He'd fallen hard for her. The relationship didn't end well, however, and Allina had found herself helping Kent through it. That's when her feelings for him changed, when she realized she viewed him differently.

Allina iced the cake, giggling when she thought of the urban meaning of the word. After she was finished, she set the table. She'd inadvertently cooked too much food and considered calling Syd and Morgan over for dinner. Her friend had called her earlier to apologize for letting her drink so much tequila, and had mentioned that she didn't feel like cooking.

Deciding to check in with Kent before she called Syd and her family over, she ambled toward his room. As she approached his door, he swung it open and practically ran her over.

"Oh, shit," he said, holding on to her elbow as she stumbled back.

Bracing herself against the wall, she smoothed a hand over her shirt. "It's okay, I—" She looked up at him and gasped. "Oh my goodness."

He was standing before her in nothing but a towel. The stark white towel hung low on his hips. The smooth lines of his hard stomach and his pecs glistened with water. Her fingers tingled with a need to touch the hard planes of his body. *Oh my!* Once she realized she was staring, she looked away quickly and turned her back to him. Too late. The sight of his muscular physique and strong legs had been seared into her brain. "Oh, um, I'm sorry. I didn't know you weren't dressed. I…I thought…I was just coming to ask you if you'd mind me inviting Syd and Morgan over for dinner." She squeezed her eyes shut. But it didn't help. "I cooked too much food and I didn't want it to go to waste," she babbled on. "Oh my God."

His hand on her shoulder stopped her. "Allina, it's okay. I don't mind."

Glancing at him over her shoulder, stealing one last look, she said, "Okay. I'll...just...I'm going back in the kitchen."

She made a break for the kitchen as fast as she could. Even though she'd done her best to not turn back, she couldn't help but shoot him one last glance before she rounded the corner. Once she was in the safe haven of the kitchen, she sagged against the counter. The smell of his soap and the feel of his hand on her elbow were etched into her mind. *Oh my God, he's hot.*

"Allina?"

She jumped, startled by his voice. Without turning around, she busied herself by opening a cabinet and pulling out a saucer. What she needed it for, she had no idea. The table was already set. "I can't call Syd because I don't have a phone," she muttered as she realized it.

"I called them myself. Brynn is asleep, and Morgan was on his way to pick up Chinese food they'd already ordered."

With trembling hands, she set the small plate on the table and turned around, hoping against all hope that he was dressed. "Thanks," she said, disappointed her buffer couldn't come to dinner and distract her from her overwhelming desire.

Thank God. He was fully clothed, in a pair of sweats and a T-shirt. Unfortunately, it didn't help her get that other image out of her mind.

"Do you think you could take me over there tomorrow on your way to work? I'd love to see the baby," she said.

"Allina, I'm sorry about earlier." He scratched the back of his neck. "I'm not used to having a houseguest and I needed another towel."

Shaking her head, she said, "No, don't apologize. It was bound to happen, right?" *Bound to happen? Geez, Allina, get it together.*

"I guess," he muttered. "First thing tomorrow, I'm going

to pick you up a phone, okay? I'll be working long hours this week trying to finish a project."

She tilted her head and observed him. Kent was a hard worker, dedicated to his job. But she knew he'd rather be doing something else. "Can I ask you a question?"

He raised his eyes to meet hers. "Sure."

"How's your art? I noticed you were working on something in the office."

"I've been working on a painting to hang at the Ice Box." His face lit up when he talked about it. "I thought it would be cool to hang it behind our booth."

The "crew" had designated a big booth in the back as their own personal booth. It was private, and off to the side. Before they bought the bar, the previous owner had allowed them to purchase the booth, kind of like a VIP thing.

"Really?" she said, grinning. "Can I see it?"

"Yeah," he said.

She followed him to the office, trying not to pay too much attention to the way he glided down the hall, or his butt.

Once they were in the office, he pushed back the tarp covering the painting.

"Oh Kent," Allina breathed. She eyed the painting—of Kent, Syd, Red, and Morgan. Stepping closer, she reached out to touch it, but paused before turning to him. "Can I?"

He nodded. "Go ahead. I've been working on it a while. It's been a long time since I used oil to paint."

She touched the surface, awed by the detail in their faces. Syd was sitting in a chair, flanked by the others. "This is brilliant. What made you do it?"

"I had planned to do it as a gift to the others when we bought the place, but work and everything else got in the way."

She glanced at him over her shoulder. "I can't believe it. It's beautiful."

He lowered his gaze, shifting his weight from one foot to the other. "Thanks."

"I mean, I knew you could paint, but . . . you're awesome." She swept a hand over the painting again, right over his face. "You could probably sell this, or something like it. Do you realize how much money you could make?"

"I don't do it for money," he said.

"You should." She studied the painting further, noting the blurred Ice Box sign in the background. It was abstract but she could make it out. "Have you worked on anything else?"

"Yeah," he told her, his eyes sparkling with pride. "I have this new program where I can design all kinds of things. I've been doing little stuff for the bar, and one of my co-workers asked me to design a logo for her."

"Kent, you could actually start your own company doing this type of work. You already know your way around the computer. You could be building websites, too. That's money in the bank, and you love it."

When her arms fell to her sides, he pulled the tarp back over the painting. "I've thought about it, but I don't have a lot of time to devote to it right now. The bar is busy and work is . . . hectic."

"Well, you should definitely think more about it," she said as they made their way back to the kitchen. "Why continue to work at that high stress job when you can do something you love?"

"I could ask you the same thing," he said.

She stopped and turned to him. "I guess you could." Who knew that in trying to encourage Kent to follow his dream, she'd end up inspiring herself to do the same? It was high time she contacted Cali about that business.

CHAPTER FIFTEEN

Kent couldn't believe it.

Instead of spending his Monday night working, he was sitting across from Allina on the floor in the living room, like it was the most natural thing in the world. He'd never imagined being so satisfied, happy even, to have someone sharing his space. But she seemed to fit into his life so seamlessly he hated to think about what he'd do when she got her own place. It was the first time in a long while that he'd thought about taking a vacation from work, just so he could stay home—with her. His mouth quirked up into a smirk at the way Allina bit her lip in concentration. He hated to do this, but...

"Uno," he announced, when he set his second to last card on the floor between them.

She placed a card on top of his. "Draw two," she said with a wide grin.

If Morgan could only see him now. He pulled two cards from the deck. "You better be glad you had that card. I was getting ready to win for the fifth time in a row."

"I think your deck of cards is rigged," she retorted, looking at the four remaining cards in her hands with a slight crease in her brow. "Besides, you cheat!"

"Hey, I don't cheat. You just don't know how to play. Uno is a game of strategy."

"Bull," she retorted with the cutest scowl. "Uno is a game of luck. I can't help it if I'm dealt a sucky hand."

"Say what you will..." He played his card, laughing when she grumbled and smacked her fist on the rug. "But luck has nothing to do with it. I just have better skills."

She bit down on her bottom lip—which drove him crazy—and pulled four cards from the deck. "You get on my nerves." When she glanced at her cards, she tossed all of them on the floor and stood up. "I quit."

He looked up at her. "Where are you going? You're a sore loser."

"Be quiet. Do you want me to slice you a piece of cake?" A pretty blush spread over her cheek and he figured she'd recalled their conversation from earlier. From his view, she had pretty nice "cakes." She was thin, but well proportioned. And he was definitely past the point of denying his attraction to her.

Nodding, he watched her disappear into the kitchen, taking in the slight sway of her hips.

Showing her his art was huge. He was extremely private, keeping most of his work to himself. Surprising himself, he hadn't hesitated to show her. Her reaction made his chest swell with pride. Not only did she love it, she'd encouraged him to do more, to strive for better in his work life and in his art. Which went hand in hand.

Then he'd been treated to the best fried chicken he'd ever tasted, even better than his mother's. It was Allina's specialty. When he'd called Morgan earlier to invite him for dinner, his brother had regretfully told him they wouldn't make it, but added his request that they save him a few pieces of chicken.

Kent had secretly hoped his brother would join them because he couldn't be held responsible for the things he wanted to do to his house guest. Being alone with her would certainly make it harder to take it slow. Unbeknownst to her, Allina had been turning him on all night. Even the way she blew on her food made him want to strip her naked on the table and show his appreciation for her. He was crawling out of his skin with the desire to touch her, to help her forget every bad thing that'd ever happened to her. He wanted it. He wanted her.

Having dinner with her, taking time to enjoy her company, playing cards, felt good to him. He liked being with her on a different level, knowing that she knew how he felt about her, how important their relationship was to him. He'd expected her to be awkward, especially after catching him in his towel earlier, but she seemed comfortable and open.

Being with her had kept his mind off his mounting worries about Den and the stress of his job. She was a welcome breath of fresh air in his life. He'd meant it when he'd said he missed her.

In college, the other players on the football team used to tease him because he was so particular about the type of woman he dated. Sure, he dated women from all different backgrounds, but he preferred a certain type. Being "fine" with "cakes" for days wasn't enough.

What was the use of having a fine woman who couldn't cook? Or a woman with a fly body, curves in all the right places, but no brain in her head? Sex was great and everything, but he needed to be able to talk to her in the morning, or at night. And not about *The Real Housewives* of whatever city, discounted shoes, or splurging on unnecessary shit just because. His ideal woman would be able to cook a dinner good enough to put his mama to shame, carry on a conversation about current events, and turn him on in the bedroom.

Allina had two of those qualities down pat. The third he suspected she would, too, with the right person. *Me*. He smirked to himself, hoping he'd be able to find out sooner than later just how good she could be. She was already sexy as hell, in that *I have no idea* kind of way. Imagine how she'd be when she got an idea.

The smell of strawberries and whipped topping wafted to his nose. He opened his eyes to Allina standing in front of him, holding a plate with a huge piece of cake on it.

She grinned down at him. "I got you a big piece."

He took the plate from her and dug right in, moaning when he took his first bite. "You put your foot in this, Lina."

She sat down next to him on the floor and sampled it herself. "Yum, it is good."

It seemed like a movie, happening in slow motion. Kent held back a groan as she dipped a finger into the whipped cream, flicked her tongue across the tip before sucking it into her mouth. The resulting purr of delight that accompanied her action shot straight to his groin.

His lips parted when she did it again, closing her eyes. "Allina?" he croaked out.

Her eyes fluttered open. "Oh," she said, clearing her throat. "Yes?"

"Um…" *Think of something not sexy to say*. "Um… never mind," he said lamely. "I lost my train of thought." Which was a flat-out lie. His thoughts were still on the way her digit slid in and out of her mouth like…

"Snuggle." That word jerked him right back to the present.

Frowning, he asked, "Excuse me? 'Snuggle'?"

She arched a brow. "I said you're out of fabric softener. Can we pick some up at the store tomorrow?"

Wow. Obviously she had been talking to him while his mind was playing in the gutter. "Yeah, I'll just pick some up on my way home from work," he said, focusing on the cake in front of him.

They ate in silence for a few minutes before he confessed, "I liked being with you like this tonight. There are a lot of things going on with both of us, but it was good to just sit back and enjoy each other."

"I agree," she said softly, pushing her remaining cake around with her fork. "I had fun. Wish we had some vanilla ice cream to go with this cake."

So she could torture him more? But a little French vanilla *would* have set it off. "That would have been even better," he said, scraping the icing off his plate.

"I've been thinking," she said, changing the subject. "I want to do more with my designs. I'm tired of being scared, of everything. I've been going through the motions of life for too long, doing what everyone else thought I should do. It's time to do what I want to do."

"I hope this means you're going to call Cali?" he asked, setting his plate on the coffee table.

"I am."

He nudged her with his shoulder. "Good girl."

"And I want you to do something for me."

Arching his eyebrow, he willed his mind not to go where it wanted to go. "What would that be?" he asked huskily.

"Seriously consider doing something with your talent. Think about it..." She got on her knees and picked up his hands, holding them out at his sides. "These hands were made to do something better than sitting behind a computer doing mundane, predictable tasks. How could you be so good at encouraging others and not want more for yourself?"

"It's easier said than done, Allina. But I love that you're so supportive."

Her shoulders slumped and she dropped one of his hands. Holding on to the other one, she traced his fingers. Her touch was stirring up something else in him. She didn't speak, just focused on the lines in his palm.

The scent—her scent—wafted to his nose, and the hairs on his neck raised. It was a mix of peonies and vanilla. Not that he made a habit of memorizing flower types. His mother happened to love the large, fragrant flowers and he made sure she had them every Mother's Day. He'd even surprised her one year by hiring a landscape artist to plant some in her backyard. And Allina smelled like she had them hidden somewhere on her. He wanted to peel her clothes off, one piece at a time to find them.

The silence was getting to him, making him want to do things to her that would likely make her blush if he described them out loud. "Are you reading my future?" he joked, unable to take it any longer.

She grinned. "If I believed in that, I would. But your future already seems clear to me."

Intrigued, he asked, "Well, spit it out. How clear is it?"

"I can't tell you," she said. "But I will say that you're going to do big things."

Rolling his eyes, he shook his head. "Are you speaking in a prophetic way?"

Allina had told him once that God gives everyone gifts, one of them being the gift of prophecy. Kent wasn't religious, but he was familiar with the Bible because of his time at church as a child. He could concede that there were certain things that were not able to be explained. This had always fascinated him.

"No." She giggled and finally let go of his hand. "I know you. I see you in a certain way, unlike how you see yourself. I think you're wonderful." Her eyes widened and she averted her gaze, as if she hadn't meant to say that. She stood up and rubbed her pants. "I better wash the dishes."

She picked up their plates and hurried to the kitchen. He sat there for a few minutes, digesting everything she'd said to him. Her faith in him was something he wanted to live up to, and for the first time in a long time, he considered taking her advice. But first...

He joined her in the kitchen. She was standing at the sink, scrubbing a pan. Approaching her, he stopped right behind her. Leaning in close, he brushed his mouth against her ear. She stilled, sponge in hand. "I appreciate what you said out there," he muttered.

Slipping an arm around her waist, he pulled her closer, enjoying her breathy gasp. "Kent," she said, her voice shaky.

"I mean it," he said. "It means a lot to me."

She turned in his arms and gazed at him. "It's true."

His hands skimmed down her sides and finally settled on her hips. Squeezing them, he lowered his face until the tip of his nose bumped hers, then pressed his lips to hers.

* * *

Allina leaned into Kent's embrace as he pulled her flush against him and kissed her with such passion, her knees buckled. Fortunately for her, he was holding her so tightly there was no way she could fall. She felt his tongue seeking entrance into her mouth and she opened willingly. Her body responded in a way it had never before: her nipples tightened as his rock-hard chest pressed against hers, her legs quivered as his hands slid down her sides, over her hips and her butt. It was almost like he'd cracked her open and exposed her in some way, only to him. Only for him.

Finally pulling back, he rested his forehead against hers.

But only for a second before he captured her lips with his again. Allina clenched her hands together and jumped when she felt water dripping down her arm and onto the floor. She felt the rumble of laughter in his chest first—before he stepped back.

"Maybe this should go back in the sink?"

Still dazed, her gaze dropped to the puddle of soapy water on the floor, then to the wet sponge in her hand. She loosened her hold on the big blue thing and allowed him to take it from her. "Oh God," she whispered as he tossed it into the sink behind her. Her head fell to his chest as they both laughed.

They swayed back and forth to their own music, and she wrapped her arms around his waist.

"Look at me," he said finally. She raised her eyes to meet his. He searched her gaze. For what, she had no idea. "I want to kiss you again," he admitted.

Her cheeks burned and she lowered her eyes. What did she say to that? *Yes? Please do? I'd like that?*

Tilting her chin up again with his finger, he asked. "Is that okay with you?"

Lips parted, she nodded. He kissed her again, drawing a low moan from her. Whatever she'd been getting ready to say was forgotten when his tongue slipped into her mouth and stroked hers. She gripped his head and dug her fingertips into his scalp.

Unnerved. Allina felt unnerved, like she was caught up in Kent's whirlwind. She couldn't describe how it felt to be in his arms, being kissed so tenderly, so passionately, by him. Or how she felt when he touched her.

He lifted her up in his arms, and she instinctively wrapped her legs around his waist. He carried her into the living room, kissing her the whole time.

Lowering her to the couch, he rested his weight on her.

He trailed a line of hot kisses from her mouth to her cheek to her neck. A pang of something she'd never felt before started low in her belly. It was scary but exhilarating at the same time. She wanted more of it. She clung to him as his lips found a spot just below her ear that drove her wild. Then he moved to the delicate shell of her ear and grazed it with his tongue before nipping at it with his teeth. His hands brushed against her breasts. *Oh God. Oh...no.*

She bucked up and he jumped back, hands in the air. If she hadn't stopped what was happening, they would have made love right on his couch. She wasn't sure she was ready to go that far and it wouldn't be fair to get him all wound up and chicken out at the last minute.

"Are you okay?" he asked, his chest heaving. "What's wrong?"

She gripped her throat and looked away. "I can't...we can't do this right now."

Frowning, his gaze darted around the room. "O...kay. Did I do something wrong?"

Wrapping a hand around his wrist, she assured him, "No. It's not you. It's just...I've never done this before." His mouth opened but nothing came out, so she took the opportunity to explain herself. "I mean, I'm assuming you want to have sex with me."

His mouth clamped shut. A second later, he said, "Eventually. I don't think I was expecting it to happen today."

She chewed on her bottom lip. "Just so we're clear, I've never...I don't..."

"What?"

"I've never had sex," she blurted out. "I'm a virgin."

His eyebrows rose. "Still?" he asked.

Gaping, she smacked him on his shoulder. "Yes, still! What is that supposed to mean?"

"I'm just saying, I had a feeling you were before you got with the minister, but I just assumed that he…" He rubbed his forehead and relaxed into the cushions. "You were going to marry the guy. I can't imagine marrying anybody without…Never mind."

She assumed he was referring to that old saying, something about buying the merchandise without trying it on. "No, we've never even done more than kissing and touching above the waist."

"Oh."

Oh? Allina wanted to crawl into a hole. She knew that Kent was very experienced. He was a football player, for Christ's sake. Silly girls on campus made it their mission to bed athletes. Everybody knew it. *I'm sure, as a young man, he embraced it.*

He didn't know it, but she'd overheard him tell Red one day that he didn't have time for inexperienced lovers. She'd never been ashamed of her virginity. In fact, she embraced it and never thought she'd have sex with anyone other than the man she would marry—until now.

Allina wasn't that naïve. She didn't expect Kent to propose to her because they'd admitted they had feelings. But she found herself in the very different position of actually considering the act of making love to someone who hadn't pledged his love to her before God and a church full of people. She'd never felt that way before—not even with Isaac, her would-be husband.

Turning to her, he squeezed her thigh. "I didn't know that," he said. "But it's okay. We don't have to go any further than this."

She breathed a sigh of relief. "I'm sorry."

His forehead creased. "What are *you* apologizing for?"

"I know you don't do virgins," she said.

"Why do you say that?"

She crossed her legs and picked at the fabric of her pants. "I heard you say something like that to Red a long time ago."

He scratched the back of his head. "Allina, I think you probably took the conversation out of context."

"No, you said that you didn't have time for inexperienced women."

He leaned back, a slight furrow in his brow, as if he was trying to recall the conversation. "I don't remember that. But if I did say that, it had nothing to do with you."

Fiddling with her earring, she said, "I'm not sure if I'm ready. And I just don't want to disappoint you."

"I'm not worried about that," he told her, leaning in and planting another searing kiss on her lips. "Everything will fall into place when the time is right."

"Wait. I feel like since I'm being honest, I should say something else."

"What is it?" he asked.

She picked a piece of lint from her pants. "I hadn't planned on doing that until I got married."

He closed his eyes and exhaled. "That's...fine," he croaked.

Giggling, she said, "Kent, don't. You can tell me the truth. I know it's probably not something you've ever had to worry about with anybody else."

"Yeah," he conceded. "You're the first. But, Allina, I'll never push you to do something you're not comfortable with. Okay?"

She nodded and fell into his outstretched arms, beaming when he kissed her forehead. They stayed like that for a little while, talking about the week ahead, before he walked her to her room and went to bed.

CHAPTER SIXTEEN

Allina grinned down at her bright-eyed godbaby. It had been a few hours since Kent had dropped her off at Syd's and Allina had been excited to spend those hours looking after Brynn while Syd cleaned up around the house. Syd had named both Allina and Calisa godmothers of her daughter. It was an honor Allina took very seriously, and also one that filled her heart with incredible joy. She loved every moment she spent with Brynn and would have been perfectly happy to hold her until Kent picked her up around six o'clock.

"I'm so glad you're here," Syd said, wiping down the countertops. "And what's this I hear about you frying chicken?"

"I did," Allina admitted. "Kent tore it up last night and took some to work with him this morning. I had saved you and Morgan a few pieces but accidentally forgot to bring them with me."

"Aw man," Syd groaned. "If only you had called earlier. No matter how hard I try, I can't get my chicken to turn out like yours."

"I'll show you one day." Allina looked down at Brynn, who seemed to be studying her. "And I'll show you, too, baby girl."

Brynn gurgled and stuffed a fist in her mouth.

Syd finally took a seat across from Allina. "She loves you."

"I love her," Allina said, rubbing Brynn's soft arm.

"So, what's going on with you?" Syd asked, drumming her fingers against the table.

Allina felt a blush creep up her neck when she thought about her "talk" with Kent. She knew her friend would understand where she was coming from, having been with only two men in her life. But after Allina had climbed into bed, she couldn't stop thinking about her escalating physical attraction to Kent. It was amazing what a few hot kisses would do to a person.

"We... kissed."

Syd smacked a hand on the table. "You're kidding. Again?"

Allina nodded. "More than once."

"Lina!" Syd shouted with glee, clapping her hands. "Girl, you've been holding back this entire time. That should have been the first thing you said when you walked in here."

"I know," Allina agreed. "But you were busy getting Brynn fed and bathed. Then you started cleaning up and I was bonding with little Brynn, I had to wait for the right time to bring it up."

"You know Cali is going to have a fit."

"Cali is going to trip out. Where is she, by the way? I thought she was coming over."

Syd stood up and grabbed her phone off the kitchen island. "She was supposed to come by with Corrine. She took some time off this week. I'm going to text her." Her friend tapped at the screen, then set it down on the table. "She'll call back. Finish telling me what happened. Did he kiss you first this time? Did he *only* kiss you?"

"Syd!" Allina giggled. "You're relentless."

"Spill, then," Syd said.

Allina looked down at Brynn, who was miraculously sleeping peacefully. "Do you want to put her down?"

Syd picked up her baby and kissed her three times on her

forehead before she walked out of the kitchen. Allina wondered what Kent was doing, if he was thinking about her like she was him.

"Want something to drink?" Syd asked, shuffling back into the kitchen. She opened the refrigerator and pulled out a carton of orange juice.

"I'll have a bottle of water."

Her friend grabbed a bottle and gave it to her. "Let's go in the family room."

Allina followed Syd to the sunken family room. Morgan's house was huge and he'd designed it himself. She'd visited countless times, but everything had changed since Sydney moved in. It was like she'd brought color into Morgan's home. Instead of drab earth tones, now there were bold reds, rich browns, and a hint of green.

She plopped down on the huge sectional and Sydney sat in the La-Z-Boy chair. "I feel like a bum," Allina said, taking a sip of her water.

"Why do you say that?" Syd asked.

"I'm not doing anything. I've been working, in some capacity, since I was a teenager. Not having a job is killing me." Judge had required she get a part-time job as soon as she could drive. They weren't broke—far from it—and she hadn't been required to contribute to household bills. It was just his way of teaching her how to manage money.

"Allina, it's been like four days. I'm sure you worked at that damn bridal shop all the way up to your…well, your big day."

Syd knew her too well. Allina had refused to take a day off prior to the ceremony. She'd argued with Isaac because he'd wanted her to take a month off after the wedding and she'd refused. In the end, she'd relented and scheduled a two-week vacation. Even then, she'd told her boss at the time that she'd probably be back early.

"I need to do something to keep me busy."

"So, you're staying?" her friend asked.

Allina had already decided to stay put in Michigan. She loved it in the "Mitten" as they called it. "Yes. This is where I belong. So, I need a job. Soon, I'll have to find a place. I can't continue to mooch off Kent."

"I'm sure he doesn't mind," Syd said. "He has the money, so let him help you."

"Excuse me; I know you're not talking." Allina folded her arms across her chest and looked at her best friend pointedly. When Syd took a leave from her full-time job as an engineer for one of the automotive companies in the area to follow Morgan to Baltimore, she'd called Allina crying about how she felt weird depending on a man.

"Well, my situation was different," Syd said. "I moved to a different state. I had no support, and I was pregnant and emotional."

"Whatever," Allina muttered. "It's not that I don't think that Kent *can* take care of me. I know he can. I just don't want him to. We're not married. All we've shared is a few kisses—"

"And years of friendship," Syd added, interrupting her. "If you want to do something, help me plan my wedding. Cali could use the help."

"I actually want to talk to Cali anyway. I hope she's willing to think about going into business together again. I really want my own shop, Syd."

"Yes, Allina!" Syd shouted, her eyes gleaming. "It's about time. And your first order of business can be my wedding."

"Wait a minute. Don't get ahead of yourself. Cali hasn't agreed. I did leave her in the lurch."

But Allina really hoped Cali would agree. It would do her

a ton of good to start working on something she'd wanted to do for ages. They'd talked about opening a store that specialized in everything wedding and party planning, a one-stop shop, for years. Cali would plan and coordinate the events and Allina would design the gowns. Although the planning part wasn't necessarily her forte, Allina knew enough about the business to contribute effectively. After all, she was Sharon Parker's daughter. It was a big risk, an expensive venture, but Allina knew it would pay off in the end.

"I know she will," Syd said. "I'm going to help out as much as I can. I'll be an investor."

Allina smiled at her friend. "I love you, Syd," she said. "You've always been so supportive of me."

"As you have for me. So, tell me about getting kissy with Kent," Syd said, wiggling her eyebrows. "Was it everything you imagined?"

"He's a really good kisser." Allina flashed back to his full lips on hers, the feel of his tongue against hers. "But..." She chewed on her fingernail. "I'm a little concerned. We kind of went from zero to sixty very quickly, and I—"

"Did he take your clothes off?" Syd asked, eyes wide.

"No," Allina said, shaking her head vigorously. "Not even close. Well, not really."

"But you said..." Syd scrunched her nose. "Never mind. What happened?"

"We kissed, and he touched me—"

"Below your waist?" Syd shrieked.

"No," Allina told her friend.

Syd sat back, twisted her lip, and rocked back and forth in the chair. "Fine. Go ahead and finish the story."

"Well, he picked me up and carried me to the couch and we were kissing the whole way. Then when he laid me down, he—"

"You're killing me! Did he at least touch your boob?"

Allina burst out in a fit of laughter. "Syd, you're too much."

"What?" Her friend batted her eyelashes with an innocent shrug of her shoulders. "You're beating around the bush. I just want to know the details."

"I'm quite sure you're getting plenty of action." Allina remembered her friend telling her that she couldn't get enough of Morgan. "You don't need my little make-out information that bad."

"Yes, but I have a newborn," Syd said. "We barely have time to do anything."

"Anyway," Allina said, bringing her friend's attention back to the matter at hand. "I ended up stopping him."

"What? Why?" Syd asked.

"Because I'm not ready to go any further. We talked and I told him I was a virgin."

Syd chuckled. "How did he take that?"

Allina shrugged. Kent had said it was okay with him, but she had her doubts. He was a man who'd never had to work hard to get female attention. That he would be willing to wait for her still seemed unbelievable. "He was fine; such a gentleman. He held me for a while, and then gave me a sweet, but sexy, kiss goodnight."

"See, I told you." Syd patted herself on the back. "I knew it would work out if you were honest about your feelings for him."

Allina bit her lip. "But I need some help."

"What is it?" Her friend leaned in, perched her hand under her chin.

With Allina's history, she'd once thought it was impossible to be sexually attracted to someone. But Kent had awakened something in her. It was exciting and frightening at the same time, for so many reasons.

Taking a deep breath, Allina said, "I'm not ready, but I'm also not opposed to going further with him. I'm scared, though."

"Scared of what?"

"I don't know what I'm doing. I just got out of a relationship on Friday. What do I look like making out with someone on Monday?"

"Allina, I know I've said this before, but it bears repeating. You've known Kent forever. And you weren't really in love with Isaac." Allina opened her mouth to speak, but Syd rushed on. "Even if you were, he is an ass who has done some shitty things, including threatening you—and me."

Syd was right about all of the above. The fact that Allina had been planning to marry Isaac had little to do with love. She'd fooled herself into thinking it did. "I know. But those are not my only reasons for putting a stop to it. There's . . . the Lord," Allina whispered.

Syd covered her mouth with her hand in a bad attempt to hide her smile.

"I know what you're going to say," Allina continued. "But it's the truth. I'm torn. I want him; don't get me wrong. But I do have my faith to consider."

"Well, I'd never tell you to go against what you believe," Syd said. "I do think that Kent is wonderful, and I love him. He's funny, fine, and fiercely protective of those he loves. You could do a lot worse, but not much better. At the same time, and despite what I said earlier, I do think you did the right thing by slowing things down—for now."

"You do?"

"It's your first time, and you're not really ready. Because if you were, and it was feeling good to you, nothing could have stopped it. I really think this situation with Isaac needs to be settled before you get too involved with Kent. Take it from me. I know of what I speak."

Allina thought about what Syd said. It was exactly what Kent had told her himself. Perhaps it was better to give it some time, which meant no more kisses either.

"And as far as the other thing, you not knowing what to do...don't worry about that," Syd said. "It's natural to feel a bit hesitant. It's new for you, and your feelings are probably overwhelming right now. But when, or if, it does happen, just go with it. Don't think about it too much."

Allina toyed with a lock of her hair, staring at a picture on the mantel of all of them together. Her eyes focused in on Kent, on the genuine smile on his face. She remembered when they'd taken the photo, during a group vacation to Las Vegas. It was her first time in Sin City and she'd surprisingly had a blast.

Over the years, she'd done a lot of things she'd thought she never would and it'd turned out well for her. There was a lot she regretted in her life, but not attending the University of Michigan. It was where she'd met her friends, the most important people to her besides her parents. Thinking about good times made her more determined to set things right.

"You're right," Allina said. "I won't worry about it. Whatever is happening between me and Kent will happen on its own. But is it completely and utterly scandalous to look forward to it?"

Syd winked. "Oh yeah, very scandalous—in the best possible way."

The sound of the baby crying interrupted their girl time and Syd jumped to her feet, leaving Allina sitting there.

While she waited for Syd to come back, she dialed her parents' house. Around this time every day, her mother would be glued to the television watching some talk show or her favorite soap opera. It would be a good time to check in with her, hear her voice.

No answer.

Mid-afternoon, during the week, and Sharon Parker wasn't at home?

Allina tried her mother's cell. It went straight to voicemail. "What in the world is going on?" she murmured to herself. Trying again, she tapped her foot against the tile. The phone was ringing. She hoped her mother would answer, but for some reason, she didn't have a good feeling about it.

She heard someone pick up the phone, but her mother didn't say "Hello" in a singsongy voice like she always did.

"Mom," she called. "Mom!"

"Hi, Allina."

Allina froze. The voice on the other end of the line wasn't her mother's. It was Isaac's. Her stomach dropped. Shaking, she jumped up and paced the floor. "Isaac," she croaked. "Why are you answering my mother's phone? Where is she?"

"Don't you worry about that," he said, his voice calm.

"Where the hell is my mother?" she shouted. Her mind ran away with all the possibilities.

Syd walked into the room, bouncing baby Brynn in her arms. She frowned when she met Allina's gaze. She placed a hand over the receiver, mouthing to Syd to call Kent. Syd dashed out of the room.

What if he's done something to my mother? She knew her father would more than likely be in court. Nobody was with her mom. She wondered where the person her father had hired and who was supposed to be watching Isaac was.

"Allina?" he called. A chill ran up her spine.

"Tell me where my mother is," she hissed.

"Where are you?" he demanded. "Do you realize what you've put me through? You embarrassed me in front of my congregation, in front of my parents. What makes you think you can get away with that?"

"Where is my mother, Isaac? I swear, if you've hurt her…"

"What will you do? Huh? It's not like you're here. You ran off," he taunted. "You left her here to deal with me."

"Please," she begged. All the bravado she'd mustered seeped out of her and her shoulders slumped in defeat. "Why are you doing this?"

"Remember what I told you the morning of our wedding?"

How could she forget? His words still haunted her. *What was I thinking?* Disappearing from the church the way she had, leaving him without so much as an "I hate you" was bound to incur his wrath. She'd been so preoccupied, so enamored with Kent and starting her life over that—

"I told you that I'll never let you go," he continued, interrupting her thoughts. "Remember that?"

Allina didn't dare answer him. Instead, she asked again, "Where is my mother?"

"Did you think I was just going to let you walk out on me? You're mine."

"Stop," she whispered.

"I'm keeping you," he went on.

"Stop!" she shouted. Something snapped in her. She was tired of Isaac. And she wasn't going to let him intimidate her any longer. "You don't own me."

"I warned you," he sneered. "I told you what I'd do if you left me. Your friend, Sydney?"

"Don't say her name, you sick fuck!" Allina shouted, alarmed by her own choice of words after she'd said it.

"I'm sure she will be at her bar at some point alone," he taunted. "Maybe I'll pay her a visit."

"If you do, you'll be sorry. Morgan will mop the floor with you."

"Not if he isn't there," Isaac said, a slight edge to his voice.

"Why are you doing this?" she asked, feeling her resolve buckle. "You have too much to lose. I could go to your father, tell him what you're doing. I could go to the news, the city council…everywhere that your family has a connection. I'll tell them all about you." Her voice cracked on that last sentence.

"I told you I'd hurt you, and anyone you love, make your life a living hell. Where's your mother?" he jeered.

She'd had enough. "Nice try. You can't manipulate me anymore. You really should come up with a new tactic. Threatening me and my family is so tired. But just so you know…I don't have a problem going to your church board and telling them about that woman who implied that you and your father paid her off," she vowed. She didn't know where she was getting all this strength from but she thanked God for it. And she was going to run with it. "Now, you tell me where the hell my mother is, right now. Before I call the police and make *your* life a living hell."

There was a long pause. Then he cleared his throat. "I was just sitting here thinking about how beautiful you are," he said. "Looking at an old picture of you and Syd. You and your friend are very nice-looking ladies. I wonder what would have happened if I met Syd first. Maybe I should ask her what she thinks."

Before she could say anything else, she heard the piercing sound of Syd's scream, followed by a loud thump.

CHAPTER SEVENTEEN

Kent sped toward Morgan's house. Syd had been frantic when she'd called him earlier, telling him that Isaac had somehow managed to contact Allina. He'd raced out of the office, rethinking his promise to not drive down to Cleveland and beat the shit out of that punk.

On his way, Allina called him, assured him she was fine but he still needed to hurry. As it turned out, though, Isaac wasn't the immediate threat at the moment. His brother Den had shown up out of the blue, talking out of his mind, reeking of alcohol. Morgan was on his way, but he wasn't as close as Kent. Mama was already there.

As he drove there he pictured the scene at the house. Gripping the steering wheel, he shook the image of Syd and Allina trying to calm down a manic Den.

When he pulled into the driveway, he saw his mother pacing in front of the door, a cigarette in her hand. It had to be bad if his mother was smoking after twenty-plus years of being smoke-free. He hopped out of the car and barreled toward her.

She held her hands out, blocking him from entering. "Son, wait. I called the hospital. I'm going to have him admitted."

"What happened in there?" Kent barked, taking the cigarette from her hand and flicking it into the grass.

"It's not good," she cried. "But you have to remain calm when you go in there."

"Mama, don't," he snapped, immediately regretting his tone. It wasn't his mother's fault that Den was a fuckin' asshole. "Did he hurt anybody?"

She swallowed, wiped a tear from her cheek before nodding slightly.

Heat flushed through his body and his heart pounded as he pushed the door open. Den lay in the middle of the floor in a pile of putrid vomit and broken glass.

Syd was sitting on the sofa, rocking a restless Brynn in her arms, and Allina was next to her, watching Den. Kent scanned the room. It looked like a tornado had hit: furniture tipped over, papers scattered everywhere.

"He finally passed out," Syd said, her voice flat.

For the first time in many months, Kent wanted to beat the shit out of his brother.

He stepped over Den to get to the couch, cringing as he stepped over the glass. "What are you doing in here? You should take Brynn out of here. I'll take care of Den."

"He needs help, babe," his mother said from behind him. "I don't know how to help him."

He was sick. They had all trotted out this excuse on more than one occasion when it came to Den. Rolling his eyes, he reached down and picked up his niece. "Hey, baby," he said, bouncing her up and down. The fussy baby calmed down a little in his arms. "Let's get you out of here."

Allina looked up then and Kent froze. "What the hell happened to you?" He asked, fury racing through his veins. Allina had a small gash on her face, right above her eye.

Brynn started squirming again and he tried to placate his

niece by rocking her. With his free hand, he reached out and ran a thumb over Allina's eye, where there was a small bruise forming.

"I fell against the table," Allina explained. "We were trying to get him to calm down, and Syd had Brynn in her arms so I tried to step in."

"And?" he asked. "Did you fall or did he push you?"

Syd peered up. "He pushed her," she admitted.

Kent struggled to control his rage. A verbal threat was one thing, still punishable by an ass-whooping. But physically laying hands on a woman? Kent cracked his knuckles, the urge to beat Den's ass taking him over again.

"Mama had him calmed down for a bit," Syd said. "Then he flipped out again and started throwing things."

"I jumped in front of him and he pushed me out of the way," Allina said. "I don't think he even knew it was me. He was so out of it, trying to talk to Syd."

Kent glanced back at his brother. Turning to Mama, he handed her the baby. "Can you take her out of here?"

"Mama, she may take a bottle right now," Syd said.

"I'll go too," Allina said, standing up.

Kent traced her cheek with his thumb. "You need to put something on that eye," he told her. "I'm so sorry."

She framed his face with her hands. "Stop. It's not your fault. But your mother is right. He needs help."

Mama gripped his sleeve. "Kent, don't be too hard on him. He's sick."

He watched his mother and Allina disappear around the corner and turned to Syd. "You need something?" he asked her.

"A drink. My nerves are frazzled. I can't stop shaking."

Nodding, Kent went to the kitchen to fix Syd a drink and check on Mama and Allina. When he returned minutes later, he handed his sister the tumbler he'd filled with cognac.

"He scared the shit out of me," Syd said. "I've never seen him like this." She scanned the room, shaking her head. "Morgan is going to kill him."

"No he won't. But I can't promise he won't kick his ass." He picked up a pillow off the floor and tossed it on the couch next to her. "Shit. I can't promise that *I* won't hurt him when he wakes up."

Just then, a groan from the floor drew their attention. Kent started toward Den, but Syd grabbed him. "Just... leave him there."

He looked at his sister as she watched Den. Her eyes were haunted and dull. She'd been through countless episodes with Den, seen him through numerous hospital visits. Kent had had his share of run-ins with Den's mental illness, but it was Morgan and Syd who had taken the worst over the years.

Den grumbled and rolled over onto his knees. His brother looked dazed and confused; his eyes were wild and his clothes were dirty. Kent was angry, but more than that he was sad. Growing up, Den had been like Superman to him, fearless. Unlike Morgan, he hadn't been privy to the different things that Den had done until much later. He'd known Den because he was such good friends with Morgan, but he'd always been the cool older brother to him.

Morgan used to tell him things, but at his young age, Kent didn't have any concept of the dark side of life. His parents were well-respected, successful people who'd barely had an argument in front of him, while Morgan and Den's biological parents ran illegal businesses out of their home. They'd had criminals and junkies and prostitutes parading in and out of their house for a long time. It was no wonder Morgan had put up a barrier and Den had turned to alcohol and drugs.

When Kent convinced his parents to take Morgan in so he

wouldn't be shipped down to Alabama, he hadn't expected Morgan to turn him down. He remembered that day like it was yesterday. In his ten-year-old mind, he'd figured out the reason for Morgan's hesitation and took care of it by asking his mother and father to take Den, too.

His parents had agreed, and he'd instantly had two brothers. Being an only child, he'd been ecstatic. Den had given his parents a lot of trouble, but they loved and supported him through everything. And soon, he'd started caring about his life. Instead of skipping school, he worked hard to bring up his grades and graduated. That's not to say he didn't have his events. But he'd worked through them.

Looking at him now, Kent wasn't so sure his brother could be helped. First of all, he had to want it. Obviously, he didn't.

"When did you get here?" Den grumbled, struggling to his feet.

Kent saw Syd wipe her eyes and ground his teeth together. "What the fuck is wrong with you?" he growled. "Do you realize you could have hurt someone? Wait a minute, you did hurt somebody."

"What are you going to do about it?" Den slurred.

Unable to help himself, he fisted his hands in Den's shirt and jacked him up. "How about I show you?" Then he flung him to the wall. His brother slid down to the floor. Kent loomed over him. "I'm not playing with you, Den."

Morgan burst into the house from the back, rushed over to Den, and lifted him off the floor. "Den, you piece of shit, I'll break your fuckin' neck."

Around this time, Kent would normally step in and pull Morgan off Den. Always the peacemaker. But this particular time, he couldn't bring himself to do it. Allina wasn't even officially his girlfriend and he wanted to maim Den for pushing her and hurting her in the process. He couldn't imagine the rage Morgan felt knowing that Den had pushed himself into their home and terrorized his fiancée while his infant daughter was there.

"Morgan, stop," Syd begged. "Please."

Kent didn't know when Syd had got up, but she was pulling Morgan off Den. Syd turned to Kent and pleaded with him to help her pull the men apart. Reluctantly, Kent grabbed Morgan.

He heard sirens in the distance and assumed it was finally the help his mother had called for arriving.

"Kent, let me go," Morgan said through clenched teeth.

"No, this isn't helping. Don't you think Syd and Mama have been through enough? I know you're pissed. Hell, I'm mad as hell. But look at him." He pointed to Den, slumped over on the floor. "He's in no shape to fight. It wouldn't be a fair one. Get him once he's sober and healed."

Morgan wrenched himself out of Kent's hold. "Get him the hell out of my house before I hurt him." Then he stormed out of the room with Syd right on his heels.

Kent sighed, dropping his head.

"Kent," Allina said. His eyes snapped to hers. "Are you okay?"

"I should be asking you that same question."

There was a firm knock on the door, and Kent answered it. The paramedics had arrived.

* * *

When Den had barged in earlier, for a brief second Allina had thought it was Isaac. She'd rushed to the front of the house just in time to see Den push through the door. He was yelling and carrying on. The mad look in his eyes, the glare toward Syd and Brynn, were unsettling to say the least. He'd been spouting off all these things about how Syd belonged with him, how he couldn't let her go, how Brynn should have been his baby. Despite how angry Den had been in the past, none of them would ever have believed he would physically hurt Syd. Then again, she hadn't believed Isaac was capable of murderous threats either.

Syd held her composure, though. Her friend spoke in calm, gentle tones. She didn't argue with him, only pleaded that he settle down and think about what he was doing. It seemed to be working until Den spotted a picture of Morgan, Syd, and baby Brynn on a table. That's when he proceeded to destroy the living room, and that's when Syd broke down and Allina had taken over. By that time, Mama had arrived and was also trying to diffuse the situation, to no avail.

When Den passed out Allina made sure Syd and Brynn were okay, then dialed her father. Apparently her mother had lost her cell phone but she was fine. Judge was not happy Isaac had somehow gotten hold of it. Her father promised to check in with his PI, just to make sure Isaac was still in Cleveland. Allina didn't share anything about Den with her father, but she'd assured him she'd call as soon as she got back to Kent's.

Then Kent arrived. It took every ounce of strength in her not to leave Syd's side and run into his arms. The only way she could stop herself was to not look at him and just let his voice sooth her frayed nerves. She'd wanted to weep when she finally did glance up at him. The rage in his eyes, the vein throbbing in his neck, was unmistakable. He wanted to hurt his brother. And she really believed he would have if it hadn't been for them.

She couldn't help but wonder if a similar scene would happen when she finally came face-to-face with Isaac. Her ex-fiancé wasn't bipolar, but he was obviously unhinged. Why else would he be threatening to hurt people?

Now, hours later, they were back at Kent's place. Allina sat with her feet propped up on the coffee table, her sketch pad in hand. She'd been trying to keep her mind off the incident at Syd's house but she couldn't stop thinking about it.

She'd already talked to her father again, who'd informed her that Isaac was still in the area, still locked up in his house. Allina breathed a sigh of relief. It had been a game to Isaac. He'd really just wanted to terrorize her, manipulate her into going back.

Her thoughts turned back to Kent. He was quiet. She'd filled him in on everything that happened before Den showed up on the way back home, but he hadn't said much. Instead, he'd gone into his office after he'd made sure her cut was cleaned and covered. She wanted to go in and talk to him, see where his head was, but she decided to give him some time. After all, he'd just seen his brother carted off in a straightjacket.

"Are you hungry?" Kent asked from behind her.

She twisted around to face him. He was leaning against the threshold, wearing a pair of sweats and a wife beater, and he had a small box in his hand. She couldn't make out the writing on it from that distance.

"I could eat," she told him, surprised she had an appetite after the events of the day. "Do you want me to fix something?"

"Nah, I'll order a pizza." He ambled over toward her and plopped down next to her. Setting the box on her lap, he said, "Your phone. It's turned on and everything. I got it after I dropped you off this morning."

Gripping the box, she opened it and pulled out the phone. "Thanks. I really appreciate it."

"I programmed it and everything. All the important numbers are in there, and I set you up a new e-mail address, too. You can go in and change your passwords."

She snuck a glance at him, a small smile on her face. Kent was the complete opposite of Isaac, in his actions and his words. Isaac had told her once that as her husband he'd want to know her passwords to everything. At the time it had bothered her but she'd blown it off, telling herself that it was for her own protection.

"The phone has everything," he said, shifting in his seat to show her a few apps. "And I found this sweet Sketchbook app." He reached over and scrolled through her apps.

Once he located it, he clicked it open. But Allina wasn't paying that app any mind. Or the next two he pointed out. She was too busy taking in his smell and enjoying the way his arm brushed against her when he was talking. The hint of a drizzle of water on his shoulder reminded her that he'd just gotten out of the shower.

"Then there is an app called Moodboard that will help you—"

Before he could finish his sentence, Allina kissed him. Long and hard. It was a direct contradiction to what she'd decided earlier after her talk with Syd, but in that moment she couldn't think of a reason to stop herself. And the way he kissed her back told her he couldn't stop either.

Pretty soon, they were stretched out on the surface of the couch, him lying on top of her and her cradling his body with her legs. She was dizzy with the need to explore him further, to let him explore her. His lips against hers, his hard body on hers, was driving her insane—in a good way.

His thumbs slipped beneath her thin shirt, brushed the skin there lightly. He swept his mouth over her neck, then her shoulder, biting down gently on her skin.

Pushing himself up on his arms, he looked down at her. "Allina?" he breathed. "We should probably—"

Leaning up, she kissed him on his chin and he groaned before taking her mouth in his again. He nipped at her lips, taking his time. That feeling in the pit of her stomach intensified with each touch, each kiss.

Pulling back again, he slowly pushed her shirt up, baring her body. His fingers were hot against her skin, blazing a trail of fire, leaving her trembling with need. When his hand found her breast, she held her breath. With his eyes on hers, he cupped her mound in his palm. He unhooked her bra and slid it off before he gently circled her nipple with his thumb. Dipping his head, he suckled her into his mouth, rolling his tongue around her bud.

Her heart pounded and her blood hummed as he kissed his way to her other breast. Digging her fingers into his shoulders, she arched her back and turned her head to the side. A low purr escaped her mouth. *A purr?* Before this, Allina would never have guessed she was capable of making such a sound. She'd heard how good it felt from her friends, who had never been shy when talking about sex. But she really hadn't expected it to feel *this* good.

Kissing his way back up her body, he captured her bottom lip in his. They jerked apart when they heard a soft knock at the door, followed by the doorbell. In her haste to get away from him, she rolled over and slid off the couch, landing on her butt with a loud thump.

"Oh, shit," he said, pulling her to her feet.

Scrambling, they rushed to fix their clothes. He pulled the back of her shirt down and pushed her hair out of her face. When he got to the door, he looked back at her. She nodded her approval and he opened it.

Syd was on the other side, holding the baby. "Can I come

in?" she asked, a deep frown on her face. "Morgan's parking the car."

"Yeah, come on," Kent said, taking the diaper bag from her and ushering her in.

"I can't stay there right now." She tugged Brynn's little jacket off. "We tried to call you. What were you doing?"

Allina's cheeks blazed and she averted her gaze.

"Nothing," Kent lied. "I must have had my phone on silent. I didn't hear it."

"We were going to visit Red, but Corrine is having her little friend over tonight and I didn't want to bring my sour mood over there."

"Do you need to stay here all night?" Kent asked.

"No," Syd said. "I just needed to get away from the house. We packed the baby up and went for a drive. Ended up here. I hope you don't mind."

"Of course not," Allina said, taking the sleeping baby from Syd. "We were just getting ready to order a pizza."

She exchanged a look with Kent, motioning with her head for him to confirm what she said.

"Yeah," he said, catching on. "You're just in time."

"Thank you," Syd whispered, unshed tears in her eyes.

Allina smiled at the disappointed look in Kent's eyes. It was a good thing that Syd had shown up. Otherwise, she and Kent would have done something they might have regretted in the morning.

CHAPTER EIGHTEEN

Too much cognac. Too much drama.

Kent's head was throbbing. He'd stayed awake practically all night, working on his painting, and ended up falling asleep at his desk. As he shuffled to his room he squinted at the sunlight streaking in. He just needed to lie down for a minute, get his shit together.

The blinds were drawn in his room. *Thank God.* He slid under the comforter and closed his eyes, hoping sleep would come soon. He was emotionally drained and just needed some rest.

When he heard the light snoring, his breath hitched and he slowly turned his head. Allina was sleep, next to him. In his bed. *Did I have that much yak that I don't remember telling her to sleep in my room?*

Poking her, he whispered, "Allina?"

She moaned in her sleep, rolled over, and burrowed into his side.

"Allina?" he called again.

"Yes," she grumbled finally. "I'm tired."

"You're in my bed," he told her, fighting the urge to lift up the cover. Not that he thought she was naked. She was very obviously clothed in at least a shirt; there was no skin showing at all.

"I know," she said. "Syd and Morgan are in my bed."

It was all coming back to him. They'd stayed up late, drinking and talking. Morgan got pretty smashed and Syd was tired as hell. Kent had insisted they stay over and Allina offered her bed to them.

"I told you to get in the bed last night," Allina mumbled. "But you insisted on staying up to work in your office."

He stroked her skin as she stretched. Despite nothing happening between them sexually, he could definitely imagine waking up next to her in the morning every day. Seeing her face first thing in the morning was definitely good for him.

She peeked her head out from under the covers and kicked them off. Yep, she had on a shirt *and* his basketball shorts. "Good morning," she said, rolling onto her stomach. "What time is it?"

"Early," he told her. "I have to go to work in a few hours. Thought I'd try to go to sleep for an hour."

She perched her chin in her hands and gazed down at him. "Do you have to?"

Running his hands through her curls, he smiled. "Yes. I left early yesterday and I have a lot to do."

Leaning down, she brushed her lips against his. "Okay," she said, tracing his jaw with her finger. "I'll make you some breakfast."

"You don't have to. I'm okay stopping to get some on the way to work."

"That's fine. I was thinking about going to visit Cali to talk business today."

"You want to drop me off at work so you can use my car?" He grazed a finger down her shoulder because he simply could not keep his hands to himself. "Or maybe I can rent you a car?"

"No, Kent. I'm going to owe you so much money." She

feathered her fingertips over his brow. "Besides, I told you my father gave me money. I just need to open an account to get it. "

"And I told you it's not a problem. I want to do it for you—because you don't ask. And I can."

She tapped his chest with her finger. "What I want you to do is take me to the bank so I can open an account and deposit my check."

"Done. I'll come by on my lunch hour and we can handle that. Actually, I'll take an extra hour so we can get you a rental car."

"Okay. I'm not going to argue with you. Just know I'm paying for my own rental." She dropped her gaze. "I think we should talk."

He couldn't help but roll his eyes. A conversation about Isaac wasn't something he wanted to deal with at that particular moment. Especially when she was pressed up against him so intimately. He knew it was something they'd have to deal with sooner than later, but...*not now*.

"About us."

He raised his brows. "What about us?" Kent agreed that they needed to discuss the fact they'd been moving at warp speed since she got there. But he wondered if they should table the inevitable discussion for later. Yes, they should probably put the brakes on it, take it a lot slower. But he just wanted to enjoy her in his bed.

"Can we talk later?" he asked, kissing her shoulder. "I'm tired, baby."

"I want to go to Cleveland," she announced.

He blinked. *I didn't expect that.* "What?" he asked.

She sat up, hugging her knees to her chest. "I can't hide forever. I have to handle this thing with Isaac before we go any further with us. It's only right."

He rolled his eyes. He adored Allina for many things, but this penchant she had for seeing things in black and white, right and wrong, bugged the hell out of him sometimes.

"That's not a good idea. He's crazy as hell."

"What else am I supposed to do? Hide here forever? Avoid visiting my parents? He's not going to control my life like that. He's not going to dictate to me what I can and can't do. I have to face him at some point. Why not on my terms? This whole thing with Den, watching Syd deal with him the way she did...What if Isaac comes here? Syd will be the one he goes to, and I can't take that chance. She's already been through too much. He's my problem and I have to deal with him—soon."

"I'm not down for that," he said with a frown. "You need to stay your ass here." *Forever*, he wanted to add.

Something flickered in her eyes, and she turned away.

Sighing, he said, "Fine. I'm going with you." There was no way he'd let her deal with that man alone. "I'll talk to my boss, take a few days next week, after this project is complete. We'll deal with this together."

She caressed the side of his face. "You don't have to, but I appreciate it."

"If you feel like you need to do this, then I'll support you." And while he was there, he'd make sure Isaac thought twice before he threatened anyone he loved again.

* * *

After work, Kent went to the Ice Box to handle some business there. When he walked in, he noticed Syd in their private booth. He waved at the manager before he made his way over to her. The crowd was light, which was normal at around four o'clock. The work crews would be arriving any minute.

"What's up?" he asked, approaching his sister.

She rolled amber-colored liquid in her glass, a deep scowl on her face. "Red just left," she said, her voice flat. "It took a minute to calm him down. Den could have hurt me and my baby."

Kent hung his head. "Pour me one."

Syd filled an empty glass with the dark liquor. "Your brother better be glad Red didn't see him yesterday. I'd be bailing him out of jail right now."

Kent didn't know what to say. There had never been any love lost between Den and Red. The two could barely stand each other, and Kent knew it was because of the way Den had treated Syd over the years.

She finished her drink and glanced at Kent out of the corner of her eye. "What are you doing here?"

"I stopped by because I got a call from the printer. They were supposed to deliver the new flyers I designed and I wanted to take a look."

"Long day at work?" she asked, her voice even and calm. Almost too calm. It was a departure from the Syd who'd come to his house, shaking and concerned. It was a completely different Syd from the Syd who'd begged him not to hurt Den.

"Every day is a long day at work," Kent grumbled. "Syd, I'm not going to make any excuses for Den. I couldn't even muster up enough energy to pull Morgan off him—until you begged me to."

She snickered. "How did *you* not kick the shit out of him when you saw Allina's face?"

It was a question he'd asked himself many times since he'd left Morgan's house the day before. He'd gone over the events of the afternoon until he couldn't stand to think about it anymore. The only answer he could come up with was the same one they'd been giving for years, with a small caveat. "He's sick—pathetic and sick. When I thought about it, I figured his hell was one that I couldn't put him in. He'd already done that himself. And he's my brother. As much as I hate what he did, I still love him."

She didn't say it, but he suspected she felt the same way. "It's over now," she mumbled. "You and Allina looked very cozy. What's going on with that?" she asked, changing the subject.

Kent smiled to himself. "It's different. But she wants to go home."

"Back to Cleveland?" Syd asked, incredulous. "What the hell for?"

"She said she wants to prevent him from coming here and looking for her through you. You've been through enough. And she's ready to stop hiding."

"What do you think about that?"

"I don't like it, but she has a point," he said. "I'm going with her, though."

"I hear that. Take care of your woman," Syd said with a grin.

"Shut the hell up." He wrapped an arm around her neck.

"Stop acting like that's not your girl," Syd laughed. "It's easier if you just give in to it."

Kent wanted to confide in his sister. He had, on many occasions. "I want her," he admitted, after a long minute of silence. "But she's . . . too innocent, too good."

Syd gazed at him, studied him. "Do you think that you're not? Good, that is."

He rubbed at the middle of his forehead, eyes closed. "It's not that I think I'm bad. I just wonder if she really knows what she's getting herself into with me. I fuck shit up. You know relationships are not my strong suit. Plus, she's all... religious. And I'm not. She doesn't have a lot of experience with men and her past... I'm still not sure she's told me everything even though she says she has."

"I know the feeling. There is a part of her I could never reach."

He tapped his glass against the countertop softly. "Shouldn't I know what really makes her Allina before I enter into a relationship with her?"

"Well, I think the real question is what do you want? How do you feel about her? It has to be more than you just '*want her,*'" she said.

He thought about that a minute. If he was honest with himself, he could admit that Allina was perfect for him. She respected him as a man, but she didn't let him do whatever to keep him. He hated weak women, women who would let him control them. He didn't want a pushover. Any woman he was with would have to be strong but feminine, giving and sweet. Everything that Allina was.

"She's a virgin," he blabbed, sneaking a glance at Syd before focusing on his drink. He really had no idea why he'd had her pour him one. The hangover he had this morning should have prevented even the urge to have any alcohol.

Syd giggled, dropping her head on the bar. When she finally looked up at him, he could see the amusement in her eyes. It could have been the bourbon, though. "And that bothers you?" she asked.

"I hope you already knew that," he said.

She covered her mouth, concealing her smile. "I did."

"What am I supposed to do with that?"

"Gee, I don't know. How about take it slow?" she suggested.

"Syd, how slow is too slow? And how fast is too fast?" He was probably overthinking it. Allina's virginity shouldn't be a problem for him. "Do I really want to be someone's first?"

"Does she want to do it?"

He shrugged. "I don't know. I feel like she does. When we're...doing things, she responds. But I can't compete with God."

Syd burst out in a fit of laughter. He chuckled right along with her, glad to see her smiling. "Kent, you're killing me. You're thinking about this way too hard."

He knew that.

"Listen, I think if you two end up sleeping together, it will be because she's ready. Not because you corrupted her, or seduced her into submission." She stood up and held out her hand to him. Once he was on his feet, she squeezed his hands. "Thanks, Kent."

"What are you thanking me for?"

"Being you," she said. "And you're good enough. The best. Allina is lucky you love her."

Frowning, he stepped back. "Who said anything about love?"

"You took her in, bought her everything she needed, cared for her during one of the worst times of her life... that's love." She patted him on the shoulder. "Deal with it. I better go call Morgan before he shows up here. Bye, brother."

Planting a kiss on his cheek, she turned and walked to the back toward the office. Syd was wise in that get-on-your-nerves way. And she hadn't said anything that wasn't true. He did love Allina. But he wasn't ready to tell her—and he wasn't sure she was ready to hear it.

CHAPTER NINETEEN

The sound of the front door slamming brought Allina out of the kitchen. Kent had told her he'd be working late, so she hadn't expected him this early. Glancing down at her attire, she cringed. She'd just finished showering, her hair was in twists, and she was in a huge pair of his sweats and a thin camisole. Quickly, she untwisted her hair and shook it out. Picking up a towel, she scrubbed the blemish cream off her face and smoothed a hand over her clothes.

When she walked out into the living room, Kent was standing at the door, skimming through his mail, a frown on his face.

She smiled. "Hey, I wasn't expecting you."

Grunting, he said, "I left work a little early because I had to stop at the bar. I have some…" He glanced over at her and paused.

Suddenly, Allina was nervous. Fidgeting, she tugged at the shirt and tucked a lock of hair behind her ear. "Is everything…okay?"

He didn't respond, only continued to stare at her.

Swallowing, she inched closer to him. "Kent? Are you okay? Did something happen at the club? Or with Den?" Allina knew that Kent had been preoccupied with his brother's troubles. She wondered if he'd heard from Den.

Is he upset with me? Allina had to admit that dropping that bombshell on him about going back to Cleveland might have seemed a little out of the blue, but she felt she needed to do it.

After he'd left for work, she'd pondered their conversation about Cleveland and dealing with Isaac. While she still felt she couldn't hide forever, she wondered what it would accomplish if she went to see him anytime soon.

More than that, how could she embrace the potential of a relationship with Kent if she hadn't disclosed everything to him? He still didn't know the whole truth about her aunt's death. She didn't know what to do. One minute, she wanted to put a halt to their budding relationship, the next she wanted to be with him. Her feelings were growing every minute, every hour she stayed with him.

Spending the short time with him in his bed that morning had been a dream come true. He was a total and complete gentleman, which made her feel some kind of way. She found herself wishing he weren't such a gentleman, that he'd make a move on her. Yes, she'd made a promise to herself to never have sex outside of marriage. She'd also never felt the way she felt for Kent about anybody else.

Kent finally eased closer to her, still not speaking, his gaze still intense. She wondered what he was thinking. Normally, she'd want to retreat, back away. But she remained rooted to the spot.

When he was standing directly in front of her, he reached out and brushed his thumb across her cheek. She bit down on her lip, then released it. She decided to forge ahead, to continue talking and hope he'd respond soon. "Kent, I just finished dinner. Do you want to eat?"

His gaze dropped down to her lips, then back up to her eyes. "You."

Allina gasped. A response might have been appropriate, and she tried her best to formulate the right one. But before she could, his lips came down on hers. Raising a hand, he cupped her face and slid his other one around her neck.

She clung to him desperately and kissed him back as hard as she could. Swept away by his roaming hands, his expert tongue, and his smooth lips, she nearly stumbled backward. But instead of falling, she felt his strong arm wrap around her waist. Lifting her up against him, he walked her back toward his bedroom.

Kent pushed the door open and hurried inside, kicking it closed with his foot. He lowered her down on the mattress and broke the kiss, his lips traveling down her neck and over to her ear.

"Tell me now if you want me to stop, before we go any further."

Her eyes fluttered opened. "No." Shocked by the desperation in her voice, she swallowed roughly. "I mean...don't stop."

His breath fanned across her ear and her nails dug into his arm.

"I want you," he admitted against her ear. "So badly, Allina. I want this. I don't think you know how much."

Hooking his thumb under one strap of her tank, he eased it down, placing a wet kiss on her shoulder before he did the same with the other one. Slowly, he lowered the straps even further. She purred in contentment when he cupped a breast and took her nipple into his mouth, circling the tip with his tongue.

His hands traveled down her sides to the waistband of her sweatpants. When his knuckles brushed against her stomach, she shivered. Once he untied the drawstring, she lifted her bottom so he could tug them off.

Allina had never been so ready, so willing, to let a man have his way with her. The fact that she was practically naked seemed like an afterthought. She didn't want Kent to stop what he was doing; she wanted him to keep going.

He traced invisible circles on her skin with his thumb and brushed his lips against her belly button, snaking his tongue around it before dipping it inside. He kissed his way back up to her mouth and touched his lips to hers again. Once, twice, and again. The soft, sweet kisses only increased her need for him. She wanted more. Sweeping her tongue in his mouth, she moaned when it melded with his in a duel for control.

She groaned when he pulled away, placed short kisses against her jawline. "Please tell me," he murmured against her skin. "Can I have you? All of you?"

The word "yes" came out of Allina's mouth on a breathless whisper. "Please," she begged.

She had no idea what she was actually pleading for, but she needed something. And only he could give it to her at that point. Her body buzzed like electricity was flowing through her veins; her heart was racing in her chest.

His hand gripped her thigh, then inched up closer to her core. She exhaled slowly, anticipating his next move, wondering how she'd be able to handle the rest of the dance. She already felt out of her element, but it was so good to her, she was willing to fumble through it just to keep him near her.

Rubbing his nose under her ear, he whispered, "I want to make love to you all night." He kissed her chin, then captured her bottom lip with his.

When he pulled back and peered down at her with those sexy hooded eyes, she felt a flood of warmth take over her body. Kent's eyes bored into her like pools of fire.

Placing a gentle kiss on the corner of her mouth, he said,

"I want to feel you under me, and around me. Tell me you want that, too."

Allina couldn't think straight, let alone form a coherent sentence. Instead, she nodded her response.

"Tell me, Allina," he urged, slipping his thumb into her panties. "Tell me you want that, too."

Oh. My. God. She wanted to tell him that she wanted to feel him over her and inside her. It was the truth, after all. Her heart was racing and she wanted the feeling to last. The only word she could get out at that point was "yes." Again.

Bracing himself on his forearms, he looked down at her again. "I want to make sure you're ready. I don't want to take this too fast."

"I'm ready," she whispered, even though she was pretty sure she couldn't fathom the concept of "ready" with her mind in a fog.

"We'll see," he said in a husky voice. Lowering his head, he took her mouth in another scorching kiss. When he pulled away, his lips lingered on hers, deliberately drawing out the kiss. With a sexy smirk he started his descent, leaving a trail of toe-curling kisses down her neck, over her breasts and her stomach.

Allina's back arched off the bed as his mouth conquered her quaking skin, lower—and lower. Pleasure washed over and through her and settled low in her belly. Slowly, he eased her panties down. When she felt his breath on her core, she tensed. But then his tongue was on her, and she practically leaped off the bed.

Her first instinct was to push him away, but it was too hot, too good, to tell him to stop. Allina couldn't catch her breath as he feasted on her, sucking her into his mouth, taking her higher. The feeling in her gut seemed to unravel; time seemed to slow as she trembled beneath him. He was winding her up, taking her higher with every flick of his tongue against her. Then she shattered.

Squeezing her eyes shut, she screamed as it overtook her. Her body was moving of its own accord and she couldn't make it stop even if she tried. She gripped his shoulders and closed her legs tightly. Fortunately for him he'd already pulled back, because she probably would have hurt him if he was still down there.

Finally, she relaxed against the mattress and tried to catch her breath. A few seconds later, she opened her eyes and found him watching her, a small smile on his face.

"Okay?" he asked.

Nodding, she placed her hands over her cheeks. "That was...intense."

He gave her a quick kiss and settled in next to her, pulling a blanket over her body. "You're beautiful when you come," he told her, kissing her brow.

"Am I?" she asked, rolling onto her side.

"Yes, you are."

"I don't want to sound too naïve, and I'm not even sure why I'm admitting this to you, but I had no idea it felt like that."

He smirked, squeezing her hip. "I don't think anybody could describe the feeling accurately. There's no one word for it."

"That is definitely the truth."

"Any regrets?" he asked.

She frowned. "Why? I mean, do you have any regrets?"

He shook his head. "No, but you did have some concerns about...sex."

Allina thought about that for a minute. Technically, what he'd just done was a form of sex. But it didn't feel wrong to her. It felt liberating.

"Honestly?" she asked.

"Always."

"I know we didn't go all the way, but I feel like we still shared something significant. And it felt right."

He leaned in, placing a soft kiss on her mouth. "It did, didn't it?"

They lay like that, facing each other, taking one another in. It wasn't awkward like she'd imagined. It was comfortable. Then her mind started spinning, thinking about everything that had just happened. He'd taken her to a new level. But what about him?

"Kent?" she asked.

He brushed his fingers over her shoulder, gazed at her. "Yes."

"What about you?"

Frowning, he said, "What about me?"

Allina hadn't been around the block, of course. But she did know about the things a woman could do for a man. "Don't you want me to—?"

"Stop," he said, placing a finger over her mouth. "We can get to that later."

"But I—"

"Baby, we have time. I just...I couldn't help myself today."

Allina searched his eyes. "I can't imagine not feeling the way I feel about you. The way I've felt for so long. That's why I thought I should go to Cleveland, put an end to this Isaac thing once and for all. I want this to work. I'm ready to be with you—in every way."

Perhaps it was the fact that he'd made her see stars that she felt the need to reveal how much he meant to her. But she didn't regret it. She needed him to know. Allina braced herself. After everything they'd shared, she hoped he didn't still want to slow things down between them. She didn't think she could bear for him push her away.

"Despite what we've both said, this thing between us wants to move forward. I told you that I wanted you. I do. Don't you feel that?"

She nodded. That much was obvious. He'd just…

"But I agree with you. As much as I want to make love to you"—he rubbed her earlobe, then slid his thumb down her neck—"it's better if we don't right now. There's still so much that needs to be resolved. I want your first time to be special. We don't have to rush it."

He wrapped his arms around her and she rested against him. Allina didn't think she could love Kent more than she already did. But the fact that he was so concerned about her first time, about her feelings, made her heart open up even more.

* * *

Kent woke up the next morning with Allina in his arms. Even now, he still couldn't believe what he'd done. He didn't know what had come over him. When he got home, saw her standing there in those too big sweatpants and little tank, her curls all over her head, he couldn't help himself. His talk with Syd had put things in perspective. It wasn't hard to admit that he wanted Allina. She *was* beautiful. But admitting there was more than simple lust was what propelled him forward.

He hadn't expected to go *that* far, though. Before he could stop himself, he'd turned his seduction up a notch, whispered things to her that he knew she'd never heard from another man. He'd admitted how much he wanted her, and begged her to tell him that she wanted him, too. Then she did. And he let himself go there, tasting her like she was his last meal.

It had been hard to pull away from her before they went too far. He wasn't sure how he'd managed to do that. But he did it—for her and for him. They'd spent the rest of the evening eating, talking, and kissing. Nothing else. The level of intimacy he'd shared with Allina was something he'd never had. He was determined to do this the right way.

He'd even gone so far as to suggest she sleep in the other room. That conversation didn't go over quite like he'd expected. They actually had an argument about it. He finally gave in and now, in the light of a new day, he was faced with another dilemma. Allina was tucked into his side, her leg hooked over his and her head against his chest. And he was hard as hell.

Gently, without waking her, he tried to slide out from under her. Instead of moving, she wrapped an arm around his waist and inched her leg up higher, brushing against him. Grunting, he closed his eyes.

How the hell did I get myself into this? He guessed the better question would be *How do I get myself out of this?*

Sighing, he tried again, lifting her arm up and trying to roll away from her. Except she stretched and he felt her breasts against his side. Groaning, he closed his eyes. It would be so easy to wake her up and take her right then and there. But he'd meant what he said. She needed to be sure she was ready.

It was obvious they were speeding past the point of no return and he didn't want to get burned. He didn't want to just be the man who took her virginity. He wanted it to mean something. When they finally made love, it had to be right for both of them. She deserved that much.

"Kent?" she mumbled.

Looking down at her, he smiled when he noticed her eyes were wide open. "Good morning," he whispered.

"Morning." She smoothed her hand over his chest and slipped her fingers below the waistband of his sweats.

"You hungry?" he asked, stopping her hand from going even a little bit lower. Touching him below his waist was a surefire way to get him to abandon his noble intentions.

"Sure," she grumbled, drumming her fingers against his stomach. His breath caught when she placed a kiss on his chest. "Are you going to make breakfast?"

"If you're okay with cereal and a banana, yeah."

She giggled. "You're funny. You know how to cook."

He shrugged. "Not really. You see how my refrigerator looked before you got here?"

Lifting her head up, she grinned. "Well, it's a good thing I'm here. And I love to cook."

Caressing her face, he leaned in and kissed her soundly. "How about you take a break and let me take you to breakfast?"

"Okay," she said.

He swung his legs over the edge of the bed and sat there for a minute. Ticking off the seemingly endless list of things he had to do in his head, he wondered how he would swing everything *and* still spend time with Allina.

His mama wanted him to meet her at the hospital for a conference with Den's doctors and he really didn't want to go. But he knew he had to. His father had told him he had to take care of his mother, and he took that very seriously. If going to the hospital to be a support to his mother was what she needed, he'd do it. Even though he was still pissed as hell at his older brother.

"Are you okay?" she asked, rubbing his shoulders from behind him. She kissed his temple and rested her head on his shoulder.

Leaning his head against hers, he said, "I'm fine. Just thinking about everything I have to do today. Which is a lot."

"Go into business for yourself. Then you can make your own schedule."

There it was again. For years, Morgan and Red had been on him about starting a graphic design business. Even Syd had implored him to do something different. But Kent always changed the subject, always found a reason to squash the idea. Yet when Allina said it, he almost believed it could happen.

He squeezed Allina's hand, brought her palm up to his mouth and kissed it. "I just don't know. It's a big decision to make and I'm not sure it's a good idea yet."

"Think about it," she urged. "You definitely have a knack for business and a charm that will certainly attract a diverse clientele. I just hate to see you work so hard, day in and day out, and not feel accomplished at the end of the day. You have so much more to give and you deserve to be happy doing what you love."

"I am happy," he said. *I don't even believe that.*

"I get it." She intertwined her fingers with his. "I am the same way. Working for a company is safe, almost guaranteed. Health insurance, paid time off...those are perks of employment. You know when you're going to get a paycheck. It's consistent. I could even see if you needed the steady money. But you don't. You have an additional stream of income in the bar. It's a win-win."

"I love that you believe in me." He stared into her sincere eyes. "You bring up valid points. Every time I think I can step out there, quit my job, and do what I want to do, I think about my father. He spent so many years working, for us."

Kent's father had grown up poor and made it his mission to never end up in that same predicament as an adult. Even if that meant he missed Kent's football games and family vacations. His dad always told him a man who doesn't work is a man who goes hungry. It had been instilled in Kent from the time he could walk and talk.

"My father worked hard, too," she admitted softly. "But one of the things I appreciate about him is that he always told me the sky was the limit. It was me who didn't believe it, especially after what happened to me. But…" She shrugged. "I don't know. Maybe I'm starting to believe it."

"Why now?"

"I have no idea. I just do. I think me and Cali are on the verge of something great. And I absolutely love designing gowns and helping women with their big day. Even if I never have mine."

Her words tugged at his heart. It made sense that she might have figured marriage may elude her, especially because of what had happened between her and Isaac. "I think you are on to something. I also think you'll have yours." Kent wanted to say so much more, but he couldn't. Not right then.

"I better get dressed," she said, sliding off the bed.

Rubbing his head, he stood up and stretched. "Hey," he said, pulling her to him. "Thank you, for everything."

She fisted her hands into his shirt and grinned up at him. "You're welcome, but I haven't done anything."

He kissed her shoulder. "You're you."

After a few lingering kisses, they finally tore themselves away from each other and got dressed for breakfast.

CHAPTER TWENTY

*T*he doorbell rang and Kent rushed to answer it. "Hold on," he called. When he reached the door he looked through the peephole.

Damn. He recognized the man on the other side of the door. He just hadn't expected him to be at his house. Sighing heavily, he disarmed the alarm and opened the door.

The older man standing on the other side assessed him. "Kent?"

"Yes. Come in, Judge Parker."

Allina's father walked in, checking the place out as he stepped over the threshold. Kent closed the door and waited. With hands stuffed in his pockets, Judge turned around.

Kent wiped his palms on his jeans and held out a hand. "Good to meet you."

In all the years he'd known Allina, it had never been a priority to meet her parents, especially her father. He'd met her mother in passing one time a few years ago, and he was perfectly fine with it.

The older man squeezed Kent's hand. "Good to put a face to a name, finally," Judge replied.

What am I supposed to say now? They stood like that for a bit, studying each other. He wondered what the older man was thinking. Then it occurred to him: he was probably wondering if Kent was sleeping with his daughter. For once, he hoped Allina didn't come out of the bedroom in his shorts and T-shirt.

He scratched the back of his head. "Coffee?"

Judge gave him a curt nod. "No, thank you. I had some already."

"We weren't expecting you. Is everything okay?"

Kent wasn't a nervous person by any means. And he'd never had a problem talking to anyone. But this was the father of the woman he loved. He couldn't afford to fuck it up. The Judge's opinion meant the world to her.

"I wanted to talk to you and Allina in person, about Isaac. Is she here?"

Nodding, Kent said, "She's in the back. Have a seat." He gestured toward the couch. "I'll go get her."

Only he didn't have a chance to get her because Allina walked out—fully dressed. *Yes*.

"Kent, I think I want to…" Her voice trailed off when she saw her father. "Daddy?" Judge stood up and opened his arms. Allina ran right into them.

Moments later, they were all seated around the kitchen table, Allina sipping on a cup of tea, and Kent nursing a mug of coffee.

"I have some interesting information about Isaac and the mystery woman," Judge said.

"Did they find her?" Allina asked, concern in her eyes.

"She's not missing," he answered. "She's hiding."

The Judge started his story, explaining that he'd found Karen through her aunt. The older woman had had plenty to say about Isaac and his family.

"Rumors of cover-ups, payoffs." Judge clasped his hands together. "Not just with Isaac, but his father too."

Allina's brow furrowed. "What—?"

"Apparently there are a few women who have been hurt by him," the older man continued. "Isaac has a history of physical and emotional abuse toward young church members, countless accusations of sexual harassment, but Bishop Hunter always manages to make them go away."

"How did this woman know all of this?" Kent asked.

"Karen told her," Judge said simply.

But Karen almost didn't live to tell the story. After she left the church the day of the wedding, she was on her way to her aunt's house when she was almost run off the road. She was so spooked she went to her aunt's house and begged for help.

"But Isaac was still at the church," Allina pointed out. "He couldn't have done that."

"He didn't have to," Kent chimed in. "If his family is as powerful as you say, he could have asked anyone to do it."

That was unfortunate since these were supposed to be God-fearing Christians. Kent had seen his fair share of shady clergy, but he thought this family took the cake.

"Exactly," Judge agreed. "You have to understand, Isaac could have easily made a call after he realized that you'd overheard their conversation. Actually, I wouldn't be surprised if the Bishop knows about what happened and approved it."

Allina shook her head. "No. I don't believe that."

Kent glanced at Allina incredulously, shocked that after everything he'd done, she was still giving Isaac the benefit of the doubt.

"I don't put anything past them," Kent said, meeting Allina's gaze directly.

"Was Karen in a relationship with Isaac or something?" Allina asked her father.

"No, but her sister was. Karen admitted she was only involved for a payday. Then she started to feel guilty. That's why she was at the church, threatening to come forward."

"So the woman in the church was the sister of one of his ex-girlfriends?" Allina confirmed.

"Yes. Karen's sister was so afraid she left town to get away from him and never returned. Isaac made her life hell," Judge said, picking up where he'd left off. "So I convinced her aunt to get me in touch with the sister. She gave me a phone number."

Allina clutched her throat. "You're going to see her?"

"*We're* going to see her," Judge corrected her. "That's why I'm here. She's in Windsor."

* * *

Allina tapped her foot against the tile, let her father's story sink in. Kent had left for work. She knew he hated to leave when they were on the verge of ending this, but he had a meeting he couldn't miss. It helped that Kent knew she was in good hands. She'd been happy to see her dad when he arrived, but she wasn't prepared for what Judge had shared with her.

Sitting across from her father, she studied the piece of paper with the number scrawled across it. The woman's name was Carla, and she was less than forty miles away.

Windsor, Ontario, was located south of Detroit, across the Detroit River. It was a thirty-minute drive from Belleville. What were the odds that they would be so close to each other? Allina wanted to meet Carla so they could talk in person. But she wasn't sure what the other woman would want to do, considering she had fled for a reason.

She stood up and walked to the refrigerator, pulling it open. She needed time to process everything she'd heard. Isaac was a predator. Threatening women wasn't a new thing. He'd been doing it for years. *How did I not know that?* Suddenly, her appetite was gone and she pushed the refrigerator door closed.

"What if she doesn't want to see us?" Allina asked.

"Her aunt said she's expecting your call." He glanced at his watch. "Are you ready?"

"I just can't believe this." Allina rubbed at a brow.

"You want me to do it?"

"No, I'll do it." Allina froze. "Where's Mom?"

"Working on a fund-raiser for her nonprofit. She wanted to come, but I thought it was best if she didn't. I figured it would be easier for me to sneak away. With everything I found out, I wouldn't put it past Isaac to have me followed so he can get to you."

"Are you sure it's safe leaving her alone?" Allina couldn't get over the story. She sucked in a sharp breath. "What if he's been following you the whole time?"

"I'm not worried about your mother. She's protected. And if anyone asks around, my staff will tell them I'm giving a guest lecture at Indiana University."

Her father explained that he'd had his judicial attorney purchase an airplane ticket for him to Bloomington, Indiana, while he'd purchased a ticket to Detroit Metropolitan Airport. Both flights left around the same time. He'd boarded only one.

Allina ran her finger over the phone number. The sooner she got some answers, the sooner this would be over. Then she could move forward with her life. With Kent. Forcing a harsh breath out, she picked up her cell phone and dialed.

When she heard the click signaling someone had picked up, Allina said, "Hello? I'm looking for Carla Little?"

"Hi." The high-pitched voice came over the receiver. "This is Carla Little."

"My name is Allina Parker. Your aunt gave me your number?" Silence on the other end.

"Thank you for talking to me," Allina added. "I appreciate it."

"I-I wasn't going to," Carla admitted softly. "But my aunt convinced me to let her give you my number."

Allina was grateful to the aunt for helping them connect. "I'm glad you did."

"How can I help you?"

Figuring it was best to get to the point, Allina told Carla, "I was supposed to marry Isaac, but I ran out on the wedding. He's made some threats, intimated that he wasn't going to give up so easily and I just wanted to talk to you. I need to know what I can expect."

"Expect the worst," Carla told her plainly. "Because he's definitely capable of it."

Allina swallowed. Hard. "What did he do to you?" she asked.

"I'm not even sure I can talk about it. There are things he did that no one knows about. Simply leaving him was not enough. I had to practically disappear."

Holding her stomach, Allina slid down into a chair and glanced at her father. "I thought I was doing the right thing," she confessed. "Marrying in the church, to someone who was so well loved in the community. But he's awful."

"Why did you leave?" Carla asked.

"I heard him, in the pastor's study, the morning of the wedding," Allina explained. "He was talking to your sister. She accused him of something." She relayed what she'd overheard about the talk of money for a cover-up. The memory of the conversation still made her feel cold.

"Believe it," Carla said. "My sister shouldn't have done what she did, but it's all true. There is so much about that family that is wrong on many levels. Isaac's father has paid off numerous women, going back to Isaac's teenage years."

Apparently, Isaac had a history of being overly aggressive with the young women of the church. Carla told Allina that one family in particular had threatened to press criminal charges, but Bishop Hunter arranged a payoff to keep them quiet. Another girl attempted suicide because of the things Isaac had done. "And those are only a few examples," Carla finished. "He found me once. I moved again."

Allina's chest tightened. "He's already called me," she whispered. "I don't even want to think about what he'd do if he came here.

They didn't speak for a moment, as Allina processed the information she'd been given.

"I had to leave the country," Carla said, her voice thick— probably with tears.

"I know. My father told me. I'm in Michigan, the Detroit Area. I came back here to be with my friends."

Carla didn't respond for what seemed like an eternity. As time dragged on, Allina wondered if she should say something else. She had so many more questions.

"I have to stop him," Allina breathed. "He can't continue to do this. There has to be something, anything, I can use to get him to back off."

"I have something," Carla said. "I collected some information and took it to the police in Cleveland. But with my checkered past and his family's reputation and standing, I didn't get anywhere."

Curious, Allina asked what Carla meant about her checkered past.

Instead of answering, Carla suggested, "I can meet you. In Detroit."

Allina closed her eyes and let out a breath she hadn't even realized she was holding. "Okay. When?"

"How soon can you get downtown?"

"I can be there within an hour." Allina knew she'd told Kent she would stay put, but she couldn't *not* go, especially when there was a good chance she could end this once and for all.

"Meet me at in the lobby of the Detroit Marriott at the Renaissance Center. One hour."

Before Allina could ask how she would know who Carla was, the call ended.

Peering up at her father, she said, "She wants to meet." She jumped up and rushed into the bedroom. After she changed into a pair of jeans and a T-shirt, she grabbed one of Kent's baseball hats and put it on.

Her father was waiting at the door when she came out. And they left.

Briefly, she wondered if she should call Kent and leave him a message, just so he would know where she went. But then she figured she would be back before he got out of his meeting. Her father's presence could very well frighten off Carla, but she hoped it wouldn't.

The car ride was quiet. Traffic into downtown Detroit was busy as usual and Allina weaved through slow cars to make it to her destination on time. Construction along the Lodge Freeway delayed her arrival and she was fifteen minutes late. She hoped Carla hadn't left before she got there.

To expedite time, she used the valet service and rushed into the hotel with her father on her heels, taking the elevators up to the lobby floor. Stepping out, she scanned the area.

"Daddy, I think you should head over to the bar. I don't want her to be scared off."

"Are you sure?" Judge asked. "I don't know about leaving you."

"I'm fine," she assured him.

Reluctantly, he agreed and ambled off toward the big bar in the middle of the lobby. Allina did another quick sweep of the immediate area. There were people milling about, hotel guests checking out and businessmen in expensive suits sitting at the new bar in the lobby. Hanging her head, she shook it. How was she supposed to know Carla from a random woman visiting the hotel?

"Are you Allina?" a voice behind her asked.

She whirled around, smiling kindly at the woman in front of her. "I am. Are you Carla?"

The woman nodded. "Yes."

Allina apologized for being late, explaining the traffic situation. Then they headed for the café that was situated off the lobby, on the other side of the bar. They ordered drinks and settled into a secluded table.

Allina observed Carla as she took a sip from her mug. If Allina wasn't one hundred percent sure that she was an only child, she would have had to call her mom to ask if there was a possibility that she had a sibling somewhere. The similarities between her and Carla were remarkable, jarring even.

Carla was fair-skinned, almost as light as Allina was. They were built the same, both thin and tall, with brown eyes and light brown hair. One noticeable difference was their hairstyles: Carla wore her hair straight in a bob cut while Allina preferred her natural style. Looking at Carla across the table from her, Allina wondered if Isaac had got with her because she reminded him of the woman in front of her. He definitely had a type.

Eyeing the big manila envelope that Carla set on the table, Allina waited for her to break the ice. When minutes passed, Allina spoke up, unable to take the silence any longer. "Thanks for meeting me. I really appreciate it."

Carla nodded and traced the rim of her coffee mug with her finger. "When I met Isaac," she started, "he was so charming, so handsome. I was eighteen years old, had just accepted the Lord in my life after a horrible childhood. I joined his father's church and he befriended me. I'd been through so much—even at that age—that I thought no man would ever want me. But he did. And I was happy."

Even their stories were similar. Allina had often wondered if any man would want her because of her past, the things her aunt did to her. She, too, found God after a horrific childhood.

"We fell in love and it was good for a while," Carla continued. "I was his first."

Shocked, Allina thought back to a conversation she'd had with Isaac about sex. He'd lied to her, then, told her he was a virgin waiting for his bride. She'd thought it endearing at the time, and so sweet. Leaning forward, Allina asked, "When did it change?"

Carla shrugged, picking at the edge of the envelope. "Things started unraveling after he proposed."

Allina's breath caught and she squeezed her eyes shut. He'd made it clear that she was the only woman he'd ever thought good enough to be his wife. "You were going to be married?" she asked incredulously.

Nodding, Carla stared past Allina. "He asked me to marry him at his parents' house. I accepted with no hesitation. But he changed. I noticed he had some strange tendencies, quirks. He was so controlling. He didn't want me to go anywhere without him, and if I did, he had to know where I was and who I was with. He demanded I dress in a certain way, style my hair the way he liked, act how he wanted me to act."

Allina felt nauseous. She'd fallen for and explained away those same tendencies. When he'd told her that he didn't want her going out without him, she'd told herself that he just wanted to be near her. Isaac had bought her clothes, telling her that he loved to see her in certain things. He paid for her to get her hair straightened because he said he loved the way her hair fell down her back. All those things seemed innocent enough at the time. And she'd willingly obliged his wishes.

"Finally, I'd had enough." Carla's downturned facial features, the way she constantly looked down, and the distant stare told Allina about her state of mind. Her heart went out to the woman who'd been through so much. "I left him. And I suffered for it."

"What did he do to you?" Allina asked, bracing herself for Carla's answer.

"I lost everything. He got me fired from my job. My boss just happened to be a member of his church and a close, personal friend of the bishop. He terrorized me. I'd go home and he would be sitting in my living room."

Allina stared at Carla, unblinking. She clutched her throat, unable to find the right words to say.

"Everywhere I'd go, he'd be there," Carla added, seemingly unfazed by the emotions Allina was sure were visible on her face. "I moved three different times, to different places. I went to stay with family, and he always found me. I reported him, filed petitions for Personal Protection Orders. The courts would always deny my requests and the police..." She shook her head. "They didn't give me the time of day."

Allina shuddered. "But he was basically stalking you. You couldn't find anyone to help you?"

"His family is very powerful; you have to know that. Over a fifth of the police force are members of that church. Trust me, I tried. Then I gave up."

"Is that when you ran?"

Carla let out a humorless chuckle. "Not exactly. It was obvious that he wasn't going to leave me alone. I'd resigned myself to never getting away from him. He'd already been threatening my family, the people I love."

Allina thought about Isaac's disguised threats against Syd and her parents. She couldn't put them through that. And what if he found out about Kent?

"But he didn't stop there." There was something in Carla's tone that made Allina look at her. Her eyes were empty, sad. "He killed my mother."

CHAPTER TWENTY-ONE

Allina's hand flew to her chest. "What?" she asked, meeting Carla's now steady gaze. She couldn't have heard the other woman right. Isaac *killed* her mother? Murder?

"He killed my mother," she repeated, this time more slowly, each syllable more pronounced.

"That can't be true," Allina said, shaking her head rapidly. "He wouldn't kill somebody." Despite all the evidence that Isaac could possibly be a sociopath, Allina could not fathom him committing actual murder. Probably because that would mean he really was capable of anything, even hurting her and the people she loved.

"The last time I talked to my mother," Carla explained, "he was with her. He'd shown up at her house while we were talking on the phone. She must have thought she hung up, but I was still on the line. They argued. She accused him of ruining my life, making it so I couldn't do anything. He promised he'd do worse if she didn't tell him where I was. That was all I heard before the call was disconnected."

Allina listened intently as Carla finished the story. After the infamous phone call, Carla tried to reach her mother. When she wasn't able to get in touch with her, she'd panicked and called an old friend to go over to the house to check on her. Carla's mother was dead. They found her slumped over on the toilet.

The coroner deemed the death an overdose, even though Carla insisted her mother never did hard drugs. Carla had rushed back to town only to find her mother's house had been seized by the police department. She hadn't even been able to go in and get the cross her mother wore around her neck.

"Of course, I was never able to prove that it was him," Carla cried, wiping a tear from her cheek. "But in my heart, I know he had something to do with it."

Allina didn't know what she'd expected when she met Carla. But even the worst-case scenarios she'd thought up paled in comparison with the truth. "Is that when you changed your name and moved here?"

She smiled sadly. "A friend of my mother's put me in touch with this guy who helps women disappear. And that's what I did. I didn't even go to my mother's funeral because I knew he'd be there, waiting for me. The only person I've been in contact with is my aunt. Karen and I aren't really close. We have different mothers. Isaac never knew I had any sort of relationship with my father's side of the family. So, despite being told to never contact anyone I know again, I talk to my aunt every now and then. It gets lonely here without family."

Allina imagined the isolation would be like hell on Earth. "I don't know how you do it."

"I don't," Carla said. "I suffer anxiety, I can't sleep. I live in seclusion, barely venturing out. I have minimal interaction with the world. The only people I see regularly are my neighbors, my doctors for the medication I have to take, my shrink, and the delivery man who brings my groceries. I live my life in fear that he will find me and finish what he started."

"Why did you agree to meet me?"

Carla slid the huge envelope toward Allina. "Because maybe you can help us."

Allina picked up the envelope and opened it, skimming through the pages. There were names, dates, and notes. All about Isaac and the many women he'd tormented through the years.

"That's the file I gave to the police," Carla said. "I'm pretty sure they burned the originals but I had copies. My aunt told me your father is a judge. They'll believe *you*."

Except Allina had a deep, dark secret of her own. A past that was as damning as Carla's.

"Take that," Carla instructed. "Use it against him."

"What will you do?" Allina asked, suddenly feeling responsible for the woman in front of her.

Hunching her shoulders, Carla grumbled, "Maybe I can go home one day, see my family. Who knows?"

"The number you gave me...Is that your permanent phone number?"

Carla shook her head. "No, but you can use it. I really hope you can get that monster off your back—our back." She stood up. "I better get going. I borrowed my neighbor's car. And she has to get to work in a few hours."

Allina stuffed the papers back into the envelope and stood. "I'm so glad you came," she told Carla. "You have my number if you need anything."

Carla gave her a curt nod and started to turn away when Allina reached out and embraced her. Carla tensed and jerked back away from her, but Allina couldn't bring herself to let her go. Carla didn't hug her back, but she heard the woman sniffle.

Finally drawing back, Allina wiped the tears that had fallen from her own eyes. "Take care," she said, squeezing Carla's hand. Seconds later, Carla disappeared around the corner.

CHAPTER TWENTY-TWO

Allina had handed her father the huge envelope of evidence the minute she'd walked out of the hotel. Later that day he left for home to turn the evidence in. Fortunately, the Judge knew a few heavy hitters of his own—in the FBI. He turned the file over to them. The next week Isaac was arrested and scheduled to be arraigned.

With the threat from Isaac gone, Allina felt like a huge weight had been lifted, like she could finally move forward. She and Kent continued their little dance. Every day, he'd leave for work after they'd spent the mornings with each other, kissing and touching. Every day, she hoped he'd take things a little further, but he didn't. Wash. Rinse. Repeat.

It was frustrating her to no end. And now she was just ready to forget the BS and let him take her, preferably in his bed because it was comfortable. Unfortunately, after that one night, she'd never slept in it again—and he'd never touched her in *that* way again.

To keep from obsessing about her predicament, she'd thrown herself into work. She and Cali had finally talked and agreed to give the business another try. Thankful for her trusty rental car, she was able to get out of the house, come and go as she pleased. She was able to buy fabric and a new sewing machine. She was back in business.

* * *

As she turned the corner and drove down Syd and Morgan's street, she thought about their upcoming wedding. She pulled into their driveway a short while later and made her way to the door. Everything was getting back to normal for Syd, so she'd asked Allina to come over and show her some of her dress designs.

Her friend opened the brand-new front door with a smile. There were workers all over the place, fixing walls, repairing the wood floor, and painting. Her friend looked relieved to be moving past the ugliness of the altercation with Den.

"I'm so sorry for the mess." Syd motioned her inside. They stepped over tarps and tiptoed into the back of the house. "They've been going strong for a while now. I'm so glad Mama took Brynn. She would have been so irritated with the noise."

Allina set her sketch pad on the kitchen table. "It's cool. I'm just happy they are fixing everything. It'll be over before you know it." She sat down at the table and crossed her legs. "How are you?"

"I'm good. Tired, but I'm a lot better. Den is going to stay in a facility for a little while. That helps. I hope he can get himself together."

Kent had already told her Den's status that morning. He'd spent the past few days going back and forth with Mama and Morgan about where they would send his brother. In the end, they decided it was best that he be placed somewhere farther north, an hour or two away. That way he wouldn't be distracted.

"Good for him," Allina said. "Maybe it will stick this time."

"Enough about that. Let me see what you got."

Allina opened her sketch pad and pulled out her phone to show Syd what she'd worked on using that app. Syd's eyes lit up as she looked at the gowns. They talked fit, color, and whether she wanted lace or tulle or both. Cali arrived a short time later and joined in the conversation, laying out her vision for the wedding.

Syd had decided on an intimate wedding, no more than fifty people. She wanted the space to be romantic, chic, and sexy. While she was talking, Cali and Allina were jotting down notes. Allina already had a few ideas for how to tweak the dress to match the theme.

"Wow," Cali said, closing her notebook. "I think we have enough to work with. Allina, when are you going to start on the dress?"

Shrugging, Allina finished the outline of a new sketch. "I'm thinking it will take me about a week to finalize my sketch. Then I can start putting it together."

"You're going to be a beautiful bride," Cali said.

Allina noticed a flicker of sadness creep across Syd's face. She hoped her friend could embrace her pending marriage without thinking about Den and everything that had happened between them.

"So, now that we're done," Cali said, shifting in her seat to face Allina. "Are you going to sleep with Kent?"

Allina's head jerked back, and she almost slipped out of her chair. "What?"

"Oh God, Cali," Syd said, shaking her head. "What a question to ask."

Allina's face burned and she ducked her head, picking at the edge of her sketch pad. "My sentiments exactly," she murmured.

Over the years, she and Cali had clashed on a lot of issues. They had different philosophies on life. Cali was more straightforward and Allina held a lot back. But when it came to men, Allina had always admired Cali for knowing what she wanted and with whom. Syd had told Allina once that Cali thought Allina looked down on her because of her views on sex, but it was just the opposite.

"What's taking you so long?" Cali teased, a mischievous grin on her face. "I mean, he's fine. You're beautiful. Get busy."

Well, when she said it like that… "Cali, you do realize that it isn't a decision that should be entered into lightly?"

Cali exchanged a knowing look with Syd before turning her attention back to Allina. "Have you kissed him more than once in a sitting?"

"Yes," Allina told her friend. "We've kissed a lot, actually."

"Have you kissed him anywhere other than the mouth?" Cali asked.

"Yes, I've kissed him on his neck and other parts of his face."

"Oooh, you're getting hot and heavy," Cali said sarcastically, wiggling her freshly waxed eyebrows. "Has he touched you below your waist?"

Allina gaped at her nosy friend. "Wh-what? Um…" She scratched the back of her neck, remembering his tongue on her. "No," she lied, fidgeting in her seat. *Please, let her not push this*.

"Cali, stop," Syd said. "Can't you see she's uncomfortable?"

"Better to talk to us than fumble with Kent," Cali retorted. "So when are you going to let him touch your stuff?"

Allina's face flushed hotter. Wanting to huddle in a corner, she sank into her chair. "I don't know."

"Better yet, when are you going to let him touch your stuff with his stuff?" Cali prodded.

"Hey, I haven't committed a crime," Allina told her persistent friend. "You've been with Red too long. Stop badgering me."

"Look, you have to be prepared. Or you'll get caught with your pants down with no idea how to work it."

Syd choked on her drink, spraying it on the table. "Oh my God, Cali. You're ridiculous."

"Come on, Syd," Cali said with an innocent shrug. "You know I'm right."

Allina swallowed. It was the perfect time to let her frustrations out about Kent's gentlemanly behavior. "Um, I guess... well, we did something. Then, we didn't. And I'm a little frustrated," she babbled.

"Why?" Syd asked, leaning forward. "What happened?"

Sighing, Allina finally answered, "If I tell you this, you can't say anything. Ever." Both of her friends nodded. "Kent will kill me if he finds out that I told you."

"What is it?" Cali asked, tilting her head to study Allina. Then she leaned back in her chair. "Oh my God, *did* he touch you below your waist?"

"Yes." She groaned.

Syd and Cali wore identical grins, a mile wide; then they gave each other a high five.

"That's what I'm talking about!" Cali shouted.

Allina just wanted to hide. Closing her eyes, she rushed on, "But he won't... I want him to... He stops..."

Cali placed her hands flat on the table, inclining her head. "What? He won't, what?"

"Ugh, it's hard to say it," Allina grumbled, clenching her hands into fists, then releasing them.

"Allina, you can tell us," Syd said, concern in her hazel eyes.

Raking a hand through her hair, Allina blurted out, "He

doesn't want to go further than that. He did it that one time, but he won't again. He won't even let me touch him either." She slapped a hand over her mouth.

Her friends stared at her, eyes wide and mouths hanging open. The back of her neck tingled and her chest tightened.

"When you say he won't let you touch him, what exactly does that mean?" Cali asked. "I mean, did you try to grab his balls? Polish the bishop?"

Syd jumped up and covered Cali's mouth with her hand. "Cali, shut up. Allina, don't pay attention to her."

Closing her eyes, Allina wished she could blink and be in the safety of her car. She may have been stuck at second base, but she knew what Cali meant. The thought used to mortify her. "I can't believe I'm talking about this."

"We're not," Syd stated firmly. "Right, Cali?"

Cali nodded. When Syd removed her hand, Cali rolled her eyes and shifted in her seat.

"I want to," Allina admitted softly. She'd told him she was ready to be with him, and she meant it. Mostly. Her attraction to Kent seemed to grow by leaps and bounds. "But he keeps putting a halt on it. Frankly, it's irritating."

"So the one time that he touched you, did he... what actually happened?" Syd asked.

Cali jerked her head back and glared at Syd. "So you get to ask the questions, but I can't?"

"Stop, Cali," Syd hissed. "I'm just trying to help her figure out what the problem could be."

Allina waited as the two bantered back and forth about the correct way to ask a question and how much was too much to know about Kent and Allina's potential sex life.

"Stop, guys," Allina said finally. "This isn't helping."

"I'm sorry," they both grumbled simultaneously.

"Maybe he's holding back because he thinks that's what

you want?" Syd asked. Ever the sensible one. "I mean, Allina, you've always been a good girl. And he's not so good a guy—in his mind. You need to make sure that you really want to go this far with him. I mean, you've waited this long to have sex for a reason. I'm sure that's on his mind, too."

"Yeah, but obviously, she's ready," Cali mused.

Suddenly, Allina was hit with doubt. Syd had a point. She was the good girl, content to follow the Word. "I think I'm ready?"

"You think?" Syd asked, a skeptical look in her eyes. "Allina, you're a virgin. This is a big deal. Do you realize how things will change if you decide to give it up?"

"I do. I've thought about it. And this isn't the first time."

"Can I ask you a question?" Cali asked.

A question from Cali, the wrong question, could derail the conversation again. But Allina nodded.

"Why didn't you go there with Isaac?" Cali asked. "I mean, you were supposed to be married. Did you never get close with him? I guess what I'm trying to say is...why Kent? Why now?"

Allina pondered the question. The answer was clear to her. It was Kent because he was Kent. She couldn't explain it without sounding completely vague. Isaac was the man she was going to marry, but it wasn't because he was the love of her life. He'd been attractive and kind to her when they began dating, and up until the wedding day—for the most part. She'd considered it, but he was a minister. It seemed inappropriate to engage in premarital sex with a man of the cloth before they were married.

Even more than that...Isaac wasn't Kent. He'd never awakened that desire in her that Kent seemed to open up with one touch, one kiss. It was the feeling that she'd always had around Kent that made her want to give herself over to

him. She knew she'd be safe, that he would treat her respect-
fully. She trusted him.

"There has never been another man for me, not since I
fell for Kent all those years ago. Don't ask me how I could
feel that way for someone I'd never even kissed, but I did. I
can't explain it. It's not even logical. And I'm not sure it's
supposed to be," Allina admitted softly.

She glanced up at her friends and noticed Syd dabbing
her eyes with a Kleenex. "Are you crying?" Allina asked.

"I guess I'm just emotional," her friend answered. "That
was beautiful. I know the feeling. Trust me. And I'm so
happy for you."

"Are you nervous?" Cali asked, suspiciously unable to
look Allina in the eye.

Is she crying? Allina wondered if her other friend was
"just emotional," too. She smiled. "No. I'm not. I thought I
would be, but I'm not. He's seen me and I didn't feel shy or
scared. That's why I know this is right. He's right."

Cali cleared her throat and pounded her fists on the table.
"Then Kent needs to shit or get off the pot."

Allina laughed. "You're crazy."

"What?" Cali asked, as if she hadn't just used the old
analogy she'd heard many old people use as a child. "We've
got to get you laid. And quick. I'm thinking *you* need to step
up your game. A few candles, a tight dress, and some kick-
ass stilettos and Kent is all yours, baby."

"Don't listen to her," Syd said. "Look, just be honest with
him. No games, no tricks, just tell him what you want."

Allina thought about Syd's advice. Could she really just
put it out there for him? She had been raised that a man
should always be the aggressor. She'd already kissed him
first, told him how she felt first. It would make her feel better
if he was the one who made the first sex move.

"Then there's the nagging feeling I have that maybe he's just not that physically attracted to me," Allina said.

"What?" Cali shouted. "Are you kidding me? Why wouldn't he be attracted to you? You're hot. I don't have busted girlfriends. I told you what to do."

It was Cali's way. She was fiercely protective and always ready for a fight. Allina loved her for it. "I can't do that, Cali," Allina told her. "I can barely walk in heels let alone wear some skimpy outfit and act like someone I'm not."

"How do you know how you are? You've never been in the situation before, never had hot sex on a bed, a counter, or a couch. Who's to say you aren't a freak up under those two-sizes-too-big clothes? Hello."

"I really hate to say this, but she does have point," Syd said.

"Who has a point?" Red asked, strutting into the kitchen with Morgan right behind him.

"I do," Cali chirped. "Hey, babe." They greeted each other with a kiss.

Morgan leaned down and planted one on Syd. He looked up at her and grinned. "What's up, Allina?"

"Hi." It warmed Allina's heart to see her two friends happy in their relationships. It gave her hope that she could be with them sometime in the future. With Kent. That's what it all boiled down to. Even though her relationship with Isaac had crashed and burned, she was willing to step out there with the right man.

"Where's Kent?" Morgan asked. "I've been trying to reach him all day."

Allina shrugged. "I guess he's at work. He said he had a couple meetings."

"He'll probably call when he's done," Morgan said. "Syd, did they finish?"

Syd nodded and stood. "Most of it," she said as they left them in the kitchen to go look at the living room.

Red slid into Syd's vacant chair. "What were you all talking about?"

"Allina and Kent," Cali said, rubbing his hand affectionately. "And sex."

Oh God.

Red's eyes widened. "Oh hell no."

"Wait, baby." Cali tilted her head, peering at Red. "Maybe you could settle this."

He covered his ears and shook his head rapidly. "I don't want to hear about Kent and Allina doing anything."

Cali pulled his hands from his ears. "This is for a good cause."

"I don't care," he argued. "Let Kent and Allina handle their own sex life. You stay out of it."

Allina dropped her head on the table. *I need to get out of here.*

"Listen, as a man," Cali forged ahead, obviously not caring that both of them were traumatized by the conversation. "What should Allina do to get Kent's attention?"

Allina peeked up at her friends.

Red appeared to be mulling the question over, because he stared at the ceiling. Then he met Allina's gaze. "Show him some leg. I'm hungry." He stood up and walked to the fridge.

Cali smacked her hand on the table. "See? I rest my case."

CHAPTER TWENTY-THREE

Where the hell is she?

Kent glanced at his phone. It had been almost an hour since Allina had called and told him she was on her way back. Morgan and Syd lived only fifteen minutes away. She should have been there by now.

The alarm sounded, signaling the front door was open. He heard Allina announce she was back and he relaxed. She must have stopped by the store. Realistically, he knew it wouldn't be too long before she would start doing things on her own, leaving without him, but he liked coming home to her smiling face in the evening. And he loved waking up to the smell of hot coffee and Allina in those damn basketball shorts. The weather was warming up, so she'd taken to sleeping in a tank instead of a T-shirt. A little skin went a long way.

They'd been steadily getting closer and closer to doing the deed, and he'd had to keep reining them back to reality—by making sure she went back to her bedroom at night. He'd decided that waking up with her body pressed against his was not an option if he wanted to slow things down. Of course, she seemed willing. He saw it in her eyes, felt it in the way she'd always find a way to be near him and the way she kissed him. But he wasn't sure she was really ready, and he needed to know beyond the shadow of a doubt. It was killing him. He'd taken too many cold showers for his liking.

Sighing, he turned back to his laptop. A co-worker had hired him to do some graphic work for a start-up business venture. It had started with a logo, but now he was working on the company's website. Allina's words kept ringing in his head, egging him on to make something happen with his designs. *Can I really do this, though?*

A few minutes later, the bedroom door swung open. Allina poked her head into the room. "Got a minute?"

He nodded and set his laptop down on the bed next to him. "Yeah, come in."

When she entered, he almost forgot to breathe. His eyes followed her across the floor. She was wearing nothing but a nightgown. A see-through one that barely covered her knees, leaving her toned legs visible. It clung to her body as she sauntered over to him. Under the thin material, he could see the outline of her full breasts. *Is she doing this on purpose?*

She climbed on the bed, crossing her legs.

"What's up?" he managed to say.

"I've been thinking, about the last few nights."

Shifting, he cursed his mind and his body for skipping straight to the gutter. Her leg brushed up against his and he fisted his hands in the sheets. It was either that or pull her on top of him.

He watched her smooth a hand up her leg and before he could stop himself, he reached out and mimicked her movement, pulling her closer to him.

"Oh," she whispered, biting down on her bottom lip. The same lip he wanted to bite down on himself.

"What about the last few nights?" he asked, his gaze flickering from her lips to her eyes then back down to her lips.

"I really enjoy spending time with you, and I love kissing you." She paused, dropped her gaze. "I want—"

He couldn't stop himself even if he tried. He braced a hand on the back of her head and pulled her into a kiss. Lifting her up effortlessly, he set her on his lap, never breaking the kiss.

When he reluctantly pulled back, it was only to breathe before he went back in for more. Urged on by her soft moans, he lowered her to the bed and climbed on top of her. He placed soft, wet kisses down her neck to the skin above her breast. As his mouth moved lower, he lifted her short nightgown.

His blood seemed to burn hot, and the desire to make love to her eclipsed everything. He gazed down at her, took in her flushed skin, swollen lips, and hooded eyes. Leaning down, he brushed his lips against her ear.

"I want to make love to you," he whispered. "Now."

"Yes," she breathed.

Perfect. She was absolute perfection to him—warm and soft in all the right places. He wanted to make this right for her. And not just that night. He wanted to build his life around her, take his time showing her just how good it could be. He cared about her that much.

Slowly, his hand inched up her thigh. When his fingers brushed against the band of her panties, he slipped them under and pushed one of them into her heat. She sucked in a deep breath as he prepared her, moving his fingers in and out. He smiled when she lifted her ass off the bed in time with his movements. He circled her clit with his thumb and was pleasantly surprised when she ordered him to keep going. Picking up the pace, he added another finger. It didn't take long before she stiffened and cried out as her orgasm washed over her. Rubbing his nose against hers, he bit down on the inside of his cheek. His body was throbbing with a need to be inside her, but at that moment, it was all about her. It was her first time, and he wanted it to be good for her.

She opened her eyes and smiled at him, a seductive grin. And he knew he'd die remembering her face. He brushed her hair back and placed a gentle kiss on her forehead, then her nose, and finally her lips.

"Are we really going to do this?" she asked.

"Only if you're okay with it." *What the hell will I do if she says no?*

"I am," she said, searching his eyes. "I want to."

Without another word, he slowly slid her underwear down her legs and tossed it behind him. Then he pulled her nightgown up and off. Finally, she was lying under him naked. He took a minute to smooth a hand over her skin, enjoying the way she shivered underneath his palm. Tracing her navel, he watched as she threw her head back and to the side. He took the opportunity to kiss her neck before trailing his mouth down her body to her breast.

Suckling one mound into his mouth, he flicked her nipple with his tongue. He felt her nails digging into his shoulder and lifted himself up. "Are you okay?" he asked, gazing down at her beautiful face.

Instead of answering, she pulled him into a wet kiss before she tugged his wife beater off. "I can't be the only one without my clothes on," she said, winking at him.

Fumbling with his shorts, he cursed when he realized he'd tied the drawstring into a knot. He tried to untie it, but it wouldn't budge. Her hands on his made him pause. Slowly, she worked the knot until it came loose and pushed his shorts down.

He yanked his nightstand drawer open and rummaged inside it for protection. *Damn it.* He was liable to shoot someone if he didn't have any condoms. The gleam of the silver package caught his eye and he pulled it out.

She watched as he opened the wrapper and put it on. Once it was in place, he relaxed between her legs, her skin against his. She ran a finger over his jaw. Gripping her thighs, he lifted them up and gently pushed inside her.

Her mouth fell open, but no sound came out. Holding himself still, he gave her a minute to adjust to his size. She was so wet, so tight, so *his*. When her eyes fluttered open, she grinned and he knew she was feeling no pain.

Starting slowly, he thrust in and out. His mouth covered hers as they moved to their own rhythm. Everything about her had him teetering dangerously close to the edge—from her perfume, her smile, her hair...to her legs. But he wouldn't fall over yet. It had to be good for her, memorable. As he picked up the pace, he ground his teeth together. He wasn't sure how much longer he could stand it.

He felt her breath, hot on his ear, heard her whisper in his ear that it felt good. His heart swelled in his chest. She wanted him, she'd chosen *him* to be her first. He was the man she trusted with herself and he wanted to live up to it. Because no other man would ever get this close to her, if he had a say.

Damn. He started to unravel, and he looked down at her. "Look at me," he ordered softly.

She complied, her big, expressive eyes locked on his.

"I want you to come for me, baby," he coaxed. "Let go."

He felt her insides quiver, signaling she was close. She squeezed his hips with her thighs and he pushed into her one last time. Then she fell over, pulling him with her.

They lay there silently, him still on top of her, still inside her. She was trembling hard beneath him. *Oh shit, what did I do?* He didn't think he could deal if she looked at him and told him she'd made a mistake—especially when it had felt so right to him. Bracing himself, he looked down at her, shocked when he saw that she was laughing.

Suddenly self-conscious, he frowned. "You're laughing?"

Beaming up at him, she giggled. "I was just thinking about something Red said."

Confused, he asked, "We just got done... we finally made love and you're thinking about Red?"

She ran her hands over his shoulders. "It's not what you think."

He tried not to feel annoyed. He really did. But after a bout like that, she *should* have been spent, clinging to him, and only thinking about *him*. Not Red's ass. And certainly not laughing at something Red said.

"Do I even want to know?" he grumbled.

She laughed and brushed her lips over his. "Seriously, it's not what you think," she repeated. "Cali asked him what I should do to get your attention."

"And?"

"He told me to show you some leg."

Wow. His friend had sold him out. Years ago, he'd confided to Red that Allina's long legs were one of his favorite things about her. "I guess he was right," he confessed, chuckling with her.

* * *

Allina rolled over, perching herself up on her elbow. Kent was asleep next to her. They'd spent the past few hours basking in the afterglow of her first time. Just thinking about it made her blush. She'd never known sex could be so enjoyable. She'd shattered into a million pieces and he'd put her back together again.

She let her fingers trace his hard muscles. There was something about his sharp intake of breath when she'd touched him earlier that made her feel powerful. She relished the fact that she could affect him the way he had affected her. Lying next to him, watching the slow rise and fall of his chest, she purposed within herself to enjoy the ride. She wanted to learn everything he wanted to teach her.

So far he'd already taught her the art of resting her body. After they'd made love a second time, he carried her into his bathroom and gave her a sponge bath. Of course, the "rest" came after he showed her that the bed wasn't the only good place to make love.

Now her body was screaming at her, but she didn't care. She just wanted to be with him. She nuzzled into his side, smiling when his arm wrapped around her.

"You're up?" he asked.

"I couldn't sleep."

"That means I didn't do my job," he joked. His hand was splayed over the small of her back. He smoothed it lower.

"Oh, you did your job." She dragged her fingertips over the taut muscles of his stomach. "I'd always heard it was a painful experience so I didn't really expect much."

He leaned back and opened one eye. "Seriously? You thought I was going to go out like that?"

Grinning, she nodded her head. "I thought it was a given. Everybody I know has had an awful first time."

"Everybody?" he asked, raising his brows.

"Yep."

"Hm."

She cringed, thinking about what would have happened on her wedding night with Isaac had she not left. Kent had made losing her virginity special. He was gentle and sweet and giving. "I'm glad it was with you," she said after a moment. She hugged him, closing her eyes when he kissed her forehead.

"I'm glad it was too."

She flicked a loose thread in his sheets with her finger. "What happens next?"

Making love to Kent, as good as it was, didn't change their circumstances. Or did it? They weren't an official couple or anything, hadn't made any promises to each other. But she knew that she couldn't imagine her life without him. She wanted to hold on to what they shared with everything she had. Except she wasn't sure he felt the same way.

"What do you mean?" he asked, drawing a circle on her shoulder.

She turned to look at him. "I mean, with us?"

He swept a thumb across her jaw. "I don't know."

Allina didn't want to be one of those women that Kent said he didn't have time for, the virgin who attached herself to his hip after one night of sex. But denying herself the opportunity, the chance, to be with him, would be akin to denying herself water, or access to her sewing machine. Her survival seemed dependent on him. Because she was in love with him. She'd realized that she'd always been in love with him, even when she was with Isaac.

"This is new territory for me," he continued. "I don't usually have sex with my friends."

She winced at his use of the word "friend." *Is that all I am to him?*

"It was a joke," he told her, chuckling.

She let out a slow breath that she hadn't realized she was holding.

"Of course you're not just my friend, Allina." He gazed at her. "You're so much more than that. I wouldn't have made love to you if you weren't. What happened between us is no accident. It's not a mistake because I went into it willingly, with both eyes open."

"What are you saying?"

"I'm saying I want to be with you. Not just like this, but I want to work toward something—with you. I don't want you to move out. I'd rather you stay, with me."

Her hand flew to her chest. "Are you asking me to move in with you permanently?"

"I'm asking you not to leave."

Allina was floored. She wasn't sure what she'd been expecting, but she knew that wasn't it. He wanted her to stay with him. Could she? Instead of feeling elated, she felt guilty. He was being honest with her, open. And she was hiding something so terrible that it could destroy everything.

Swallowing, she told him she didn't want to leave. "But I can't make that big of a decision right now. Everything is still so new between us."

"I get it," he said. "There's a lot to consider. We don't have to rush."

That eased her mind a little.

"But I do want to make something clear."

Frowning, she peered up at him. "What's that?"

"I want to be sure you know that you're my girl." He smiled, his white teeth on display. "Because I'm sure that's what you really want to know."

She laughed. "You do know me well. I did wonder if we would have an official title change."

"Exactly. So will you go steady with me?"

Caressing his face, she pulled him to her, kissing him deeply. "Does that answer your question?" she muttered against his mouth.

He cupped her cheek and slid his other hand around her neck. "Sure does." Then he kissed her soundly. "Now get some sleep," he ordered with a light smack on her butt. She leaned into him and finally let herself drift off to sleep.

CHAPTER TWENTY-FOUR

$\mathcal{A}$llina studied her reflection in the mirror—in Kent's master bathroom, in nothing but her tank and panties. Tilting her head to the side, she brushed her unruly curls from her face. She *felt* like another person, like she was finally let in on a secret that she hadn't been privy to for a long time.

Twisting, she looked at her back, her shoulders, and her neck. Every part of her had been thoroughly loved. Not just sexually, but emotionally and spiritually. Kent had made sure that her first time was a memorable experience. Her fingertips grazed her swollen lips and she smiled.

"Are you coming back to bed?" Kent asked from the doorway.

She glanced at him over her shoulder and smirked. Tearing her eyes away from his bare chest, she forced herself to focus on the task at hand—brushing her teeth. She'd snuck into the bathroom before he woke up to take a hot shower. "In a minute. I didn't know you were up."

"I called out today. So I'm all yours. All day," he added with a wink.

She gripped the edge of the countertop as he neared her. When he wrapped his arms around her from the back, she leaned into him, grinning when he brushed his lips against her temple.

"You didn't have to do that. I know you have a project." Allina was deliriously happy that they would be able to spend the day together

He rested his chin on her shoulder and gazed at her through the mirror. "I want to. Besides, we have a lot to do."

Frowning, she asked, "What do we have to do?"

He kissed her shoulder, then her neck. "I'm not done with you." He turned her around and perched her up on the bathroom counter.

Wrapping her arms around his shoulders, she arched a brow. "And what exactly do you plan on doing to me?"

He pressed his lips to hers in a fervent kiss, and she opened for him without hesitation. Kissing him used to be a dream, something unattainable but thought about often. Now she knew what it was like and it was still all she could think of. Kent Smith was too sexy, too hot for his own good. *No, for my own good*.

Soon, her thin tank and underwear were tossed behind them. His talented fingers skimmed her slit and she winced in pain, letting out a muffled grunt. But she squeezed his hips, hoping he wouldn't pull away. She could handle a little pain. *Right?*

When he finally broke the kiss, she groaned and cradled his face in her hands. "You caught that, huh?" she whispered.

He chuckled. "Absolutely." He kissed her forehead, scooped her up in his arms, and carried her back to the bed. Once they were settled under the covers, he wrapped his strong arm around her waist and nuzzled against her from behind. "You need a break."

"I guess," she mumbled, twisting her neck and giving him

a quick kiss, before relaxing against him. Small gestures like this, the way he seemed to always know how to take care of her, only made her want to be with him more. He was her perfect angel, like heaven on earth. She didn't think she'd ever get enough of him. Her heart skipped a beat whenever he was near.

That's why she knew she loved him, would go anywhere with him. They hadn't said the words to each other, but she didn't need to hear them. His love shined on her like the hot sun, enveloping her in a warm cocoon.

"We're good just like this," he said, nipping at her ear-lobe. "We can chill here for a little while, maybe go out to dinner later, someplace intimate."

She smiled. "You're so good to me. I don't know what I would've have done if I hadn't shown up at your door."

"You would have been just fine."

"Eventually," she said, tracing his fingers. "I didn't know that at the time. I was scared, distraught. For the first time in a long time, I thought about giving up on myself. But you took care of me, encouraged me. It means a lot to me."

He turned his palms up and intertwined her fingers with his. "That's what we do for each other."

Allina wished she would have listened to Kent when he'd warned her about Isaac. Instead, she'd been blind and defensive, intent on proving something. What she had to prove, she didn't really know. Maybe it had been about some warped need to show that she could get the guy—the good and handsome guy. Only Isaac wasn't as good as he let on. That was her fault, too, for not paying that close atten-tion to the signs. Now she could see them clear as a bright, sunny day. The way he'd always try to control her, tell her what to wear and how to style her hair. It'd started as a seemingly innocent request to straighten her hair when she preferred to rock a natural style. She'd complied because she wanted to please him. Then he'd insisted she wear certain skirts because they were appropriate for a minister's future wife. Before she knew it, she barely recognized herself in the mirror.

But she realized that everything happened for a reason. If she hadn't turned into the runaway bride, she would have never ended up with Kent. Although the road traveled was full of winding roads and rough terrain, she couldn't regret it. It had brought her there— to Kent. In a sense, she had Isaac to thank. Not that she would ever do that.

"What are you thinking about?" Kent asked.

Snapping herself out of her thoughts, she shifted in his arms. "Just thinking about how I can't bring myself to regret the last several months."

"Even the worst parts?"

"Yep. Things would be very different if I hadn't gone through what I did."

As much as she had hoped they would turn into more than friends at some point, the chances of that happening had been slim to none. Kent was too noble and she was too shy. She would have just settled for hanging out with him every weekend, chatting about work and the drama within the crew. They never would have kissed and she never would have been invited to his home after eleven o'clock.

"We certainly wouldn't be here," she added. "You were there for me, even when I couldn't recognize it for what it was."

"You're not exactly the person you were when you moved back to Ohio. You're different, but the same—if that makes any sense."

"It does," she agreed. Allina recalled a conversation she'd had with Syd a while ago. Her friend had implored her to try to see the different sides in a situation, the grays or the occasional burst of color in her black or white world. Allina couldn't fathom it at the time because she'd always believed in right or wrong, cut and dry.

She'd let herself believe the persona Isaac presented to her because he was everything she'd fooled herself into thinking she needed. But it wasn't what she actually wanted.

"I've learned a lot," Allina told him, kissing his palm. "I don't want to take anything for granted. I want to live my life with the people I . . . care about." She stopped short of admitting she loved him, although she suspected he already knew.

"Good," he told her, running a finger across her shoulder. "I'd say you're on your way. You really took me by surprise."

She'd wanted to ask him the night before, after the first time they made love, but she couldn't bring herself to say the words. "About that," she grumbled.

He perched himself up on an elbow and peered down at her. "What?"

Covering her face, she said. "Do you . . . did I . . . Was it good for you?"

His eyes widened and a whisper of a smirk spread across his face. "Did it seem like it wasn't?" he asked, a glimmer in his dark eyes.

"I don't know!" she shouted, pulling the sheet above her face. She felt the rumble of his body as he laughed. "It wasn't like I knew what I was doing."

"You caught on quickly," he told her, tugging at the sheet. "But this conversation is pretty awkward with your face covered up."

Kent finally won the tug-of-war they had going on with the sheet and he yanked it off her. She slowly opened her eyes and he was smiling down at her.

"It was very good for me," he told her, kissing her deeply. "Very good."

Now, if only I can get you to stop being so nice and do it again. When his eyes widened and he barked out a laugh, her mouth fell open. "Oops. I said that out loud, didn't I?"

"Wow, you just..." He scratched his head. "You really just said that."

Allina felt her ears burn and she buried her face in his chest. "I'm so embarrassed."

"Don't be," he said, smoothing a hand up and down her back. "And I'm not that nice. But you do need some time. You're sore. Making love to someone who is writhing in pain and not pleasure isn't my idea of a fun time." He tipped her chin up and locked eyes with hers. Leaning down, he took her bottom lip in his mouth, kissing her long and hard. "But we have time, baby. No worries."

"Whatever you say," she grumbled, turning around so that her back was to his. They spooned for a few minutes, enjoying the silence and each other.

Long-term happiness had always seemed to evade her, but she'd decided to enjoy the time she did have with him and hope to have more. After all, there was still her past and Isaac to contend with.

"I love you," he murmured against her neck.

Allina sucked in a deep breath and turned around to face him. Gazing into his eyes, her own filled with tears.

"I should have said it before we..." he whispered. "I'm sure you always imagined your first time being with someone who loves you, and I wanted you to know that I did...I do. I won't ever intentionally hurt you, or try to change you into something you're not. I don't want you to be anyone but yourself. I love your big hair, your wild and unruly curls, your face, your eyes—everything about you. And it's not because you gave me a part of yourself that I probably didn't deserve. It's because you're you. My Allina, my baby."

"I can't..." Allina was overcome with emotion. In her wildest dreams, she never thought he'd declare his love for her the way he just had. It was so pure, so real, so sincere. "What you said...just confirmed what I already knew. But I'm glad you said it because I love you, too. And I've waited for this moment for a long time. Longer than you'll ever really know."

He rested his forehead against hers. "I never thought it would feel this good to hear you say that." Then he kissed her.

Maybe it was the words, the emotions, or the love hang-over? But Allina was helpless to deny what was in her heart. She wanted Kent; she loved him. And she would show him every day of her life just how much he meant to her.

Later on, Allina stared at Kent while he slept. She grazed her fingers over the bare expanse of his chest and ran a finger over one of his nipples. His skin was so smooth, his muscles so firm.

She froze when he shifted, grumbling something incoher-ent. When his soft snores filled the room again, she contin-ued her journey. Softly, she feathered her fingers down his stomach to the edge of the sheet draped low on his hips.

Lifting up the sheet, she looked back at him before she slipped her hand under it. When her hands closed around him, his eyes opened.

His eyes glazed over with desire as she stroked him. Feel-ing bold, she brushed her lips over his, sweeping her tongue over his lips. He opened for her then, letting her take control of the kiss. She tightened her hands around his erection, sat-isfied when he groaned into her mouth.

Breaking the kiss, she met his gaze and kissed him again

before trailing her lips down his neck, then his chest, then his stomach. Giving him one last look, she took him into her mouth, swirling her tongue around the tip.

Kent's hips bucked off the bed when she took him deeper into her mouth, applying a little suction before she grazed the underside with her tongue. She repeated the motion again.

She giggled when she heard him mutter a curse. And she groaned herself when his hands tangled in her hair. He breathed out her name as she slid her mouth down and then back up again. Pulling away to catch her breath, she went back in for more.

"Allina," he murmured. "You have to stop."

But she couldn't. She wouldn't. Surprisingly, she liked it. And she continued exploring every inch of him with her tongue. Using her other hand, she cupped his balls and squeezed.

When she applied more pressure, Kent growled, hooked his hands under her arms, and pulled her up until she was lying on top of him. Flipping them over, he kissed her.

"What?" she asked.

"You're killing me," he said, chuckling. "I'm not sure you're ready for what was about to come next."

Allina knew what he was talking about. She hadn't really thought about it until he said it out loud. "Kent, why don't you let me please you for a change?"

"What are you talking about? You're good."

She pursed her lips and tilted her head. "Stop. I'm serious."

"I am, too." He brushed his lips across her collarbone. "Very serious. You're good." He glanced at her, and his eyes softened. "Okay," he said. "I have an idea."

CHAPTER TWENTY-FIVE

Later on, Allina suggested they meet their friends at the Ice Box for dinner. When they walked in hand in hand, she suddenly felt nervous. *Would they know?* It had been on her mind on the car ride over and she wondered if her friends would be able to take a look at her and see that she and Kent had done it.

The crew was already seated at their private booth. Morgan and Red were in a heated discussion about the NBA playoffs and Cali and Syd were discussing wedding stuff.

Syd noticed them first and waved them over. "Hey, guys! Get on over here. We were wondering when you two would show up."

Allina felt a blush creep up her neck when she thought about why they were late. Kent had decided to teach her a little lesson in sixty-nine. She didn't think she'd be able to see after that experience. She found herself looking forward to his teachings. She wanted to learn everything he wanted to teach her.

Allina slid into the booth next to Syd and Kent pulled up an extra chair and immediately rested his hand on her knee.

"Girl, you look radiant," Cali said, taking a sip of wine. "You're glowing. What have you been doing?"

As if it wasn't bad enough that Cali had called her out in front of everybody, the table descended into silence as every single one of her friends sat there and studied her like she was a lab specimen.

Morgan frowned. "Cali is right, for once. You look good, girl."

Red winked at her. "Mmm-hmm. Looks like someone showed someone else that leg."

Allina's gaze darted to Syd's smiling eyes, then to Red's smirk, and finally Cali's mischievous grin. *They know.* Her eyes snapped to Kent. He shrugged at her, but she hadn't mistaken the glint in his eyes.

Sinking down in her seat, she yelled, "Stop looking at me like that, shit!"

That made matters worse because they all fell out laughing—even Kent. *Traitor.* She pushed his hand off her knee.

"Come on, baby," Kent said, picking up her hand and giving it a little squeeze. "I didn't mean to laugh, but you cursed. And that *is* funny."

He stood up, planted a scorching kiss to her lips, and motioned for the fellas to join him at the bar.

Once they were gone, Cali leaned forward. "All right, now...spill."

"Yes," Syd agreed, fanning herself. "Because Kent just laid one on you and it was hot!"

Oh Lord. "You two need to quit," Allina said. "What happened between us is nobody's business."

Allina knew her friends wouldn't let it go, so she braced herself for the barrage of questions.

"Oooh, you did it," Syd said, wiggling her eyebrows. Her friend tapped a nail on the table. "Look at you, Allina. You're relaxed...you even walk different."

"And you got your hair all out, on full display," Cali added.

Allina rolled her eyes. Cali had been telling her for years to let her hair free and stop wearing buns and ponytails.

"Okay," Allina admitted, glancing behind her for Kent. "I did."

Cali and Syd gave each other a high five and burst into another fit of giggles. Allina whispered to the ladies about her night with Kent, making sure she checked over her shoulder for the guys because she'd hate for them to hear her.

Once she finished her story, she leaned back in her seat and crossed her arms over her chest. "So, there you have it. No more details." Allina wanted to keep the best parts to herself.

Syd gave her a hug. "I'm so happy for you. More importantly, I'm happy that you are happy."

Allina was happy. It was the happiest she'd ever been. "I am. I remember in college when you two would talk about sex, I would think about the person special enough to pop *my* apple."

Cali's mouth fell open. "Your apple?"

Allina's gaze darted back and forth between her two best friends. "Yes. You know the saying…popping your apple?"

Syd snickered. "Allina, baby." She patted Allina's hand gently. "I really am so ecstatic that you've experienced something so wonderful with the right person. But I think you mean 'cherry.'"

Her friends once again laughed at her. She jumped when her phone vibrated. Shaking her head at her giggling girlfriends, she answered the call. It was her father's number.

"Hi, Daddy," she chirped. Allina had wanted to call her parents all day, especially her mother, because they could talk about anything. But she hadn't gotten around to it.

There was no answer. "Dad?" she called again. Hanging up, she frowned. She had a fleeting thought about the time Isaac had called her from her mother's phone, then dismissed it. Isaac was in jail. Or at least she hoped he was.

Her father had told her that he would fight to have bail denied. Knowing Judge knew plenty of people made her feel secure.

"Is everything okay?" Syd asked, the glee in her eyes replaced with concern. "Was that your dad?"

Allina shrugged. "It was his number, but when I picked up, no one was on the line."

"Maybe the call dropped or something?" Cali suggested.

"Yeah, you're probably right," Allina said. "I'll call him later. Better yet, let me use one of the offices to call him now. Do you mind?"

"Sure," Syd said. "Use mine."

Allina got up and headed toward the back of the bar where the offices were. She hoped everything was okay.

* * *

Kent watched as Allina got up and went to the back of the bar. He'd asked the guys to join him at the bar specifically because he thought Allina might need a minute with her girls. He was curious about the conversation because of all the laughter. At one point, he'd seen Cali and Syd throw each other a high five and he wondered what exactly they were chatting about. Obviously, it was about him and Allina, but he would probably never know what Allina had shared with her friends.

Although he'd had every intention of moving slowly with Allina, in the end he couldn't do it. She'd let him make love to her. She'd trusted him with her body. He had to live up to it. That's why he'd confessed his love to her. He felt she deserved to know his true feelings. And he'd meant every word he'd said to her.

Now what? It wasn't like they had specifically determined they would live together, get married, and start a family. She was already staying there, but knowing Allina, she wouldn't want to live with him permanently. Kent wanted her to stay; he wanted her with him every day. As far as he was concerned, they'd wasted enough time. But he figured he had to let things come organically if he wanted their relationship to last.

He felt the smack of Red's hand on his back. "So, you and Allina? Together or nah?"

Morgan barked out a laugh and gulped his beer down. "I would say together, judging by that public display of affection earlier."

Kent shook his head. "Whatever. Shut the hell up. Did I clown you when you were chasing after Cali's ass, Red? Or you, Morgan, when you were sleeping with your brother's ex?"

Morgan scowled. "Low blow, brother."

Kent knew Morgan wasn't really hurt or offended. Throwing barbs, showing no mercy...that was their way of bonding. But they always told the truth to each other, no matter what. It was a code he tried to live by in everything. The truth hurt only when you tried not to face it. It was best to take the pain with the punches, and keep it moving.

"Yeah, man." Red asked the bartender to bring them another round of beer. "When did this become about us? For once, *you're* in the hot seat. I seem to remember you gladly dispensing your opinion when I was going through with Cali."

"Oh, yeah," Morgan agreed. "He had a lot to say when I was dealing with my shit."

Speaking of Morgan's *shit*, Kent asked, "Did Mama tell you about Den?" On their way to the bar, Mama had called Kent to tell him that Den had checked himself out of the hospital and disappeared. "She can't reach him."

Morgan grumbled. "Yeah. I'm not sure what she expects me to do. When I wanted to go see him at the hospital, she told me not to because she thought it would set him off. Honestly, I don't want to see him anyway."

Morgan had basically put his own life on hold multiple times for Den, and Kent couldn't blame him for feeling the way he did. But he also understood why Den didn't want to see Morgan. He hated being in the middle, but his main concern was his mother.

"Mama's worried. I don't want her stressing herself out. She's getting older, tired. She started smoking again. I don't like that," Kent said. His mother was the ultimate caregiver. It made her feel good. To know that she couldn't help her own son was driving her crazy.

"Yeah, she even called me," Red confessed. "Even knowing I can't stand Den. She asked me to check in with some of my contacts in the police department. She said she'd be willing to pay someone to find Den."

It didn't surprise Kent that his mother had called Red. She was desperate. "Well, if it makes her feel better, help her."

"I couldn't tell her no," Red said. "I'm going to make a few calls—for Mama. But I'll tell you this... if Den does anything else to hurt Syd, I will fuck him up. I'm sick of him."

Kent nodded. He understood Red's frustration with Den. Shit, he was frustrated with his brother and growing weary of Den's antics.

"Enough talking about that asshole," Red said. "You just need to come out with it. What's going on with you and Allina?"

"Shut the hell up, man," Kent said. "I'm not telling you shit."

"Well, how about I tell you something?" his friend said. "Don't fuck it up. Allina is a good girl. She's like a sister to me. I'll have to kick your ass if you hurt her."

Kent snorted and waved his friend off. "Please."

"I'm serious," Red said.

"Bruh, are you sure you know what you're doing?" Morgan asked. "Women like Allina are not to be played with."

"Did I say I was playing with her?" Kent opened his new bottle of beer and took a swig. "I know who Allina is, better than you and Red. I know what I'm doing."

"Just go ahead and admit you're so gone." Morgan twirled his beer bottle in circles on the bar top. "You know you love that girl."

Red laughed. "Exactly."

Kent glanced at his watch. It had been more than a few minutes since Allina went into the back. He'd wait a little before he went to check on her.

"I told y'all, I'm not telling you shit." He tipped his bottle toward them. "Drink up."

A few minutes later, Kent knocked on the office door and peeked in. The office was in shambles; papers were strewn everywhere. The chair was tipped over, drawers were pulled out. And Allina was sitting on the floor, hugging her knees.

Rushing to her, he knelt down in front of her. "What's wrong?" He brushed her curls back. When she peered up at him, he noticed her tearstained cheeks and puffy eyes. Clenching his jaw, he asked, "What happened, Allina?"

"I called my dad." She sniffed and wiped her nose with the back of her hand. "Isaac was released on bail. Well, actually on personal recognizance. I guess his father pulled some strings in the governor's office."

He clenched his jaw, grinding his teeth together. The

thought of that man running free made his blood run cold. "Did your father say anything else?"

"Just that he would put his guy back on him, to keep an eye on him." She peered up at him, through wet lashes. "I thought it was over. I thought Isaac was out of my life for good." She let out a bitter snicker. "Basically, he really is making my life a living hell."

"Son of a bitch," Kent grumbled, cracking his neck from side to side.

"When I got the call from my dad's phone and he didn't answer, I was so worried that something had happened to him. Will it always be like this?" she cried.

He pulled her into his arms, stroking her back tenderly, whispering words of comfort to her. If only he could punch a wall or somebody's face, anything to relieve the tension that had set into his bones. Somehow he didn't think his partners would understand if he stomped out to the bar and started a fight with one of the patrons.

"Isaac threatened my father," she murmured.

Jerking his head back, he frowned. "What?"

Allina disclosed the details of her phone conversation with her father. "When Isaac was released from custody, he phoned Daddy and threatened him, my mother, and, of course, me."

Fortunately, Judge wasn't easily intimidated. The protective husband and father had threatened to slap Isaac with a Personal Protection Order if he didn't stop harassing them.

"But knowing Daddy, he probably issued a threat of his own," she continued.

Kent glared at everything, but nothing in particular—the wall, the stupid little calendar Syd had on her desk with that old lady saying stupid things about men, the plant that was almost dead on the windowsill.

He inhaled deeply as she finished her story, hanging on to the little bit of control he had left. His temper was dangling from a short, thin piece of thread and he was liable to blow.

"Something in me just snapped," she explained, gesturing to the mess around them. "I'm so damn frustrated," she shouted. "I want him out of my life."

Her eyes were fierce with determination as she went into her plan. Kent listened as she told him she still wanted to go back to Cleveland in the next week. She wanted to go to the church to speak with Isaac's father, Bishop Hunter. If he couldn't get Isaac to back off, no one could. If that didn't work, she'd press charges herself for harassment.

"I'm done hiding from him," she hissed. "I'm not going to take this lying down anymore." She stood up and brushed off her clothes. "I uprooted my whole life, left my stuff behind to get away from him. He thinks he can just control me with fear and intimidation." She paced the office, swinging her arms out in frustration. "I'm happy. I'm finally content with my life and he can't take that from me. I won't let him. Damn it, he will not win this fight."

Kent stared at his girlfriend with what he was sure was a stunned expression on his face. What a difference a few minutes made. He'd walked in on a seemingly defeated Allina and was now faced with a kick-ass, take-no-prisoners Allina. He liked it. Smirking, he asked, "Are you going to need some help with this plan? Because I'll definitely bring my fists with me."

Kent had never wanted to knock some sense into someone more than that son of a preacher. *He better hope I don't get a hold of him.*

She laughed. "Only if I can punch him first."

He jerked her to him and kissed her. "You're feisty," he murmured against her cheek.

"I have too much to lose."

"You won't lose me," he said. "I promise."

Gazing into his eyes, she pulled him into another kiss.

Need and desire slammed into him, but he tried to think of food or football or bleach... anything to keep himself under control. They were in the bar, in one of the offices. There was no way he was joining the do-it-at-the-Ice-Box club his friends had formed over the last year.

But her hands were moving fast, unbuttoning his shirt, tempting him to take it there: to take her against the wall or on the chair or on the floor.

"Allina?" he murmured against her relentless mouth. "We're in the bar."

"I know," she whispered. "I don't care. Make love to me. I need you to, now."

And he didn't want to disappoint her. Before she could say anything else, he pushed her up against the wall, pinning her hands above her head. One hand slid down her side, over her hip and to her leg. He hoisted it up and stepped closer, pressing himself into her, thrusting against her without even taking her panties off. She was wet. So wet he felt it through his pants. But he couldn't stop. He continued to push into her, harder, more forcefully. She sucked in a deep breath and her eyes rolled into the back of her head. When her legs buckled, he picked her up and continued to move against her until she cried out. It didn't take long for her to come, and he muffled her cries with his mouth.

Once her trembling subsided, he slowly moved back from her. She drooped back against the wall and almost slid to the ground, but he held her up. "You're okay," he whispered. "Come on."

She stared at him in awe. "You just... with my clothes on."

He placed a finger against her mouth. "It's okay. But we

have to get out of here. Syd will kill us if she knows we, uh..." He swallowed. "Did this in her office."

"But you..."

"I'm fine." He buttoned his shirt and glanced at her. "Are you?"

She nodded. "I love you."

"I love you, too."

"And I meant what I said. He's not going to ruin this thing between us."

That will never happen. "Don't worry, he won't." Kent cradled her face in his hands. "Allina, we're going to be fine. As long as we're honest with each other."

She averted her gaze, shifting her weight from one foot to the other. Bending down, she started picking up papers and putting them back on the desk. His hand on her wrist stopped her.

"Do you want to go home?" he asked, tilting his head and trying to meet her gaze. "I'll have someone clean up in here later."

Nodding, she grabbed her cell phone and stuffed it in her pocket. "That would be good."

They walked in silence out to the main area of the bar. The crew was back at the booth. He veered off in their direction with Allina right by his side.

"We're going to head back to my place," he announced.

"Is everything okay?" Syd asked, munching on a fry.

"Yep," he said. "I'm tired."

He didn't even try to make up a good lie. Judging by their looks, he would say they knew it, too. Kent glanced at the empty beer bottles and wineglasses. They were well on their way to being drunk. For a minute, he wished he could stay and chill with them. After all, knocking back drinks with his family had been his life for a long time.

Allina brushed his arm with her hand. "We can stay if you want."

He glanced at her and smiled. *Why the hell would I stay with these fools when I could go home with her?* "Nah, I'm ready to go."

Allina gave quick hugs to everybody and told Syd she'd call her the next day. Kent whispered to his brother that he should keep Syd out of her office until he could clean it up. Then he gave his boys dap, and he and Allina left.

CHAPTER TWENTY-SIX

*A*llina jolted awake when she heard a knock on the door. She glanced at the clock. After they'd left the bar, she and Kent had gone back to his place to watch a movie and cuddle. But he'd gotten a call from Mama and had to rush over there to help her out.

She sat there for a while after he left, thinking about Isaac. What would she do if he found her? She had no way to protect herself. After her aunt died, Allina had started going to the gun range. Every time she visited home, her father would take her. Once she turned twenty-one, she bought her first gun and got her license. Not many people knew that about her, because they call it "concealed" for a reason. Having a gun and being able to shoot made her feel safe, especially when she would work late at the bridal shop.

Since she'd left Ohio with literally nothing but the clothes on her back, her pistol was still safely tucked away in her bedroom closet—back at her parent's house.

"Allina?" Kent's voice called from the other side of the door. "Baby, you in there?"

Scrambling off the bed, she raced to the door and pulled it open, throwing herself into Kent's arms. After a few seconds, she closed her eyes when his arms wrapped around her and squeezed.

"What's going on, baby?" he asked. "Are you okay?"

"I'm fine. I missed you."

He shot her a super sexy smirk and gave her a lingering kiss. With their mouths still joined together, she smiled.

"I missed you, too." he said, swatting her on her butt.

Hesitating, she bit her lip. "I have something to ask you."

"What is it?" He kicked his shoes off.

She searched his eyes before blurting out, "I need your gun."

He stepped back, eyes wide. "What? What the hell for? What happened, Lina?"

With trembling hands, she raked a hand through her hair. "I've been thinking about this since we left the Ice Box. I need to feel protected, Kent. I know you're here with me, but what about when you're not? He's already threatened Syd. I'd just feel safer."

His face went blank; the muscle in his jaw twitched. Stomping to the closet door, he yanked it open with such force she thought the door was going to come off its hinges. Lowering himself to the safe, he punched in a code and pulled on the handle. He lifted a small box from the inside and stood to his full height.

She followed him over to the couch and sat down next to him. He opened the box and pulled out his handgun. "Not that I think you're going to need this, but I want you to know where it is and how to use it."

Wrapping her hand around the grip of the gun she gently took it from him. Studying the pistol, she said, "I know how to use it." When their gazes locked, she couldn't hide the smirk on her face at the surprise on his. "I have a Concealed Pistol License," she explained. "My father taught me after..." She didn't finish that thought. She didn't want to bring her aunt into the conversation.

His mouth fell open.

"I learned at a very young age, thanks to Judge," she told him. "I don't have my piece here, but it makes me feel better to know where yours is." Giving him the gun back, she said," You can put it back. I just needed to know how to get to it."

He opened his mouth to speak but then clamped it closed. "You're full of surprises today. Come on." Kent showed her how to get into the safe, and let her practice punching in the code a few times. When the gun was back in the safe, and they were seated on the couch again, he held her hand in his. "For the record, I don't believe that he will do anything to Syd. He doesn't have a death wish. But it's not out of the realm of possibility for him to figure out where you are. Because of that, I want you to be able to defend yourself."

She rested her other hand on top of his. "Thank you. I hate this. I hate not knowing what he's going to do next. I don't want to be a prisoner forever."

"It's not forever." He squinted his eyes as if in deep thought. "I just think he's hoping to scare you enough to get you to run home. He's not used to this 'bout' it side of you."

She snickered, dropping her head on his arm. Kent could always make her laugh. She appreciated it most of all during times like these. He pulled her into his side and kissed the top of her head. "Thanks, Kent." She wrapped her arms around his waist. "I love you."

"Love you, too," he murmured.

"I have something to tell you, Kent," she said. It was time she told him everything. If they were really going to make a go at this, she needed to be honest. She would hate for Isaac to really know something incriminating and blow her family secret sky high. And she didn't want Kent to be blindsided. But she didn't dare look at him while she was telling him.

"What is it?" he asked.

"It's about my aunt," she began. "About her death." Reaching for his hand, she took a deep breath. "There is more to the story than I told you before."

"Just say it," he said.

"Well, everything I told you about the night she died was true, up until the moment that my mother caught her... doing what she did." Closing her eyes, she willed herself to keep going. "The truth is, my mother was enraged at what she saw. They fought. Everything happened so quickly. One minute, my mother was defending me, screaming at Aunt Laura for violating me. The next my aunt was dead. My mother killed her."

Kent tensed and jerked his head back. Using his finger to tilt her chin up, he looked at her. "What?" he asked, his eyes searching hers.

"My mom...she killed my aunt."

"Wow," he said. "What...what did you do?"

Allina struggled to continue. In a sense, she was betraying her parents by telling Kent what had happened back then. They'd all come to an agreement that no one would ever know. Now she was telling her new boyfriend?

"I threw up," she answered lamely. "I mean...I just stood there, shocked."

He frowned. "Wait a minute. Your mom never went to jail. So the courts must have deemed it self-defense."

"Not exactly," she mumbled. "My father came home and saw what had happened. He was devastated. The circumstances were awful and his sister was dead. I don't think he really even thought about it. He went into protective mode." She lowered her gaze. "He covered up our involvement, made it so everyone would think an intruder killed my aunt."

Kent nodded slowly, like her words were sinking in. "Basically, he panicked and did what he thought was best."

"Yes," she said. "And I think Isaac knows because he keeps telling me he knows things about me."

Kent took a quick breath. "That's why everything surrounding the wedding and Isaac has brought all those memories of your aunt to the surface. I had a feeling you were holding something back from me. That's it. You've been carrying this guilt all these years."

Choking back a sob, she slumped forward and ran her hands over her face. "When Isaac said that, my mind instantly took me back there. I can't let it get out, Kent. My parents would be destroyed. My father's reputation, ruined. He's a judge, an officer of the court. Isaac said he would ruin my father's reputation. And my mother...she could go to prison. I could, too. If he knows..."

Allina didn't want to think of the ramifications. It was bad—all bad.

He held her against him. "Baby, don't. What are the odds that Isaac would find out about something that happened that long ago?"

"But what if he does know?" Isaac's family had many connections. She'd never asked her father how he'd pulled it off, covered up the murder. What if Judge had help, had trusted someone he thought would keep his secret? What if that person betrayed him? Judge seemed so sure that Isaac would never know, but what else could Isaac have on her family that would destroy them?

"If he does, then we'll deal with it. I promise you. No matter what he does, I have your back."

She leaned into him, grateful that he'd reacted the way he

had. She'd entrusted him with not only hers, but her parents' livelihood. As scary as it was, she felt a sense of peace because she'd finally unburdened herself of the secret that had haunted her for so many years. And it felt good to know she wasn't alone, that she had someone who loved her in spite of it all.

Allina was staring at the ceiling after midnight, though. Punching her pillow, she rolled over to her side away from Kent. He'd fallen asleep hours ago, but she was still wide awake. Kicking the covers off, she growled. She'd expected to rest after being so open with Kent earlier, but sleep evaded her. It was no wonder, though. There was still so much going on. Isaac had threatened her before. What would prevent him from trying to carry out his promise to hurt her? For all she knew, he was biding his time, waiting for the perfect opportunity to hit her where it would hurt.

"Shit," she heard Kent say before he slid off the bed and padded into the bathroom.

A few minutes later, she heard his feet shuffling across the plush carpet. Then she felt the bed dip as he lowered himself down onto the mattress. She wanted to throw herself into his arms, beg him to take her until morning—anything to stop her from thinking about her situation for at least a couple hours.

She felt him against her back, the skin on her legs tingling as he swept his palm up her leg, lifting up her thin nightgown as he traveled. When his hand slipped around to cup her she moaned.

"You want me to help you go to sleep?" he murmured against her ear.

"Yes," she breathed, trying not to sound so desperate.

He kissed her jawline and down her neck. Tilting her head toward him, he brushed his lips against hers—again and again. Deepening the kiss, he sucked her tongue until she groaned. She shifted until she was lying flat on her back and reached out for him, but he gripped her wrists with his hands and pinned them above her head.

Using his knee, he pushed her thighs apart. Still gripping her wrists with one of his hands, he feathered the fingers of the other one down her body, stopping to tease her nipples before pausing at her panties.

Allina couldn't breathe; she squirmed against the mattress as the ache in her belly intensified with each caress. His hot tongue mated with hers, drawing a whimper of pleasure from her throat. He pushed her underwear down and slipped a finger into her heat, hooking it upward. Her orgasm came swift and hard. She quaked as it rolled through her.

She expected him to keep going, to climb on top of her and take her, but when he removed his finger and let her go, she frowned and glanced at him out of the corner of her eye. He was staring down at her, a soft and seductive smile on his face.

"Kent?" she croaked.

He kissed her again and rolled over on his back, pulling her on top of him. Instinctively, she straddled his waist and sat astride his lap. He sat up, too, rubbing his hands up her spine.

"You ready?" he asked softly. "Ride it like you want it," he commanded softly.

Allina's mouth fell open. He'd never talked to her like that. Most of the time he whispered sweet declarations of how much he cared for her and how he loved her. To hear him be so...blunt, though, made her heart pound wildly in her chest and the hair on her arms and neck rise. She liked it—no, she loved it. *Has he been holding back with me?*

"Uh, I don't..." She didn't want to say she'd never done

this before, because he was well aware of her lack of experience. But his erection, hard against her, was making it impossible to concentrate on anything else.

"It's okay," he said.

Allina lowered herself on top of him, and she closed her eyes as he filled her. Letting her head fall back, she enjoyed the shiver that shot up her spine as he pulsed inside of her.

"Oh God," she groaned, framing his face with her hands and pulling him in to kiss. She swept her tongue along his bottom lip, grinning against his mouth when she heard a low moan escape.

He planted both hands on her hips, guiding her slowly at first as he grinded into her. Their movements were natural, like they were meant to be this way with each other. She rocked her hips back and forth, enjoying his quick intakes of breath as the pace increased. She felt like a boss. With every thrust, every kiss, she was set free.

Their lovemaking was different this time, more urgent. Like they both needed it to survive. His hand wrapped around the back of her neck as he gently bit down on her lip. Aroused to the point of frustration, she raked her fingernails over his back. Kent had taken up residence in her soul. All five of her senses were infused with him.

His hands seemed to be everywhere: splayed on her back, running down her sides, sweeping over her shoulders, and cupping her breasts. When her orgasm ripped through her, she cried out as she shook against him. She vaguely heard him growl out her name because everything seemed to go still, silent as the shockwaves rippled through her.

When her surroundings came into focus again, she collapsed against him, hugging him to her like he was her lifeline.

He fell back against the mattress with her in his arms. His heart pounded against her chest.

After a few minutes, she peered up at him. His mouth twitched into a sexy half-smile and a burst of heat filled her stomach. *God, I love you.*

"I love you, too," he murmured, kissing her brow.

She hadn't realized she'd spoken out loud, but she didn't care. She was content and she'd shout it to the whole world if she had to. Her eyes drifted closed. The heaviness in her chest had disappeared and she took a breath, savoring the moment.

* * *

Kent's alarm blared and his eyes popped open. Allina was still lying on top of him, and he was still inside her. It had been hours since she'd made him come so long and hard that he thought he'd heard the "Hallelujah Chorus" ringing in his ears.

The woman he loved, the woman on top of him, had shocked him with her energy. Her desire to be with him, to learn from him, touched his heart.

He never wanted her to feel afraid or like she'd have to defend herself with a gun. But he was glad that she wasn't cowering in fear anymore. She needed to be aware, ready for anything. He made a mental note to talk to Morgan. He would feel better if he was able to find out more about Isaac and what he was capable of. That way they could keep an eye on the situation. He didn't see why Isaac would risk his cushy life and freedom by coming here, but he also didn't want to take any chances. If Allina got hurt, he'd have to kill that man.

Tickling her back, he whispered. As much as he wanted to wake her up and do it again, he had an early meeting that he couldn't miss. "Allina, baby. Wake up." She wiggled her ass and he muttered a curse. "You . . . you have to get up."

"I'm tired," she whined, nuzzling her face against his chest.

"I know. You can go back to sleep. I just need you to roll over."

She sat up straight, her eyes still closed. Beams of sunlight streamed in through his blinds, shining on her glowing skin.

He tried to fight his body's response but, considering her position and her beauty, he knew it was a futile attempt.

When she realized where she was and what she was sitting on, her eyes bulged out of her head and her gaze dropped down. Her mouth fell open and she swallowed visibly.

She shifted. He moaned. His pulse raced when her eyes locked on his again.

Fuck it.

He flipped her over on her back, chuckling at her yelp of surprise.

"What are you doing?" she asked, a wide grin on her face. "I thought you had an early meeting."

He winked at her. "I have some time."

About an hour later, Kent stood before his full-length mirror, buttoning his shirt. He was late. Again. *It's for a good reason.*

He glanced back at Allina, who was watching him silently. "I don't plan on being at work all day. Remember, I have a big meeting and you won't be able to reach me for a while," he reminded her.

"Okay. I'll probably try and get some work done on a wedding Cali wants me to help with."

"Do you remember how to get into the safe?" he asked.

"Yes." She scooted out of the bed and grabbed her nightgown off the floor. Slipping it on, she followed him to the living room.

Gripping her shoulders, he squeezed. "I'll call you when I can."

"Okay," she said with a quick nod.

"And if you need anything and you can't reach me, call Morgan or Red."

"Yep, I got it."

"And make sure you—"

Allina pulled him to her, cutting him off with a kiss. He gripped her hips, tugging her closer to him.

Reluctantly, he broke the kiss, pressing his forehead against hers. "I just want you safe," he told her.

"I know. And I promise I'll take care of myself," she assured him.

Right. Her reassurance didn't stop him from feeling nervous. He rubbed the back of his neck and gave her another kiss. "I have to go."

"Bye, babe," she said, waving at him. "I'll be fine."

Turning, he walked out the door, locking it behind him. *She better be.*

CHAPTER TWENTY-SEVEN

Allina yawned and stretched as she woke up. Rolling over, she smiled. Kent was scribbling in his sketch pad. "You're up," she said. "What time did you get in last night?"

It had been a few days since Isaac had been released from jail. Her father had been keeping her in the loop about his whereabouts, but she was still on edge. Kent had worked late at the Ice Box. She'd tried to wait up for him, but fell asleep watching Lifetime.

"About midnight," he answered, setting his book down on the nightstand and smoothing a hand up her stomach. He ran the pad of his thumb over her nipple. "I was hoping you'd wait up for me," he murmured.

"I was trying to, but..." Her words died there when he leaned down and ran his tongue over her lips before he slid it into her waiting mouth.

Every single kiss left her breathless, craving more. Her nerves tingled as his hands moved over her body, as he plied her with his expert fingers.

She smoothed a hand down his chest until her fingers brushed the waist band of his boxer briefs. Slipping her hand underneath the thin fabric, she wrapped around him and stroked him up and down until he let out a low groan.

He lifted her shirt up and off as she pushed his underwear down. Raising her hips to help him, she watched him tug off her panties and toss them behind him. Rolling on top of her, he rested between her thighs. "I love you," he murmured against her lips.

Smiling, she whispered, "Show me."

His lips met hers again in a hungry kiss as he entered her. When she opened her eyes, he kissed her nose and withdrew only to push into her again. She locked her ankles behind him. They settled into a slow rhythm at first, taking their time with each other. Rocking her hips against his, she marveled at the friction they created and the synchronicity of their movement. Making love to him was unlike anything she'd ever imagined; being with him was everything.

Eventually and inevitably, though, the need for completion grew and the pace picked up. They raced to the finish, clinging to each other as they moved in sync, in a rhythm created solely for them, to a beat only they could hear. Allina needed this, she was desperate for his loving. She needed him. *Just. Like. This.*

The world melted away and the only thing that mattered was Kent, inside her, in that moment. There was no place she'd rather be, no person she'd prefer to be with.

As waves of pleasure rolled through her, she met his powerful thrusts with a fire of her own. Her eyes rolled to the back of her head and she dug her nails in his scalp as he pounded into her. When her eyes drifted open, his hooded eyes met hers. Grabbing her wrists, he pinned them over her head and pushed into her faster. Harder. She felt her body unravel and shudder beneath him, screaming his name as she exploded. His lips met hers, muffling her cry. Soon, he was right behind her, growling out her name.

They lay still for a moment, still...joined together in the

most intimate way. He captured her lips with his one more time, then rolled off of her.

"Wow," she breathed.

Picking up her hand, he brushed his lips against the inside of her wrist and chuckled. "Exactly."

Being with him got better each time. Not just the act itself, but the all-around experience. Waking up in his arms and going to sleep dreaming about his kisses.

When they weren't together, Allina kept busy working on a business plan with Cali and putting the finishing touches on Sydney's wedding gown.

"I missed you," she murmured, brushing her lips against his chin. "How's Mama?"

Kent had been spending a lot of time taking care of Mama. She'd taken sick over the weekend and Allina suspected it had more to do with Den being missing than anything else.

He shrugged and trailed his fingers down her shoulder. "She's okay. I go back and forth between wanting to find Den and wanting to beat the shit out of him for putting everybody through this."

"I'm sorry, babe," she said. "I hope he gets the help he needs."

"Let's hope so." He kissed her brow. "I talked to my boss, took next week off."

She and Kent had made plans to head to Cleveland by the end of the week. Ultimately, she was still hoping Isaac would just slither away with his tail between his legs. But she knew that was unlikely. He was stubborn and entitled, and he wouldn't give up. And she wanted to be prepared for the worst.

"I called Red today. Did he tell you?" she asked.

"I haven't talked to him today. What's up?"

Allina had contacted Red because he knew people. And it just so happened that he knew someone who worked for the Prosecutor's Office. She'd asked Red to ask his "friend" if they could send the police file on Isaac. Her father had been coming up against a brick wall trying to get it.

"Good. Hopefully, we can put this behind us very soon. What are your plans for the day?"

She rested her head on his chest. "I'm meeting with Syd at the bar."

"Okay. I have to stop by Mama's house after work. Do you need me for anything today?"

"No, I'm good. Go on to work, and I'll update you if I hear anything."

He placed a quick kiss to her lips and hopped out of the bed. After she joined him in the shower, she made him a plate of leftover fried chicken and he left for work.

* * *

After his morning meeting, Kent closed his office door and walked over to his desk. His project was almost done and he couldn't wait. Tempted as he was to give his notice and say "Deuces" to his boss, he had to be careful. He would quit soon enough. Then he could start on what he really wanted to do.

His cell phone beeped and he picked it up. The number was blocked, which made him curious as to who would be calling in the middle of the morning. He'd already spoken to Allina earlier.

Tapping the talk button, he answered. "This is Kent."

"It's me."

Kent sighed, gripping his phone. "Den? Where the hell are you? Mama's been worried sick."

He'd spent the past few days nursing Mama back to health. After a trip to the emergency room, the doctor had sent her home with a dose of antibiotics for walking pneumonia and strict instructions to rest. But his mother wasn't the resting kind. She'd been beside herself worrying about the ass on the line with him.

"I'm sorry," Den grumbled. "I had to leave that hospital. I needed to get myself together. Find my own way for once."

Kent wanted to blast Den for once again failing to consider anyone but himself. "What is that supposed to mean?"

"I left the hospital and checked myself into another one, in Traverse City."

Traverse City was about 240 miles north of Ann Arbor. Kent had never been there himself, so he didn't know much about the area—except that it was on Lake Michigan and was the Cherry Capital of the World.

"Den, if you're going to just check yourself into a hospital and not actually do the work it takes to get better, there's no point."

"That's why I'm calling you," Den said. His voice sounded hollow, flat. "I wanted to apologize for everything. Can you tell Syd that I won't bother her again?"

"Why do I have to tell her?" One of the biggest lessons his father had taught them was to take responsibility for their own actions. Den failed at that best. "You did it, you fix it."

Grumbling, Den said, "That's so easy for you to say. Your life has never been anything but easy."

"Den, fuck you," Kent snapped. "You're a selfish son of a bitch. You walk around here thinking somebody owes you something. At the end of the day, you have to be responsible for your own shit. Everything you're going through? You caused. Take your damn meds!"

"I don't know why I called you."

"Why *did* you call me?" Kent asked curiously. "Den, you checked yourself out of the hospital and disappeared. You didn't tell me, Morgan, or Mama where you were! That's some bullshit."

"I had to get out of there, man. I feel like the only way I'll get through this is to be far away from her. Looking at her baby, her happy life with my brother? That sucks."

"I'm sure it does, but whose fault is that? Let's not forget, you and Syd would be married if you hadn't cheated on her in her own bed. You need to grow the hell up. Man up, and get your shit together. Because if my mama gets sick because she's worried about your ass, I will fuck you up."

"That's what I'm trying to do, Kent," Den said in a gruff, defeated tone. "I called you because I need your help."

Kent knew it was coming. For someone who hated drama, tried his best avoid it, he always found himself smack in the middle of it. And eight times out of ten that drama was not a direct result of something he did.

But no matter how much he wanted to tell his brother to take care of his own shit, he couldn't. He didn't want his mother to take on any more stuff and he wanted Den to succeed. If his brother actually followed through, everyone's life would be better. But most of all, Den would be the man they all knew he could be.

"What do you need?" Kent said.

About an hour later, Kent walked into his mother's bedroom. Mama was sitting in the bed, propped up on a mound of pillows, watching her favorite soap opera.

"Hey, Mama," he said, kissing her forehead and climbing on the four-poster bed with her.

She patted his knee. "What brings you here in the middle

of the day? You know my story is on." She covered a cough and blew her nose. "We can't talk until it's over."

Kent chuckled. Growing up, he always knew that every afternoon between twelve-thirty and one-thirty, his mother was not to be disturbed. Although his father made a lot of money in his job, his mother worked as a part-time nurse. And her shift always started after three o'clock. Once he was old enough, he'd told her about herself. She'd cracked up with glee that he had caught on to her.

Glancing at his watch, he noted that her soap was just beginning and settled in to watch it with her. He'd been around long enough to know who Victor and Nikki were, and the stories recycled so much he could catch on quickly.

On the next commercial break, she shot him a look out of the corner of her eye. "Can you believe that man ran her off of the road? This is getting good."

Kent shrugged. "Ma, you know that chick isn't dead. I don't even know why you fall for it."

"Don't you have some work you need to do?" she argued.

"Are you seriously going to kick me out for a TV show?" he retorted. "Besides, I do have something I need to talk to you about—"

She shushed him. "Hold on. Wait until the next commercial."

Grumbling, he pulled out his phone. While cheesy music played on the TV, he checked his e-mail, sent a few texts, observed the lines in his hands, and played his next move in online Chess. *Yes.* He did a fist pump when he moved his Queen. *Checkmate, Roc.*

He set his phone on his lap and waited. Like he'd expected, a ding sounded, signaling he had a text.

The text from Morgan simply read: *That's some bullshit, man.*

Kent snickered and responded: *Next time, play to win*.

"Kent?" his mother called, cutting his gloating off. "Commercial. What did you want to talk to me about?"

He glanced at her. "It's Den. He called me."

Her tired eyes lit up. "Really? Is he okay?"

Nodding, he explained, "He checked himself into a different hospital up north. But he wanted me to tell you that he's doing well and he wants to make you proud of him again."

Mama's chin trembled and she covered her mouth with a hand. Closing her eyes, she shook her head. "I'm so glad he's okay. Can I call him?"

"Not right now," he informed her. "Maybe in a few days."

She slumped forward and wept quietly. Kent rubbed her back slowly. He'd promised Den he would help him. Watching his mother react with such relief, seeing the love for her son glistening in her eyes, he would do whatever he could to make sure Den stayed on track this time. And maybe, in the process, other relationships would be healed. Namely, Morgan and Den's brotherhood.

Kent's birthday was coming up soon. The last one had ended with Den storming out of Morgan's place after breaking a few dishes, then getting into a car accident. This year, he thought it would be a great gift to have his entire family under one roof again, celebrating. No fighting, and no drama.

Clearing his throat, he gently shook his mama. "Ma, you have to stop crying. You're killing me, here."

She chuckled and turned to him, brushing tears from her cheeks. "I'm sorry. I know how you hate that. I'm just so relieved. I've been so worried."

He smiled at the woman who'd made them all the center of her life for so many years. He wanted her to be happy. "I know. But you don't have to worry anymore. Just focus on getting better."

"Does Morgan know that Den is safe?" she asked.

He nodded. "I told him on the way here."

She laid her head on his shoulder, her television show forgotten. "Now I can rest."

"You should have been doing that anyway." He squeezed his mother's hand. He studied her hand in his and remembered so many nights when she would hold his hands while he struggled to fall asleep after a bad dream or horror movie. "It's going to be okay."

"So, tell me about Allina."

The abrupt change in subject didn't shock him. He snorted. "You don't waste any time, do you?"

Then she peered up at him, a loving smile on her face. "Well, I know that she's been staying with you. And I know she's had feelings for you in the past. How do you feel about her?"

"You're nosy," he teased.

"Hey," she said, nudging him with her shoulder. "I'm your mother. I need to know these things. Besides, I won't be around forever. I'd love to see all my sons settled with *good* women who love them and treat them well. And I need more grandbabies."

He barked out a laugh. "You're way ahead of yourself."

"Well?" she prodded. "Are you going to answer my question, son?"

"What question?" he joked. "Just kidding. I care about her." A big understatement, but he didn't want Mama to go off and start buying wedding invitations.

"You love her, don't you?"

"I have to go, Mama." He stood up. "I'll stop by after work, okay?" He gave her a hug and headed to her bedroom door. Before he walked out, though, he stopped and turned around. "I do, Mama."

She grinned widely and nodded.

"But don't start thinking about weddings and babies," he added. "Let's let Morgan and Syd have their time." Then he left.

* * *

Strolling into the Ice Box, Allina hollered for Syd. The bar was scheduled to open mid-afternoon. There were contractors in the building working on the bathrooms. She grinned at the huge bouquet of flowers sitting on the bar. She eyed the red vase and ran a finger over one of the daisies. It was full of her favorites—red roses, daisies, Peruvian lilies, and lush greenery. It even had a few mini carnations. She sniffed one of the big roses.

"Hi," Syd said, coming from the back. Her friend walked behind the bar and scribbled something in a binder. "I'm sorry. It's hectic around here this afternoon."

"No need to apologize." Allina glanced at her watch, then back at her friend. She noted the way Syd pinched her lips together as she groaned, and she wondered what was wrong with her friend. "What's up, Syd?"

Without looking at her, Syd shrugged, "Frustrated. Mama is sick, Den is gone to God knows where, and Morgan has clammed up."

"Well, I'm sure Morgan is just on edge because of everything that's happened. He'll come around."

Syd scrunched her face, then relaxed. "I know. It's just hard to concentrate today. I came in this morning and some guy was waiting in the parking lot; he asked if we opened for breakfast."

Curious, Allina asked, "What did he look like?"

"Regular. Like he'd just hopped out of bed and decided to go for breakfast. But then he started asking me questions. And you know how I am with strange men."

Allina nodded. Because of Syd's experience, she didn't take to new men well. Most of the men she allowed in her life, she'd known for years. Allina could relate to that because she was the same way, except it applied to strange men *and* women. She didn't like new people, period. She had her friends and that was that.

"Well, what kinds of questions did he ask?"

"If I was the owner, if I knew the owner. Those types of questions. For a minute, it sounded like he was a detective or someone who had a vested interest in the answers. Anyway, I thought we said we were meeting a little later?"

Allina flipped open her book, prepared to show off her masterpiece. "I was just so excited to show you what I came up with."

Syd bit down on her pencil, a deep frown on her face. "I can't wait to see it," she mumbled. "Give me a second."

Her attention drawn to the bouquet of flowers, she leaned in, taking another whiff. Allina loved the smell of fresh flowers. Humming, she said, "Beautiful flowers. Is Morgan buttering you up for something?"

If he was, Allina had half a mind to call Morgan and tell him he needed to step his game up. There were no Gerbera daisies, which were Syd's favorite. In fact, Syd didn't care for carnations either. She said they reminded her of high school Valentine's Day celebrations.

Syd looked up. "Hm? Oh, those aren't mine. They came this morning—for you."

Frowning, Allina asked, "For me? Did you see who they came from?"

Syd twisted her mouth, obviously focusing on the paper in front of her. "Um, no. I just set them up here because I knew you were coming."

Allina twisted the vase, searching for a hint of the sender. "No card." There was nothing, not even a sticker on the vase with the name of the florist.

"It was probably Kent," Syd mumbled. "Did he know you were coming here?"

"No. I just told him this morning." Maybe Syd was right, though. Kent had probably wanted to surprise her.

"Call him," Syd ordered. "I'll be right back." Her friend disappeared in the back.

Dialing Kent, she waited for him to pick up. When the low timbre of his voice carried to her ear, she smiled. The sound of his smooth voice made her stomach flutter in excitement. "Hey, babe," she greeted him.

"Hey," he said, his voice muffled.

"Are you busy?" she asked.

"A little. Is everything okay?"

"Well, I won't keep you long. I just wanted to thank you for the flowers."

"What flowers?" he asked.

She froze, feeling rooted to her spot. If Kent hadn't sent the flowers, then who... "Stop playing, Kent," she said, her voice shaky. "You know you got me this beautiful bouquet. It has all of my favorite flowers in it."

"I'm not playing. I didn't buy you flowers, baby," he insisted. "But I'm interested to know who bought my girl flowers. Did you check the card?"

Blinking rapidly, she picked up some papers lying on the counter. She scanned the immediate area, checking under the stools and on the floor. Allina hoped the card had simply fallen out of the vase. When she didn't see it, she talked back into the receiver. "I have to go. I'll call you back, okay?"

She ended the call. There was only one other possibility.

"What's wrong?" Syd asked, approaching her. "Your face lost all its color. Did you call Kent? What did he say?"

Allina jumped at the sound of Syd's voice. Her gaze flitted around the room. "Nothing," she said. "He was saying, uh, he told me, um … He didn't buy the flowers," she stammered, grabbing her phone. "Has anyone strange been in here?" she asked Syd. "Other than that man you saw."

Syd walked around the bar to stand in front of her. Her friend gripped her shoulders. "Allina, what's going on?"

Holding her stomach, she leaned against a chair. Just as she started dialing her father, his picture flashed across her phone. He was calling her. Allina's stomach rolled. She held up one finger, signaling to Syd to hold on a minute. "Daddy?" she said, answering the call.

Her father's voice came through the receiver, "Hello? Allina?"

"Yes, what's going on?"

"Isaac's gone."

Allina clutched the phone, tried to not panic. Taking a deep breath, she asked, "What do you mean? You lost him?"

"My guy … he lost track of him. I think it was some time during the night."

"Oh my God," Allina whispered, shuddering at the thought of Isaac being somewhere out there watching her.

Her gaze flashed to the flowers. Breathing became difficult, and she slumped forward, leaning on a bar stool. Syd rushed to her side, sweeping her arm over her back.

"Where are you?" Judge asked.

"I'm at the bar with Syd."

"Where's Kent?"

She told her father Kent was at work, in meetings all afternoon. "What if he...?"

"I'm coming up there now," her father said. "I'm leaving now. If I can't catch a flight, I'll drive."

Before Allina could protest, tell her father that she would be fine, he ended the call. Turning to Syd, she explained the situation. Her attention turned to the flowers again. "If Kent didn't buy me those flowers, there's one other person that could've: Isaac."

Syd's eyes widened. "That would mean—"

"He must know where I am. He must have figured it out. I mean, it's not like I've been hiding. I let my guard down when I thought he was in jail. He could have had someone here all along watching me. Now that Judge doesn't have eyes on him... what if he comes here?"

Syd grabbed the vase and walked it to the back.

"What are you doing?" Allina scurried after her. "Where are you taking those?"

"I'm throwing this shit in the trash," Syd said. She kicked the kitchen door open and tossed the flower-filled vase in the huge bin by the back door. "I'm calling Morgan."

"No," Allina blurted out. "Please, don't. He'll tell Kent and I want to be the one to tell him."

CHAPTER TWENTY-EIGHT

Allina raced back to the condo and hurried up to the front door, fumbling around in her purse for her key. Rolling her eyes, she muttered a curse to herself for not connecting the house key to the car keys. An envelope fell out from between the doors when she opened the screen. Bending down, she picked it up. It was for her. Tucking it under her arm, she shook her purse. When she found the keys, she pulled them out and rushed into the house, closing the door and locking the dead bolt.

Allina paced back and forth, stopping at the window every few seconds. Peering outside, she wondered if he was out there, watching. If he was, then he knew about Kent. He probably knew about her and Kent, too.

Earlier, Syd had convinced her that Isaac might have sent the flowers to the Ice Box as a scare tactic. He knew Syd worked there, after all. There really was no good reason to panic yet. So she'd left Syd at work, promising she was going straight home and that she would tell Kent everything.

Allina glanced around the empty condo. Kent probably wouldn't be home for another couple of hours. She dropped her purse on the table next to the door, pushed her hat off, and headed to check her e-mail. Red had said he would forward her any information he received. Along the way, she made sure all the windows were closed and every door was locked.

Her phone rang as she neared the office door. Without looking at the caller id, she answered. "Hello?"

"Did you get the flowers?" Isaac growled.

She froze with her hand hovering over the office doorknob. Allina gripped her phone. Her first reaction, fear, was quickly replaced with anger. With her chin held high, she said, "I figured they were from you. I threw them out."

"Don't make me hurt you, Allina," he threatened. "I just want you to come home with me so we can work this out."

"How did you get this number?"

"Don't worry about that," he said.

Frowning, she yelled, "What is wrong with you, Isaac? By now, something should have clicked in your head that I don't want to make anything work with you. I left you for a reason. What do you want?" she growled.

"Did you get my letter?" he asked.

Remembering the small envelope in the door, she hurried back to the front table where she'd dropped it, picked it up, and ripped it open. Gasping, she pulled out the pictures. They were grainy, but definitely of her—walking into the Ice Box with Kent the other night, the same night she found out he'd been released.

There was another one, and this one made her legs weak. It was a picture of her mother, walking with some friends. Her heartbeat thrashed in her ears.

"Are you there?" he said. "You must really think I'm stupid. I realized your father had someone following me, so I decided to bide my time. I figured you'd go back to Michigan, so I had a friend start at the Ice Box. It didn't take long to figure out where you were staying, once he spotted you. You weren't very discreet."

"Stop playing games with me!" she screamed. "If you hurt my mother, I swear to God—"

"Who is he, Allina?" he questioned. "Who is the man you're with?"

With trembling fingers, she twisted the door handle and burst into the office, immediately turning the computer on. "None of your business," she fired back. She went to the side window, peeked out, and closed the blinds.

"I have to admit, I wasn't going to let you know quite so soon that I knew where you were. But when I saw that picture of you with that man, I knew I had to step up my plan."

"So why send flowers to the Ice Box? Huh? If you knew where I was, why not just send them here?"

"I just wanted to make it very clear that I can get to you, your friends, and your mother any time I want. Did you really think you were done with me?" he said.

She double-clicked on the Internet icon. "What do you want, Isaac?"

"You," he sneered. "I'm coming for you."

A loud beep sounded in her ear and she jerked the phone away from her and looked at the screen. He'd hung up on her. She called Kent. No answer. She tried her father. Voicemail. Frantic, she dialed her mother. Busy signal. Frustrated, she chucked the phone across the room.

He killed my mother.

She clenched her jaw as a sharp pain shot through her chest. Carla's words taunted her now. What if he had done something to her mother? Wouldn't her father have called her by now? *Unless he did something to him, too.* Eyeing the door, she jumped up and ran to it, slamming it shut and locking it. *On second thought*... He could be right outside, ready to barge in and do something. She wasn't ready.

Sucking in a deep breath, she unlocked the door and ran toward the front of the house. The shrill sound of her phone ringing made her whip around and go back into the office. She picked it up, relieved when she saw it was her father.

"Daddy, thank God."

"Allina?" Her father's shaky voice came over the receiver. "There's been an accident."

No.

"But everything is fine. Your mother was on her way to meet me when someone sideswiped her car and ran her off the road."

Oh God, no. Exhaling deeply, her lower lip trembled and her eyes flooded with tears.

"She's fine, though. Not hurt, just shaken up."

"I'm coming there right now."

"No," her father ordered. "Stay put. I brought her to the hospital for a quick checkup just to be sure. Soon as we're out of here, we're coming to you."

"Okay. Okay," she muttered to herself, as well as her father. "I'll stay here."

For all she knew, Isaac could still be in Ohio. He did say he hired someone to watch her and torment her. After all, he was out on bail. If the authorities knew he'd stepped over the state line, he'd be picked up in a heartbeat.

Shaking her mind free, she opened the closet and dropped down to her knees. She punched in the code, opened the safe, and pulled out the tiny box that held Kent's small gun. Looking inside the big safe, she noted there was another pistol, a bigger one. She considered taking it, but decided against it.

"Allina? Baby, are you still there?" her father said.

Nodding as if he could see her, she said, "I'm here."

"Your mother wants to speak to you."

A beat later, she heard her mother's voice. "Hi, baby."

"Mom?"

"I'm okay, babe. Soon as we get out of here, we'll head up there. Just...don't worry. It's going to be okay. Isaac doesn't know where you are, so you'll be fine."

Allina didn't have the heart to tell her parents that Isaac knew exactly where she was. It would only worry them more.

"I love you, Mom," she said, brushing her face against her sleeve to wipe the tears that had fallen. "Please, be safe."

"Aw, I love you, too. You be careful, sweetie." She heard her mother telling someone in the background that she needed a towel. "Owen...wait...okay. Allina, baby, I have to go. The doctor's here. We'll call you when we leave here."

Once Allina ended the call, she pushed the heavy safe door closed, made sure it was secure, and stood up. She opened the box and pulled out the gun and the ammunition. Allina made quick work of loading it. Turning it in her hand, she prayed she wouldn't have to use it.

Massaging her temples, she walked to the bathroom and set the gun on the countertop. She turned on the faucet, let the water get cold, and splashed it on her face a few times. Peering up at her reflection, she cringed at her pale skin, droopy eyes, and overall crazy-looking appearance.

She needed to talk to Kent. But when she grabbed her phone to dial him, another call came through.

She clicked on the answer button, but didn't say anything.

"Allina?"

Isaac's gruff voice made her skin crawl, but she remained silent.

"I'm going to give you one more chance to come to me willingly. I don't want to have to hurt your mother."

She was so tired of him saying the same thing over and over again. Same threat, different day. Only he didn't know that she had already talked to her parents. They were safe, and would be there soon.

"Didn't you try to hurt her already?" she asked. "Didn't you try to have someone run her off the road earlier?"

"I don't know what you're talking about," he told her. But Allina knew better. She might not be able to prove it, but she was sure he had something to do with her mother's accident. It wasn't a coincidence.

"You don't, huh? What makes you think I'm going to come to you willingly?"

"I'm staying at the Westin Hotel at the airport, room 434." When she didn't respond, he continued, "Don't bring that black bastard you've been hanging out with. Come alone. Just me and you. We have something to settle."

Like hell. Allina held her breath. The only sound in the room was the pounding of her heartbeat in her ears.

"Oh," he said. "No games. I do know what really happened to your aunt. And what your father, the judge, did to cover it up."

CHAPTER TWENTY-NINE

$\mathcal{K}$ent entered his condo. He hadn't talked to Allina since earlier. There was something about her tone that didn't sit right with him. She'd asked him if he'd sent her flowers and then practically hung up on him. He'd had to go into another meeting so he hadn't had a chance to call her back. Once it was over, though, he'd called her but she didn't answer. So he'd packed up and left the office, telling his boss he was going to finish his work from home.

He'd gone back to his mother's house after work to check on her and make sure she ate something. She'd talked his ear off about Syd's wedding and Sunday dinner. He hated to, but he had to sneak out while she was in the bathroom because he was anxious to get home and check on Allina.

On Kent's way home, Morgan called. Allina had called his brother to let him know that Isaac had found her. He'd hung up on his brother and called Allina. Again she didn't pick up.

Now he called out, "Allina?"

Pausing, he listened for her. The condo was quiet: no television, no radio, no off-key singing, no clinking of pans in the kitchen...no Allina.

His gaze traveled over the room, and his eye caught on the black box sitting on the table. Stalking over to the table, he yanked the box up, letting it fall open. The box of bullets fell out but the gun was gone.

He tried Allina's phone one more time, but he was pretty sure she wasn't going to answer.

Hanging up, after leaving her another message, he dialed Morgan. While he waited for his brother to pick up he walked through the house, checking all of the rooms.

"What's up, Kent?" Morgan grumbled.

"Allina's gone," Kent said. The bedroom was empty and his bed had been stripped down to the mattress. "And so is my gun."

He heard Morgan let out a string of curses. "Have you checked the house? See any signs of a fight?"

"I'm walking through," he told Morgan. When he got to the laundry room, he opened the lid on the washer and saw the bedding inside. "Did she say anything else to you?"

"No. Just that he'd found her and she needed to reach you. I'm leaving work right now," Morgan said. "I'll go to the bar, check on Syd. If you need me, just say the word." They decided that if something went down, it would be best if Morgan was with Syd, since Isaac had issued a threat against her.

"I'll call you if I hear from her," Kent said before he ended the call.

Kent pushed the office door open. The computer was on. He stepped over to the desk and peered at the monitor. Next to the keyboard was an envelope. After he shut the computer down, he picked up the envelope.

A couple of pictures fell out onto the desk, of him and Allina at the Ice Box, and of Allina's mother. That fuckin' asshole had someone following her, which meant he knew where Kent lived. The longer he stared at Allina's face in the pictures, the cloudier his vision got. He could only imagine the terror Allina had felt when she saw the pictures.

There was a second envelope on top of the printer. He picked it up and pulled out the paperwork. *Son of a bitch.* Inside was documentation highlighting Isaac's past, from payoffs to complaints of sexual assaults to court orders denying personal protection orders. There was also an obituary for a woman named Tina Pollard.

He called his brother again and told him about the pictures and the envelope. Morgan then told him that he'd already called Red to give him an update.

A gamut of emotions spread through Kent. On one hand, he was terrified. Allina was gone, and he didn't know if she'd left on her own or if someone had taken her. If she'd left on her own, with his gun, then she'd felt she needed it. If she didn't leave on her own, then whoever took her had his pistol. Either way, the situation was bad.

On the other side of his fear was anger. He wanted nothing more than for her to be safe. And he wanted to beat the brakes off Isaac. He wouldn't be satisfied until he made that man bleed, damn the consequences. Because he knew who Allina was with. In his heart, he knew she was with that goddamn minister.

His phone rang and he recognized Red's number. "What's up, Red?" he said.

"Are you still at home?" Red asked.

"For now." Kent went back into the living room.

"Any idea where she is?"

"No," Kent grumbled. "But I need you to do something for me. I have an envelope full of shit on Isaac. When I see you, I need you to take a look. We're probably going to need your skill set."

"That must be the file I sent *her* earlier," Red said. Kent heard Red tell someone he was out of there. "I'm on my way," Red told him. "Be there in twenty minutes."

Kent picked up his baseball cap from the floor and set it on the table. A piece of paper was sitting on the table, with Allina's handwriting on it. "I think I know where she is," he said to Red.

"Where?" Red asked. "You want me to meet you somewhere else?"

"Meet me at the Westin Hotel at the airport, room 434." Kent walked over to the coffee table and snatched up his keys. "I'm on my way there now." Kent balled up the piece of paper in his hand and tossed it in a small trashcan on his way out the door.

Kent sped to the hotel, grateful that he lived five minutes from the expressway. From there, he was able to make it to the airport in record time, ten minutes to be exact.

* * *

Allina walked into the nearly empty hotel lobby. She searched the area for the elevators. When she spotted them, she dashed over to them and punched the up button.

Stepping into the elevator, she pressed the 4 button and leaned against the wall as it ascended. Clutching the huge white envelope in one hand and cupping the bottom of her purse with the other, she peeked out of the elevator. She'd made two copies of the file Red sent just to make sure Kent saw it when he got home. She looked right, then left, and walked out, going down the hallway toward room 434.

Dragging her feet, she approached the door. She'd practically left a trail of bread crumbs for Kent to find. The only problem was she wasn't sure when he'd actually see it. Although she was hesitant, she'd tried to call him and it went straight to voicemail. Thinking back to what he'd told her earlier, she hoped he would get off work early and head straight home.

When she finally reached the room, she opened her purse and pulled out her cell phone. She stuffed it into the back pocket of her jeans. Lifting her hand, she knocked.

Isaac answered the door dressed in a pair of dress slacks and a button-down shirt. Narrowing his eyes at her, he stepped aside and motioned for her to come in.

She sidestepped him, careful not to brush against him as she passed. She didn't want any part of her to touch him, not even her purse. Her hair was pulled back into a tight bun so that he couldn't pull it, and she was wearing gym shoes in case she had to run.

Whirling around, she glared at Isaac. "What do you want?"

"I've come to take you home. We have a wedding to plan."

Frowning, she threw her arms up in the air. "Are you nuts? There is no way I'm going to marry you."

"If you don't want to go down for killing your aunt and your father to go to jail for hiding it, you will."

Allina retreated, blown away at his accusation. Only he didn't have it right. He thought *she* killed her aunt. Still, he could do serious damage. Her family would be implicated if the prosecutor had good cause to reopen the case. She couldn't let that happen.

"Now, I bought you a plane ticket," he said. "We're going back in a matter of hours."

"I'm not going anywhere with you," she said, her chin held high.

"Do you really think you have a choice?" he asked, cocking a brow at her.

When she'd first met Isaac she'd thought he was so handsome, but the man standing before her now was ugly, inside and out. She scowled at him. "If you think you have the up-per hand, think again," she snapped. "You're delusional. I didn't kill my aunt. An intruder did that. You're a freakin' fugitive, however. You're going to jail. And your father will not be able to get you out of it this time."

"They don't have anything on me," he said, waving a dismissive hand at her.

"See this," she held up the envelope. "Proof that you've been crazy as hell since you were a teenager. Looks like they're building a pretty decent case against you. You'll be lucky if you ever see the light of day again, especially since you killed Carla Little's mother."

Isaac blanched at her, his eyes growing wide. "What did you just say?"

"You heard me," she said. In reality, Allina had read the file. She'd watched enough *Law and Order* to know the evidence against Isaac was shaky at best. All circumstantial. She needed to goad him into a confession. "You want to talk about what you think you know about me. I told you, I know a lot about you, too." She flung the envelope at him, reached into her back pocket, and grabbed her phone. Pushing the button, she shoved it back in there while he looked through the file. "You're going down, and then I'll be free."

"Where did you get this?" he asked.

"Don't you worry about that," she tossed back at him. It was something he seemed to have grown fond of saying to her when she asked him a question. "You're done. By the time all your dirty deeds come out, you'll be lucky if you find any supporters. And I'm sure the bishop will wash his hands of you as well."

The sting of the slap that came next brought tears to her eyes and she staggered back from the force of it. She glared at him, her hand on her cheek. She grimaced in pain as the fire spread through one side of her face.

The ire in his eyes gave her pause. She eyed the door, looked around the room for a blunt object, then darted for the door but he grabbed her around the waist and hauled her back. She stumbled backward but managed to remain standing. When she fumbled to open her purse he grabbed her by her neck, pulling her to him.

Allina clawed at him as she struggled to breathe. "Let me go," she gasped.

"See what you made me do?" he mumbled in her ear. "You're not so big and bad now, huh?" His breath on her skin made her cringe. He yanked her purse away and tossed it across the room. It landed next to the bed with a muffled thud.

He shoved her hard and she fell to the floor and tried to crawl to her purse, but he grabbed her leg and dragged her across the room. Kicking and screaming, she tried her best to connect with his chin, his gut, his stuff... something. She hoped someone would at least hear her frantic cries.

With one move, he picked her up and threw her on the bed. Climbing on top of her, he growled, "Do you let that fool get on top of you like this?" he asked. "You let him touch you?"

Allina looked in his eyes. There was nothing there but contempt. She bucked under him, "Get off of me!" she shouted.

His hand brushed against her breast and she stiffened. "I'm not going to just give you up. After all the time I put into you? Let some other man rub his hands all over your body? I don't think so."

Cupping his hand over her mouth, he murmured against her cheek, "You're so beautiful. Your skin and your mouth drive me crazy. So crazy that I can't stand the idea of him touching you, making love to you. You're mine. Not his."

She felt a tear stream down the side her face and into her ear. But she refused to buckle for him. She would fight until she couldn't fight anymore. Struggling under him, she glanced at the lamp on the nightstand.

"See, I figure you're just a little hardheaded," he said, squeezing her neck. "It's a habit I can break."

He pushed against her, and she felt his erection against her belly. Eyes wide, she bucked even harder.

"It's better if you just give in," he said. "Isn't that what your little boyfriend told you? I told Carla that as well. She didn't listen, because of her stupid mother. That's why I had to get rid of the woman."

Trying another approach, she stopped moving. He licked her face and she whimpered. Her tears flowed freely. Steeling herself, she waited until he removed his hand from her mouth and tried to kiss her.

"Get. Off. Of. Me." She bit down on his lip and when he jerked back, she kneed him in the groin. He keeled aside in pain, rolling off the bed and landing on top of her purse.

She jumped out of bed and bolted for the door, but he managed to grab her ankle and yank, sending her crashing to the floor.

Grunting when her shoulder landed hard, she kicked at him with as much force as she could. She finally got leverage and her heel connected with his neck. He let go of her and she scrambled to her feet.

Her purse was still too far away so she made a run for the door. When she swung it open, Kent was standing there.

Allina trembled with relief. It was all she could do to not rush into his arms and let him carry her away. But Isaac's voice stopped her from rejoicing when he said, "Get away from her before I shoot her."

CHAPTER THIRTY

Kent's relief at seeing Allina was short lived. Isaac had his gun pointed at them.

Allina turned around and gasped. "No," she whispered.

Kent stepped in front of her and raised his hands up at his sides. He didn't have time to think of what he'd just heard. When he'd heard her screams, he'd sprinted down the hallway.

Even though he wasn't looking at her at that moment, he couldn't get the image of her red cheek and scared eyes out of his head. He couldn't think about that right now though. He had to deal with the preacher.

"Hold on," he told Isaac, trying to keep his voice even. "You really don't want to fire that gun in this hotel."

"Shut up," Isaac barked. "I told you to get away from her."

"Look, man," Kent warned. "You might as well forget it. I'm not letting you near her. Now put the gun down."

"Who are you?" Isaac demanded.

With his eyes still trained on the gun, he answered, "A friend of Allina's."

Isaac snorted. "A friend? I'm not an idiot. I know that you're more than a *friend* to Allina. She is staying with you, right?"

"Does it matter?" Kent struggled to keep his temper in check. Every time he thought about moving forward, he saw the glint from the gun in Isaac's hands. He couldn't risk it going off and hitting Allina, and he didn't want to get shot himself.

"Just answer the question!" Isaac roared.

"I did answer your question," Kent said. "I'm a friend." He felt Allina's nails digging into his biceps.

"What kind of friend?" Isaac insisted.

"A good one." Kent knew he was being coy, but the man in front of him seemed unhinged. Telling Isaac what he was to Allina could likely set the man off. "Aren't you a minister? Your father is Bishop Hunter?"

"What do you know about it?" Isaac asked.

"I know more than you think," Kent replied. "I'm sure your father wouldn't want a scandal. Maybe you should put the gun away and leave here."

Kent's eyes remained on Isaac. When he noticed his arms lowering, he lunged for him. He barreled into him, knocking him into the desk. The gun slipped from Isaac's hand and slid under the bed.

Allina screamed his name, distracting him, and Isaac got him in the jaw. A weak hit, but that shit still hurt. Growling, Kent lifted the stupid man up and slammed him back down into the desk. He heard the wood splintering under Isaac's weight, and when he fell to the carpet, Kent delivered a swift kick to his abdomen—or two. He rushed toward Allina.

"Are you okay?" he asked.

"Kent!" Allina shouted. "The gun."

He looked down and saw Isaac crawling toward the gun. But before he could get to it, Isaac grabbed it and pointed it at him. He drew back, holding his hands out in front of him. His eyes were focused on the barrel of the gun and nothing else. His gaze swept around the room, and he'd jumped right toward the bed when the gun fired.

"No," Allina yelled. "Kent!"

He rolled to his back, but Isaac had already managed to stand up. The gun in Isaac's hand was pointed directly at Kent. Out of the corner of his eye he saw Allina spring forward and swing the heavy bedside lamp, hitting Isaac in the head. The man fell to the ground like a dead tree.

Allina stared at her ex-fiancé, her mouth open. "Oh my God!" she gasped.

Kent's gaze fell to Isaac, who was knocked out cold. Blood seeped onto the carpet from where Allina had hit him, but it wasn't an overwhelming amount.

"Is he dead?" she cried. "Did I kill him?"

Jumping off the bed, he reached the preacher and felt for a pulse. Shaking his head he said, "No."

Before he could tell her to call an ambulance and the police, Red rushed in. His friend stopped in his tracks when he saw Isaac lying in the middle of the floor.

"Holy shit," Red stopped and stared down at Isaac. "Damn. Did you kill him?"

Glaring at Red, Kent said, "No. He's not dead."

"The police are on the way," Red explained. "The front desk had already alerted them because someone called them about the commotion."

Kent stood up and pulled Allina into his arms. She pushed against him and stepped back.

"Wait," she said, grabbing the phone out of her back pocket. "I recorded everything. He said he killed Carla's mother."

Kent couldn't help the pride that swelled in him at Allina's tenacity. He gently took the phone from her hand and gave it to Red.

Turning into him, Allina buried her head in his chest and sobbed.

A few minutes later, the cops were all over the room. Red was off to the side answering questions because Allina was still crying. Rocking her slowly, Kent murmured words of comfort in her ear until an older police officer approached them. The cop asked him his name and wanted an account of what had happened in the room.

Allina looked up then, her eyes tired and dull. "Officer, I can tell you what happened."

Kent was proud of Allina as she gathered herself enough to explain everything to the officer. While she was talking, the paramedics rushed in and tended to Isaac. The minister had regained consciousness, but still needed medical attention.

Allina paused in the middle of her story when they wheeled a handcuffed Isaac out of the room. She tugged at her ear and let out a ragged breath before she continued.

Kent hated that she'd gone through something so similar to her aunt's death. He imagined her instinct to protect him was a lot like the way her mother had felt when she'd walked in on Allina's aunt molesting her.

He couldn't say that he wouldn't do the same thing if put in that position. In fact, he was very sure he would have shot Isaac himself, given the chance.

The officer finished up his questions and gave them his card. Kent directed the officer back over to Red. When he and Allina were as alone as they could be in the middle of a crime scene, he brushed a hair away from her eye. "Are you okay?"

It was a silly question, but he asked anyway.

"I guess. I just want to go home."

"Then we're going home," he told her, helping her to her feet. "I'm sure Red can handle everything."

They walked slowly toward the door. Red nodded at them and blocked their exit. "I'm going to push for attempted murder, stalking…everything I can try for. I've already contacted a colleague of mine at the Prosecutor's office to give him the heads-up."

It probably wasn't ethical, maybe it was even a little shady, but Kent appreciated having friends in high places. "Good. On top of everything else, maybe he'll die in prison."

The thought occurred to him that Isaac might still pose a credible threat. Although he hadn't had a chance to talk to Allina about why she'd come to the hotel, he suspected it had to do with Isaac somehow knowing about her parents' involvement in her aunt's death.

If Isaac did know, then Kent was confident the minister would use anything and everything in his power to stick it to Allina and stay out of jail himself. Kent intended to make sure Isaac would never hurt Allina again.

The car ride home was quiet. Allina sat in the passenger seat, staring out at the passing scenery. He'd managed to convince her to leave the rental car she'd been driving at the hotel. They'd pick it up in the morning. Kent wanted to ask her what she was thinking about but he figured he'd give her time to process everything that had happened.

When they arrived at the house, his condo was lit up. Scanning the lot, he noticed Morgan's truck. Shifting the car into park, he turned to Allina. "We have company, Allina."

She nodded and wiped her eyes. "Okay."

"Before we go in, do you want to take a minute?"

Her gaze, glistening with unshed tears, locked on his then. Taken aback by the emotion shining in her brown orbs, he reached out to her, but his hand stayed suspended. He didn't know what to say, what to do at that point to make her feel better, other than being there with her, letting her know that he loved her no matter what.

"I wasn't going to go," she said. "But he'd sent those flowers, left those pictures, had my mother run off the road."

Confused, he asked, "What?"

"Yes. My dad called and told me. She's fine, thank God." She stared ahead, a dazed look on her face.

"My first instinct was to lock myself in the room and wait for you to get home," she continued, "but he called and demanded I meet him. I figured I needed to confront him and get him to confess to the murder, and I'd record him. But things went left when he slapped me."

Fury rolled off Kent in huge waves. He could tell she'd been hit, but hearing her actually say it made his blood simmer.

"Kent, he hurt me," she whispered softly.

His mind raced. When he'd barged into the hotel room earlier, he'd only had a quick glance at her before having to focus all of his attention on Isaac and the gun. From the file he'd skimmed, it seemed as if Isaac had done more than harass some of the women in his church. Kent had seen the effects of sexual assault firsthand when Syd was brutally raped in college.

"I mean, for a minute, I thought he was going to…" She shook her head and balled her hands into fists before releasing them again. "He was on top of me, he kissed me, taunted me. He would have. But I fought him off."

"Don't think about it," he told her, stroking the top of her hand with his thumb. "He didn't. That's really all that matters."

"It was bad," she continued. "Thinking that he could possibly rape me. But when he pointed that gun at you? I— something kicked in and I didn't think. I had to stop him."

"You did the right thing," he assured her gently, taking her hand in his.

"I can't lose you," she said.

Caressing her face with his hands, he swept his thumbs under her eyes and pulled her into a kiss. She tugged at his shirt with one hand while her other cupped the back of his head.

"You won't lose me," he promised. "You believe me, don't you?"

She nodded. "I believe you."

* * *

Allina leaned into Kent as they entered the condo. Syd greeted them at the door. It had been a long, crazy day but Allina was happy to see her friend.

They'd sat silently in the car for twenty more minutes. He didn't ask her to talk anymore and she didn't. He just held her hand. That was what she needed most.

"Girlfriend," Syd said, hugging her tightly.

"I'm glad you're here," Allina told her friend. Morgan was there too, holding the baby, and she smiled at her godchild. The brothers greeted each other in their usual way, with a distinct handshake that she'd seen them use only with each other. She'd always meant to ask what that was about.

"Do you need anything?" Syd asked, rubbing a hand up and down Allina's back.

"I could use some help in the bedroom," she told her friend.

Syd nodded and stepped to the side, allowing Allina to lead the way. Once they were in the bedroom, Allina sat down on the bed.

"I noticed the comforter and sheets were in the washing machine," Syd said, climbing up next to her. "I threw them in the dryer. They should be done shortly."

Allina wanted to confide in Syd about her experience with Isaac, but frankly, she was exhausted from talking about it with Kent. "Thanks, Syd. I really appreciate all of your help."

"Anytime," Syd said. "Red called. He's on his way."

"Can I ask you a question?" Allina said.

"Go ahead."

"How much trauma do you think one person can handle?" Allina asked.

"I wish I knew," her friend said. "Seems like there is always something lurking around the corner. Are you ready to talk about what happened tonight?"

Allina shook her head. "I don't want to talk about it again. I'm just tired."

Even though she'd said she didn't want to discuss the events of the day, she knew she'd have to talk about them eventually. Just not that night.

"Well, you need to rest," Syd said. "Morgan and I are going to take the baby home. She's cranky and I'm exhausted, too. We just wanted to be here when you got home, make sure you didn't need anything."

"Thank you, Syd. I..." Shaking the image of Isaac holding that gun on Kent out of her mind, she forced herself to focus on her friend. "I love you, Syd."

"Aw, I love you, too."

They embraced again before Syd walked out of the room. Allina lay back on the mattress, pulling a small blanket over her. Ten minutes later, Kent appeared in the doorway. She smiled at him. "Everybody gone?"

Nodding, he joined her on the bed. "Yep, even Red."

"I'm so tired," she told him, yawning.

"Well, let's get you in the shower first. Then I'll put you to bed."

The hot water beating down on her body was just what Allina needed. She turned and let it massage her back. It was hard to believe how things had changed in the blink of an eye. One minute, she was deliriously happy, ready to conquer the world. The next, she'd been fighting for her life.

The terror she'd felt in that hotel room was akin to the fear in the pit of her stomach the first night her aunt had snuck into her bedroom, and the night her mother had killed her. Closing her eyes, Allina wondered if she'd ever be able to get the image of either event out of her mind.

Kent had been great. He'd listened when she just wanted to talk about it, get it out. He'd let her cry, scream, vent. She loved him for it. She heard the sound of the door closing and called out, "Kent?"

"Yeah, babe."

Even the sound of his voice filled her with undeniable peace in the midst of her storm. Before she could tell him she'd be done in a minute, the shower door opened and he stepped in, immediately pulling her into his arms.

They stood like that for a minute, the water raining down on them. When she pulled away, she peered up at him. "Thank you," she cried, tears streaming down her face. "Thank you so much."

"Don't thank me," he rasped out, his voice thick. "Now let me take care of you."

He took a washcloth, poured her soap into it, and swept it down her neck, her shoulders, and across her chest. Turning her around, he rubbed it up and down her back. Kneeling down, he moved the cloth up and down her legs. Then he shampooed her hair. The gesture was so heartfelt, so sincere,

Allina wanted to weep. Kent hadn't come into the shower to arouse her or make her tremble with need. His soft touch, the tender way he washed her, was his way of loving her.

Once he was done, he washed himself quickly and turned off the water. He grabbed a towel, dried her off, and wrapped it around her before he found another towel for himself, then picked her up and carried her back into the bedroom.

The bed had been made with clean sheets and a different comforter. He'd set out one of his T-shirts for her. Unwrapping the towel, he tugged the shirt over her head. He pulled the comforter back and smoothed his hand over the sheet and fluffed the pillows.

"I can put you some tea on," he said, handing her the hair tie she often slept in.

Clutching the thin silk band in her hands, she smiled up at him. "You're spoiling me."

He smiled at her. "For the rest of your life," he said.

She felt a soft pang in her heart at his words. She didn't want to look into it, or assume he meant more than what he'd said.

"Kent?" she asked, grabbing his wrist when he started toward the door.

He glanced back over his shoulder, "What do you need, baby?"

There was so much she wanted to say. The only problem was knowing where to start. So she figured she'd start with the nonemotional stuff. "I want to call my parents. I haven't heard from them. They're probably on their way here."

"I talked to your father," he said. "Told him what happened. Your mother is fine, but the doctors want to keep her overnight because she had some dizziness."

"I have to talk to them."

"I know. He's waiting for your call."

He handed her his phone and she dialed her father. The thickness in her father's voice when they talked, made Allina tear up as well. They chatted for a few minutes, then she talked to her mother. Her parents assured her that the doctors were keeping her only as a precaution. Allina felt relief wash over her.

When she hung up, she turned to Kent. "Thank God, she's okay. I don't know what I would have done if she wasn't."

"I'm glad she is, too."

Biting down on her bottom lip, she asked, "Kent?"

"Yes?" He brushed his thumb over her chin.

Allina told Kent to make sure all the doors and windows were locked.

There was still the matter of her bringing the gun with her to the hotel. The police had confiscated it, but Red told Kent he'd do his best to get it back to him by the end of next week. Red was confident the prosecutor wouldn't try to charge Allina with anything since she did have a valid license to carry.

"Oh," she said. "And Kent?"

He raised his eyebrows. "Yes, baby."

"I love you."

Grinning, he placed a kiss on her lips. "Love you, too."

CHAPTER THIRTY-ONE

Four months later

$\mathcal{K}$ent ran a finger down the curve of Allina's nose and over her lips. He smiled when she stirred. He'd spent the better part of an hour just watching her sleep, the way her hair fanned out against the white pillow, the soft rise and fall of her chest, the cute way she moaned. He let his gaze travel over her again, groaning at the sight of her. The moonlight streaming through the window, the way the thin white sheet barely covered her body... made him want to take her again right then. But their last bout of lovemaking had knocked her out.

It had been a hard four months since the hotel room incident, as they called it. Things had started to settle down recently, though—except for that awkward moment when Judge found out Allina had every intention of staying with Kent. He figured it had a lot to do with the realization that they were also sleeping together. While he'd managed to charm Sharon Parker quickly, the Judge was harder to win over. The older man was skeptical at first, but once Kent sat down and had a talk with him about his intentions, the older man softened his stance.

Isaac was arrested while in the hospital. Red made sure his friend at the Wayne County Prosecutor's Office leveled every charge possible at the sadistic minister. And that was just with the Michigan court. Isaac still had to face trial in Ohio for murder. Of course, Isaac pled not guilty.

Even though Allina had denied it, the fool had still tried to blackmail her and her parents by threatening to reveal to anyone who'd listen his suspicions about who really killed Allina's aunt. Allina had lost sleep over it, and Kent had tried to comfort her. Somehow, after Allina's father paid a visit to Isaac, that problem just went away. Kent had his suspicions on what a conversation between the two men might have been like, but he kept his thoughts to himself and assumed there were some serious threats passed from her father to the minister.

The not-so-surprising influx of women who'd been victims of the crazy preacher contributed to the sensationalism of the trial. Every day for a week straight, a new woman appeared and came out with tales of the many horrible things she'd been subjected to at the hands of Isaac while attending Christian Dreams Church. All in all, eight women came forward. Lawsuits were filed and parishioners had begun to leave the church in droves.

The Hunter family washed their hands of their son amid the scandal and publicly spoke out against him to save face. During the discovery proceedings, attorneys for Bishop Hunter presented a signed affidavit from the sickly man stating that he'd had no idea his son was capable of such heinous acts, and had never participated himself in any payoff of any alleged victim. The outburst in the courtroom that followed was one for the books. Isaac accused his father of not only paying women off, but of being the aggressor himself.

The next day, Isaac's high-priced attorney submitted a

motion to the court to withdraw from the case. Isaac was forced to deal with a public defender. Kent suspected Isaac's financial backing had disappeared when he tried to implicate his father in the wrongdoings.

Although most of the women were only at the trial for solidarity because the statute of limitations had passed on their own claims, Kent had delighted at the trepidation on Isaac's face when he saw the women sitting there. It was especially satisfying when Carla Little appeared in the courtroom, shocking Isaac so much he fell out of his chair.

Unfortunately, they didn't get to see Isaac found guilty in a court of law. The coward ingested a large of amount of rubbing alcohol along with other cleaning supplies and died of an overdose.

"What are you thinking about?" Allina asked, her husky voice interrupting his thoughts

Smoothing a hand down over her stomach and hips, Kent lowered his mouth to her forehead, then her nose, then her mouth, kissing her until she trembled underneath him.

"You're so damn beautiful," he said before he touched his lips to her neck and her shoulder. "Beautiful," he mumbled against her skin. He made his way down to her hardened nipple and suckled it into his mouth, enjoying her short, desperate intakes of air.

He couldn't get enough of her, and he'd shown her that most of the night. Everything about her seemed tailor-made for him. It had been days since they'd been able to spend some time together. Between her new business with Cali, her parents being in town, the court proceedings, and his job, they'd barely been able to talk.

Kent hadn't given his two-week notice like Allina wanted, but he did register his new graphic design company with the state. It was definitely a leap of faith, but he was almost ready to make the change. He'd already signed contracts with four companies in the area, two of them referrals from Red and Cali.

Her hands trailed up his back, looping loosely around his neck. "I can't believe we're here," she breathed. "In Vegas."

Kent had surprised Allina with tickets to Vegas to get away for a while. A smile tugged at his lips as he nipped at her earlobe and kissed the spot on her neck right below her ear.

"Aren't you glad we came?" he asked, rolling on top of her and kissing her in the way that drove her mad. Grasping one of her thighs, he hitched it up and slipped inside her.

She gasped against his mouth and dragged her nails across his back.

They made love at a leisurely pace, eyes locked on each other. When her eyes drifted closed, he knew it was time to pick up the pace. As they raced toward completion, he marveled at the way she matched him thrust for thrust. It was a rhythm they'd perfected in the past few months. He felt the tremors pass through her body before he heard her. Seconds later, they both found their release together.

Once their labored breathing calmed, he pulled back. "You didn't answer my question."

She frowned and stared at him through her lashes. "What question?"

"I asked if you were glad we came?"

"Of course," she said simply. "I needed to get away before the holidays and Syd's wedding."

Morgan and Syd were marrying during the Christmas season because Kent's darling sister was a Christmas nut. Allina had been working nonstop on her friend's dress and running around with Cali to finalize details.

"I love my friend, but she is a bridezilla," Allina said,

giggling. The sounds of laughter coming from her plump mouth made him feel warm inside. *God, I love her.* "I told her to stop changing her mind every day about flowers, music, and up-lighting."

He laughed. "Yeah, Cali cornered me in the bar last night and begged me to talk to her because Morgan and Red had refused to say anything."

Allina dropped her head on Kent's chest as she shook with laughter. "Cali is a mess."

Vegas without the crew wouldn't have been the same, and it worked out that all of their friends were able to come with them. The girls had spent the first day shopping while he and the fellas gambled.

"Have you talked to Den yet?" Allina asked.

Kent's relationship with Den had improved over the past months. The brothers had been talking more, which made Mama feel better. Things were still tense between Morgan and Den, but Kent had a feeling it wouldn't be long before the two would be able to mend fences. Syd really was better off with Morgan and Den knew it, too. He'd all but admitted it during one of their visits.

"I have," he told her. "He'll be home before Christmas." After Den's stay in the hospital he'd chosen to move away, figuring it was best to have a fresh start all around. Kent supported his decision.

"Good. I know Mama will be happy to see him."

He picked up her hand, twisted the ring that was now on her finger. He brushed his lips against her palm. "I love you, Mrs. Smith."

Grinning widely, she said, "I love you too, Mr. Smith." Her brown eyes were gleaming as she smiled up at him.

"Any regrets?" he asked.

"No," she said, kissing him softly. "Not a one."

* * *

"I want to make an honest woman out of you."

Allina recalled the moment Kent had said those words to her. It wasn't an elaborate event. He didn't take her for a romantic dinner at a fancy restaurant or to a show or even to a baseball game to propose on the big screen. His proposal had been simple and understated.

They were at home, playing Uno. He was kicking her butt as usual, but instead of doing his usual fist pumps and gloating he'd pulled out the ring box and said, "You're *my* Uno."

It was the corniest, sweetest thing anyone could have ever said to her. She wasn't sure if she'd shared with him or not, but in college, she and her friends used to always talk about finding their *one*. And he'd told her she was his *one*.

In pure Allina fashion, though, she'd fallen back in her chair. This time she ended up with a concussion. He'd rushed her to the emergency room. In front of the doctor, a nurse, and Syd, he told her he wanted to make an honest woman out of her. The nurse and Syd cried, and Allina couldn't even speak to say yes.

She couldn't help but smile at the sight of her husband of three hours. "I can't believe I'm your wife," she breathed, staring at the beautiful diamond ring and matching band on her finger.

"I can," he told her, sweeping his lips across her brow. "Your father was going to kill me if I didn't marry you."

She laughed. "So, you married me to spare your own life?"

"Yes." His eyes locked on hers. "But not because of your dad. Life without you is not possible. So, in a sense, I am saving my own life by making you my wife."

"You just made a rhyme?" she asked, chuckling. "You are so corny now."

With a wide grin, he said, "I know. What have you done to me, woman? Got me over here waxing poetic, saying crazy shit. Next thing you know, I'll be baking cakes and making crafts with you."

She laughed again, and this time he joined her. "Saying yes was the best thing I could have ever done," she whispered, tears filling her eyes.

"If I recall, you didn't *say* yes. You just nodded rapidly."

She smacked his chest playfully. "Be quiet. I couldn't find the words."

"You couldn't find the *yes*?"

Giggling, she pinched him. "Stop. You know what I mean."

He planted a lingering kiss on her mouth. "I know, baby."

In the months following "the hotel incident," Allina had thrown herself into work. She'd made herself focus on anything but Isaac and the pending trial. Allina kept in touch with Carla and was happy when the other woman informed her that she was moving back to Ohio to stay with family.

After Isaac committed suicide, Allina had cried for days. Not because he was dead, but because it was over. There would be no rehashing everything that had happened and her aunt's death would still be considered a random act of violence. She didn't have to see him or hear his voice ever again.

"Babe?" Her husband's voice snapped her out of her thoughts.

"Hi," she said, smiling at him.

"Hey," he murmured. "You okay?"

"I am. Today was exactly what I wanted."

Frowning, he asked," Are you sure?"

They'd gotten into an argument when Allina told him she didn't want a wedding. She'd already been there, done that. She'd suggested Vegas originally, but Kent had nixed that idea because he thought it was crazy.

But Allina's business was picking up and she didn't have time to plan her own wedding. And she didn't want to. Stubbornly, she'd refused to talk about a wedding anywhere until after the New Year—until he'd surprised her with the tickets to Vegas.

Their wedding had been exactly what she'd envisioned when she'd suggested it—just them, their friends, his mama, and her parents, under the moonlight. They'd chosen to write their own vows. They both promised to support each other always, to love each other through everything. Kent added a promise to eat her fried chicken in sickness and in health.

Syd and Cali stood up for her, while Morgan and Red stood up for him. Corrine was the flower girl and Brynn was the ring bearer. Cali found a cute little wagon that they used to wheel her growing and busy godchild down the aisle in. That was all Allina needed. It was quick and painless.

"I'm so sure," she replied, checking out the band on his left hand. It was dark and masculine, just like him. "I just loved that everybody who mattered to me was able to make it."

He nuzzled her neck. "As long as you're happy," he mumbled against her skin, "I'm happy."

Allina lowered her gaze when his hand brushed over her stomach. "When do you want to tell them?"

His thumb swept over her lower abdomen. "At breakfast," he said. "I guess your father probably knows we've been sleeping together since we live together, huh?"

She gaped at him. "Really? You're worried about the Judge?"

Shaking his head, he said, "No. I was just saying…"

Kent was joking. That much she knew. He had developed a wonderful relationship with both of her parents and she was grateful for it. She held his hand against her stomach. "Next year, this time, we'll have a little Kent running around."

The positive pregnancy test had almost sent Kent to the hospital with chest pains. But he quickly recovered and immediately hired a Realtor to find them a house. In less than seven months, she would be a mother. She was excited and terrified at the same time. But she wouldn't trade the feeling for anything.

"I hope so," he said. "Because any daughter of mine is getting locked in the attic or something until she's thirty-five."

"You're crazy," she said, giggling. After a few minutes of comfortable silence, she said, "Kent?"

"Yeah, babe."

"Thank you." She had no idea where she'd be right now if she hadn't ended up on his doorstep all those months ago.

He looked down at her, the love he felt for her shining in his eyes. "For what?"

"Just say you're welcome."

"Okay. You're welcome."

She leaned in and kissed him. "I love you."

"I love you more."

When her fiancé's latest dirty deed is too big to ignore, Sydney Williams calls off their engagement, walks out on Den... and into the arms of his brother, Morgan. Having secretly loved Sydney for years, Morgan is determined to finally make her his—but Den won't give her up without a fight.

Please see the next page for an excerpt from

The Forbidden Man

CHAPTER ONE

Don't move."

Sydney Williams glanced at her watch. "Allina, I have to go. I'm meeting Den in thirty minutes." In a few short months, Syd was finally going to marry her longtime love, Caden Smith, affectionately known as Den.

Sydney flinched when she received a playful whack on the behind.

"I told you to be still. I'm almost finished. There. You can turn around."

Sydney sucked in a deep breath then turned and looked at her reflection. The white silk, floor-length gown fit her perfectly. Smoothing a hand over her hip, she eyed the tiny crystals adorning the plunging neckline. It was simple, understated—exactly how she wanted it.

"What do you think?" Allina said, biting her thumbnail as she stepped back. "I think it looks much better with your hair up."

"It's beautiful. Den's going to love it." Sydney ignored the look her friend gave her and the quick rolling of her eyes. Sighing, she took one last glance at herself, turned around, and raised her arms. Allina unzipped her and she rushed into the fitting room. "I appreciate this, girlfriend. You're truly gifted," she told her from behind the curtain.

Tossing the gown over the door for her friend, she dressed. When she was finished, she slipped into her sandals and pulled the curtain open. Allina was zipping up the garment bag.

"I'm ready to invest when you're ready to go out on your own," Sydney said, rummaging through her purse. "It's time."

"It'll be ready for you Friday after five o'clock," Allina said, changing the subject. She tucked a stray braid that had fallen out into her neat bun.

Before Sydney could go into the countless reasons it was better for Allina to venture out and open her own boutique, her cell phone vibrated. Muttering a curse, she shook her bag and felt around for the cell phone. Sighing heavily, she grabbed a hold of it and pulled it out. After a quick glance at the anonymous number, she was tempted to ignore the call—except she was planning a wedding and it could be someone calling to confirm something.

Grumbling a curse, she answered, "This is Sydney."

"I wasn't sure you'd answer." The nasal-toned voice of her fiancé's ex–booty call, Laney, immediately put Sydney in a bad mood.

"Can't make the right choice all the time. Why the hell are you calling me?" Syd snapped.

"I just thought you'd want to know—"

"And how did you get my number?" She dropped her purse on the chair.

Curiosity prevented her from hanging up on the other woman. It was no secret she couldn't stand Laney, but she couldn't help but wonder why she was calling her. "Look, I'm doing you a favor," Laney said. "The least you can do is treat me with some respect."

Syd's interest turned to dread at Laney's snide tone. The

last "favor" from Laney had almost destroyed her relationship with Den. It took months to get over the fact that he'd cheated on her while she was away at graduate school. She gripped her phone. "Laney, what the hell do you want?"

Allina, who'd just returned from the back, stopped in her tracks at the mention of that name.

Placing a hand over the receiver, Syd mouthed to her friend, "I'm fine. Go ahead and finish what you were doing."

Allina didn't look convinced, but walked away anyway, glancing back as she headed toward the counter.

"I'll just cut to the chase," Laney sneered.

"Please do." Something told Syd to have a seat, but she remained on her feet. Although the other woman couldn't see her, she didn't want to give even the slightest impression that she was affected by anything Laney had to say. "I don't have all day."

"If you think you're going to be happy with Den, you're fooling yourself."

"What do you know about it?" Sydney asked with a snicker.

"Everything. I know that Den has been lying to you for months. He told you that you could trust him. That he'd never hurt you again. That he wanted to start fresh, confess everything . . . the random woman at a bar story . . . then he realized that he couldn't live without you . . . couldn't wait to make you his wife."

Syd felt sick to her stomach as Lancy droned on. The fact that this woman knew all of her business wasn't the worst part. It was what she feared was coming next that was giving her fits.

"Sydney, did you hear me?" Laney called through the receiver.

She swallowed, then cleared her throat. "Just say what

you need to say and stop wasting my time with this shit, Laney."

"And I'll bet you believed him, too." Laney laughed, and the sound made Syd's skin crawl. "The thing is, he may be ready to make you his wife, but he surely can't keep that promise of never hurting you again, because *I* was the woman at the bar and it definitely wasn't a random hookup. We've been seeing each other for months now—at your house, in your bed."

Closing her eyes, Syd barely flinched when the phone landed on her toes, then the carpeted floor, with a thump.

Allina rushed over to her. "What's going on?"

"Oh God," Syd cried. "This can't be happening."

She vaguely felt Allina nudging her, heard her begging her to say something, anything. It seemed like everything was happening in slow motion. Over the last eight months, she'd spent thousands on the details, the plans, the invitations...Oh God, her family was coming. They'd purchased tickets and paid for hotel rooms. What would they think of her? How would she face them?

"Sydney!" Allina yelled, shaking her out of her thoughts. "What's wrong?"

Syd wouldn't bother calling Den to confirm Laney's story. In her heart, she knew the other woman was telling the truth. She was sure it had happened just the way Laney described. And it wasn't because Laney was such a truth teller. It was only because Den had lied to her more times than she cared to admit, more times than she ever told anyone. He'd promised her he was a changed man, but she knew change didn't come easily to Den. She wanted to drive to his job and embarrass him in front of his employees, demand that he explain himself, order him to do something—anything— to make this seem less real, less devastating. Would there be

anything he could say to justify this? Wasn't it her fault for
believing the lies, taking him back, and choosing to never
hold him accountable every single time he'd hurt her? Yet,
even as her heart seemed to split open and the pain crept into
her bones, she couldn't muster up any blame for the man she
loved. No, there was no one to blame but herself.

Blinking, Sydney zeroed in on her phone lying on the
floor and picked it up. She didn't bother checking to see if
Laney was still on the line. She turned it off and tossed it
into her purse.

What the hell am I going to do now?

"Do me a favor?" she asked Allina, grabbing her keys and
heading toward the door. "Call Calisa. Tell her to cancel...
everything."

"Wait," Allina called to her before she opened the door.
"Don't just leave like this. Something happened. You're upset and crying. You can't drive like this." She walked over
and took Sydney's purse from her hand. "Come on. I'm closing up. Keep me company?"

Sydney wiped her eyes angrily then plopped down on an
empty chair. "Allina, I know you have an event this evening.
You don't have to stay with me."

"I have a few hours." Allina sat down next to her and
squeezed her hand. "I'm here for whatever you need, okay?"

"I need a drink." She pulled some tissue from a dispenser
and blew her nose.

"I have some wine in the back," Allina offered. "We keep
it for bridal parties."

"Bring it out and let me wallow."

"Syd, what happened?" her friend asked again, concern
in her brown eyes. She ran her hand over Syd's back.

"He cheated on me," Syd said on a sigh. "Again. With her.
Again."

Allina shook her head, disgust playing on her features. "That fucking . . . piece of shit."

Syd knew that her friend didn't care for Den. It'd been painfully obvious for months. Hell, it'd been years since she'd heard Allina curse, and she'd said "fucking" and "shit" in the same sentence. But Lina wasn't the type to voice her opinion about someone else's relationship. Never had been. She'd always supported Sydney's decisions even if she didn't agree with them.

"You don't have to say it, Lina. I already know you hate him."

Allina sighed heavily, but continued to focus on the end-of-the-night receipts.

The silence from her friend did nothing but heighten her anxiety, and she realized she wanted—no, needed—to hear her thoughts. Exasperated, she told her, "Fine. Say it."

"What's there to say?" Allina shrugged. "He's an ass, but you already knew that."

Ouch. Allina always did have a way of making things very plain. So plain it irked the hell out of her.

"He hurt you again," Allina continued. "I can't say I'm surprised, but I do think it's better that you found out now instead of after you married him."

Syd grabbed hold of Allina's wrist. "Please don't say anything, not even to Kent," Syd begged.

Syd had tried to play matchmaker for Allina and Den's brother Kent for years. But the stubborn duo had refused to see the potential in each other that she had. Instead of dating, they were firmly in the "we're just good friends" camp.

"I never do." Allina smiled slightly and patted her hand.

Releasing her hold, Syd stood up and pulled on her shirt. "Where the hell is that wine?"

Allina disappeared into the back of the store and emerged

a few minutes later with a bottle of Red Moscato, Syd's favorite. Pouring it into a cup, she held it out to her.

Instead of taking the cup, Syd grabbed the bottle and put it to her lips.

"Allina?" Syd belched and muttered, "Excuse me."

"Yeah?"

"What am I going to do?" Syd felt like she was going to choke on her tears. It was hard to even think straight. She had no clue where to start. "How am I going to tell everyone? My dad, Red…" Gulping down more of the wine, she covered her mouth when another burp escaped. "Oh God, Red is going to kill him."

Syd knew her twin brother, Jared, or Red as they called him, wasn't Den's biggest fan. He'd always felt that Den didn't appreciate her and took her for granted. Every chance he got, he told her that Den didn't deserve her loyalty.

"Red is going to be fine, Syd. He's an attorney. He knows how to keep his cool."

"It's really my fault," she confessed. "I shouldn't have taken him back again. I knew he wasn't ready. When he proposed, I knew it wasn't right. He did it during my lunch hour, for Christ's sake. Who does that?"

The quick, unromantic proposal had been the talk for weeks within their small circle of friends. Even Den's brothers thought the approach was rather trifling and had told him so countless times. Syd, on the other hand, made excuses for Den: it was romantic to her, they hadn't been able to schedule a dinner, or it was always her dream to get proposed to in an ordinary way. That last excuse was kind of true. She did envision a proposal during a random weeknight dinner or during their favorite television show. Sitting in the drive-thru at Mickey D's? Yeah, somehow that didn't make the cut, but she was happy and couldn't wait to become Den's wife.

Allina scratched her head and peered up at the ceiling.

"Allina, I know you have something to say. You always hold back. It's the reason you never told Kent that you have feelings for him that go beyond just friends, or why you don't have your own shop. You're a kick-ass seamstress, with a good business sense. But you never speak your mind, say how you really feel about stuff."

"Maybe it's not my place," Allina said, her pale cheeks now a dark shade of crimson. "And you promised never to say anything out loud about Kent and my true feelings for him."

Syd smiled. "I'm sorry. I did promise, didn't I? Kent would be lucky to have your tall ass on his arm. You're so beautiful. Just wish you'd realize it." When Allina didn't respond, Syd finished off the bottle and set it on a table nearby. Her friend was modest as this day from hell was long, so it was no use ever paying her a compliment. "You have another one of these?" she asked after a few minutes of silence.

Allina glanced at her before heading to the back. Syd couldn't be sure, but she swore she saw it on Allina's face... pity. Her friend thought she was pitiful. Maybe she was.

When Allina returned, Syd reached out to grab the bottle. But Allina held it back. "Syd, maybe you should slow down. You still have to drive."

"I'll slow down when you tell me what you're really thinking."

Sighing heavily, Allina sat down. "Okay. I just think you deserve better. Den is okay—charming, funny, and attentive when he wants to be. I don't think any of us doubts that he loves you. But love and respect are two different things and one or the other isn't enough to sustain a relationship on its own. He's hurt you so much... Sometimes it's better to let it go than to keep trying when a relationship isn't working."

"I love him." Her words sounded hollow even to Syd's own ears. Allina hadn't told her anything that she hadn't already thought herself over the past few months.

"I know you do, sweetie. But Den has issues. You said yourself that sometimes you feel like you can't even leave him alone because you're so worried he won't take his meds, or he won't make it without you. In the meantime, it's like you're willing to accept everything he throws at you."

Den's bipolar disorder had wreaked havoc in the lives of those closest to him, especially her and his other brother, Morgan. He had a habit of not taking his meds when he was busy. A part of him always wanted to test the limits, see if he could do without the Lithium.

"You don't understand," Syd told her. "He needs me. And I owe him."

"You don't, Syd." Tears gathered in Allina's eyes and she turned away to wipe them. "I just wish you'd realize that and maybe take this as an opportunity to start fresh."

"Start where?" Syd dropped her gaze to the floor. "I've been with him so long I don't even remember life without him."

"But you've also sacrificed so much for him and the relationship. You've made excuses for his behavior, blamed everything on his disease. What if he's just being himself? Ask yourself why he cheated on you with her in the first place."

Syd had asked herself that question so many times. "I wasn't here. I moved out of the state. How could I expect him to be faithful when I wasn't sure I was coming back?" It was the blanket answer she'd repeated to herself so often she believed it.

"You moved to go to graduate school," Allina said, obviously not accepting the bland excuse. "You went to help your sick father."

"Still, we didn't make any promises when I left," she insisted, even as she realized her defense of Den was more out of habit. The fact was, Den hadn't proven himself worthy of her loyalty in a long time. Just like her brother said.

"Well, you're back now." Allina picked up a safety pin off the floor and tossed a used tissue into a small waste bin. "It's been years and it seems that you're in this perpetual state of cleaning up behind him."

There it was again. The cold, hard truth. And she couldn't deny it any longer.

"He made a promise when he proposed to you, Syd," Allina continued. "He broke it. You have to decide if you're going to keep accepting that, because you know he's not going to take responsibility for his actions. It's always someone else's fault."

Allina was right. She had given Den more than enough chances and she was tired. The relationship was beyond repair at this point. And even if it wasn't, she wasn't sure she'd want to fix it. As much as she loved him, she had to face the fact that it just wasn't going to work, and he wasn't healthy for her. The wedding was off.

* * *

Morgan tapped on the door to the small storefront, then pressed the bell. He'd rushed over when he'd received Allina's call begging him to come and pick Syd up. She'd spouted something about heartbreak, wine, and weddings, so he dropped everything and raced there. As he waited, he wondered what he'd find when the door opened.

Allina opened the door. "I'm so glad you came."

"What's going on?" he asked, ducking under the low-hanging bell and stepping into the shop. He heard the radio blasting Destiny's Child and what sounded like...singing, loud and off-key.

"I tried to take the bottle away from her, but she's in a mood," Allina told him. "I would stay but I have an event. I tried to call Red, but he's not answering. Calisa didn't pick up either. I even tried Kent. So you're it."

"Where the hell is Den?" Morgan muttered, shaking his head and running a hand over his face. He cringed when Syd hit an awkward high note. "You still haven't told me what's going on, Allina."

She sighed. "That's...not an option. I'm sorry if I interrupted your evening, but I didn't know who else to call. I'd tell you what happened, but I promised I wouldn't."

He muttered a curse under his breath. "Where is she?"

"Back there," she answered, pointing to one of the private bridal rooms in the rear of the store.

Morgan followed her toward the music. Although Allina hadn't technically spilled the beans, he'd already guessed that his brother was the reason Syd was belting out through-with-love songs at the top of her lungs. Obviously, Syd was in no condition to drive. And he wanted to throttle his older brother for undoubtedly breaking her heart. Again.

Rounding the corner, he stopped at the sight of Syd sprawled out on the couch singing Dru Hill's "In My Bed."

"Oh, shit," Morgan grumbled.

"Tell me about it," Allina mumbled under her breath. She stood over Syd and nudged her. "Hey. Morgan's here."

Syd's eyes widened. "Morgan? What is he...?" She pointed at him accusingly. "What are *you* doing here?"

"Syd," he said softly, approaching her. "What are you doing?"

"Singing," she said simply. "And drinking."

He bent down to Syd's level. Pushing a few stray curls out

of her face, he took a good look at her, noting that her hazel eyes were bloodshot and her mocha skin had a pink flush to it. Sure signs that she was drunk. "Are you going to tell me what happened?"

"I don't know." Syd shrugged. "Can I trust you?"

He chuckled, amused by the question. "You know you can."

"I don't know." She traced his cheek with her fingers. "You're his brother. Do you know you have dimples just like him?"

He squeezed her hand and gently removed it from his face. "You can trust me."

"But you don't look like him," she said, her voice low and hoarse. "You have nice facial hair. And you're much taller and thinner. Between me and you," she whispered, "I think Den is going to get fat in a couple of years. He eats too much pizza."

"Tell me what happened," he said, trying to get her back on track.

"He cheated on me with that whore, Laney. Again," she slurred, picking at the mound of curls on the top of her head, pulled into what she often referred to as a bitchy bun. "He fucked me over. I mean, the first time I was away. I gave him that one because I lived in another state at the time. And even though she ended up pregnant...I still forgave his ass." She sobbed and dropped her empty paper cup on the floor.

Morgan remembered the drama surrounding Den's first affair with Laney. The woman had gotten pregnant and couldn't wait to tell the world. Den had refused to 'fess up even though they all told him to tell Syd before she found out from someone else, namely Laney. Eventually, Syd found out the truth when Laney followed her through the mall, taunting her with the sordid details of their ongoing relationship. Shortly after, though, Laney suffered a miscarriage.

Syd squeezed his arm, jarring him from his thoughts. "I forgave him again a week ago when he confessed that he'd slept with some random woman he met in a bar," she cried, her tears falling unchecked down her cheeks. "He said it happened months ago, before he proposed, when we were having that rough patch. But it was really last week. And then I find out it's *her*. He played me. And I let him. Again. She called me, ya know," she babbled on. "She wanted me to know that he fucked her in my bed. He couldn't even take her somewhere else."

"Son of..." Allina groaned. "You didn't tell me that earlier."

"I didn't want to say it out loud," Syd admitted quietly. "Allina already thinks I'm stupid for taking him back in the first place. You probably pity me, too."

"I don't, Syd," Allina said, her voice cracking. She dropped to her knees next to Morgan. "I'm here for you."

"You do," Syd told Allina. "You probably think I'm going to take him back again."

Morgan looked at Allina, who stared down at the floor. He guessed she really did believe Syd would take his cheating brother back. Probably because she always did. Sometimes it would take a few days, a few months, but she always took him back. He'd spent a lot of time trying to figure out why. In the end, he figured her reasons for making excuses for Den's behavior matched his own. He'd spent most of his life doing the same thing, years of ignoring the bad and concentrating on the good. In spite of all Den's flaws, they'd seen the man who protected those he loved with everything he had; the man who could make anyone laugh no matter the circumstance; the smart, talented businessman...a man worth saving.

Glancing back at Syd, anger coursed through him. The Den he wanted to save seemed lost to him. It had been a long time since he felt the need to make excuses for his brother, and that was partly because of Syd. Mostly it was because Morgan resented Den. He'd given up a lot for his brother, but ultimately had made the decision to pull away because he was tired of being pulled into Den's hell. This latest debacle was simply Den being Den—selfish, careless, and impulsive. And he hoped Syd was finished with him for good this time.

"Come on, babe," he said, picking Syd up and cradling her in his arms.

"Are you going to take her home?" Allina asked, her eyes filled with unshed tears. "I mean, are you taking her home with you?"

He nodded as he made his way through the store with Allina right on his heels. "I'll keep trying to reach Red," he told Allina. "In the meantime, I'll make sure she's taken care of. Thanks for calling me."

"Morgan? Her purse," Allina called. She hooked Syd's tote on his arm. "I was going to say tell Den to go screw himself, but just take care of my friend. I parked her car in the garage. It'll be good there overnight."

He nodded. "For what it's worth, I want to kick his ass, too."

Calisa isn't the chocolate hearts and red roses type of woman. She's perfectly content with a friends-with-benefits relationship...until Jared. She's not ready for what he's asking, but her heart can't seem to keep him out. Now Jared must find a way to convince Calisa to let go and take a chance on him.

Please see the next page for an excerpt of

His All Night.

CHAPTER ONE

This has got to be the worst date ever. Calisa Harper stabbed at her overdone pasta, twirling it around her spoon. For a minute, she felt guilty even thinking that. Joshua Clayborn was one of the most eligible bachelors in the Detroit area, with his dark skin, firm body, and long money. There were hordes of women waiting in the wings to get to him, but he'd picked her. Still, having dinner with him was akin to watching golf or, better yet, sticking a thousand needles in her eye. One word—no, make that three: boring as hell.

She glanced at her phone, torn between opening up her current game of Candy Crush and browsing through her e-mails. This couldn't be the life.

"Why are you so quiet?" Joshua asked, his dark eyes on her, assessing her.

Eyeing the door, she shrugged. "You seemed like you weren't done talking." She smiled at him. "About your house, your car, your job," she muttered under her breath, not even caring if he heard her.

He reached across the table, picked up her hand in his. Rolling her eyes, she forced herself to at least pay attention to the man. It wasn't every day she was treated to dinner by a hot millionaire. *Hot* was the only thing good about Mr.

Clayborn, though. What was the use of having a good face but all the charm of dry paint? At least with paint, she could choose her own color.

"Calisa, you're so beautiful," he said.

She could agree with that, she thought with a smile. Her black, low-cut, form-fitting dress left just enough to the imagination, stopping at the knee. Long layers fell down her back like ocean waves. Topping off her look with a pair of five-inch, red-bottomed pumps, she knew she looked good.

"Thank you, Josh. You look good, too."

"What do you want to do tonight?"

"Red." Her eyes widened, mortified that she'd actually said that out loud. Scrambling to cover up her mistake, she tried to think of anything *red*. Red rover, red robin, red... "Redeem my points at the casino," she lied, shifting in her seat.

He seemed to accept her answer because he ticked off the casinos in town and mentioned his preference. Nodding, she agreed to go to the MGM Grand. *Maybe I can lose him on the floor?*

The sound of boisterous laughter sounded in the restaurant, and her attention shifted to the bar. Her body stiffened at the sight of a group of men in business suits and the harem of women surrounding them. One in particular stood out, with his smooth golden skin, short wavy hair, and dimpled smile. He chose that moment to look up, locking eyes with her across the room and tipping his glass in her direction.

Knowing he would be in the city and actually seeing him were two different things, since the Detroit-Windsor area boasted a population of 5.7 million. Jared Williams was hard to miss, though. He had a way that drew her to him. Cool, calm, and collected with an irresistible swagger. No wonder she wanted to do him. It seemed as if that was all she ever wanted to do. Only they had strict rules; rules she tried to never break.

Joshua went on and on about his contacts and his contracts in the city and she...watched as "Red" charmed all the women around him. She gulped down the rest of her wine, bothered that the sight of him getting so much female attention made her stomach burn. It was a feeling she'd been getting used to, especially over the past year.

Jared and Cali had known each other for a long time. After all, he was her best friend's twin brother. Sydney had been more like a sister to her from the moment they laid eyes on each other. Red came with the package, except that the underlying attraction between them prevented her from ever viewing him as a "brother." About five years ago, they'd acted on that desire and entered into a *no-strings* type of relationship. They had fun, then they had sex, then they went home.

When Cali saw one woman slip her card to Red slyly, she stood up abruptly, bumping into the table. "I'm sorry," she said, interrupting Joshua mid-sentence. She rubbed her sore knee. "I have to use the restroom." She dropped her napkin on the table, grabbed her clutch, and limped off toward the ladies' washroom.

Closing it behind her, she leaned back against the bathroom door. She did a quick glance under the stall doors to see if she was alone. Once she was satisfied that no one could hear her, she groaned out loud and let out a string of curses. Exhaling, she turned to the mirror and pulled out her compact.

She heard the click of the door latch behind her, but continued to touch up her makeup.

"How's your date?"

Whirling around, she nearly toppled over when she lost

her footing. Shocked, she rushed to the door and swung it open, peeking outside. She closed the door and turned to face a smirking Red. "What the hell are you doing?" she hissed. "This is the ladies' room."

He shrugged, his hazel eyes raking over her body. "I was just checking on you. You bolted from your table so fast, I thought something was wrong."

"How is it that, of all the places in the city, we end up at the same restaurant?"

"Coincidence," he told her. "Holiday party. The firm likes to go all out."

"Really? Red, it's not even December yet."

"They did it early this year," he explained, brushing a piece of hair behind her ear. "They're calling it a harvest party."

"Why didn't you tell me you were coming here?" She forced a frown onto her face even as her insides were melting at the smell of his cologne.

"Didn't think I had to. But since you're here, you could always join me." He traced the vee on her dress, sending shivers up her spine. "Why don't you get rid of the stiff and come up to my room?"

Tempted as she was, she wasn't going out like that. "No," she breathed, suddenly feeling very...hot. "I have a date."

Slowly, he edged closer to her. She retreated until the hard doorknob dug into her back. Reaching behind her, he flipped the lock on the door, the click echoing in the empty bathroom. Sucking in a deep breath, she waited, anticipating his next move.

His fingers flitted across the hem of her dress and he inched it up a bit. Kneeling down, he slipped his hands under her dress and slowly pulled down her underwear. She held her breath, wondered what he would do next.

"Step out of them," he ordered in a low, deep voice.

Bracing her hands on his shoulders, she stepped out of her lace panties. With a smirk, he stood up, tucked the thin material into the inside pocket of his suit jacket, and pulled out a tiny key card. He placed it in her hand and closed her fingers around it. "Room 1179," he murmured, his lips a mere inch away from hers. Closing her eyes, she took in the smell of cognac on his breath and leaned closer.

His soft laugh brought her mind back to their location and she opened her eyes. She opened her mouth to speak, but he placed a finger over her lips.

"Shh. Try not to think about what I'm going to do to you, while you're on your date." Swinging open the door, he walked out, whistling.

She hated him—in the best way.

* * *

Jared Williams flung his hotel room door open, surprised when Cali burst through it straight into his arms. He kicked the door closed as she kissed him deeply and passionately. As they backed up toward the bed, touching and kissing along the way, she undid his tie and slid it off. She flung it over her head and went to work unbuttoning his shirt. Grunting when the backs of his knees hit the frame of the bed, he felt for the hook to her dress. It had a line of tiny buttons going up the back, and he struggled to undo them with his big fingers. *To hell with it.* Frustrated, he gripped the end of it and pulled, sending buttons flying into the air.

"Fuck, Red," she grumbled, shoving him back. "You ruined my dress."

"Sorry," he said, but he wasn't. Wrapping an arm around her waist, he yanked her back to him.

Her head fell back as he nipped at her neck, pushing her dress down to the floor. Pausing, he stepped back to appreciate her. She was standing before him in a black push-up bra and a sexy-ass pair of *do-me* pumps—and nothing else. She was perfect. Her brown skin seemed to glow in the dim light and he hardened at the sight of her.

She tugged on the waistband of his pants and unzipped them, freeing his straining erection. "Step out of them," she said, with a wink and a smile.

Doing as he was told, he kicked the pants behind her and pulled her into another wet kiss. They fell back on the bed, her on top. She straddled his lap and eased herself down onto him. He closed his eyes, gritting his teeth. He wanted to make this last. They stayed like that a moment, staring at each other. Soon, she was moving those hips, grinding into him in a way that often made him forget his name. She was truly the best he'd ever had and he couldn't get enough of her. He wanted to possess her, claim her in a way he never had before, and make sure she knew that she'd never find another man that would mean as much to her as he did. Gripping her hips, he flipped her onto her back and pushed himself into her harder, enjoying her yelp of surprise.

He looked down at her, taking in her long, dark hair fanned out on the pillow, her lips between her teeth and her eyes on his, and slammed into her again. They moved, each of them matching the other, settling into a rhythm that seemed innate—like it was meant to be. She wrapped her arms around him and whispered, "Don't stop."

Hooking his arms under her knees, he thrust into her—deeper, harder each time until he felt her constricting around him. Knowing she was close, he slipped a finger between their bodies and pressed down on her clit. Her body stiffened, and she screamed out his name as her orgasm shook through her. Soon, he was right with her.

Arms and legs tangled together, they lay there panting, trying to catch their breaths. Lifting his head, he ran a finger across her cheek, smiling at the light sheen of sweat across her brow. Her hair, once flowing down her back, was wet with perspiration.

Being with her was the highlight of any day. The need to touch her, feel her against him, had him making up excuses to end up where she was. Yet, ending up at the same hotel that night had been a happy coincidence. And he took full advantage of it. He brushed his lips over her shoulder and rolled off of her, onto his back.

She turned to him, propping herself up on her elbow. "You are so naughty," she whispered with a giggle. "You know I couldn't concentrate the rest of the night, right? Imagine Joshua's surprise when I ended our date before he had the chance to bore me with more details of his life."

He chuckled, turning to face her. Seeing her with another man had irritated him more than he ever thought it would. And the knowledge that she'd ended her date to be with him made him want to puff out his chest with pride. He slid a hand over her hip and squeezed her thigh. "Mission accomplished, then."

Red pulled her into the crook of his arms and kissed her brow. Moments like these were hard to come by with Cali. She was determined not to be *his* girl. But it was all he could think about. He wasn't sure when it had snuck up on him, but he wanted Cali to be more than his *no-strings* booty call. Hell, she was already one of his closest friends.

"Why don't you stay the night?" he asked softly. He already knew the answer, but he couldn't stop himself from asking.

"I can't." She brushed her lips against his chest. "I have an early meeting."

Although he wasn't surprised, it still stung. There was something irresistible about Calisa Harper and he wanted to take advantage of their time together. He wanted this night to stay. But she always put up the walls, always found a reason to pull back.

Leaning in, she kissed him and then scooted to the edge of the bed. She picked up her dress and held it up to him. "You are so going to reimburse me for this dress." He watched as she pulled it up and stuck her arms into the sleeves.

"I wish I could say I was sorry and mean it," he admitted.

"Ha-ha." She put on his shirt and buttoned it up. "I'm taking this home."

"Guess you can add it to your collection, huh?"

Over the course of their…relationship, Cali had managed to stockpile many of his clothes, always making up an excuse why he couldn't have something back. He supposed it was par for the course.

"You don't have to leave, you know," he told her. It was the same thing, different day. No matter how much fun they had with each other, she'd always leave him wanting more.

"You know the rules. No sleepovers." She walked over to him and kissed him again, holding his chin with her hand. "I'll call you later!" she shouted as she flung open the door and walked out of the room.

About the Author

Elle Wright was born and raised in Southwest Michigan near Ann Arbor. She learned the importance of reading from her mother and it was also her mother who, later on in her life, gave Elle her first romance novel: *Indigo* by Beverly Jenkins. From that moment on, Elle became a fan of Ms. Jenkins for life and a lover of all things romance. An old journal she wrote back in college became her first book (which she still wants to publish one day).

You can learn more at:
TheBasementLevelFive.blogspot.com/
Twitter @LWrightAuthor
Facebook.com/LWrightAuthor

FALL IN LOVE WITH FOREVER ROMANCE

"Everything I love in a romance!"
—LORI FOSTER, *New York Times* bestselling author,
on *Bringing Home the Bad Boy*

RETURN OF THE BAD BOY
By Jessica Lemmon

Fans of Gena Showalter, Olivia Miles, and Jaci Burton will love Jessica Lemmon's hot alpha heroes with dark pasts and hearts of gold. Rock god Asher Knight is forced to put down roots when he finds out he has a three-year-old son. But is his newfound stability enough to convince Gloria Shields to finally surrender her heart to this bad boy?

THE WAGER
By Rachel Van Dyken

Seattle millionaire Jake Titus has always made Char Lynn crazy. He's too rich, too handsome, and too arrogant. But now Jake's stopped acting like a jerk and turned on the charm, and Char knows she's in trouble. The *New York Times* bestseller from Rachel Van Dyken is now in mass market.

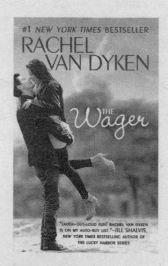

#1 *NEW YORK TIMES* BESTSELLER

"LAUGH-OUT-LOUD FUN! RACHEL VAN DYKEN IS ON MY AUTO-BUY LIST."—JILL SHALVIS, *NEW YORK TIMES* BESTSELLING AUTHOR OF THE LUCKY HARBOR SERIES

FALL IN LOVE WITH FOREVER ROMANCE

THE WEDDING PACT
By Katee Robert

New York Times and *USA Today* bestselling author Katee Robert continues her smoking-hot series about the O'Malleys—wealthy, powerful, and full of scandalous family secrets. In THE WEDDING PACT, Carrigan O'Malley has a parade of potential suitors, but the only man she wants is the head of a rival ruling family. To be with Carrigan, James Halloran will have to fight not only his enemies—but his own blood.

HER KIND OF MAN
By Elle Wright

I'll never let you go… Allina always dreamed of hearing those words. But when her fiancé utters them—it's a threat. Forget walking down the aisle; it's time to run. Back to Michigan. Back to Kent. Kent will do whatever it takes to make Allina feel safe, beautiful, and desirable. But as the two grow closer, and their passion pushes deeper, it's clear that something bigger than a botched wedding still lingers between them…

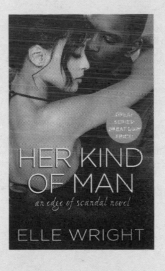

FALL IN LOVE WITH FOREVER ROMANCE

MATT
By R. C. Ryan

In the *New York Times* bestselling tradition of Linda Lael Miller and Diana Palmer comes the first in a beautiful new series by R. C. Ryan. When lawyer Vanessa Kettering and rancher Matt Malloy are forced to weather a terrible storm together, they're drawn to each other despite their differences. Can they survive the storm without losing their hearts?

HOW I MARRIED A MARQUESS
By Anna Harrington

When an old family friend comes to retired spy Thomas Matteson about a rash of mysterious robberies near Blackwood Hall, he jumps at the chance to be back in the field. What will he do when the suspect turns out to be the most beautiful—and beguiling—woman he's ever seen? Fans of Elizabeth Hoyt will love this sexy historical romance.

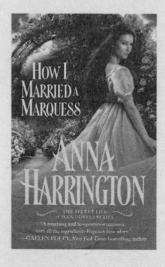